Praise for *The Last Romanov*

"You will be sucked into a story that holds you to the finish...a great book for a reading club or discussion group."

—Blogcritics.org

"Crackles with tension and imagination—an engaging story splashed upon a broad canvas. Mossanen mines an emotional landscape, rich in myth and characterization, offering an innovative perspective on what may have happened to the Romanovs. Savor the magic and enjoy the journey."

—Steve Berry, author of *The Jefferson Key* and *The Columbus Affair*

"Deeply rooted in an exotic time and place, ornamented with the observed detail that comes from exhaustive but discerning research, suffused with authentic historical drama, and populated with irresistible men and women who come fully alive on the page, all of which are [Mossanen's] trademarks as a novelist...a master storyteller works her powerful magic yet again."

—Jonathan Kirsch, *The Jewish Journal*

"*The Last Romanov* spins a magically laced, bejeweled look at the end of Russia's Romanov family, as seen through the preternatural eyes of the long-lived woman bound to their fate. From the sumptuous halls of the Alexander Palace to the cramped back-alleys of the Jewish ghetto, this haunting tale of prophecy and redemption sweeps us into an opulent world of glamour, myth, tragedy, and unforgettable humanity."

—C.W. Gortner, author of
The Confessions of Catherine de Medici

"A lyrical, magical, and utterly captivating story of redemption and the triumph of the human heart. *The Last Romanov* brings a tumultuous era of history to rich life and re-creates in sumptuous detail the world of the Imperial Russian court. Darya's story will hold you spellbound."

—Anna Elliott, author of *Georgiana Darcy's Diary*

"A thrilling, exotic sojourn in the opulent drawing rooms of Imperial Russia as the Bolsheviks tighten their noose, recounted by a member of the doomed Imperial Family's inner circle. Unimaginable luxury and abasement and the magical properties of nature form the backdrop to stories of love and enduring loyalty despite a drumbeat of tragedies. The beautiful, opal-eyed Darya, veiled in butterflies, lives on hope and ambergris to reunite with her lover amid the chaos of the Soviet Union and to discover whether the heir to the Romanov throne survived."

—Jenny White, author of the Kamil Pasha mystery series

"With the assured hand of a master storyteller at the height of her game, Mossanen leads us deep into the intimate world of the last Romanovs. She weaves history and magic into a riveting page-turner that brings to life the enduring mystery of a gilded court teeming with unforgettable characters who interact with history to create a vivid, engrossing tapestry that will haunt the reader long after the last page is turned."

— Robin Maxwell, bestselling author of
Signora da Vinci and *The Secret Diary of Anne Boleyn*

"*The Last Romanov* shimmers with tantalizing mystery and brilliance. Readers will delight in sharing the journey of the bold and self-possessed Darya through the corridors of the Russian Imperial Palace during the final days of the Tsar's reign as she cares for the young and sickly heir, finds herself the beloved muse of a celebrated Jewish artist, and grapples with Rasputin's revelations about her ancient past. Filled with rich period detail, *The Last Romanov* is a testament to the enduring power of love and honor, but most of all, hope."

—DeAnna Cameron, author of *Dancing at the Chance*

"You are slowly seduced like a great lover, with untold secrets, fascinating family interactions, hidden relationships, steamy passion, and mystical characters. Engagingly satisfying from start to finish."

—Moll Anderson, lifestyle expert and author of *The Seductive Home*

The Last Romanov

The Last
Romanov

A Novel

DORA LEVY MOSSANEN

sourcebooks
landmark

Published by Sourcebooks Landmark, an imprint of Sourcebooks, Inc.
P.O. Box 4410, Naperville, Illinois 60567-4410
(630) 961-3900
Fax: (630) 961-2168
www.sourcebooks.com

Library of Congress Cataloging-in-Publication Data

Levy Mossanen, Dora
  The last Romanov : a novel / Dora Levy Mossanen.
      p. cm.
  (pbk. : alk. paper) 1. Romanov, House of—Fiction. 2. Women—Russia—Fiction.
3. Courts and courtiers—Fiction. 4. Russia—History—Nicholas II, 1894-1917—
Fiction. 5. Soviet Union—History—Revolution, 1917-1921—Fiction. I. Title.
  PS3612.E94L37 2012
  813'.6—dc23
                                            2011044182

Printed and bound in the United States.
VP 10 9 8 7 6 5 4 3 2 1

ALSO BY DORA LEVY MOSSANEN

Harem

Courtesan

———

For my father, Sion Levy, of blessed memory,
And for my mother, Parvin Levy,

My Beloved Teachers

And for Hannah Sophia and Macabee Ryan Ascher,
My Shining Stars

———

"What else should our lives be but a continual series of beginnings, of painful setting out into the unknown, pushing off from the edges of consciousness into the mystery of what we have not yet become."
—Malouf's Ovid, *An Imaginary Life*, David Malouf

"I am thinking of aurochs and angels, the secret of durable pigments, prophetic sonnets, the refuge of art. And this is the only immortality you and I may share, my Lolita."
—*Lolita*, Vladimir Nabokov

— 1887 —

T HE HOWLS OF WILD aurochs echo deep in the ancient forest as Boris Spiridov spreads his hunting coat over a mattress of leaves and Sabrina Josephine, daughter of a grand duke and favorite in the Romanov Palace, squats down as if she has spent her entire life in this forest. Tall and solid behind her, Boris anchors her weight against his legs, his hands supporting her under the arms. She spreads her knees wide, summons her enormous reserves of strength, and pushes once. A girl is born. A girl with black curls and skin the color of copper. A girl with exquisite golden eyes, one a translucent opal that reflects the depth of her emotions.

Chapter One

— 1991 —

D ARYA BORISOVNA SPIRIDOVA IS startled awake by a persistent knock at her front door. Butterflies flutter against her skin, weave their way around her silver curls, rustle under the covers. A cloud of butterflies floats out of the bedroom and into the vestibule.

Draped in a shawl of fine satin, the cane of Tsar Nicholas II in one hand and an oil-burner in another, she quietly slips across the corridor of the crumbling Entertainment Palace to confront the massive oak door.

Little Servant appears, carrying a tray of piroshki and a tumbler of vodka. His smile reveals a mouthful of gold teeth that cost Darya a pearl-encrusted cross. "May I help, Madame?"

She raises one hand to keep him at bay. With the glint of mischief in his eyes and a habit of materializing at the most inconvenient times, the dwarf can be a nuisance. "This one is for *me. I* will answer."

She tightens the shawl about her shoulder, her curls casting shadows in the dim light of the oil-burner as she tackles the many locks and bolts. The door heaves and clangs, then swings open with a great groan, and she comes face to face with a slit-eyed young man in a uniform the color of the Crimean shores.

"*Dobroye utro!*" He greets, bowing low, one hand touching the brim of a fox-furred shapka tottering on his narrow, conelike head, the other offering a cream-colored vellum envelope.

At the sight of the Association's familiar seal on the envelope, her hand flies to the miniature Fabergé egg she wears on a chain around her neck. The Russian Nobility Association is a ragged assembly of leftover aristocrats, descendants of the Scherbatovs, Golitsyns, Bobrinskois, Yusupovs, and Sheremetevs. Before the motherless Bolsheviks destroyed Russia, these aristocrats would roll their shiny carriages along the Nevsky Prospekt on the way to the Mariinsky Theater or from one palace or another, where, cuddled in furs and dazzling in jewelry, they would spoon pearly Caspian caviar and click champagne flutes with their Imperial Majesties, Tsar Nicholas Alexandrovich Romanov and Alexandra Feodorovna. They communicated in French with their children and Swiss governesses, in English with their nannies and British friends, and in Russian with their servants.

These exiled aristocrats still dream, plan, and plot to reinstate the monarchy, although they dismiss her own search for the Tsarevich, Alexei, as a mad woman's last delusion.

"*Spasiba*, son." Darya murmurs her thanks to the ruddy-faced messenger. She steps back to shut the door, but the boy remains rooted at the threshold, enthralled by the 104-year-old woman with mesmerizing eyes, one an orb of cracked opal. Not the type of milky opal mined from the crevices of the earth, but a lucid golden shade, defiant and full of mystery.

"You are so beautiful, so different!" He hears himself blurt out, his tongue tripping over itself. "Is it true that your opal eye can read the thoughts of animals?"

Darya aims her cracked gaze directly at him. "Humans too, *Golubchik*, my dear fellow. I see everything, even what I'd rather not." At her age, she has learned to accept many things…accept the crack in the opal that was caused by long-ago grief, a tragedy witnessed, a black stain that should never have happened. She has learned to accept the curiosity her eye stirs, accept that her beauty, unmarred by time or misfortune, is an oddity too. So, despite her impatience to learn what the envelope holds, she decides to answer the courageous boy, who reminds her of Little Servant twenty years before, when he appeared at her door with a mouthful of bad teeth and two fat-nosed civets in his arms, claiming his parents had been exiled to "the camps." He said he did not care that everyone thought she was a sorceress and her butterflies were Romanov spirits. In truth, he said, her eccentricities suited him well, since he was different too. He promised to work hard in return for food and shelter and claimed that his wild cats were trained to pluck red coffee cherries from bushes he promised to plant in her garden, cherries that would yield the most aromatic coffee. She had simply opened the door and let him in. And now, despite his penchant for lighting the fireplaces in her absence, his lengthy silences and the excellent vodka he distills have become agreeable additions to her solitary life.

She rubs the envelope between her palms and offers the uniformed young man a smile that reveals her own impeccable teeth. "Would you like a bottle of my homemade vodka?"

He shuffles in place, uncertain of the right protocol, whether to accept or politely refuse. Deciding on the safest course, he replies, "I don't drink, *spasiba*."

She lets out a rare laugh that originates in her bowels and bursts out into a volcanic mirth. "What a pity! A daily shot of good vodka keeps you healthy. But I understand, boychick, I really do. You are young, untouched by tragedies, drunk on life. Still, if you change your mind, you are welcome to a bottle of my excellent vodka."

"Is vodka the reason you look so young... Pardon me. They say you are old, but you don't look old at all. *Are* you old?"

"Old! Wash your mouth, boy." She cocks her head at him, searches his eyes for some evidence of malice or derision, and finding only the innocence of youth, she adds, "The secrets to my long life are my passions, obsessions, and dreams that have not changed one bit since I was seventeen, living in the Belovezh Forest with birds of paradise and wild animals. If anything, I am more driven today. Go, now, and share this with your young friends."

There is more to the secret of her longevity, of course. A chunk of ambergris she discovered on the Crimean shores remains essential to her youthful appearance. And her optimism, this ability to sustain herself on hope and a diet of memories, helps too. Even when the mix of memory and guilt will not be assuaged by the hallucinatory berries in her garden, she refuses to lose hope. Hope that the Tsarevich survived the horror of that long-ago night and, despite his age, remains in good health. Hope that she will, once more, hold him in her arms and cover his face with a million tender kisses.

"May I ask another question?" the boy says.

"*Ne budet-li*, be careful what you ask, young man," she replies, a puff of butterflies huddling in her cupped hand.

"Is it true that you were Tyotia Dasha of the Tsarevich, Alexei Nikolaevich Romanov?"

"The answer is yes. *Da*! I was his lady-in-waiting, his beloved auntie Dasha. Now, go! *Schast'ya i zdorov'ya*! Good luck! And remember our Tsarevich in your prayers," she replies, a cloud of butterflies fluttering around her like ornaments.

Finding her less intimidating than he was led to believe, the boy exclaims, "People say you are a sorceress and these butterflies are Romanov spirits that keep your enemies away and help you…"

"You talk too much, son. Close your mouth or you'll start burping fat toads." She gives him a gentle push with her cane and shuts the door behind him. She waves away two insistent butterflies that land on the envelope and snaps the cane at a rat that scurries across the hallway to peck at her heel. Other rats come and go, content with meager leftovers. This beady-eyed one is as greedy as every revolutionary Red that crossed her path, every bastard communist and worm-eating antimonarchist who soils his pants at the sight of her.

She breaks the seal on the envelope and pulls out a vellum note.

Her heart loud in her chest, her gaze skips over the gold-embossed inscriptions. Emissaries of the Russian Nobility Association summon her to an emergency meeting at Rostislav Perfumery. Four in the afternoon, sharp. An important matter requires her immediate attention. What could have prompted this tight circle of monarchists to summon her *now*? She kept an eye on them through the years, following their pathetic failures to find the heir to the throne, her precious charge, her sweet Alyosha, the man who would restore the monarchy. Year after year, one or another pretender to the throne materialized, crooks and impostors with no ties to the Romanovs, not a drop of royal blood in their dry veins.

She folds the note, reflecting upon her own continuous quest around the polluted Ekaterinburg streets, the traffic-choked boulevards, soot-covered buildings, and stinking buses to scrutinize anyone who might bear a remote resemblance to her Tsarevich, her adorable prince, with melancholy eyes that reflected his suffering. She continues to travel around the country to listen to whoever might claim to have information about a Romanov, meet with one impostor after another, inspect the geography of their faces, and heap ash on their lying heads.

Little Servant reappears with his tray. "Your breakfast, Madame?"

She slips the note back in the envelope and frees a butterfly that found its way in. "Not today."

"Important news, Madame?"

"Yes, yes, an important meeting I need to attend."

"Right now, Madame?"

"No, in an eternity. Well, not quite, but so it seems. I will have to be at the perfumery in four hours."

"Perhaps Madame would like me to warm up the banya? That always helps."

"Yes, thank you. Please do." She will bathe, shampoo her hair, and enjoy a hallucinatory berry or two, a tumbler of scented vodka to pass the time. She likes the sense of lightness that every immersion in the banya brings. Bathing is a necessary ritual, her daily conduit to the past, all the way back to her childhood and her beloved parents.

The dwarf hastens to prepare the banya, intent on pleasing his mistress who, unlike others, regards him as an equal rather than a stepped-on cockroach to be swept up with the trash. As long as he can remember, he has been addressed as Little Servant, despite the fact that, apart from his height, the rest of his features are quite large: protruding eyes, hooked nose, shovel-like hands and feet. He likes living here, safe from curious stares, where he can dress as he pleases, in loose, colorful satin pants and shirts that remind him of Backschai village, where he came from. His room, despite the flaking paint and smell of mildew, is opulent by his standards, and he likes to occupy a bed that once belonged to the Grand Duchess Anastasia. He shuffles into the garden with its patch of berries, giddy butterflies, wild civets, and the vodka distillery where he ferments black figs, molasses, cumin, and currants. And he walks the same path the Tsar and Tsarina had walked seventy years before.

Set in the center of five acres of land, perched on a hill over-looking the city below, the Entertainment Palace is where Nicholas II and Alexandra Feodorovna held symphonies and ballets after a long day of formal responsibilities. Once surrounded by groves of birch, linden, and cedar, the landscape now chokes with robusta and hybrid arabustra bushes Little Servant planted when he came here with his wild civets.

The civets continue to breed and multiply. They creep among the bushes at night and pluck coffee cherries, chew off the fruity exterior, and swallow the hard innards. Every morning, Little Servant steps out into the garden and separates, from the many clumps of civet dung, the beans that have been refined by the civets' gastric juices. Then he embarks on brewing the rarest of sweet coffees with the aroma of vanilla and chocolate.

This miraculously preserved backdrop that masks the ruins of the Bolshevik Revolution and years of civil war is the only imperial residence the communists and antimonarchists did not confiscate, for fear of the multiplying butterflies they regarded as the lingering spirits of the Romanovs.

Little Servant steps into the banya, a bathhouse built decades ago that, apart from the missing roof, remains in acceptable condition. Testing the water and finding it warm and pleasant, he stirs in a generous amount of essence of eucalyptus and orange blossom, stacks towels, and places a jar of scrubbing salts and birch whips close by. He picks five hallucinatory berries from the garden and arranges them on a decorative fig leaf in a bowl. He goes to fetch his mistress.

"The banya is ready, Madame," he formally announces.

She emerges, tossing her shawl behind and stepping out of her nightgown as Little Servant picks them up and folds them carefully on his arm. He observes her immerse herself in the aromatic water, admiring the miracle that she is. Her muscles are firm, her skin the shade of cloves of cinnamon, her golden eyes reflecting the splendor of a woman who is secure in her beauty. He never tires of searching the Entertainment Palace for something that might explain the secret of her eternal youth: an elixir, an incantation, a magical herb. Perhaps something that might add a few centimeters to his height.

He has wondered more than once whether the secret of her youth might be related to the fragrance emanating from the ever-present miniature Fabergé egg slung from a gold chain around her neck. It is a superb piece of jewelry, no larger than his thumbnail. Deep green enamel dotted with brilliant diamonds and pearls in the center of which is the likeness of a beautiful red-haired woman. When snapped open, its bold, inebriating scent is like a lover's playful slap.

Little Servant restrains Darya's hair with a scarf and adjusts a pillow behind her head. He fetches the bowl of berries. She drops two plump, shiny ones in her mouth, sucks the nectar, savors the familiar bitter-tart taste. She calls out to Little Servant to bring back the bowl of berries he is carrying away.

"Be careful, Madame, freshly picked off the vine and quite potent."

"So much the better," she replies, plucking an obstinate butterfly from the bowl and collecting the rest of the berries, enough to keep her excitement at bay until the meeting this afternoon.

Darya rests her head on the pillow, sighs contentedly, and shuts her eyes to imagine a time 104 years ago, a time before her birth, a time when aurochs roamed wild in the Belovezh Forest and Sabrina was a woman free of care.

Chapter Two

— 1887 —

G RAND DUKE BORIS SPIRIDOV raises his binoculars to his eyes and gazes at an endless vista of forest rich in game— stag, elk, and bison—dotted with meandering streams and sandy paths, ancient oaks, pine, and white firs. The imperial entourage is expected at his Belovezh Estate in eastern Poland, and Boris, second cousin to Tsarevich Nicholas Alexandrovich Romanov, looks forward to the excitement of the chase and the pleasure of spending time in the company of the ladies.

A vast expedition has been planned to hunt the elusive aurochs, a fierce species of European bison, raised and maintained for the hunting enjoyment of the young Tsarevich. In the last year, however, the cunning aurochs have multiplied, trampling the delicate nesting grounds of the rare birds of paradise the Tsarevich dispatched to the forest. The birds, with their lacy plumes and dazzling shades, are on the brink of extinction. And the Tsarevich is not pleased.

Boris gallops from one hunting lodge to another, calling out in his authoritative voice how the serfs should prepare the lodges, adorn them with carefully selected artwork, bring in provisions, disperse fire logs, clear the brush, and mill oats to mix with meat as hound forage. As for how to prepare the private lodge of Princess Alix of Hesse, the Tsarevich's companion, he is at a loss. What added amenities would a woman require? A net over her bed to keep the mosquitoes away? A bouquet of flowers and a box of chocolates? Recalling her long reddish hair, he makes his way toward the main lodge to fetch the set of silver-backed hairbrushes that had once belonged to Catherine the Great and which he had acquired at auction.

At dusk, he is back in the saddle, straight-backed and alert to the slightest sound carried on a gathering breeze, a red cravat carelessly tied in a loose bow, his shirt and billowing sleeves as white as the dolomite cliff towering behind him. He hears the gallop of approaching hooves, followed by the wooden roar of wheels, snippets of speech, and then the ring of laughter.

Boris flips the reins and canters toward the source of laughter.

The imperial entourage advances like thunder. Tsarevich Nicholas is on horseback. Princess Alix Viktoria Helena Luise Beatrice of Hesse and Rhine is on his right, riding sidesaddle on a honey-colored stallion from the imperial stables.

Wearing oversized earrings and bright-colored scarves, flung about her neck as if to gift wrap her laughter in her throat, is the red-haired Sabrina Josephine, the daughter of the Duke and Duchess of Corinin, a small European principality known for its two mines that supply Europe's royal families with the much-coveted pink diamond.

A large contingent of serfs clad in scarlet livery are followed by dozens of trunks and a hospital on wheels, a mobile kitchen, the master of hounds to his majesty, and large packs of borzois, grooms, and falcons.

Ninety-eight huntsmen—aristocrats and Romanov grand dukes—rein their Arabian thoroughbreds into a trot to keep at bay the churning dust gales, an inconvenience to the ladies.

Sabrina adjusts a shotgun slung over her shoulder and reins her dappled steed into a trot to keep pace with the princess. "My dear Alix, are you tired? Perhaps you might want to rest. How far are we?"

"Not far, not at all," Princess Alix replies. "It is my back, you know, as always. But how are you, dear? Your cheeks have no color. Apply some rouge, tuck your hair behind your ears…yes, the right side…good. I shall personally introduce him to you. You will be pleased. Grand Duke Boris Spiridov is of royal blood and a fine gentleman at that."

Sabrina struts her steed closer to the princess. "Don't be upset, Alix, but I'm more interested in the hunt than in the grand duke."

"I don't know what you see in this sport, my dear. Perhaps this time you'll find the grand duke more interesting than shooting aurochs. Promise to withhold judgment until after you meet him."

"I shall," Sabrina replies, steering the steed away from a clump of daffodils.

Farther back, behind the serfs and the thoroughbreds, Jasmine the Persian Dancer—invited by Boris Spiridov to entertain the imperial entourage in the evenings—is astride a brown stallion. Her muscular thighs hug the saddle; her white-knuckled hands grasp the reins. Her dark hair, studded with sparking rhinestones, is braided on top of her head and covered by a veil the color of the sky. Her dulcimer accompanies her in a leather box on the back of a mule.

She is furious, her heart an aching rock in her chest. Throughout the trip, hundreds of ravenous male eyes have been trailing her every move, the flip of her wrist sending the horse into a canter, the sway of her ample buttocks on the saddle, the wink of a date-black eye behind her veil, the flash of her ankles when her pants ride up. Yet, to the Tsarevich, she is nothing, stone dead, as if she never was. As if he did not recently shower her with gifts and adoration, did not enjoy numerous quiet evenings at a secluded café, where they held hands and gazed into each other's eyes, discussing poetry, Persian music, the many enchantments of the dulcimer, and how he, the Tsarevich, Nicholas II of Russia, feared the inevitable day he would have to occupy the throne.

And now, here he is with his German consort, whose frail legs, Siberian smile, and mournful gaze would banish the germ of any passion before it has a chance to bloom. Jasmine aims her stare at the Tsarevich, lifts her veil, and wraps it around the braid on top of her head. Even seated as she is on the saddle, a head taller than Alix of Hesse, he refuses to take note of her. But she will not go unnoticed, the dancer vows. She did not travel for days by train and on mule from Azerbaijan to Russia to be tossed aside by any man, not even the heir to the Russian throne.

Sabrina retrieves her lorgnettes from the saddlebag and gazes at a man on horseback in the distance. He seems alert, waiting, his red cravat and hair flapping in the breeze. He canters straight toward her, coming into clearer focus, wild fair hair, sunburned complexion, reins clasped in hands as solid as a blacksmith's. Sabrina removes the rifle from her shoulder and lays it on her lap. One hand grasping the pommel, the other resting on the rifle, she tilts her head and gazes intensely, mercilessly, at the advancing Boris Spiridov.

His stallion comes to an abrupt stop in front of her, nose to nose with her steed, its flanks heaving, front hoof pawing the ground as if to charge. Boris holds her gaze. This red-haired woman, who rides as a man does, wears no gloves to protect her hands, her large earrings a riot of colors. He takes count of her every feature: the rounded lines of her cheeks that blush under his gaze, her mischievous green eyes that do not shy away, her languorous smile that frames the corners of her lips like tiny question marks.

She acknowledges him with a slight nod.

He lifts his hand to the brim of an invisible hat, flips the reins, and changes course.

The Tsarevich and his beloved Alix are his guests, and they must not be kept waiting. He canters on toward the German princess, helps her down from her stallion, and welcomes her with a kiss on her hand. She offers him one of her rare smiles. She gestures with a great flourish of one hand toward Sabrina. "My dear friend, Princess Sabrina Josephine of Corinin. You must know her father, Duke Joseph Leon IV of Corinin."

"Yes, my lady, I certainly do. We hunted together in Peterhof," Boris replies, leading the princess toward the Tsarevich, who hands the reins to his groom and walks toward Alix. The Tsarevich is a man of strong build, not tall. The eager expressions in his eyes are readable to everyone. He longs to have Alix to himself, to show her around the grounds, to introduce her to the birds of paradise. But most of all, he wants to hold her in his arms and assure her that despite her Lutheran upbringing and his parents' strong anti-German sentiments, he will marry her one day.

Boris greets the Tsarevich with a bow and a kiss on each shoulder. His cousin is not as tall as he, but his strength and energy make him a worthy adversary in their hunting expeditions, so much so that, in his eagerness, the host has sent word out that the hunt tomorrow will start at an earlier hour than customary.

Princess Alix pulls out a gold-embossed box from her purse and hands it to Boris. "I meant to give this to Sabrina, but it was forgotten in the excitement of our journey. Be kind enough, Grand Duke Boris, to assist her with the lock."

Boris bows his respect to the princess. "My honor, of course, if it will please my lady Sabrina Josephine."

Sabrina is on the saddle, caressing the shotgun on her lap, a feral glint in her eyes. She gestures toward the box in his hand. A gentle, persuasive tilt of the head asks what he is waiting for.

Boris opens the box to find a superbly crafted miniature Fabergé egg necklace, encrusted with pearls and diamonds, resting on velvet. He takes his time to snap the egg open and admire the image of Sabrina Josephine's profile hidden inside. Clicking it shut, he loops the delicate gold chain around two fingers and walks toward the red-haired woman. He grabs her around her waist and, with one powerful motion, lifts her off the saddle, setting her down to gaze into the depth of her teasing eyes. He reaches out to lock the chain behind her neck, their breath mingling for a fleeting instant, before the catch snaps shut and Sabrina turns away to thank Princess Alix.

The guests are led to their lodgings, where cotton-gloved footmen welcome them with warm piroshki, jellied ox tongue, and brandy-laced tea. Tomorrow will be a long and strenuous day, and rest is essential for the imperial entourage.

For Boris Spiridov, tomorrow is already alive with the scent of the redheaded woman.

———

At dawn, the blare of hunting horns echo through the forest. The earth gleams with early autumn dew. The leaves are a kaleidoscope of reds and oranges. Sunrays warm the sandy paths, and winter chill is a fading memory. The serfs have cleaned the fireplaces in the imperial lodges and started new fires. The pantries have been stacked with provisions: grape leaves stuffed with nuts and dates, buttermilk pancakes, fresh caviar from the Caspian, port, brandy, herb-scented vodkas, and cases of 1787 Château Lafite.

Paths have been cut through the enclosures and shooting positions set up. Packs of dogs and houndmen were dispatched to cut off the aurochs from behind. Falcons, trained to ignore the birds of paradise, have been flown against smaller prey: hares, squirrels, and all types of birds. Having sensed looming danger, many of the wild animals and their litters have retreated deep into the shadows of grand oaks and pine.

The imperial party in hunting attire—coats cinched with leather belts, pants tucked into knee-high boots—pour out of their lodges onto a vast clearing spread with silk carpets and set with tables brimming with delicacies: beef stroganoff, sturgeon, black caviar, red blinis, stuffed suckling pig, and pelmeni pastries with reindeer meat roast. Serfs, grooms, and servants replenish the food and serve all manner of libation.

Boris Spiridov's large-eyed, strong-backed hounds, having rested for three days and been kept inside the day before, yelp excitedly at the aroma of biscuits and mushrooms frying in butter. Hot mead and spiced brandy are ladled into jewel-encrusted cups, and toasts are raised to the young Tsarevich and his honored guest.

Princess Alix of Hesse is not fond of hunting. She would much prefer to spend her time introducing herself to the birds of paradise, stroking their colorful feathers and feeding them ripe figs and grapes. But with this massive hunt about to take place and aurochs on the loose, she decides not to stray too far from the main lodge, remaining behind with other women, servants, children, and their nannies. Conveying her prayers and good wishes to the men, she gestures to her lady-in-waiting to walk back to her accommodations.

Sabrina Josephine emerges from her lodge, followed by her long-haired borzoi. She wears a leather skirt cinched at the waist with a brass-buckled belt, the hem grazing heavy riding boots, her oversized earrings shimmering like aspen leaves, her silk blouse draped low to reveal her plump cleavage. She lingers at the threshold to gauge her surroundings, her dismissive gaze gliding over man and beast as if none is worthy of her universe. Shouldering her rifle, she strolls to a table and pours herself a cup of mead, which she raises, wishing everyone long life and victory. She drinks the libation, hands the cup to an attendant, then crosses the clearing and, undaunted by the dangers ahead, walks deep into the thirty-thousand-acre forest that is alive with birdsong, the chatter of insects, and the snorting and whinnying of thoroughbreds.

Boris leaps off his mount and hands the reins to his groom. He steps away from the ranks of men and follows the woman whose laughter had echoed in his chest the entire night. He is responsible for the safety of this bold woman, a guest on his estate, and he will make sure no harm befalls her.

He quickens his step as she vanishes behind one tree then another, surefooted and swift as a lioness in familiar territory. He pursues the flash of her gold earrings, the blaze of her curls, the flip of her skirt as she appears and disappears from view like a cat on the prowl. She whistles to her dog as she crosses a clearing of decaying leaves, an undergrowth of aspen, and splashes across a shallow pool, the hem of her skirt darkening with mud. For an instant, he loses sight of her, and then a beam of sunlight catches the silver glint of her rifle. His silent steps hasten toward her, his rifle at the ready, alert to the distant cry of hounds and rising voices of huntsmen on the scent.

Then silence. He freezes in place.

Sabrina has anchored the butt of her rifle against her shoulder, the barrel pointed slightly to the left. Her borzoi's ears are pricked, a low growl emanating from him.

Boris comes down on one knee, releases his safety catch, and points the barrel of his gun with the precision of a veteran hunter.

The metallic click of the safety catch sounds explosive among the gathering of trees. Sabrina glances in his direction, a silent warning for him not to interfere. The cunning aurochs will allow no more than a single shot. A wrong move, an accidental sound, could be fatal.

The raging animal emerges from a narrow path between two massive firs. With his harplike horns, flaring nostrils, and fur dark as obsidian, he lumbers toward Sabrina.

She aims her rifle and fires a single bullet between the animal's eyes. An excruciating howl reverberates through the woods, alerting the huntsmen that the first aurochs has been felled. The animal shudders, disturbing the wet underwood and raising the stench of decay. She finishes off the aurochs with a second shot.

Cheeks flushed, face beaded with perspiration, a drop of blood blossoms on her lower lip, which she has bitten in her excitement. She pulls out a hunting knife from her belt and slowly, calmly, approaches the aurochs and severs the right forehoof, a strong, clean cut through skin, bone, and sinews.

Boris steps out from behind the trees and strides toward her. She holds his gaze, reaches out for his hand, and places the forehoof in his palm, closing his fingers around her trophy.

He wipes her lips with his thumb, raises it to his mouth, and licks her blood.

She lets loose laughter that hums like a hundred harps. The moment she saw him on his black stallion with his wide chest and big hands against the backdrop of that great cliff, she knew he would belong to her.

She unbuckles her belt, lifts her skirt, and tucks the hem into her waist.

Boris falls to his knees and slides his hands up her thighs to her linens and slips them low, his caressing tongue between her breasts as she eases herself onto him and the humid carpet of moss and earth.

———

Nine months later, mother and father hold their newborn daughter in the Belovezh Estate they have made their home since the day of the imperial hunt. Half-naked among pine trees, comfortable with the wild animals and a population of aurochs that continues to diminish since Sabrina and her borzoi arrived, they gaze at their daughter until the half dome of the sun rises above the jagged edge of the dolomite cliff and the skies turn into a fury of colors.

She is beautiful, they whisper to one another. Look at her golden eyes, they murmur. But God works in strange ways. What, they wonder, is the Lord attempting to tell them? Why is their daughter born with an opal eye? Not dull and lifeless as mined opal can be, but gold-colored, vibrantly translucent, observing them with the unexpected wisdom of second sight.

Boris tells Sabrina that this child, their daughter with an opal eye, must be a punishment for some unknown sin he might have committed. Sabrina will not hear of it. She is certain that their daughter is a blessing that will further embellish their love.

Chapter Three

— 1894 —

S ABRINA JOSEPHINE HOLDS HER seven-year-old daughter's face between two hands and kisses her on her opal eye. "You are special, my darling. Different than other girls. You'll change our world one day. This I know. But to do that, you'll have to keep evil at bay. Come, I'll teach you a secret. Turn and spit three times behind your left shoulder to ward off the evil eye."

Darya plants her hands on her hips, cocks her head, and replies that she does not believe in the evil eye or any other such superstitious nonsense and that she will certainly not spit like a fool behind her shoulder. She is unaware that in a few hours, she will do just that, and in ten years, she will spit not only in the face of bad luck trailing behind, but here, there, and everywhere, each time she is ambushed by a looming sense of foreboding.

Sabrina adjusts her rifle behind one shoulder, bunches up her ruffled skirts, and plunges her suede boots into a stream running the length of the Belovezh Estate. Her carefree laughter peals about the forest as she wades across the stream, water hissing and splashing around stones and boulders. She skips past a rock, down one corner, winds her way around a pebbled path, then climbs a set of planks set to divert the stream toward a wide meadow. She does not care that her suede boots are darkening with mud, water rising up her legs and the hem of her velvet skirts. She likes all manners of stylish attire but also this freedom, the Belovezh Forest, and to live as one with wildlife, lush vegetation, birdsong, and the call of animals. Home for more than seven years, this is where she and Boris continue to plan vast hunting expeditions for the pleasure of Nicholas II, who is the Emperor now. And to his wife's endless joy, the billing and cooing birds of paradise, with their vibrant colors, flowing feathers, and penchant for procreation have multiplied, their love chatter bouncing around the forest. The demanding females are drawn to the most eccentric costumes: the goldie with its narcissistic mating cry that sounds like a trumpet, the *Carola parotia* with its wiry whiskers and exaggerated courting rituals, the ribbon-tailed *astrapia* with its cumbersome diaphanous tail that has a way of attracting numerous mates, and the whispering blue bird of paradise with its modest ways that is especially endearing to Empress Alexandra.

Sabrina gestures behind with an open palm to Darya, who quietly slips her hand into hers. They walk like that together, hand in hand, ducking under branches of ancient oaks and white firs spread out in all directions. A squirrel scurries past, startling them both. Darya does not like to be surprised. She would rather know what is around, be prepared for the unexpected. Their surroundings become spare, almost bare, a sliver of sun appearing between congregating clouds until, wet and satiated from their long walk, they step out of the stream and into an open meadow dotted with tiny daisies, all types of foliage, and beaten-down wild herbs.

Darya pulls her hand out of Sabrina's. "Look, Mama! Why are they all staring?" A distance away, in the center of the meadow, all types of animals—deer, rabbits, squirrels, foxes, even rats—have emerged from their hiding places as if summoned by order of the Emperor himself.

"Remarkable," Sabrina mutters, struggling to conceal her alarm. "Why would all these animals come out in full view in this open field when they are surrounded by predatory beasts?"

But this is not what concerns Darya. She is certain they have come out to punish her, come out as one to reprimand her for being a bad girl, for doing something very wrong.

"Do you see it, Mama?" she asks Sabrina, turning up to the sky as if the darkening clouds hold an inexplicable threat.

Sabrina detects nothing. All she sees are clouds the shade of metal, hanging low and heavy in the horizon. But she has learned to trust Darya's instincts, especially when it has to do with animals. She has learned early on that Darya, with her gaze that can travel far and bore into hidden places, can see things others don't.

"A storm is on the way, darling. We better return before the animals become nervous and Papa sends a troop looking for us."

It has happened before to Darya, this sense of fear that makes her self-aware as if she were standing outside her body, observing herself with critical eyes and not liking what is revealed. Or is it the way the animals glare at her with their kohl or red-rimmed eyes and the rest of their faulty design, which leaves all their proportions disturbingly out of balance. Long or short, skinny legs folded at awkward angles. Thick or thin twitching whiskers. Piercing eyes of all shapes that grab and hold her in a condemning grip.

Then she sees it. A deer in the center of the crowd, splayed in an awkward position, its gaze fixed on her.

"Mama, look," she cries out. Even from this distance, she can tell that all four hooves are skinned and raw as the bloody chicken livers their cook fries with red peppers and heaps of diced onions. She runs around the meadow, kneels to check one plant after another, breaks a flower off the stem, yanks an herb by the roots, tastes and sniffs the leaves. "Weeds, just weeds!" she complains, crushing a flower in her fist.

"Dasha! Stop digging in there," Sabrina calls out to her daughter. "Now! Before something bites your fingers off."

"Oh! Mama, can't you see it needs help?"

"What, darling, what needs help? Be careful, I said!"

But Darya hears nothing but the faint reverberations in her head, the secrets of identifying hawthorn berries, calendula leaves, lavender petals, and arnica in the forest. How to extract their essential oils to create a healing paste.

Sabrina shakes the water off her skirt, adjusts the rifle over one shoulder, and tightens her wide belt. Her loop earrings dance in a fury of copper shades as she runs to catch up with her daughter, who has cut a path through the animals and is already kneeling by the deer.

"It happens in the forest, Dasha, because of the carnivorous pitcher plants. They secrete a sticky substance that lures the animals into a puddle of enzymes and acid that eats into their skin and flesh. It's a wonder this one escaped. There's nothing we can do but put the poor soul out of its misery."

But Darya will not hear of death. Neither will beast nor nature. The surroundings become still, paralyzed, stilted and heavy with what might happen if Sabrina fires her rifle. Not one leaf or petal moves. The birds of paradise are mute. The drone of insects has ceased. Not one single roar or warning grunt can be heard from the aurochs. Sabrina does not notice the frozen surroundings, but Darya does. She records the stillness. Suffers a sharp pain in her opal eye. Fear squeezes her insides, crawls up to claw at her throat, and rises to coat her tongue with the pungent taste of ash. This is the moment she will always remember, a moment of discovery when bad luck might have crept up on her from behind, cold and silent and hair-raising.

She turns and spits three times behind her left shoulder. "There, Mama, will this kill the evil eye?"

Sabrina locks the rifle and slings it back across her shoulder. "This is what I've been told, Dasha. I see you've become a believer."

Darya touches her opal eye. "Is this the evil eye, Mama?"

"Oh, darling, don't say that! On the contrary. It's magic. The reason you are different in a beautiful way. I could hardly bear to think that part of you might be living in the dark."

"But what is wrong with me, Mama? Why is my eye different?"

For a fleeting instant, Sabrina wonders if her daughter is being punished for the sin of her parents, for their having consummated their relationship out of wedlock. But her daughter was born of love, Sabrina muses, and as such, she must be rewarded, not punished.

So, in the forest, surrounded by all types of beasts with obstinate glaring eyes and a sickly deer with skinned hooves that Darya cures with a soothing touch and a concoction of healing plants— Sabrina tells Darya, "I don't know, my darling. I don't know why you were born with an opal eye, why you are different. I wish I knew. What I know is that you are our special blessing, mine and your father's. You are magic, my darling. You will change the world one day. That's all I know. Perhaps one day you'll find out the truth."

Chapter Four

— December 1903 —

SIXTEEN-YEAR-OLD DARYA HAS BEEN summoned to the Livadia Palace, the summer residence of the Imperial Family. The Empress is not well. Dr. Eugene Botkin, the court physician, has determined that in addition to sciatica, the Empress suffers from an inherited weakness of the blood vessels, which can lead to progressive hysteria. He has ordered her to visit the Nauheim spa for a cure, but the Empress will not hear of it. Convinced that nothing short of a miracle can cure her, she refuses to follow Dr. Botkin's orders, take medication, or be subjected to any further medical procedures.

In a letter to Sabrina Josephine, the Empress acknowledges she has been ill nearly all the time. She can rarely appear at formal events, and when she does, she is afterward long laid up. Overtired muscles of the heart, her letter states. "I have rested," the Empress writes, "but am not cured. I need to get well for the sake of my family. I have decided to travel to Yalta to rest at my beloved estate. You wrote that Darya Borisovna seems to possess a healing touch. Perhaps she might heal me too. Bring her to me."

Having traveled to Yalta by train for long, dreary hours, surrounded by nothing but the flat emptiness of the Ukrainian steppe, the lush Yalta panorama is a welcome sight as Darya and her parents make their way to the Livadia Estate. Stretches of beach glitter like crushed glass. A replica of a Greek boat on shore is reminiscent of a long ago past, when Greek sailors settled here to sell handmade gold jewelry that remains buried in plains and ancient burial mounds. All around the pine-lined boulevards, venders hawk red garlic, the popular snack of the region. Families stroll under the shade of ancient *zemlyanichnik*, the red-bark, broad-leafed evergreens. The tropical park of Prymorsky looks down upon the dark waters below, unaware that in less than two decades the entire political and cultural geography of the region will change and a statue of Lenin will be erected here.

Darya flips her shoes off and digs her toes into the warm sand. Suddenly her mouth fills with the taste of bitter ash. It has happened before. Each time she feels a sense of foreboding, originating in her belly and rising like bile to coat her tongue.

"What is it?" Sabrina Josephine asks. "Is it visiting the Empress?"

"I'm not certain, Mama," Darya replies. "I think I am ill myself."

Boris presses his thumb to his daughter's wrist to count her pulse, checks her eyes and the color on her cheeks. Her pulse is fast, but other than that she seems to be in good health. "Come, it's nothing that a moment's rest won't cure," he says, leading her to a seaside bench.

They sit there, all three, facing the sea. Darya is in deep thought, fearing she will fail to help the Empress. It is true that she has cured animals such as the deer with the skinned hooves by applying a concoction of leaves, wild flowers, and roots and the aging borzoi with valerian roots steeped in chamomile. She also treated the scurvy that inflicted the grooms with a pomade of beeswax and essence of lemon peel, relieved the stable hand of miserable spells of hay fever with syrup from the sap of trees, and eased the ache in her father's muscles after a hunt with salve from the marrow of exotic flora and fauna crushed with feverfew leaves and chickpea paste. She had even saved her father from the lethal venom of the fierce snake. But it is different with the Empress. The problems Her Majesty suffers from seem to stem from her heart. This is what Boris and Sabrina say. This is what all the newspapers claim. What does she, Darya, know about the human heart?

Sabrina unlocks her necklace, cups her hands around the jeweled Fabergé egg, and tells her daughter that it has helped her at times of difficulty. Snapping the egg open, she says, "Come closer, darling, and inhale."

The marvelous scent emanating from the enameled belly of the egg strikes Darya with unexpected force. Against her will, she finds herself reaching out as if to touch some pockets of past pain, some powerful emotions she does not yet understand. She is crying uncontrollably, eye-stinging tears that startle Boris and Sabrina.

"Why, darling?" Sabrina asks. "Ambergris is pure magic! Take advantage of its healing potential."

But Darya is inconsolable. She tells Sabrina that the scent evokes the woman who came to her last night in her sleep. She appeared at midnight like a warning, teetering at the fringes of Darya's dream. Appeared with a certain unnerving calmness, a prayer book in her hand.

I am the Ancient One, she said. *I come to you from long ago and far away. I will be here to guide you, warn you of looming misfortunes, of births and deaths and blessings.* She held her book up and told Darya to see her name inscribed in fiery letters. *Do not be afraid,* the Ancient One encouraged. *Come closer.*

But Darya did not move. "This is not my name," she whispered.

You are both women, the Ancient One replied. Then, one by one, she lifted the churning veils concealing her to reveal a dazzling smile.

Darya was comforted. The woman had a kind face. Then, as suddenly, her features began to soften and melt and drip. Her windblown blouse and skirt, which Darya had found beautiful, began to stiffen, shrink, and tighten like metal chains, hampering her fluid movements. She walked with great difficulty, as if fighting tidal waves, struggling ahead toward a ritualistic fire into which she disappeared. Darya startled awake, chilled to the bone, her opal eye throbbing in its socket.

"Listen to the Ancient One, darling," Sabrina advises her daughter. "Pay attention. She must be wise beyond our understanding. What was the other name in the book the Ancient One showed you?"

"I don't remember, Mama, I was scared. My nightgown was stuck to my body when I woke up. I felt like a prisoner. I couldn't breathe."

Sabrina presses the jewel into Darya's hand. "The scent calms me, maybe it will do the same for you. It was a gift from the Empress when she introduced me to your father. Come, darling, look at the valuable piece of ambergris embedded here. The scent is still strong after sixteen years. Cherish it. You can't find it anywhere. Once gone, even the Empress won't be able to replenish it."

The Livadia Estate is resplendent under the warm sun, brimming with pine clover, its lush parks sloping toward the Black Sea with its iodine-rich breezes. The imperial summer home occupies most of the peninsula, nineteen kilometers west of Yalta, where the southern coast of the Crimea spreads over the shores of Mount Moghabi. The unfortunate death of the Emperor's father, Tsar Alexander III, in the smaller palace here, prompted Tsar Nicholas II to set a future date to raze both palaces and replace them with ones better suited to the taste of the Imperial Couple.

For now, gardeners are busy pruning, shearing, clearing the ponds dotted with water lilies, scooping out a stray leaf, petal, or dead bee from the pond. Cossacks on horseback patrol the perimeter of the park. They wear red tunics, sabers swing at their sides, and black boots flash in sunlight. They raise their ushanka caps to salute Darya and her parents.

The Byzantine-style Church of the Exaltation of the Cross looks down upon the palaces below. A flock of boisterous crows circle above the Greek cross on top of the steeple as if mourning a death. The taste of ash is thick in Darya's mouth.

On the horizon, whale humps bob on the surface of the Black Sea. Boris Spiridov tells his daughter that the ambergris in the jeweled egg she now wears around her neck comes from a sperm whale like the one out there. "Did you know that sperm whales suffer from terrible indigestion, sweetheart? Their belching sounds like volcanic eruptions that echo around the hills and startle the people."

Darya smiles for the first time that day.

She is unaware that in a few years, once the construction of the new Livadia Palace is completed, she will walk the same path and explain the same phenomenon to her beloved young charge, the Tsarevich, Alexei Romanov.

Empress Alexandra Feodorovna is in her private chambers, playing Bach on the piano. Maria and Anastasia, the four- and two-year-old grand duchesses, flank her on the bench. They are all in white, encircled by luscious folds of whipped silk and organza. The embroidered silver threads in the Empress's sleeves and high collar are dazzling; the pearls around her throat and diamond-studded golden red hair are magnificent.

Margaretta Eagar, Irish governess to all four grand duchesses, stands behind the piano, ready to take the children away for their afternoon nap before settling down with her newspapers.

At the sight of guests being led in, Miss Eagar claps twice, announcing nap time. But the grand duchesses hop down from the piano bench and run toward Darya, who whisks them up into her arms. The Empress holds on to the piano and pulls herself up to greet Darya and Sabrina with a hug. Boris bows and plants a kiss on her hand. He steps back into the shadows, relinquishing the arena to the ladies. His main responsibility on this trip is to look after the safety of his wife and daughter on the long travel here and back home.

The Empress is indeed ill, Darya muses, appearing frailer than she has seen her on previous occasions. No color on her cheeks. Even her eyes have lost their gray-green spark. Darya's heart turns into a painful fist in her chest until the Empress begins to chat with Sabrina.

"Here you are, my dear missed friend. Come make yourself

comfortable. How radiant you look. And you, Boris Spiridov, you must be tired, but Nicky is expecting you. He holds smaller meetings these days as he finds discussions and opinion exchanges more useful in small groups. Four ministers just left, so join him in the study. He is eager to take you for a swim. I have not been good company to my poor family these days. And you, dear Darya, how are you? Olga and Tatiana are here. They'll be happy to see you. I like that necklace on you; it brings back fond memories. Come, Sabrina Josephine, tell me all about your latest hunting adventures. We so enjoy the expeditions you arrange. And my birds of paradise? Are they well? No longer bothered by those vicious aurochs, I assume."

The butlers serve cups of hot tea with cakes and English biscuits, sweet vatrushka, and sweetmeats set on small white-draped tables. Although it is not yet suppertime, an extra table is set with blinis and fresh caviar.

Darya dislikes caviar, nor can she bear to have hot tea, but to please the Empress, she accepts an offered cake, takes a bite, and offers the girls a bite each. What she craves are the wild berries heaped in a bowl on top of the piano that the imperial children pick for their mother.

Maria taps on Darya's necklace and attempts to open the enamel egg. Anastasia pulls on one of Darya's black curls, coiling it around one finger, then another. Darya wraps her arms around them, gives them an affectionate squeeze, plants a kiss on each of Maria's blue eyes, which the family affectionately calls Maria's saucers.

Anastasia reaches out and pokes Darya's opal eye.

The pain sends Darya reeling.

"Anastasia! No!" The Empress scolds the two-year-old. "You hurt Darya."

Her eye on fire, Darya attempts to catch her breath. There she is again, the Ancient One, somewhere on the fringes of her pain, no more than a shadow, a fleeting imprint behind her eyelids. She is saying something, whispering words that Anastasia's whimpering snuffs out.

"Don't cry," Darya attempts to soothe the child. "I did this once too, because I thought it didn't hurt. But it does."

The Empress orders the children to nap. She kisses the tip of her two fingers and touches them to her daughters' cheeks, sending them away.

Finally, Sabrina asks the Empress about her health. "Not well, my dear, not at all. And the family is making it more difficult for me to recuperate. I suffered a miscarriage, my dear. Terrible. And Nicky's sisters are insinuating that the pregnancy was psychological, blaming Philippe Vachot. Poor chap, he's an innocent mystic who's been doing everything in his power to influence the gender of the baby. But alas! It was too early to know. Xenia went so far as to call it a minor miscarriage, and the other sister spread rumors that it was a hysterical pregnancy. So hurtful, my dear. I wish people would not meddle in my affairs."

Sabrina shifts her chair closer to the Empress and drapes an arm around her shoulders. "My poor Alix. I didn't know. How you must have suffered. When did it happen?"

"Six months to the day. We were devastated."

"You must come to us then, as soon as you're well enough to travel. The Belovezh air will do you good."

"Yes, I promise. Now, tell me about yourself and all about Darya Borisovna. How is she doing in her studies?"

Sabrina tells the pleased Tsarina that Darya is fluent in English now and explains how well she is doing in her spiritual studies. So well, in fact, that in a short time she has become more knowledgeable than the mystic the Empress dispatched to the Belovezh Estate to counsel and hone Darya's healing powers.

"Come, my dear. Come closer." The Empress gestures to Darya, sitting quietly, attempting to ignore her eye, which only makes it throb harder.

Darya takes the offered seat next to the Empress, suddenly content to be here, content to be close to the unexpected warmth emanating from the Empress. Darya's heart settles. The Empress is not ill. Lonely, perhaps, and craving the company of her friend. It is not easy, after all, to be disliked by her in-laws, who consider her arrogant and aloof and regard her as a German with an atrocious French accent who lacks the necessary vitality to produce an heir to the throne. In return, the Empress, in the spirit of the Orthodox faith, only trusts the common people who believe in the inalienable right of the autocratic system, not the aristocracy with their lack of faith and depravity and their unending criticism of her ways. They even critique her taste in art and clothing, which they find middle class and less than imperial, and they go so far as to count with lurid interest the number of times the Empress smiles in public.

The truth, which Darya has heard from her mother, is that when the Tsarina was six years old, diphtheria assailed her home, the palace in Hesse Darmstadt. Within a few weeks Alix lost both her mother and sister. The tragedy caused the cheerful, sensitive, and obstinate little girl to withdraw, a habit reinforced by the Victorian tutelage of her grandmother, Queen Victoria of Britain. Even now, years later, the Empress seldom allows anyone into her private shell, and when she does, it is only to a cherished few: her husband, her daughters, her friend Sabrina Josephine, and perhaps Darya now, who finds herself explaining to the Tsarina how the mystic has taught her to create healing unguents with the plethora of herbs and minerals found in the Belovezh Forest: angelica for pleurisy, bayberry for the chill, black walnut to purify blood, chestnuts to arrest convulsive coughs, and black haw to tone the female reproductive organs.

"Fascinating! Come, Darya. Come with me to the prayer corner." The Empress goes to the back of the room and kneels in front of a wall of icons illuminated by candles. "Let us pray together. You, too, Sabrina, join us. There's power in numbers."

Sabrina sweeps her skirts up, raising the scent of earth and pine and patchouli, the forest scent that has become a second skin. She lacks the patience to stay still and pray, longs to explore the hills on horseback or join the men for a swim in the sea.

Hers is a life of activity, riding, hunting, and loving. Prayers are imparted on the run.

The three women bow their heads as the Tsarina murmurs her prayers. The Empress is preoccupied with the list of healing salves Darya just mentioned, unable to concentrate, even as a crowd of saints of all sizes, shapes, and colors view her with mournful eyes. She is adding and subtracting days to calculate the date of her next menstrual cycle, reflecting on the many times she has not only disappointed Nicky but an entire empire. She turns to Sabrina, rests her hand on her arm, and glances questioningly toward Darya.

Sabrina knows her friend, understands that her modesty holds her back from communicating freely in Darya's presence. "Darya is ready, Alix. I've taught her everything I know, and what I have not, she is learning from her animals. You may discuss any subject you please."

The Empress gazes at Darya, not a hint of her inner conflict reflecting on her face. "The herbs you mentioned, my dear, have you come across others perhaps that might induce the female to produce a boy?"

Darya is unable to conceal the many clashing emotions that creep up into her eyes, turning them deeper gold. She is over-whelmed with a feeling of joy, replaced by unimaginable sadness, and as quickly by a sense of indistinguishable uncertainty, as if she is about to open a door and step into the unknowable.

"Yes, Your Majesty, I can name a number of herbs that might help a woman produce a boy. But you don't need any, Your Majesty. You are with child. A boy. An heir to the throne."

A shadow of a smile brightens the Empress's features. She rises to her feet with a sense of unexpected solidity. She stares into the distance, fingers touching the pearls at her neck, raising the brilliant string, an absent motion as if she is dreaming a better future.

It would take another twenty days for the Empress to believe that she is indeed with child and to allow herself a sliver of hope.

Chapter Five

DARYA BORISOVNA BRAVES THE smoke and commotion of Ekaterinburg and walks toward Rostislav Perfumery, where emissaries of the Nobility Association await her arrival.

She wears a wide-brimmed bonnet woven with golden braids and a fawn mantle trimmed with decaying ostrich feathers. She aims her cane like a weapon at the hostile streets, blaring traffic, belching factories, and rushing pedestrians. She averts her gaze from the wooden cross erected on the site of the Ipatiev House, the spectacle of which has been chipping at her heart, breaking a piece off every time she passes. For seventy-three years the house where the Imperial Family was slaughtered stood here like a filthy wad of spit on the face of the Soviet government, before being demolished fourteen years ago. Now rumors abound that the government intends to build a memorial Church-on-the-Blood here to commemorate the Romanovs.

A legacy of shame taints Ekaterinburg, infusing generations with the need to forget. Brains have become dense and murky. The Romanov executions are regarded as a legend rather than a stain on the canvas of history. Generations seem unable to conceptualize facts, a nation feeding on folklore. Darya, with her elaborate hats topped with faded, artificial flowers and her flounced gowns of the Romanov era, is an unwelcome reminder.

How in the world did she not realize then, not until it was too late, that a volcanic brew of discontent bubbled under them all? Such ignorance, she berates herself, such lack of judgment to invite that wandering monk, Grigori Rasputin, to court. By the time she realized what she had done, the revolution had spiraled out of control. The Bolshevik Red Bastards deceived the people with a grand illusion of a Soviet state, set brother against brother, executed countless millions, and left a ravaged Russia in their wake. The end of the Romanovs, the Bolsheviks had supposed, their relief echoing across seas and oceans. But they were mistaken, the enemies of the monarchy, they certainly were. There is a reason why she survived that black night in the basement in Ekaterinburg. A reason why the Tsarevich has survived too.

The bells of the Church of the Trinity announce four o'clock. She arrives at the perfumery and takes a moment to collect herself.

The store window is packed with shiny bottles nestled in crushed satin the color of the Siberian aquamarine brooch the Tsarevich Nicholas gave his fiancée three months before their wedding. Yes, Darya remembers well the excitement with which the Empress showed her the signed initials of Fabergé work-master Henrik Wigström on the brooch. She wore it often. The Tsar enjoyed seeing his beloved wife bedecked in imperial regalia and shimmering in jewels. He insisted that his massive collection of gifts to her be carried in large hardwood boxes wherever the family traveled.

A "Store Closed" sign dangles behind the perfumery's glass door. It is not surprising that the meeting is held here.

Rostislav Alekseevich Dalevich is a staunch monarchist. His perfumery is the hub of all types of political rumors that have to do with the Romanovs. He is also a craniometrist and a forensic anthropologist, whose expertise the government often seeks.

Rostislav is Darya's most important link to the outside world. He is the man in possession of the latest news. Together they have mourned the rise of Bolshevism and atheism and celebrated

Leningrad's vote to take back its rightful name, St. Petersburg. They followed with skeptical interest as Communism came to an end two years earlier, Germany was reunified, and Boris Yeltsin administered the dissolution of the Soviet Union.

She lifts her necklace and takes a deep breath from the Fabergé egg, the emanating scent evoking delicious memories of her mother.

Darya braces herself and rings the bell. The door is unlocked from inside, and Rostislav ushers her into his sun-splashed perfumery with its floor-to-ceiling windows, chrome walls, and immaculate glass counters. Bottles of varying colors sparkle on shelves and counters. Crystal, silver, and Lalique stoppers of different shapes and designs—seeded with turquoise beads, onion-shaped church domes, mythical forms—adorn bottlenecks. Plants, herbs, and flowers are immersed in clear cylinders filled with alcohol, undergoing the process of enfleurage for extracting essential oils.

She follows the perfumer across the shiny linoleum floor, averting her gaze from his scarred profile, caused by an accident in his youth that consumed half his face, leaving the other side as smooth as a baby's bottom.

It happened when his father, a forensic anthropologist, went mad in the years of anarchy, ordering his son to study the science of examining cadavers. But Rostislav wanted nothing to do with malodorous, putrefying bodies. He liked to distill the essence of flowers, to measure and weigh and mix all types of petals to compose aromatic formulas. One day, finding his son's nose poked into a fistful of rose petals, the father had, in a burst of rage, hurled a bottle of acid at the boy. Just like that, the left side of Rostislav's face was burned into a permanent grimace.

Now, he leads Darya into a room with pastel wall-to-wall carpeting and whitewashed walls, aluminum chairs, and a round table on which a bottle of champagne chills in an ice bucket.

Two men, emissaries of the Russian nobility, and a woman, executive secretary of the association, rise to greet her. She acknowledges them with a brief nod and takes her seat among the few who have the courage to face her, the few whose political ideology resembles her own. She studies the group, their expressions and mannerisms, stares intently at their unflinching gaze to determine their honesty. In these unstable times, when people are either afraid to talk or have no qualms about convicting innocent citizens, everyone is suspect. Having concluded that they are neither on God's side nor the devil's, she addresses them with guarded anticipation.

"What can I do for you?"

The executive secretary tugs her skirt over stout knees. "Thank you for granting us a few minutes of your time. As you know, the last six years have brought a change in our country with glasnost and perestroika—"

"An important junction in our history," the younger man adds, pomaded hair and aristocratic forehead glistening in the white light from the great windows.

Darya struggles to stop her opinions from bursting out of her mouth. She has no faith in glasnost or perestroika, is certain that not even a single Baltic state has truly become independent. The full dissolution of the Central Committee of the Communist Party will not happen until each and every godless Communist is buried upside-down like rotten radishes.

The silver-haired, square-jawed emissary coughs twice and lights a cigarette. His voice is raspy. "It's time to stabilize Russia. Unify our national identity. Fill the ideological vacuum the Communist regime left."

"How, may I ask, do you intend to achieve that?" Darya asks, a note of impatience creeping into her voice.

"What do *you* propose?" The gray-haired man throws the question back at her.

A bitter smile appears on her face. "Need you ask? To reinstate the monarchy, of course."

"Exactly! And this is our intention."

She aims her incredulous gaze at them. "Good heavens! Is this the truth?"

"It certainly is. We have been planning for years. In fact, preliminary preparations to reinstate the monarchy are in progress as we speak."

Darya gasps, digs her fists in her pocket. "Then you must have someone in mind for our next Tsar."

"Possibly," the executive secretary replies. "And that's the reason we called this emergency meeting. Rostislav Alekseevich, please explain the rest."

The perfumer abandons his seat, adjusts his jacket about his wrestler's shoulders, and begins to pace the room. "This is classified, you understand. Please refrain from discussing it until the government makes a decision. Seven days ago, Boris Yeltsin authorized the opening of the Ekaterinburg grave believed to be the burial site of the Romanovs. I was asked to appear at the government morgue to help a group of forensic anthropologists identify the recently exhumed remains."

Darya doesn't know what to do with her hands, her wild heart, the many clashing voices in her head. She had, for years, mapped the plan for a day such as this as she went about looking for the Tsarevich, imagining how she would greet him, embrace him, ask for his forgiveness. The quest became her life's goal, the nucleus of her universe. It kept her alive in hope of purging the sins she committed in her past life, so much so that the thought that he might have perished with the others did not occur to her. And now Rostislav is telling her that the remains of the Imperial Family have been disinterred. What if the Tsarevich is discovered among them? What if her life's quest to find him proves to be nothing but an old woman's pitiful longings? She finds a hallucinatory berry in her pocket, is about to drop it in her mouth, but decides against it. She cannot escape into the past, not now.

With great relish, Rostislav continues to recount the events of the last few nights, every detail down to the decor of the morgue, where the walls are the color of urine and he keeps on dropping bonbons in his dry mouth to mask the taste of death.

"It was terrible, I tell you! Dreadful beyond belief. The bodies were chopped to pieces, burned in sulfuric acid, and buried for decades in a shallow grave. The bones were no longer sheathed in flesh, of course, but had to be boiled clean before the meticulous labor of identification began." The next six nights Rostislav had dined in the morgue while the bones boiled in large vats that emitted the stench of decay. He chewed on a piece of bread rolled around a slice of cured ham, periodically setting his plate on the pot handle, where steam kept his meal warm. He conducted a silent discourse with his father. He had become a forensic anthropologist, he boasted to his long-gone father, but not any ordinary cadaver-poking anthropologist. He was examining the remains of the Imperial Family. Every now and then he checked the bubbling brew of remains and popped yet another bonbon in his mouth.

"It's hard enough to identify the two hundred and six bones in the human body. But nearly impossible to recognize chemically degraded bones that were exposed in a shallow grave for seventy-three years. For hours we reconstructed shattered thigh bones, bayonet-crushed skulls, burned and disintegrated vertebrae. Quite difficult, but in the end, we managed to provide tentative, preliminary results. More needs to be done, of course—sample preparation, DNA extraction, PCR amplifications, extensive DNA tests using samples from relatives—to prove the authenticity of the remains. Before conclusive results are announced and even then—"

"To the point, Rostislav Alekseevich," Darya interrupts. "We don't have all day."

"The remains," he replies, "belong to the Romanovs."

"Are you certain?" Darya asks. "Swear on your mother's grave!"

"Please, Darya Borisovna, do not insult me."

Darya stands up and walks to the great windows, the bright

light sharp as razors. She has an urge to pray, but to whom? To what? The windows face the backyard, where carefully delineated beds of daisies, magnolias, begonias, and lilies sprout as colorful as the bottles displayed inside. When did spring arrive? Will next year be different? Will she notice the change of seasons? Rejoice at the blooming flowers? Feel the autumn leaves crunch beneath her feet? Feel the first fat snowflakes piling on the brim of her hat? She turns to face the perfumer, her throat dry, her tongue heavy. She wets her lips and asks the question she has been avoiding for seventy-three years. "Did you identify the remains of Alexei?"

"This is what I'm getting to, Darya Borisovna. You are making me nervous; can I ask you to sit down?"

She stands paralyzed, unable to move, until he approaches her and asks if she is all right, if he can offer her a glass of water, which makes her let out a loud sigh, because she realizes that nothing will calm her now, not even Little Servant's potent vodka. "I don't want water, Rostislav. Just answer my question."

"Your answer is that I have no doubt, no doubt at all, that the bones of the Tsarevich, Alexei Nikolaevich Romanov, heir and Grand Duke of Russia, were *not* among the remains!"

All eyes are on Darya, and it takes a moment for her to process the good news and another moment for her muscles to function again. Going to the small table, she grabs a flute of champagne, raises it in a rare gesture of joy, and drinks it in three quick gulps. She seizes the perfumer's hand and gives it a few affectionate squeezes. "Thank you, Rostislav. You confirm what I knew all along. Here, have some champagne!"

The executive secretary pats her lips with a napkin. "You should know, Darya Borisovna, that we received a recent telegraph informing us that a claimant to the throne has been living quietly in Russia."

"Where?" Darya cries out. "Right here? The Tsarevich himself? His son? Grandson perhaps?"

"You may find that out for yourself. Being the only surviving member of that Imperial Court, you are best suited to confirm, or refute, this person's claim. A meeting can be arranged."

Darya clutches her cane, the contours of her body acquiring a new youthfulness. "When? Where?"

"As soon as you are ready to travel to the estate of Grand Duchess Sophia Sheremetev."

Chapter Six

KNIFE IN HAND, DARYA risks the steep stairs to the upper level, making her way across the hallway of her home. Along the walls remain faded traces of frames of all sizes, the theft of which she never stops to grieve, her memories of the Imperial Court—coronations, births, anniversaries, deaths— etched on those canvases.

The same impudent rodent that gnawed at her toes this morning scrambles behind her and up the steps, intent on raiding her secret hiding place and digging its greedy teeth into her treasure. She lifts her cane to plunge the silver tip down in one fast motion. Her arm held high, it occurs to her that enough is enough. Ekaterinburg has seen its share of death.

She shoos the rodent off with a flip of the cane, pressing her lips to the handle, the double-headed eagles, the cane's shaft smooth with polishing oils—sandalwood, ginger, and patchouli. She glances around to check if she is alone, an unshakable habit from the past. A smile on her plump lips, she mimics the Tsar, raises his cane above her head, and waves it with agility improbable for her age, as if the Tsar were reprimanding his only son for concealing himself beneath the dinner table at a state gala held in the Entertainment Palace. He had removed the high-heeled shoe of the Grand Duchess Chostayovska and planted it on the table in front of his father. The Tsar had ordered his son to return the "trophy" to its rightful owner, which the Tsarevich had, but not before dropping a plump, juicy strawberry inside. The grand duchess had squeezed her foot back into her shoe, a horrible smile pasted on her rouged face. The child was not allowed to attend formal events for several weeks after that.

An unfair punishment, Darya had bristled, since it was not often that Alyosha's health allowed him to attend such ceremonies. As far as she was concerned, a firm warning from his father would have sufficed. Still, he was a good father, Nicholas II; he certainly was.

Making her way down the hall, Darya takes a moment to acknowledge the mounted aurochs head above the door to the salon, its dull gaze a permanent reminder of her parents. This, too, is a long-held habit, as if ignoring the first aurochs Sabrina hunted might unleash more misfortunes. She wiggles two fingers in her pocket and a breeze of butterflies emerges to soften her mood, adorn her hair, and burrow into the faded ermine embellishing her collar.

She unlocks the door and steps inside. The salon is an oval-shaped theater, where she once shared a tumbler or two of vodka with the Imperial Family and their guests, where she continues to enjoy her evening vodka laced with hallucinatory berries. Just enough to stir her memories to life without blotting out her present. The Corinthian columns, flaking stucco, and patterned parquet floor are reminders of a distant opulent era, resplendent with imperial silver, porcelain, crystal, and exotic flowers shipped from the imperial greenhouse at Tsarskoe Selo. This is where Château Lafite, Mouton Rothschild, and Larose were in endless supply and the French champagne, Monopole from Charles Heidsieck in Rheims, bubbled like eternal springs. Where dinners were followed by ballets performed by the Mariinsky Theater corps de ballet, and ornate menus with the imperial warrant, supplied by his majesty's court printer, A. A. Levinson Moscow, were a much coveted souvenir of an evening of art and music and culinary bliss.

Now, a lattice of cobwebs clings to the chandelier that hangs over a stage. A finger-depth of water from a leak overhead encircles the stage that should have rotted decades ago, but excellent wood and craftsmanship hold it together. The sound-making machine for wind, thunder, and rain and a device that once raised the orchestra pit so the theater could be used as a ballroom were plundered in front of her eyes when the revolution was still in full force. She had crouched behind the velvet curtains then, her mourning heart a bloody fist in her chest, her veins jumping at her temples as the thieves combed through every niche and corner, poking their bayonets up the shaft of the fireplaces, ripping the blue damask of the Louis XVI sofas and armchairs, yanking the French goblin tapestry off the wall, carting away the massive silk carpet, a gift from Sultan Abdul Hamid II of the Ottoman Empire. She was thirty-one years old then and did not know how to utilize her greatest asset; a glare from her recently cracked opal eye would have sent any thief bolting to the nearest exit.

She lingers in front of the last portrait Avram had painted of her, which the Bolshevik bastards found no use for. She strokes the canvas, the grief palpable in every brushstroke. She is naked in the painting, reclining on a dais, her nipples erect, her soft curves half-lit by the chandelier, her grief-stricken eyes gazing at the painter with a blend of wonder and adoration.

In the gold-framed, tarnished mirror above the fireplace, she gazes at the ancient woman with hair like silver seas. With steady thumb and forefinger, she plucks out a black strand woven among her curls. Her bug-eyed servant has strict orders not to light the two fireplaces in the salon or any of the thirty-six others around her home. It took a chunk of ambergris and the powers of a wandering monk for her to understand why fires thrust her into fits of shivering, piercing her marrow like gusts of Siberian winds.

Wrapped in a blanket, Little Servant walks around the Entertainment Palace in winter, setting small blazes to keep himself warm, unable to comprehend what sort of blood runs in his mistress's veins to make her react in such a strange manner.

She squats by the fireplace, checks the flue for dirt or rat droppings. Finding none, she flicks off a fleck of dust from the gold molding around the hearth, and then pulls out a large package from a hidden niche up the flue.

She unravels layers of fabric to reveal a porous, waxy chunk of ambergris, the ashy shades variegated like marble. She caresses the ambergris, rubs her palms together, raising them to her nose to drink in the perfume of ages, the high and low tides, the warmth of sun-drenched waves, lightning in the Crimean skies, hot sand flowing between her toes. The salon fills with the scent of ocean breeze, warm honey, and crustaceans, sending her reeling back to the day her mother gave her the Fabergé necklace, back to her life with the Romanovs, and to Rasputin and that fateful day by the Crimean shores when she discovered this ambergris.

Spreading her fingers across the surface, she measures half, then three-fourths, then a bit more. This much she owes to the Tsarevich. Bracing herself, she raises the knife and brings it down with a swift motion, dissecting the ambergris.

Like a warning, something pokes out of the cut section. With great trepidation, she passes her palm over the buttery surface to discover what might be embedded in it. Her fingers catch upon the object, smooth and hard. She grabs the tip and carefully loosens it, jiggling it this way and that, a bit more pressure to dislodge it without causing damage. Out slides a miniature enamel hand splayed as if in prayer. With two fingers, she carefully grasps the little hand, never letting go, afraid it might break or slip back and bury itself again. Her breath painful in her chest, she coaxes out the rest. An amulet! A mythical childlike figure with pointed emerald ears and an opal stomach gapes at her with ruby eyes.

She lets out a cry of disbelief, closes her fist around the amulet and then opens her hand again to take a closer look. Her heart thrashing about, she rests the amulet on her open palm and checks the back, her forefinger verifying an engraving. Hastening to the window, she flips the curtains open, raising a cloud of dust and letting in a shaft of light that is not much help. She needs her magnifying glass. It is illogical that her eyes pierce through people's chests to decipher their emotions but have trouble reading small characters. She rifles through a stack of yellowing newspapers on a side table, in the drawers of the ornate cabinet, behind the portrait leaning on the mirror above the mantelpiece. She half-opens the door and calls, "Little Servant! The magnifying glass. Immediately!" She paces back and forth, cursing the slow dwarf, who must be drunk on berries.

A tentative scratch on the door. "Madame. Your magnifying glass."

She thrusts her hand out and grabs the glass, lowering it over the engraving, moving it up and down, back and forth. Unable to trust her eyes, she wipes the glass with her skirt and gazes at the engraving with the possessed eyes of a nonbeliever.

Alexei Nikolaevich Romanov August 12, 1904

The memory of the Tsarevich's christening day remains vibrantly alive after eighty-seven years. A great honor was conferred upon her that hot summer day. A young, inexperienced orphan appointed to carry the heir to the Russian throne to the baptismal font. Even then, she already felt the Tsarevich with her heart, with every nerve in her body, deep in her bone marrow. That day she had pinned this very amulet to the Tsarevich's baptism robe, slightly to the left, just above his heart. The amulet disappeared several years later. With its loss, the Romanov fortunes turned for the worse.

She gropes for an understanding, which is out of her grasp for now, fastens the amulet to her dress, then goes to the full-length mirror of mottled glass on the other end of the salon to check herself. The baptism comes to life in the mirror. The Imperial Family, dignitaries from around the world, diplomats, grand dukes and grand duchesses congregated in the chapel in the Peterhof Palace to celebrate with the Tsar and Tsarina as if all were well in their world. But all was not well. Russia was at war with Japan. The Russian navy was struggling. A series of defeats ignited the people's anger. Discontent with the Imperial Family, for their presumed indifference to corruption in the government, was simmering around the nation. Unions were formed by liberals, socialists, Marxists, and populists. Seeds of a revolution were being planted.

Darya folds the remaining ambergris in its protective layers and tucks it back onto the upper niche of the fireplace. She inspects the rest of the room for signs of intrusion, the curlicues over the window, the precise details obscure now, the once magnificent indigo faded, the rusting lock on the windows. The stem of the chandelier, covered with decaying velvet, still firmly anchored, sways slightly, as if at the hand of a playful ghost. She steps out of the salon and locks the door behind her, nudging the handle this way and that as she does with every other locked door across the upper corridor. Life has taught her to be on her guard. No telling when another dissident, another soldier, or another group of revolutionaries might burst through the door and attempt to pilfer more of her memories.

"Dinner is being served, Madame," Little Servant calls from the lower level.

"I am busy," she replies, descending the stairs.

Little Servant is at the landing, his face drooping with disappointment. "A tumbler of vodka, perhaps?"

"Maybe later, but do not wait for me. Have your dinner, let out the cats, and feed the butterflies."

She enters her room. Selecting a couple of the Empress's outfits, two sets of underwear, a pair of shoes, and another in case of a formal event, she lays them on the bed next to the ambergris. She checks a handbag with a catch of coils tipped with metal balls that snap into each other. The purse is sturdy enough to hold the precious jewels she will be carrying to the Sheremetev Estate, jewels she has been safeguarding for decades.

Her mouth is bitter with the taste of ash at the pungent memory of the day she buried the imperial jewels under floorboards in the cellar here. She cursed and screamed and grieved as she buried sapphires, rubies, diamonds, pearls, and emeralds, certain they would be returned to their rightful owner one day. She was right. That day is here.

She crosses the length of her bedroom toward the moth-filled storage room with its odor of things past their prime. She tries to avoid this place. Once the Tsar's library, the room is now storage for abandoned chests, trunks, and assorted boxes. She takes a quick look around and selects a valise, the pigskin dulled with the patina of time, the elaborate gold studs imparting an air of decadence. A faint memory of having seen this valise somewhere in the palace, or perhaps being carried by one of the servants, is sparked. She snuffs out the memory and drags out the valise, depositing it on the bed. Surprised at the ease with which the lock clicks open, she takes a closer look, discovering that the lock and the studs are made of solid gold, which, unlike humans, does not rust. She lifts the top, stirring up a whiff of mildew and stale cologne.

A folded piece of paper, a page perhaps ripped from a notebook, lies forlorn and yellowing in a corner of the spider-webbed, opium-brown lining. She steps back and observes the sheet as if it might come to life and bite her or open wide a door to intruding memories that she would rather keep at bay. The outline of some inscription peeks out under a curved edge of the paper. She picks it up with thumb and forefinger, checking every angle before unfolding the delicate sheet to reveal the handwriting she knows well. The inscription, somewhat slanted, the delicacy of certain letters with their elongated loops, the bluish purple ink, a special formula resistant to fading. Yes, she has no doubt the handwriting belongs to Tsar Nicholas II. He was meticulous, her Tsar, he certainly was, caring about every loop and precise curlicue set on paper.

A vein in her throat hammers as she settles on the edge of the bed and carefully smooths the paper on her lap. Her glance jumps up to the top of the page, seeking a headline, a date, which is missing.

It has been an especially difficult day. It is hot and we are not allowed to open windows. Sunny's sciatica forces her to remain in bed… The girls busy themselves with crocheting. And… Alexei…boredom…with his box of trinkets. At nine there was a vesper service. The day of the Feast of Presentation we had to forego church service…did not allow it. It is heartbreaking to hear…what is happening in Petrograd… How could those Bolshevik scoundrels… My soul is in turmoil. I am preoccupied with the same…thought. Mogilev! War! Such poor judgment… lifetime of torment…forgive this sin…why did you? Why? Lord…cannot…not even with Sunny…the details I shall take to my grave.

Darya turns the page around, this way and that, searching for another sentence, another word, hoping to unearth the meaning of the faded letters, any clue to illuminate the reason for the Tsar's agony. What could have burdened him with such personal torment? She passes a finger over the frayed edge, certain now that the sheet must have been torn from the journal he most likely kept when residing in the House of Special Purpose.

She folds the paper and tucks it into the lining of the suitcase, another mystery assigned to the revelations of time.

Clad in a black velvet dress trimmed with handmade gauze, flowing sleeves, and a train frayed by thousands of accidental footsteps, she lifts the suitcase and begins her journey to the estate of Grand Duchess Sophia Sheremetev.

Chapter Seven

A WARM CRIMEAN BREEZE TRANSPORTS the faraway roar of waterfalls through the window of the rented Volga, the engine coughing spurts of black smoke. Farther on the horizon, beyond the subtropical belt of thriving foliage, an ancient volcano pierces the brilliant sky. Grape-lush vineyards adorn the valleys along the cliffs. Darya's eye throbs at the memory of those far-gone years, when hundreds of bottles of red and white wine from Massandra, the Emperor's Crimean estate, were consumed during winter balls in St. Petersburg.

Eighty years have passed since she last set eyes on this marvelous landscape of jutting cliffs, deep canyons, and lush mountains that look over the Black Sea. On these shores, she found the ambergris. On these shores, Grigori Yefimovich Rasputin succeeded in breaking her resistance and thrusting her into a hypnotic trance. And on these shores, her mother, Princess Sabrina Josephine of Corinin, gave her the Fabergé egg necklace she has been carrying like a talisman for eighty-eight years.

Now, decades later, her memory intact, Darya turns to Rostislav behind the wheel. "Do what you can to move this monstrous car. You are not transporting breakable goods."

Rostislav wipes his forehead with his sleeve. "We should have checked into an inn first."

"Nyet! Never. The less time in these hateful places, the better."
Even when her continued search for the Tsarevich takes her away
from home, forcing her to rent a room, she makes a point of leaving
her meager belongings in her travel bag rather than feed them to
a closet that must have nibbled on the soiled underwear of one
or another fatherless Bolshevik. "Rostislav Alekseevich Dalevich!
Why are you so slow today?"

"See the state outdoor inspection directorates? They're packed
with policemen." She sighs, checking the cache of jewels in her
purse. A butterfly flutters out to settle on her shoulder. "Shoo,"
she scolds. "Move to the right before I spit on you." She rests
her head back on the seat, certain she will never accept what has
become of her country, never understand a generation ready to
be led by a bunch of oppressors. She unlocks her necklace and
inhales deeply.

The perfumer's pupils narrow, and as if he were in the presence
of Shesmu, the Egyptian god of precious oils and embalming, he
draws a series of deep breaths through his flaring nostrils. He is
familiar with ambergris, has often attempted, unsuccessfully, to
acquire some in the black market to use as fixative in his perfumes,
to provide a base from which to create an enhanced blend of rare,
long-lasting fragrances. He has tried numerous times but failed
to emulate with any other ingredient the uniquely subtle perfume
ambergris adds to the mix of scents in a bottle.

He wonders how Darya acquired this rare ambergris. The
harmony of inebriating scents is proof that this ambergris is far
superior to any harvested from the irritated stomach or intestinal
tracts of dead sperm whales. This ambergris was vomited into the
ocean and properly cured for decades. If he applied his expertise to
ambergris, born as it is of a pathological condition caused by indi-
gestible marine food—octopus beaks, tough shellfish, squid—he
would create an exceptional perfume that would secure his name
as the greatest nose in history.

Darya shuts the Fabergé egg and locks the clasp with a snap.

"Darya Borisovna, do you have some ambergris to spare?"

"I wish I had, Rostislav. I'd like to replenish my own necklace, not much left in it. Let me know if you happen to come across any. Will you?"

Rostislav directs his stare toward the winding road, his knuckles white around the steering wheel. She is hiding the truth from him. The imperceptible catch in her voice, the slight flutter of her eyelids, the nervous tick of her fingers on her purse are proof enough. In fact, she must have stashed some away in a safe place. Among her treasure of jewels, perhaps, which she pawns with him once in a while in exchange for cash to purchase food and other necessities. The jewels, she insists, are placed with him as collateral until she raises money to pay him back. But as far as he is concerned, they are his to keep, since the possibility of her raising cash is nil.

Darya strokes the rounded opal belly, the splayed hands and bulging ruby eyes of the amulet pinned to her dress. She feels a sudden surge of optimism. There is a good reason why the amulet concealed itself for years to show up only now.

The Volga rolls past the tropical park of Prymorsky, where the statue of Lenin looks down upon the dark waters below. Darya's mouth fills with bitter ash at the arrogance of that face. A plaque declares Lenin's 1920 decree: On the Use of the Crimea for the Medical Treatment of the Working People. "Such nonsense," she bristles. "The hateful man turned the Crimea into a mass playground, destroying the cultural heart of Russia."

"At your left!" Rostislav exclaims. "The Livadia Palace."

Her muscles tense at the sight of the Imperial Palace that holds a treasure trove of memories. Once the pride and joy of the Romanovs, it is a museum now. "Why, Rostislav, tell me why they had to turn the palace into a museum. And not even to commemorate them as saints, but to put their life on display as if they were some cheap artifact. Even their dogs were treated better. Tell me, Rostislav Alekseevich Dalevich, do you think the

Imperial Family might have predicted their fate? They were saints, after all. Divine."

"Yes, they certainly were. Yet I don't understand. So many turned against them in the end. Yes, there was poverty, of course, but the Tsar was trying to fix things. We are an impatient people, Darya. We expect our demands to be met right away."

"No! We didn't do this. The Bolsheviks did! The Reds! The Liberals! Whatever they called themselves," Darya shouts, grabbing Rostislav's arm with one hand, the other pounding on the dashboard.

Rostislav loses his grip on the steering wheel. The car veers dangerously close to the precipice. Reclaiming control of the car and of his thumping heart, he shouts, "Calm down before you get us both killed!"

"Calm! How in God's name? The bloodthirsty fanatics with their 'Declaration on Liberated Europe' destroyed everything. Is this a liberated Europe, Rostislav? Look into my eyes and tell me the truth!" Faced with his silence, she digs into her purse and finds two hallucinatory berries hiding under the jewels. She is about to drop them in her mouth but restrains herself. Today, her present is far more important than her past.

Rostislav pops the dashboard open and retrieves a few balls of chewing gum.

"When I meet the Tsarevich, I'll invite you to Massandra for a nice bottle of Madeira. Maybe two. We'll become drunk, Rostislav, as drunk as Dionysus."

"Not *when* you meet the Tsarevich, Darya. *If* you meet him. There are too many ifs in the picture. His age, for one. If he survived hemophilia and the ravages of time, he is eighty-seven, not so young. For another, no one said that this contender to the throne is the Tsarevich himself."

"The Tsarevich is alive and well, Rostislav. And I don't like your glum attitude. Focus and drive faster."

A dismissive smile on his burnt profile, he steers the car toward a peninsula-like clearing at the bend of the road and brings it to a stop at a viewing point that juts out from the mountainside. His jaws grinding the gum, Rostislav unfolds the map and spreads it out on the steering wheel. He points a finger. "There."

Perched on a cliff ahead of them is the Sheremetev Estate. There, awaiting her is the contender to the throne, the same Tsarevich with whom she had formed an emotional bond long before his mother became aware of her pregnancy.

Chapter Eight

THE VOLGA SPUTTERS ACROSS the broad circular driveway of the Sheremetev Estate. Ornate double gates crowned with the Sheremetev crest—two lions, one holding a scepter in its paw and a laurel branch in its mouth, the other brandishing an olive branch—swing shut behind them.

The European-style masterpiece of architecture created by the Italian Bartolomeo Rastrelli overlooks the warm shores of the Ukraine, one side sloping down toward the sea without so much as a fence to mark its boundaries. The estate is notorious for having changed hands twenty times in the span of two centuries, lost in drinking bouts and card games, mortgaged repeatedly, yet managing to remain in the possession of one or another member of the Sheremetev family.

This is home, Darya sighs. This is how one should live, without shame and in full view. She is familiar with the Sheremetevs, one of the wealthiest families during her youth. Unlike other distinguished families that rose and fell with the change of Emperors, this dynasty remained in favor to the very end. The Sheremetevs had served the Imperial Court as companions to the Tsarevich, chamberlain to the Tsarina, and diplomats and military commanders to the Tsar. Nicholas II granted the Sheremetevs parcels of fertile land in south Russia and the Ukraine, in addition to vast tracts of forest land, which enabled them to multiply their wealth by erecting paper mills and factories.

Although a number of family members were murdered during the Bolshevik Revolution and others fled the country, the current owner, the Grand Duchess Sophia, remained in Russia by bribing her way into anonymity and then back to a resurrected lifestyle few imagined in a postrevolutionary world. Rumor has it that the estate sought and finally found the grand duchess when she emerged from anonymity after the revolution to reclaim her property, brandishing her endless charm and a wealth of loose diamonds.

Guards at the main door descend the broad marble stairs, striding to each side of the Volga to welcome Darya and Rostislav and whisk their suitcases away.

Darya ignores the offered arm of a servant whose saucer eyes become rounder at the sight of this woman who seems to have stepped out of a sepia photograph of the Romanov era.

The double doors of polished oak are flung open, and they are led into the grand foyer that once boasted one of the largest collections of European art but, having been pillaged during the revolution, has been restocked with modern master-pieces by Chagall and Kandinsky and a portrait of wide-eyed Byzantine saints with pale locks and miniature arms and faces. Jewel-encrusted Fabergé cigarette boxes and malachite ashtrays are scattered on tables—part of a cache of inherited treasures brought back from exile. It is rumored that the duchess is in possession of thirty-six diamonds, ranging in size from eight to sixteen carats of such unparalleled color, cut, and clarity that it's impossible to set a price on them.

A flicker of hope flares in the perfumer's dark eyes. If he plays his hand right, it would not matter much to the grand duchess to reward him with one of the jewel-encrusted ashtrays strewn around the foyer like pebbles. The bankrupt government lacks the resources to import high-grade essences for his perfumes, let alone expensive fixatives such as ambergris, yet one of these ashtrays might fulfill his ambitions.

Darya checks the surroundings with delight and reverence, as if she has set foot into one of the Romanov Palaces again, as if the Tsarina would walk in at any moment and ask Darya how her charge is faring. She combs her hair with her fingers, smooths her skirt, and slides her tongue over perfectly healthy teeth as the steady tap of heels on parquet floors announces the imminent arrival of the grand duchess.

She emerges from one of the many branching halls, ushering in the scent of Rose Blanche, the Empress Alexandra's favorite fragrance. A wide-brimmed hat with an ornamental feather casts a shadow across her face. An enamel cigarette holder stands out from between her blood-red lips. She toys with a strand of pearls the likes of which Darya had only seen on the Empress, freshwater pearls shimmering like iridescent peacock fans. A fleck of cigarette ash falls on the perfect gloss of the duchess's red nail polish, and she blows it off with an expression of annoyance.

Behind her is a handsome man clad in uniform, leather belt cinching his massive girth, an ashtray balanced on his palm. His gaze shoots this way and that, then lands on Darya and Rostislav as if their mere presence is an affront to his mistress.

Diamond bangles circling a slender wrist, the grand duchess reaches out a hand to her guests. "I expected you earlier. He is here, you know. The contender to the throne. Quite a day around here, very unusual. His presence has stirred a commotion. Do follow me to the salon." She traverses the Persian carpet and hardwood floors, past a silk-paneled cloakroom with scented candles flickering on mahogany shelves and through a vestibule leading into a salon.

She settles in a chair at the head of the salon and gestures for Darya and Rostislav to take the two opposite seats. Having established them in their respective places, an expression of ennui descends on her soft-powdered face.

Every jarring note of the expensive imitation perfume the

duchess wears is an affront to Rostislav's olfactory senses. He clicks his briefcase open, removes a Baccarat bottle, twists the stopper off, and waves it under his nose. "Your favorite perfume, Madame. Rose Blanche. The exact formula without a single missing or added note."

The grand duchess pats the transparent shell of each earlobe with a dab of perfume. The shadow of a smile appears on her scarlet lips.

"A gift for you too." Rostislav addresses the handsome man, who hovers over his mistress as if to shield her from some imminent danger. "The Tsar's favorite eau de cologne of aromatic cedar and eucalyptus leaves."

"Thank you," he booms in a voice even more intimidating than his stature.

The duchess tips her chin toward the ceiling and blows out a puff of smoke. She grinds the cigarette in an ashtray with remnants of lipstick-smeared butts and addresses Darya, "You are a living legend, Darya Borisovna, and as legends go, some surrounding accounts are true and others pure fabrications. Tell me about your relationship to the Romanovs, especially to my grandmother, Tamara."

"God bless her soul. She was far too young and talented to die, and from grief no less." Darya unlocks her purse to search for remnants of a berry, a sliver of ambergris, anything to temper the assailing memories, but she takes a deep breath and quickly snaps her purse shut. "The Tsarevich was fond of her miniatures, so much so that I am not surprised he would feel safe here with Your Majesty."

"No need to address me in this manner," the grand duchess replies with an intimacy uncommon to her breeding. "Duchess will suffice. And it is premature to conclude that the contender to the throne awaiting your arrival is indeed the Tsarevich." Her gaze suddenly falls on the amulet pinned to Darya's dress. "Where have I seen this before? Was it in a photograph? Yes, I believe so."

"On the Tsarevich's lapel," Darya offers. "I made certain it was always there."

"Yes, yes. But how did it come into your possession?"

Searching the wide-set, sable eyes of the duchess and encountering no threat, a smile breaks over Darya's face. "It is a long and unbelievable story. It was my gift to the Tsarevich, and it somehow found its way back to me."

The grand duchess taps a gold-tipped cigarette on the tabletop. The warden hurries to light her cigarette. "So tell me everything, Darya. Do not leave anything out, not even the executions. Is it true that you were there? And if so, how in our Lord's name did you survive?"

"My story does not begin at the end, but at the beginning, when the Romanovs invited me into the court."

"Then start from the beginning. I know you're impatient to see the claimant to the throne, but it's important for our future monarchy that I separate fact from fiction about you and the Romanovs. There's so much myth surrounding your life, Darya. You need to tell me the truth."

Chapter Nine

— 1904 —

THE BELOVEZH ESTATE IS aflame with giant candles and Baccarat candelabras. A vast tent is set up on the clearing in front of the lodges, and the melodic notes of "The Blue Danube" float out and echo around the forest. The Empress has sent man-sized urns of lilacs from the imperial greenhouse in the Alexander Palace. The scent of roasted mutton, partridge, and truffled whitefish caviar rises from makeshift kitchens and ceramic heating stoves, mingling with the perfume of mead and pine and anticipation. It is Darya's seventeenth birthday.

Wearing a white shirt, loose tie, and unbuttoned vest, his hair sprinkled with silver, Boris Spiridov trots his stallion about the grounds, giving last-minute orders, making certain the tables are set with starched linen and silver stamped with the family emblem, libations plenty, and the cooks vigilant.

Boots crunching on the pine needles underfoot, sapphire blue skirt sweeping the ground, Sabrina Josephine advises Darya regarding the nuances of court protocol, the dangers and joys of carrying royal blood, and the art of seduction.

Her many admirers, gentlemen callers of all ages, young and old aristocrats, noblemen, and grand dukes, come from near and far, bearing all types of lavish gifts and promises of endless devotion. She, like Sabrina, believes in meeting the educated young men who might have potential. She is curious, wants to measure them for herself, gauge their first reaction. She is different, after all. That first moment of an encounter is what matters, whether they gape at her like dumbstruck adolescents or possess the wisdom and self-containment that comes with maturity and a healthy imagination. For now, no one has passed her scrutiny.

So she would rather wade the brooks, attempt to decipher her dreams, or search for yet another healing miracle sprouting from the ground. Or, most of all, she would like to take the train with Boris to Bialystok, the nearest big town, and bid by his side in auctions as he teaches her how to differentiate between an original painting and an imitation, how to bid without creating a frenzy and raising the value. She would like to visit one art gallery or another, hear his philosophy on different mediums, one work of art or another. Or discuss the miracle of imagination with artists of all persuasions, aesthetically adventurous men riveted to her translucent opal gaze.

The imperial entourage arrives bearing gifts and compliments and storks to let loose for good luck. Empress Alexandra wishes Darya a happy birthday and many more years of health and happiness.

Wild hair tamed back with one of her mother's sheer scarves, Darya is radiant in a silver brocaded dress, high-collared and long-sleeved to please the Empress's sense of decorum. She had spent hours in her dressing room, an amalgam of feathery hats, gossamer veils, rhinestone-encrusted evening gowns and gloves, lace and satin corsets, and high-heeled shoes resplendent with bright crystals, purchased from antique shops and back-alley stores. A rack is designated for hand-me-downs the Empress sends her, which a seamstress in town shortens and takes in to fit Darya. Clothing and accessories that other people throw away become precious eye-catchers on her.

The Empress hands Darya an enamel icon studded with diamonds and pearls, a copy of Feodorovskaya, Mother of God, pressing her cheek to Christ's face.

Darya curtsies. "Thank you, Your Majesty, I'll always cherish it." The icon is a far more valuable gift than any she has ever received, but she wants nothing more than to turn away from the gloomy features of the Feodorovskaya, the hollow eyes, the grief-struck lips.

The Empress gestures with two fingers. "Come closer, Darya Borisovna, this is for your ears only. I would not have made this trip in my condition if it were not for wanting to thank you in person, my dear. You were right that day at Yalta. I am with child, after all. And taking your words to heart, I'm hoping this one is a boy."

"My heartfelt congratulations," Darya whispers back. "I cannot wait to meet the little one."

"Then you must visit us when the time comes. I will send for you. The girls, too, would love to see you. Now, go, enjoy your day. I shall not keep you any longer."

The Tsar is pleased to be here, away from endless court formalities and responsibilities that leave little time for leisure. He claps Boris on the back. "Hard to believe, my friend, that seventeen years have passed since Sunny introduced you to Sabrina Josephine. You did well that day," the Emperor teases. "You added to your own family while reducing the aurochs population. Are the animals under control?"

"So much so," Boris grins back, "they seem to have altogether stopped breeding."

"We don't want that either, not at all. A controlled number is necessary for our hunting pleasure."

"Understood, Your Imperial Majesty," Boris replies with a playful salute and the click of boots. "Shall we join the ladies?"

The tender notes of a dulcimer float outside from the tent, where Jasmine the Persian Dancer is joining three drummers seated on a carpet-covered dais. She sweeps her arms up, anchors her long hair on top of her head, folds her legs under, and settles on her knees in front of a low, mahogany stool that holds her santour, a Persian hammered dulcimer. Her index fingers hooked into the loops of the santour's mallets, she sends them skipping on the taut stings, raising notes that travel to faraway places and transport the perfume of Persian roses and visions of turquoise domes, the plight of torn-apart lovers and the Rubaiyat of Omar Khayyam. A lot has changed since she was last here, at the Belovezh Forest, seventeen years back, but not her feelings toward the Emperor, who, in her heart, remains the sweet, insecure Tsarevich who once clung to her every word. She drops her mallets on the dulcimer, massages her fingers, shakes her dark mane of curls, and raises herself to her full striking height.

She is on the dance floor, pearly veils swaying and foaming about her, embroidered vest tossed to the side to reveal plump breasts packed into a beaded brassiere. Her movements are fresh, languid, her head thrown back, her throbbing neck damp with sweat, her voluptuous buttocks swaying to the clap of the drums. She is twisting and twirling, floating away from the crowd, unleashing her emotions as she sinks into a trance.

More guests stream into the tent. Women huddle farther away from the spectacle, chatter, exchange gossip, wonder why such a brash dancer would remain a favorite in court. Surrounding the dance floor are cheering men, their arousal electrifying, eyes devouring the Persian dancer, her every deliciously intimate swing.

She reaches out and snaps her brassiere open, sending it into a languorous dance overhead.

Men cheer, clap, encourage. Their alcohol breaths mingle with the odor of roasted lamb, ripe fruit, and desire.

She swings the brassiere once, twice, as if to lasso one of the men, aims it at the opening of the tent.

The brassiere lands on the left shoulder of the Empress, who has just stepped in.

A collective gasp of horror can be heard around the tent. The beat of drums, laughter, and applause cease. Maids, servants, waiters are effacing themselves, retreating behind expressions of solemn seriousness, pressing themselves against the canvas walls.

The Empress stares at the brassiere, stares at the insult of beaded lace fragrant with perfume and moist with perspiration. Her features are a mask of revulsion, her pursed lips as pale as death. She raises her gaze to confront the offender. In what appears no more than a halfhearted attempt at modesty, Jasmine bunches her skirts and presses layers of sheer gauze in front of her breasts, exposing her black lace underwear in the process.

Sabrina removes the brassiere from the Tsarina's shoulder, crushing it in one hand, the other restraining the Empress with a soft touch on her arm. "Please, Alix, I will handle this. I promise. Darya will accompany you to your lodging. She'll give you something calming."

Alix nods, shaken. She reaches out for Darya as if she might faint.

Darya has an urge to spit behind her shoulder. Looming misfortune is creeping up, sour and bitter, to settle on her tongue. As she leads the Empress out of the tent and away from the gathering crowd, Darya is unaware that by the end of this evening, she will understand what her heart already knows.

Sabrina Josephine marches the length of the tent toward the dancer who, having enjoyed the spectacle of the Empress's retreat, has found her way back to the dais.

Lace brassiere dangling in hand, Sabrina charges like an aurochs, marches up the three carpeted steps, and comes face to face with the dancer.

"My lady?" the dancer purrs down at Sabrina. "How may I oblige?"

"Like this!" Sabrina shouts, rising on her toes and looping the brassiere around the dancer's neck, grabbing both ends and yanking with all her might.

The entire tent rocks about them, wind in the trees outside, wind forcing its way under the tent. The installed chandelier sways as if by a chorus of ghosts. The scratch of scurrying squirrels can be heard. A cloud passes across the full moon, framed by the entrance to the tent.

In the absence of the Empress, the emboldened guests crowd the dais as if cheering a spectacle in a Roman arena.

Sabrina tightens her grip on the brassiere, jerking, yanking, squeezing harder. Her rage sparks off her green eyes. Her veins are pumping venom. "I'll kill you! Drag you into the forest and feed you to aurochs."

Beads of perspiration appear on the dancer's upper lip. She gasps, heaves. The brassiere is wet in Sabrina's hand. Jasmine grabs Sabrina's wrists. They lock eyes, the daring stares of cats. Boris calls out to Sabrina from somewhere, ordering her to stop. He is on the dais, attempting to loosen Sabrina's grip. Every muscle in her face strains. Jasmine's lips are turning color. Her hands fall to her sides. Boris touches Sabrina, a soft touch on her shoulder, gentle, persuasive, full of reproach.

"Sabrina!" He reprimands in a low voice.

She turns her skewering glare on him. And then she hears him utter her name again, feels his tightening grip on her arm. She releases Jasmine, sending her scrambling for breath.

———

Later in the evening, when most of the guests have retired and the dwindling crowd is drunk and swaying to a slow tango, Darya and her parents sneak into the humid canopy of trees to toast Darya's birthday and Boris and Sabrina's seventeen years and nine months of love.

They walk far into the forest, away from the music and vodka-laced air.

Sabrina and Boris amble ahead, sharing champagne from a bottle. "Come along, darling," Sabrina calls to her daughter. "Come have some champagne."

The forest is oddly still to Darya. The trees are creeping toward her. Heavy clouds press upon the fecund growth of pine and oak and ash. She comes to a stop on a narrow sandy path between the trees. She listens, struggling to decipher the silence of nature teeming with all types of animals.

Then she sees the Ancient One, her veils whipping a gale about her, floating around one branch or another, disappearing behind a stout tree trunk, and then appearing anew. One moment she is tempting Darya to follow her into the dark, into an abyss of uncertainty, somewhere far from home, the next she is crossing her hands in front of her face, the red paint on her manicured fingernails melting and dripping blood. Darya has learned to decode her dreams of the Ancient One, certain that they foreshadow some looming event, something that will transpire the next instant, the next day, the next month, the next year. But this is different. Wide awake and on the alert, she is uncertain how to decipher the Ancient One's message. Until, raising her bloody fingers, the Ancient One points to her eyes, which are changing shape, widening, deepening, darkening, becoming wild, feral.

Darya cups her hands around her mouth and calls out to Sabrina and Boris to turn back immediately because the forest is different tonight, dangerous, filled with bloodthirsty animals and silent ghosts.

One moment her parents are ahead of her, Boris wiping off the spilled champagne glistening on Sabrina's cheek as she turns to say something to Darya. The next instant, they are engulfed in a thickening gale of dust from which Boris never returns.

An aurochs charges, hooves uprooting bushes and raising dust that momentarily blinds Darya. The animal's curved horns impale Sabrina's skirt, the champagne bottle still clutched in her hand like a weapon. She calls out her daughter's name in an unrecognizable voice, attempts to say something, but is tossed with a violent shake upon the underbrush of pines and leaves. The bottle shatters against a tree. Champagne foams and hisses. Gasping for breath, Sabrina lifts herself on her knees and crawls forward to grab the broken neck of the bottle. She struggles ahead on all fours and aims the jagged glass at the eyes of the animal.

The aurochs crouches, haunches quivering, teeth gnashing, its bloodshot stare aimed at the fearless huntress. It lumbers forward with a great howl and pins Sabrina's arm down with its forefoot, grabs her hand between powerful jaws and snaps down.

Chapter Ten

CANNON BATTERIES OF THE Fortress of Peter and Paul announce three hundred salutes across Russia. The cheering populace crowds the streets. Flags wave in the hot breeze. Guns boom in Kronstadt. There is singing and dancing in the streets.

His Imperial Majesty Alexei Nikolaevich, sovereign heir Tsarevich, Grand Duke of Russia, heir to the three-hundred-year-old Romanov dynasty, is expected at Peterhof Chapel.

Tsar Nicholas II and the Empress, Alexandra Feodorovna, pace anxiously outside the church. Custom forbids the imperial parents to be present during their son's baptism ceremony. They gaze at each other with shared joy, struggling to rein in their impatience until the proper time when they will be ushered into the chapel, where family and guests are already seated.

The mercy of God has been visited upon them, and for now, their joy overshadows the catastrophic results of the war with Japan, which has been raging for the last eight months.

The great-grandfather of the Tsarevich, Christian IX of Denmark, has traveled from afar to witness the baptism of a miracle, the first heir born to a reigning Russian Tsar since the seventeenth century. He sits next to Maria Feodorovna, the dowager mother, who is regal in a brocaded gown studded with diamonds. A tiara of oak and laurel leaves, surrounded by sheaves of wheat encrusted with diamonds and centered with a citrine, shimmers on top of her swept-up hair.

Grand duchesses, distant cousins, and aunts flaunt gold-embroidered gowns, scintillating jewels, cascading diamond earrings, and diadems of all shapes and sizes. Grand dukes, princes, and uncles discuss the significance of this birth and how it will change the course of history. Court officials in gold-laced coats, elk-skin breeches, and rows of medals on their chests sit silent and stiff-backed, expecting the venerable arrival. Couriers in magnificent uniforms with gold braid and high orders on their chests discuss the dire political situation: negotiations with the Japanese to seek a warm-water port on the Pacific Ocean had broken down, leading to war and threatening a Japanese victory. Should Japan win, the balance of power in East Asia would shift significantly, and the embarrassing defeat could pitch the Russian people against their Tsarist government. Still, as a tribute to courage and bravery on the battlefield, the entire corps of officers of the Russian army and navy has been named honorary godfathers of the Tsarevich.

The grand duchesses—nine-year-old Olga, seven-year-old Tatiana, five-year-old Maria, and three-year-old Anastasia—are all dressed in lace, chiffon, and organza. They crane their necks to catch the first glimpse of their infant brother.

The imperial entourage, ladies-in-waiting, squires, and Cossacks of the Guard are seated in back of the cathedral. Among them are Lili Dehn, close friend of the Empress, and her husband, an officer of the imperial yacht, and Anna Vyrubova, the lady-in-waiting of the Empress. Also present are Tamara Sheremetev, the resident imperial artist and Creator of Miniatures, accompanied by her syphilitic husband, Count Trebla, the imperial veterinarian.

The gold-inlaid mahogany doors swing open and the grand master of ceremonies marches into the chapel. He lifts his ebony staff with the imperial double-headed eagle. Three taps of his staff reverberate around the hall. "His Imperial Majesty Alexei Nikolaevich, sovereign heir Tsarevich."

Darya Borisovna emerges through the doors, her golden gaze resting on every man, woman, and child. Her torrent of black curls tumbles over a velvet cape the color of amethyst, under which sway colorful scarves and scented petticoats that once belonged to her mother.

She is delivering the Tsarevich to the baptismal font on a pillow of gold cloth, which is fastened to a jeweled strap looped around her neck.

Murmurs of disbelief rise from the assembly. Who is this revelation, swathed in mysticism and mystery? Who is this girl who carries herself with unprecedented grace and exemplary confidence? Why is such a holy duty assigned to such a young woman?

Darya swallows her grief, adjusts the pillow on her arms and steers her way toward the central aisle, her eager steps moving toward Father Yanishev, the confessor to the Imperial Family.

A few days earlier, the lady-in-waiting in charge of this task was struck with contagious pockmarks on her entire body. The Empress, who found the advanced age of the lady-in-waiting unsuitable in the first place, had seized the opportunity to persuade the Emperor that Darya was an appropriate candidate. As she has taken up residence with the Imperial Family to spend her year of mourning in the Alexander Palace, Darya is most touched by this added kindness.

She sails down the aisle, comfortable in her skin, as if she is carrying her own son to the baptismal font. Her laced shoes tightly bound, the soles fitted with rubber to prevent her slipping, a continuing tradition to accommodate the ladies-in-waiting who are usually older, she delivers the Tsarevich to the trembling hands of Father Yanishev.

Slowly, carefully, he undresses the small Tsarevich, preparing him for the ceremony. He dips the heir into the font, then raises the infant high above his head.

The cathedral erupts into applause.

The screaming Tsarevich lets loose a stream of urine on the

ecclesiastic pendant of rubies and emeralds Father Yanishev wears on his habit. To the roar of laughter, the father declares that he is now doubly sanctified.

The grand master of ceremonies announces their Imperial Majesties. The crowd rises to their feet.

Women sink into deep curtsy.

Men bow low.

Her chestnut-red hair glowing under the chandeliers, her eyes dazzled with joy, the Tsarina is lavish in white silk embroidered in gold and covered by a velvet robe with a thirteen-foot sable-trimmed train. She wears a brooch of Ceylon sapphire mounted in gold and silver and bordered by fifty-six carats of unparalleled diamonds, which were transported in an armored car from the diamond chamber in the St. Petersburg Winter Palace. The Tsar is clad in formal regalia, medal-heavy and trimmed with gold braid and sable.

Darya reclaims the Tsarevich from Father Yanishev, wraps him in a towel, and dries him briskly. She plants soft kisses on his wrinkled forehead, brushes his peach-fuzz hair, and buttons up his baptismal robe. The Tsarevich grabs her finger and smiles at her with his mother's gray blue eyes. She pulls out a small box from her skirt pocket, snaps the clasp open, and steals a quick look at an enamel amulet nestled in blue satin. Fashioned by Peter Carl Fabergé, goldsmith and jeweler to the Imperial Court, the amulet depicts a mythical childlike figure with pointed emerald ears and ruby eyes, the belly a translucent opal, which will portend the Tsarevich's future.

"My gift to you, Loves. For good luck and endless happiness," she whispers. "It was my father's gift to me on my seventeenth birthday, and I had the back engraved to you."

She fastens the amulet to the Tsarevich's baptism robe, strokes the opal belly, the ruby eyes, not a gesture of farewell, no, not that, but a silent vow to hold her father's memory dear. She has granted his gift a prominent stage, an honor and permanence he would have appreciated.

Chapter Eleven

A DROP OF BLOOD BLOSSOMS in his navel, bubbling like a tiny underground well.

The six-week-old Tsarevich is bleeding.

The Empress presses her lips to her son's chest, slides a trembling finger across the blood worming down his belly. Moon-pale and slightly out of breath, her eyes seek the icons crowding her room to rest on the image of Our Lady of Tsarskoe Selo. Falling to her knees in front of her favorite saint, her lips move in silent prayer. She rests her wet cheeks on the lady's image, begging forgiveness. She had prayed too hard for a son, begged for an heir to the throne, forced God into submission, and He punished her by giving her a sick Tsarevich.

Darya changes the blood-soaked gauze on the infant's abdomen, adds dry ones, and secures them with bandages. She folds the blanket around him and kisses his dimpled cheeks. Her bones feel brittle as icicles from the hissing fire in the hearth. Although it is not yet cold outside, doctors have ordered the fires to keep the baby warm.

The Empress goes back to her son and bundles him in her arms as if to tuck him back into her womb. It is here, in the Lilac Boudoir, that she comes to escape official protocol and royal intrigue, to pass quiet time with her children, and to share evening tea with her husband. Her sanctuary is decorated in the Victorian style, the lemonwood furniture painted off-white, the enamel imitating ivory. The furniture is upholstered with fabric that matches the silk wall covering, a raised floral motif with a reflective weave. The fabric was selected to match a lily the Tsar once gave her.

Two tall windows, framed with curtains of Charles Berger's French mauve silk, decorated with ribbons and tassels, allow ample light during the day. It is rumored that the value of the silk fabrics and ornate trims used in the Lilac Room is far greater than the value of any of the imperial Fabergé Easter eggs.

In order to afford the family some privacy, the only entrance to the room is through heavily draped, flower-carved doors that lead to the Pallisander Room or to other bedrooms.

New styles come and go, but this room remains as it was on the Imperial Couple's wedding night, despite tremendous disapproval of the press for selecting a British design for a bedroom the Tsar shares with the Tsarina.

Those were happier times. Her son is diagnosed with hemophilia now, an incurable disease. An inherited blood-clotting deficiency transmitted by women, the doctor tells her, a capricious disease that rarely afflicts women. Among five thousand males, one is afflicted with the bleeding disease, and God chose *her* son. No one is able to predict how often the bleeding will occur or how long it will last before the blood coagulates.

Patience is suggested.

A mother has the right to be impatient. "Heal him, Darya Borisovna! Heal my son! Stop this terrible bleeding!"

"I tried, Your Majesty, with herbs, with the power of my eyes, my touch. You were there, saw how hard I tried. It is cruel that I can cure others, but not my own son." Darya sucks her breath in. She cringes in her own skin, afraid she insulted the Empress. It is not normal, she is certain, to love another woman's son so deeply. The answer, she has come to believe, is somewhere in her dreams, underneath layers of smoke concealing the Ancient One, whose appearances have become more frequent, to chide, hassle, goad, or even praise, not only at nighttime, but often in daylight. She directs a searching look at the Empress. "I hope I did not insult Your Majesty."

"Not at all, dear, you have been good to Alyosha. But why would your healing power fail you now? Perhaps I put too much faith in that."

Darya casts her eyes down. She has disappointed Her Majesty, proved herself unworthy of her trust. She waits, silent, sensing the Tsarina's disapproval, wanting to vanish and fade away. Then it occurs to her, a thought that had been simmering in the back of her mind. "I've been hearing about a wandering starets, Your Majesty, a certain Father Grigori. Perhaps he could help Alyosha. I hear that the Virgin selected him as God's mouthpiece to travel to Mount Athos and pray to the Black Virgin of Kazan in the convent of Afron."

At the mention of the Virgin of Kazan, her Russian saint, wonder spills from the Empress's mournful eyes. "The convent of Afron? But it is so secluded and hard to reach."

"Yes, despite that he made the pilgrimage back and forth by foot. May I summon Grigori Rasputin to the palace?"

"To heal Alyosha?" the Empress asks in a soft voice.

"Yes, God willing," Darya replies, relieving the Empress of the sleeping Tsarevich, placing him on the chaise lounge, and tucking a blanket around him. "And perhaps Father Grigori might help me to channel my own powers, so I may help the Tsarevich too."

"This monk, this father Grigori, will he keep quiet about our precious one? Orders have gone out to doctors to keep the matter to themselves. No one must suspect anything wrong with the heir to the throne. No one! What do you think, Dasha? Can we trust Father Grigori?"

"I do not know, Your Majesty."

The Empress walks to the window and gazes out as if to seek a miracle beyond. The sky is an expanse of pure blue, not a cloud in the horizon, no hint of a breeze to disrupt peace, and in the garden below, the hedges trimmed to perfection, the dormant rose bushes await springtime to bloom. The imperial Cossacks are at their stations, guarding the massive gates on the far right.

Inside, butlers, servants, waiters, cooks, physicians, wardrobe ladies, and poultry keepers are at their posts, making sure the palace is running smoothly.

Yet in her head and heart, everything is in turmoil as she grapples to make sense of the unfairness of it all. Why? Why is her only son suffering? She turns to the imperial basket of jeweled lilies of the valley on her writing desk. One of Fabergé's most skillful creations, a burst of gold, silver, pearls, rose diamonds, and nephrite flowers presented to her in 1896 at the Nijny Novgorad. She caresses the enamel leaves, brings her face close to the diamond flowers as if to inhale their scent. She will be patient, not because the doctors suggest, but because she trusts in the healing power of faith and prayer. God and His saints are on her side, after all.

"No more talk of Father Grigori, Darya! The Tsarevich is our future Emperor. We will put our trust in the Lord. He will heal my son."

Chapter Twelve

THE PERFECT DISK OF the sun hangs high in a cloudless sky. Scent of lilac and watered lawns permeates the Alexander Palace Park at Tsarskoe Selo, the Tsar's village, an oasis of eight hundred acres situated fifteen miles south of St. Petersburg. Followed by imperial Cossacks on horseback and surrounded by ancient fir trees, Darya and the Empress stroll in the park.

Pale-faced and sad-eyed, Darya counts the pebbles underfoot. The Belovezh Forest is only a short two-hour ride on the imperial train that brought her here, yet without Boris and Sabrina, it feels distant to her heart.

The Empress, who as the young Alix of Hesse and the grand-daughter of Queen Victoria was nearly always in mourning for someone in her extended family, has demanded that Darya follow the Victorian custom of mourning—black for the first six months and white, gray, or mauve for the second six months—except for the Tsarevich's baptism, when festive ceremonial garments were required.

Now, engulfed in gloomy grays, a sheer mousseline shawl, appliquéd dress, and high-heeled satin boots, Darya's heart is breaking. The period of mourning is about to end, and she will be expected to collect herself, thank the Imperial Family for their kindness, and return home. This must be why the Empress has summoned her. To wish her well and send her on her way. She will miss the pleasure of running into the nursery every morning, being the first to ruffle Alyosha's silk-soft hair, the first to squeeze his sleep-warm body in her arms, to change and powder and ready him for his mother. He is hardly able to talk, but when his plump tongue hits the roof of his mouth, she hears him calling her, "Da, da, da."

"You are fond of Alyosha," the Empress says. "Your dear mother had a way with children too. She is terribly missed. We were born on the same day, you know, and tried to celebrate together, just the two of us, whenever possible. Despite our differences, or perhaps because of them, we so enjoyed each other's company. I used to be fond of your Belovezh Estate. But it's different now. You must not go back, not for some time, my dear. It will be difficult."

Darya is surprised. As difficult as it will be, her only choice is to return to the Belovezh Forest. Where else is there to go?

The women stroll along Fir Avenue, toward the Dragon Bridge leading to an open meadow. The Empress drapes her arm around Darya's shoulder. "I want you to know that your mother's spirit is always with you."

As if confirming the Empress's words, a flock of winged birds of paradise alight on a branch overhead, a sighting of extravagant plumage, rare anywhere in the world, let alone in Europe and North Asia. More than a century ago, on the occasion of the twenty-fifth anniversary of the reign of the Enlightened Despot, Catherine II, eight birds were sent here from the rain forests of Papua New Guinea. A most adept breed in the art of seduction, they have multiplied, and now all types inhabit the Alexander Palace. Their extraordinary acrobatic feats and elaborate courting rituals have earned the park the dubious title of "Imperial Aviary of Whores."

The Empress strokes Darya's cheek. "Our souls fly to heaven when we die. Having gone through the process of purification, we return to earth as birds of paradise. That red one, there, must have come from your Belovezh home. It must be your dear mother's soul."

In the scorched earth hue of the bird's plumage, Darya sees Sabrina's red hair. In its birdsong, the echo of her laughter that reverberated against ancient tree bark and sent the leaves dancing. If only she had a way of conversing with the bird, confiding how she misses her mother who had the heart of a warrior and the laughter of an enchantress. How she longs for her father's wisdom. But more than anything, she wants to know why Sabrina and Boris had lost their hunting instincts that evening and had failed to heed the ominous silence of the forest.

"You were there when they died," the Empress says. "It will remain with you forever."

"Yes, Your Majesty, it will. If I had the foresight to carry a rifle that evening, my parents would be alive now."

"My poor Dasha, you must not blame yourself. If anything, the blame rests with me."

Darya slows down, her knees weak, an ache in her chest. "But what do you mean, Your Majesty?"

"It was I who introduced Sabrina to Boris. I invited your mother to accompany the imperial entourage to hunt aurochs on your father's estate. That is how your mother met your father. I usually do not make plans, my dear; only God knows how they will end."

Ahead of them, Count Trebla, the court veterinarian, emerges from behind the imperial garages, his small head swaying on his square shoulders, his left hand rocking at his side, his right tugging at the leash of a Doberman.

"Morning, Your Eminence," Count Trebla salutes the Empress with an exaggerated bow. "On our way to the infirmary. An intestinal problem, I'm afraid."

Darya tightens her shawl about her shoulders. Her hand creeps up to her necklace, her thumb and forefinger stroking the polished belly of a pearl. She dislikes Count Trebla, this mad husband of Tamara Sheremetev, the Creator of Miniatures. He is devoted to his job, trains the imperial dogs, dispenses medication to the sick, and keeps vigil at their side, but the endless abuse he inflicts on his wife is gnawing away at her life and her art so much that she seems to shrink into herself. Her miniatures, too, are becoming smaller and smaller—the likeness of the Tsarevich carved into a cherry pit, the imperial Children's Palace engraved onto ivory the size of a thumbnail, a wicker carriage hammered onto a sliver of gold.

In the last year, grieving their respective losses—Tamara her sense of self and Darya her beloved parents—the two women came to share their heartbreaks. To her great horror, Darya has learned that, at the end of each day, Trebla records in a ledger his wife's progress and failures, her strengths and weaknesses, and punishes or rewards her accordingly, which does not matter in the end, since both punishments and rewards result in sadistic sexual acts he brags about to anyone who will listen.

The Empress acknowledges Trebla with a nod, pats the dog on the head, and then resumes her walk into the park. Four imperial Cossacks on horseback keep guard at a respectable distance.

"Sweet one," Count Trebla hisses behind Darya, smacking his lips.

She swings around, narrows her eyes at him, the lowly creature who would dare address her in this manner. She holds up a fore-finger in warning.

He is too close behind her, whispering in her ear, his putrid breath insulting.

"Doggy is in licking mood, sweet one. Come, be nice."

She flicks her hand as if dismissing a dog, then walks faster to catch up with the Empress.

He is at her heels, grabbing her shawl, pulling it off her shoulders. "Why? Don't you like me? But of course you do. I like you too. Come to me, will you? Yes, of course you'll come tonight to the end of this path where…"

His every word lands a bitter insult. Is he suggesting a rendez-vous with her, the daughter of Boris and Sabrina who refused the hands of princes and grand dukes? She yanks her shawl away from his grip, aims two fingers at him like a pistol. "Go away!" she growls, surprised by the enormity of her rage.

He jumps back, as if hit by a bullet, his protruding eyes rolling back in anger, a furious rumble emanating from him. His mother, whose vulgar mouth never stopped cursing, was the same. He was less important to her than her elaborate hats and gigantic chignons piled on top of her head.

With a quick snap of his fingers, he frees the Doberman from the leash, which remains dangling like a noose in his hand. Two short whistles from him, and the dog, breathing hard and fast, leaps forward like an evil thought.

Darya's forearm is locked between the canine's jaws. His teeth pierce her sleeve, tearing skin, flesh, and crushing bones. She leaps back, struggling to free herself from the dog's powerful grip. She screams for help, but her voice is a painful knot in her throat. The Doberman's teeth are digging deeper. She will die like Boris and Sabrina. Not a dignified death at home in her Belovezh Forest, but a senseless death instigated by a jealous madman.

The birds of paradise burst into a racket, alerting the Empress who, unaware of what has been transpiring behind her, strolls ahead. She pauses. Glances behind. She grabs hold of a nearby bench. Her face is paler than the underfoot gravel. "Restrain the beast!" she calls out to Trebla, then gestures to the Cossacks, who lead their horses closer. Her voice is trembling with fear and indignation. "Go fetch a doctor. Now!"

Trebla aims a boot at the Doberman's underbelly. His features are distorted. A thread of saliva trickles down his chin. He lands one punch after another on the animal's head, triggering savage snarls. But Darya's arm remains locked between the dog's jaws.

The Empress raises her voice, "Control the beast, I said, before he kills her!"

Count Trebla digs into his pocket and flips out a revolver, aims and shoots between the animal's eyes. Birds of paradise burst into a frightful chorus, scattering a shower of leaves as they take flight to higher branches. The Doberman lets out a gut-curdling howl. The animal falls to the ground, convulsing. Blood and brain splatter in all directions.

Darya seizes her forearm. She struggles to stem the bleeding, pull the ligaments together, the raw, gaping flesh. She is oblivious to the Empress ordering the Cossacks to remove Trebla from her sight, to a swarm of flies feasting on the glazed-eyed Doberman, and to the imperial doctor who rushed to her side. He pours alcohol on her wound, applies surgical blood suction, sutures her wound with silver filaments,wrapping a bandage around her arm. To the accompaniment of the gloomy nasal blasts of the red bird of paradise, who keeps vigil on one of the lower branches, a tune, an unfamiliar melody, rises to twirl and twist like an embrace around Darya, a balm that settles on her wound to adjust bones, bond sinews, and meld flesh.

The doctor mumbles something about a forgotten ointment and unwraps the bandage to apply another curative salve.

The Empress, having partially regained her breath, abandons the bench on which she has been leaning and hurries toward the alarmed doctor, who is having difficulty controlling his trembling hands. His firmly rooted belief in the world of science and medicine is being tested by the unfolding phenomenon he is witnessing. The wound has changed form in just moments. Blood has drained, veins mended, healthy flesh replacing the damaged.

"What is the prognosis?" The Empress asks the doctor.

"I sutured the wound, Your Majesty, applied antiseptics. The rest is in God's hand."

The Empress bends closer to take a better look. "Astonishing! Have you ever seen a wound heal so fast, doctor?"

"I am at a loss, Your Majesty. I've sutured the wound with silver filaments, a relatively new material, but none of my medical pamphlets mention such a positive outcome."

"Miracles are not in the realm of medicine, doctor. Faith is."

"Of course, Your Majesty. I understand. May I cover the wound again?" he asks, reaching for bandages in his medical case.

"I don't think it is necessary," Darya interjects in a weak voice.

"How are you feeling?" the doctor asks. "You must be in pain."

"The pain is not bad, but I am tired."

"No pain!" The Empress exclaims. "How is this possible?"

Darya, too, is not certain what is happening, whether she is being healed by the soothing melody that continues to echo in her head, whether the song sprung from somewhere within her soul or from the red bird of paradise that remains on her perch, head cocked, wings fanned out in dazzling shades of red. All she knows is that this healing is very different from the others, where she had cured with herbs and all types of potions. This time she is terrified of the woman she has become, a stranger she is unable to recognize.

"May I be excused, Your Majesty?" the doctor says, placing the bandage back into his case, eager to return to his medical books to discover whether any recent breakthrough might shed light on what has just occurred.

"Thank you, doctor, you may leave," the Empress replies, her astonishment giving way to delight.

Darya crosses the main palace foyer with its earthy scent of Italian marble in winter, of melted candles from last night's ball, a hint of sweat and talcum powder. The clock in the alcove chimes four in the afternoon—metallic and final. In the Great Hall, *The Triumph of Venus* and *The Rape of Europa* look down at her from white walls. The domed ceiling above the grand staircase is a vast colorful tableau depicting Galatea, the mythological nymph loved by Polyphemus, the one-eyed son of Poseidon. Galatea reminds Darya of the Ancient One, the fluid lines of her body and her understated sensuality that contradicts her prophetic messages, her warnings, her instructions.

The Ancient One appeared again last night. Darya was a curious observer tittering on the edge of awareness, attempting to decode the message before her dream dissolved in the light of dawn. For an instant the woman's cloudy face coalesced into what was an affectionate expression of encouragement, and her eyes turned deep violet and soulful. She raised two fingers, pointed toward Darya, and something akin to a smile parted her pale lips.

Then, with startling speed and precision, she turned on herself and thrust a forefinger in her left eye. Instead of being startled awake by the horrific act, Darya clung to her dream, to the pleasant warmth emanating from the assaulted eye that remained whole and expressive and full of promise. Only when the woman turned her face away as she walked into a fire emitting bone-chilling blizzards in place of warmth did Darya release the dream, certain that a gift had been imparted to her.

She will have to wait another six years, witness the humiliating defeat of Russia's Baltic Fleet by the Japanese navy, the emergence of several radical antimonarchy political parties, and the rising influence of Grigori Rasputin in her life, before she will garner enough courage and wisdom to unwrap the gift and discover its contents.

Now, Darya's guts churning with anxiety, she climbs the grand staircase to the upper hall. The Empress has summoned her to look at Grand Duchess Anastasia, who refuses to open her eyes, eat, or swallow a sip of water. She moans and tosses in bed with a high fever that resists every prescribed medication.

Fumée d'Ambre Gris, a gift from Boris and Sabrina, is prominently displayed in the upper hall. Darya glances around and finds herself alone. She passes her hand over the canvas that carries her father's loving advice, her mother's throaty laughter. The memory of the day Darya accompanied Boris to the Poniatowski Auction House remains fresh. Her father bid on this painting—a woman swathed from head to toe in a cape like churning milk, hood raised from her face to inhale the smoke of ambergris from a brazier at her feet—as a present to the Imperial Family on the occasion of the birth of their fourth daughter, Grand Duchess Anastasia Nikolaevna.

Darya waves her memories away and takes the corridor that leads toward the children's quarters. A single repetitive note can be heard in Olga and Tatiana's shared bedroom. The Gramophone needle is stuck again. The two are enamored of the new gadget from America and spend long hours listening to the same songs.

Darya bends down to pick up a hair barrette Grand Duchess Maria Nikolaevna must have lost at the ball last night. A stain of melted candle catches her eye on the marble underfoot, and she scratches it off with a fingernail. She stops to catch her breath at the door to Anastasia's bedroom. Soft-footed servants come and go, silent, their faces creased into perpetual attentiveness. They melt away down the service backstairs and into the tunnel beneath the palace, leading to the kitchens. The scent of lamb and rice stew is creeping up from the tunnel, but from under the door seeps the odor of soap and antiseptics. Darya knocks, walks into the room, her hand on the jeweled egg slung about her neck, her palms damp with perspiration. The Empress has put her trust in her, and disappointing Her Majesty is not an option.

The Tsarina is stroking her three-year-old daughter's forehead, pressing one eye to gauge her temperature. She soaks a napkin in ice water and lays it on Anastasia's forehead.

The Empress's gaze strays toward Darya's opal eye, the spark of mischief, the wisdom in its depth. There is too much complexity in this woman for the mind to comprehend, the Tsarina muses. Had she miscalculated her potential, invested too much in her? She failed to heal Alexei, after all. How will she fare with Anastasia? "Here you are, Dasha. Thank the Lord! I am beside myself with worry. Anastasia is not well, I am afraid, and the doctors are useless."

Darya lowers herself at the edge of Anastasia's bed. She removes the napkin and wets it again in ice water. "Hello, sweetheart, are you hurting? Tell me where."

But flushed with fever, the child is curled into herself, tossing and moaning, her wet hair plastered to her head, her lips as pale as stone.

The Empress rests a hand on Darya's shoulder and squeezes as if to stress the significance of this moment. "Heal Anastasia, dear. Will you? Show me you can do it."

Darya's thoughts take flight, searching for a revelation, an incantation perhaps that might aid her. She massages the swollen glands that throb under her palms, tells the child how very much she is loved, embraces the fragile body, and holds tight until the butterflies inside her spread their wings and settle.

"Don't be afraid, my darling. Open your eyes, Anastasia. Tell me where it hurts."

But the grand duchess does not respond. Tears escape under her firmly shut eyes.

"My darling!" Darya suddenly exclaims. "Is it because of Shibzig? Are you sad you lost your little dog? How about you and I go visit Shibzig's tomb on the island? We'll take flowers and toys and have a picnic there." Lifting the child's limp body, Darya rests her head in her lap. Eyes throbbing, aching in their sockets, Darya digs deep into her well of emotions—loss, longing, fear, and love. She begs, demands, and pleads with the Ancient One for help.

Her opal eye radiates warmth, flooding her veins, her entire body. She presses her eye to the child's forehead.

"And you know what else I'll do, darling? I'll get you another dog to replace Shibzig, who is very happy and playing with his doggy friends in heaven now."

Anastasia half opens her large blue eyes. Darya helps her into a sitting position, reaches out for a glass of water at her bedside, and raises it to her mouth.

"See, darling, you are better already. Let me examine your glands. No pain? Yes, just a bit, I know, but it will go away tomorrow."

The Empress approaches Darya, cuddles her face between both hands, gazing at her for a long, tender, almost intimate moment before resting her hands on her shoulders, applying a steady pressure as if Darya might flee if she were not held in place. "Darya Borisovna, my heart is full of gratitude. You have lived up to your name, my dear, proven your healing powers. I want you to take care of my precious Alyosha. I appoint you Tyotia Dasha of His Imperial Majesty Alexei Nikolaevich, sovereign heir Tsarevich, Grand Duke of Russia."

Chapter Thirteen

DARYA STEPS INTO THE thick-carpeted, mahogany-paneled auction house that evokes monasteries where tight-lipped nuns glide across shadowy corridors. She has instructions to bid on a contemporary portrait the Empress desires, a deviation from established classical art, the customary norm of the Imperial Court.

Darya registers the multitude of tired hearts she sets into a gallop by her young appearance. Men with satin vests and heavy gold watches, thick mustaches stretched across arrogant grins that speak of wealth and greed. She recognizes one of her suitors, the bearded, heavy-lidded Prince Lukashenko, who rises to salute her, a spark in his small, roaming eyes. Among her many rejected gentlemen callers, this one was the most unimaginative, not a grain of creativity to allow for a certain sense of anticipation, a sense of excitement, of what might come if she happened to accept him. He is wearing a three-piece burgundy suit, a gold chain draped about his tight vest. The prince fumbles for his watch and, in the process, snaps off a vest button that lands on his shoe with a tiny bounce. She acknowledges him with a nod and continues on her way.

She is greeted by familiar dealers, curators, advisers, and collectors. Was it only a year ago that she accompanied her parents to this auction house to bid on a sculpture by Mordecai Matysovich Antokolsk? A week later, Sabrina and Boris were dead. Auction specialists walk the perimeters of the room, nodding to her in discreet acknowledgment. The daughter of Grand Duke Boris Spiridov and Princess Sabrina of Corinin, Darya is a recognized face and one of the few permitted to forgo the bidding paddle. Her number was supplied to the bid spotters, who scan the room and have been alerted to her bidding signal: slipping her shawl off her shoulders.

In this arena that boasts a culture of its own, a collector's behavior is as important as his bank account, seating assignments of utmost importance, as are the observed rituals between experienced bidders. Art purchased for personal pleasure and not for resale is a subjective and private decision, and she has made a point to find out the condition, the unpublished reserve price, and the level of interest in the portrait she wants. The maximum of forty-five thousand rubles the Imperial Couple allotted for the acquisition is more than sufficient, Darya is certain, a sum far higher than any bidder would consider paying.

She settles into her assigned seat, in the same preferred area allocated to her parents with whom she attended the auction in which they acquired *Fumée d'Ambre Gris.* That day, Boris taught her to appreciate the nuances of a sculpture—sloping shoulders that melt into breasts and heart-shaped faces scooped out of stone, buffed skin of marble, and the gracefully rendered folds of the garments of ancient goddesses. Here she is now, wearing a seashell-colored robe the Empress had once worn to a much publicized inaugural ceremony, wild hair shimmering like black ink, lonely in a crowded room, every seat taken except the two on her right that once belonged to Boris and Sabrina.

A drone of excitement rises in the room. Heads turn toward the entrance. Murmurs ripple and bubble and gather force. "Miraculous healings…" "Strange religious belief…" "He cured the peasant of rabies…" "Bedded thousands of women…" "Wagged his penis in the face of customers…" "Cured Mirfenderesky's gout…" "A man of God…"

A fly buzzes its way into the room, settling on the sweat-beaded head of the auction master. A faint, anticipatory hum joins the surrounding murmurs.

Darya turns toward the entrance to discover the cause of this excitement.

A pair of eyes grabs and holds her like blue magnets, unrelenting, cutting, splitting her open, exposed.

He is of medium height, with powerful legs, square shoulders, hair parted in the center and held back with a gray ribbon. A wiry beard claws at his buttoned-up jacket that has seen its share of borscht and Madeira. He wends his way toward Darya, a churning storm gathering force with each approaching footstep, a cyclonic gale in which his peasant coat flaps like bat wings. Trailed by the clang of unexpected thunder, his beard flails in the wind of his steps that carry the pungent odor of his collective sins. Darya is bewildered. Did she witness a miracle, witness him usher in the wind? Thunder? She sniffs the air, tastes the smell under her tongue and at the base of her throat, and her heart closes into a fist in her chest. The odor of bitter almonds and arsenic becomes stronger with his every nearing footstep.

Darya has learned to recognize the taste of ash, the sour, mouth-puckering taste of looming misfortunes. But she does not recognize the pungent smell woven into the fabric of this man, is unaware that it portends historical calamities that will reverberate around the world, tragedies far greater than her young mind can fathom.

He is standing in front of her, left hand resting on his heart, right hand raised in a salute, the coarse fabric of his pants assaulting her knees. He speaks in a broken way: "Grigori Yefimovich Rasputin. Ah! Darya! Your name. The sea."

Darya recoils from his grip, attempts to shutter herself from his churning stare. What else does he know about her? Does he also know that she was conceived in the forest and out of wedlock?

What business does a man of such low taste have in this exclusive auction house? "How do you know me?" she asks, shifting her legs away.

He holds his paddle below his unrelenting eyes, amplifying the power of his gaze. "I know everything about you, Darya Borisovna. Of course I do. Why? Not important. Not at all. Important is your amulet of an eye. Precious."

She straightens up in her seat, tightens her shawl around her shoulders. She wants nothing to do with this man and his sour odor.

The auction master's hammer comes down with a force, silencing the crowd. His short feet dangling above the ground under the ornate desk, he jerks his bald head behind, then jolts to one side with peculiar urgency—his way of ushering in the first object.

A violin is carried in. Burnished lights of the chandelier flicker on the slick shell of maple and spruce that has turned the shade of ebony. Legend has it that each time the violin played for a dead virgin, its shade became a bit darker until it turned black.

"Lot number one. Sixteenth-century funerary violin. Vilhelm Van Mordeh. The only black violin in the world. Excellent condition."

Silence shrouds the room. Who would want a notorious violin, known for its melancholy melodies in imperial funerals, a violin that had the power to solicit tears from the most callous? A violin reputed to have brought a tragic end to every one of its owners. Its last proprietor was a high-ranking Imperial Courtier who was trampled to death by his own stallion.

"One of a kind!" the auction master announces. "Do I have a bid?"

A red-cheeked man with pomaded, combed-back hair lifts a bony hand to flourish his paddle. Darya recognizes the dealer from whom her parents had purchased the despised *Mephistopheles*.

"Twenty-five rubles," the auction master calls out. "One! Two! Three! Going! Going! Knocked down! Funerary violin goes to bidder number fifty-three."

The man rises and, without as much as a backward glance, exits the room with short harried steps, leaving behind a sense of relief.

Another quick backward jerk of the auctioneer's head ushers in a couple of pubescent boys carrying a detailed rendition of what resembles an ornate cathedral.

"Lot thirty-three. Blueprint of the Russian Masonic grand lodge headquarters. The only known representation of its kind, rendered by the famous Soltan Kontisky, a master mason who gathered information never before revealed."

A murmur of surprise scurries about the room. No outsider has set eyes on the sacred sanctum of a lodge, where the highly secretive Freemasons hold their rituals. An altar and candles stand in the center of a windowless room. Two blocks of stone are rendered with great care, the edges of one uncut, the other polished to symbolize the ritual of preparation Masons are required to undergo. A stained-glass panel portrays a G in a square and a compass. Darya wonders if it is true that Masons undress during rituals, require tattoos, or that women are not admitted because they are inferior in the eyes of God, the great architect of the universe.

"Yes sir, louder please. One hundred fifteen. Do I have another?"

In an unmistakable plot among the bidders not to compete against one another, the work is sold quickly and without fanfare to a man sporting a Masonic ring on his small finger.

Another clap of the hammer silences the crowd. *The Victorious Samson* by Guido Reni is brought out. An important seventeenth-century Baroque painting that might have been more at home among the imperial collection than the one the Empress has set her heart on.

A slash of red toga drapes in folds around Samson's lower torso, the flesh and blood shades true to life, the sensual lines of his sinewy arm stretched up to pour wine from a decanter into his open mouth. One foot rests on the lifeless body of an enemy.

"Two hundred fifty...Three hundred...Four hundred fifty... *The Victorious Samson*, ladies and gentlemen. Do I have another bid? Yours, sir."

The evening is coming to an end. The atmosphere is charged with excitement.

The auctioneer's cheeks glow under the chandelier. "Last lot! Number sixty-six."

The two boys usher in a rolling easel covered with black satin as if leading a convict to the gallows. In a dramatic show of unison, the cloth is removed to reveal the treasure underneath.

Murmurs fill the room, astonishment, disbelief, but mostly admiration.

Darya leans forward, her heart beating in her ears. Avram Bensheimer's *The Cure* is breathtaking. It is a masterpiece, impressive in its intimacy and terrifying in the confrontational expression of the dark eyes. A scar slashes diagonally across the black and white rendition of a man's face and neck, evidence of a bullet that destroyed the exposed vocal cords, shattered half the chin and right cheek, leaving a thumb-sized hole in the skull. Yet it is not a gloomy portrait. The vibrant ribbon of red, orange, and violet the artist painted with fluid strokes to frame the scar transforms the portrait from proof of a bleak injury to confirmation of the human body's miraculous ability to heal.

Darya better understands now why the Empress wants this portrait. In the end, it is an optimistic piece of art, connoting hope and a restorative future. Afflicted with a bad back and a weak heart, it is understandable for the Empress to admire Bensheimer's ability to celebrate human frailties and the body's healing powers.

Darya leans back in her seat. Patience and timing are of utmost importance. Once each of the perspective bidders has arrived at his limit, then and only then, will she drop her shawl.

Two men in front stand up, one long-faced with a bulbous nose, the other stout, large ears flushed red with excitement. Both men struggle to be noticed. The long-faced one leaps up and down like a metal coil, the other flaps both arms like giant bird wings. She will benefit from these novices who have entered the bidding too early, flourish their paddles unceremoniously, and encourage a frantic atmosphere.

"Nine thousand…Nine thousand five hundred…Eleven thousand!"

Darya's palms begin to perspire; a drop rolls down her vertebrae. The price is rising, far more than she had expected for an unknown artist. Nevertheless, there is time.

Next to her, Rasputin is as still as stone.

Two bidders remain: an anemic man in front, his hair spiky as boar's hide, and Darya's bearded suitor, whose stare travels from *The Cure* to Darya, back and forth, as if he were bidding on both.

Darya laces her fingers in her lap. The limit allowed her for the purchase is fast approaching. Soon it will be time to act.

The auction master stands up, wiping his bald head with a checkered handkerchief. "Twenty thousand!…Thirty-five thousand!…Sir, do I see your paddle?"

Darya listens intently, notices the tension in her suitor's gestures, the excitement. But more than anything, anxiety, his trembling fingers toying with his pocket watch, shutting and opening the lid with metallic snaps. He has arrived at his threshold. The greatest sum ever paid for a Russian painting was the sum of thirty-five thousand rubles by Alexander III for *Reply of the Zaporozhian Cossacks to Sultan Mehmed IV of the Ottoman Empire*, a painting that had taken the artist Ilya Repin eleven years to complete.

Darya drops her shawl off her shoulders.

At that signal, one of the bid spotters raises a forefinger, gesturing to the auctioneer.

"Bidder number eighteen. Forty-five thousand."

She lifts her shawl and ties it into a tight knot around her shoulders. The portrait is hers. The Empress will be pleased.

Rasputin raises his paddle. Holds it up like a lure. His underarm is stained.

"Fifty-five thousand!" The auctioneer announces, sucking in his breath.

The crowd bursts into applause. The room is hot and humid

from the plethora of sweating bodies. The fly buzzes its way from the opposite end of the room to circle around a lamp shade, finds its way to the naked electrical bulb, crackling and sizzling.

"Do I have another bid? One! Two! Three!" The yellow-nailed finger of the auctioneer aims at Rasputin. "Lot number sixty-six. Knocked down! Congratulations, sir!"

Darya's head reels. She grabs her shawl, pulling with a savage tug, splitting the seams. She clutches her necklace, wanting to open it, needing to inhale the scent, longing to evoke Boris, ask where she failed. She turns to take a better look at Grigori Rasputin. He is sweating profusely, tugging at his beard with thumb and forefinger. She returns his gaze, her own unblinking, spewing fire until her shoulders slump under the torn shawl. How in the world would this man have the means to pay for such an expensive portrait?

Chairs sigh against the carpet underfoot. People begin to leave the room. Congratulatory words are exchanged among buyers.

Rasputin does not move from his chair. Neither does Darya.

One eye shutters down in a wink. His voice is resonant, even melodic. "For you, Darya Borisovna Spiridova. The portrait. Yours!"

"Then why did you bid against me?"

"Because I want something in return."

She directs a puzzled look at him.

"I want an audience with the Empress."

She is overcome by an urge to slap his oily face. How dare he! She would not have encouraged the Empress to invite him if she had met him in person. With his unkempt appearance, muddy boots, and vile stare, he is better suited to the crime-infested slums of St. Petersburg rather than the Imperial Palace. "Why would the Empress grant *you* an audience?"

His magnetic gaze leaps up to grab her. "Because the little Tsarevich needs my help."

Chapter Fourteen

DARYA SHIFTS FROM ONE foot to another, her opal eye throbbing, her heart drumming in her temples. The Empress is displeased. The Emperor is livid. Tyotia Dasha of the Tsarevich has no right raising her voice in a court of law in defense of a Jew! Yet as harshly as they continue to castigate her for attending the Kishinev trial, she does not regret having followed the Ancient One into the mist of dawn, followed her to court to witness mankind at its worst and best.

A young Jewish boy was on trial, a boy accused of murdering a Christian, although the identity of the murderer as someone else had been established beyond a doubt. The anti-Semitic newspapers *Bessarabetz*, *Ceem*, and *Svet* had insinuated that the Christian boy had been murdered so his blood could be used to prepare matzos, the flat bread Jews eat on Passover. The next day, a priest had led a frenzied mob into Kishinev. One hundred twenty Jews were killed, five hundred were wounded, and seven hundred houses were looted and destroyed. For three days, neither the police nor the military intervened.

Despite proof of the Jewish boy's innocence, not one God-fearing Christian had raised his voice in the court of law to protest the inflicted injustice until, proud and unblinking, an eloquent, defiant man whom Darya will not forget stood up to confront the judge.

"I am a Jew!" he said, as if that was enough of an introduction. "My people are like you and you." His accusing forefinger pointed at the judges, attorneys, and at every person in the courtroom. "We are fathers, mothers, workers, and artists. We love our country. Look at me! Do I have horns? A tail? Why would I use blood in my bread if you don't? You pay for my art, display it in your homes. Then go about murdering my people."

At that instant, the Ancient One spun around to confront Darya, her manicured fingernails hovering like small daggers, her fire-spewing eyes boring into Darya's conscience, prodding deep and stirring her sense of duty so that, disregarding the dire consequences, she stood up in that anti-Semitic atmosphere to defend the brave Jew.

She squared her shoulders, fastened the golden button at the neck of her pearl-studded, emerald-colored velvet cape, two ruby hairpins in her black curls raging with menace. The Ancient One was beside her, in front of her, around her, smiling, encouraging, prompting. Darya's voice rang about, silencing the courtroom. "I am Darya Borisovna, your honor, Tyotia Dasha of the Tsarevich. I speak for the Imperial Family who stand for the truth. They will not be pleased to discover that an innocent boy is on trial in place of the real murderer who, as you all know, has been incarcerated and is in custody as we speak!"

The next day, with much fanfare, the papers reported every detail of what had transpired in the courtroom. Word of mouth spread around the city like the black plague, snaking its way into the palace.

Pen poised in midair, the Empress directs her gaze toward Darya at the door. The Empress's eyes are as cold as blades. She drops the pen and it rolls to rest in a groove on her desk, piled high with paper. A prolific letter writer, she carries her writing pads with her and forgets them in every corner.

Darya tries to speak, to offer an apology, but the Empress's eyes hold her in their paralyzing grip, and she lingers at the door, hand over mouth as if to stop herself from instigating further impropriety.

"I am disappointed!" the Empress says. "You represent the Imperial Family, Darya Borisovna, and such unacceptable conduct has a negative impact on us. The Tsar is angry and there is a limit to how far I will defend you. To take sides with a Jew and make a spectacle of yourself in a court of law is inexcusable. Leave this devious clan to their own resources. They do not need your help."

"I apologize," Darya replies, the words burning her mouth. "It was foolish of me. I shall not embarrass you again."

"So unlike you, my dear. What made you go to court?"

"Curiosity," Darya blurts out a half-truth, keeping the rest to herself. The Empress is a staunch believer in dreams and their influence on daily life, but she will not understand the power the Ancient One exerts on Darya, how she had lured her out of bed and into the courtroom.

"Curiosity belongs to the young and carefree. You, Darya, although young, carry a heavy responsibility on your shoulders. Show more reserve next time. And never, ever again mention our name when it has to do with any Jew."

The Empress, fighting her fury, goes to her chaise lounge to fetch her embroidery. "Sit. I want to discuss an important matter with you." Her lips curl and she looks down at her embroidery as if the important matter is concealed inside.

"Some details about Alyosha's condition have leaked out. People are starting to talk, saying the heir to the throne might be sick. This is unacceptable. We have to stop the rumors. Or our enemies will get it in their heads to take advantage of the situation. Terrible power struggles might ensue. It could endanger the monarchy.

"Dr. Botkin tells me that future bleeding episodes are inevitable. Alyosha will have to rest and be under medical supervision. We will have to keep him out of the public eye. I had long discussions with the Tsar, dear, trying to find a way to divert attention from Alyosha's absences. In the end, the Tsar left the decision to me. I've suffered long sleepless nights; even the sleeping pills don't help." She raises her embroidery, folds it, unfolds it again, passes her palm over it, rolls one corner, then pats it back into shape. "As you know, at times of difficulty, the court tends to neglect artists and their art. So in order to present our court as a haven of peace and stability, we have decided to establish an Artists' Salon in the palace. What do you think, dear?"

Darya ponders the consequences of establishing a salon when the political landscape is becoming exceedingly volatile, violence everywhere, workers complaining about the rising prices of essential goods and the decline of wages, peasants unhappy about their wretched conditions and the unfair punishments landlords inflict on them, unrest even among the once faithful imperial Cossacks. It has been suggested that the most efficient method of ending the rising turmoil is for the Tsar to relinquish a degree of power and for the country to be converted from an absolute autocracy to a semiconstitutional monarchy that would promise a reformed political order, basic civil rights for all, especially for the disgruntled peasants, and even go so far as to legalize union activities, political strikes, and freedom of the press. The Empress considers the suggestion blasphemous. She refuses to hear of the Tsar surrendering his rightful place as supreme ruler.

Now, she intends to open the doors to her home to an artistic community teeming with dissidents. "I am not certain, Your Majesty. Our political situation is unstable. Some members of the artistic community are vocal insurgents who might further disrupt our fragile situation."

"Oh, my dear, don't be a pessimist. Concentrate on the outpouring of love toward us rather than on a small, inconsequential minority whose only care is to incite disruptions that can be easily crushed."

The Empress readjusts her position. Pain radiates across her back, her sciatica wreaking havoc on the frail muscles of her heart. She inadvertently sticks her needle into the eye of the embroidered icon on the tapestry. Flinching, she retrieves and reaffixes the needle in the bordering sky, then folds the embroidery in her lap, careful not to crinkle the face of the icon.

Darya hurries to adjust a mound of pillows behind her. "Your Majesty, embroidering all day is not helping your back."

"Idle hands, dear, are the devil's workshop. That's why I support artists who engage their hands as well as their minds. Anyway, dear, a salon requires advance preparation, time, and attendance. I am not up to assuming another responsibility. I cannot think of anyone better suited than you to take charge of the details. You were surrounded by art. You know art better than anyone I trust. I am certain that, under your tutelage, bold artistic breakthroughs will emerge that will give people something to talk about. You have my permission to select the artists. Send out invitations. The salon will be held four times a year. Choose the wording of the invitation to reflect our appreciation of art and the importance of raising the artistic consciousness of our people. Be sure to invite friends and supporters. There are many, I assure you. Compile a list of names for my review. Make sure the painter of *The Cure*, what was his name?"

"Avram Bensheimer, Your Majesty."

"Yes, yes, Bensheimer. Pity he is Jewish. *The Cure* is such a masterpiece. It remains my favorite, you know. Who ended up acquiring it in auction?"

"The monk, Your Majesty, Grigori Rasputin," Darya replies without further elaboration.

"Father Grigori!" The Empress exclaims, gesturing for Darya to massage her back. "How in the Lord's name did he outbid us?"

"He is a wealthy man, Your Majesty. People travel from all parts of the country to seek his healing powers. They reward him with great sums of money."

"I have my doubts, dear. He must have received the money from one of our enemies. Yes, I am quite certain. Even if he happens to have the means, a wandering monk would not have the aesthetic inclination to purchase a portrait such as this. At any rate, make sure the artist, this Jew, Bensheimer, is invited to our salon."

Chapter Fifteen

THE MOST PROMINENT ARTISTS of the land, four men and two women, rise to their feet. They have left behind unfinished canvases, paint, brushes, tripods, cameras, clay, and blocks of stone that beg for attention, taken precious time away to prepare for the occasion, yet the smell of paint, chemicals, and clay still clings to them as they impatiently await the Imperial Couple's arrival.

They are soon rewarded, not by the appearance of their Imperial Majesties, but by the vision of Darya, who lingers at the threshold, her sable-lashed eyes aimed at them as if at a herd of exquisite prey.

Clothed in purple crepe with a corseted waist and a bead-studded drape that trails behind, she sashays past them with an arrogant swish of her hips.

Her dainty feet sheathed in a pair of satin pumps, she loves the crash of beads behind her, loves the effect of her eyes upon them, the shock of her feral hair that frames the perfect oval of her face. Contrary to the artists, she is in her element, at home in court and surrounded by opulence.

The Portrait Hall has been emptied of its Jacobs sofas and armchairs covered in blue silk, magnificent consoles, gilded pianos, and lapis and carnelian tables. Life-sized paintings of Alexander I,

Nicholas I on horseback, Alexander II, his children, and Catherine the Great are protected with dust cloths.

Seven stations have been assembled for the artists to work in their respective mediums. A giant scaffold is erected in the center of the hall. All other necessary tools and materials—worktables, sculpting tools, easels, paints, brushes, and a Gramophone—are in place.

A beardless Cossack of the guards stands at attention, Kodak camera in hand. He has strict orders from her Imperial Majesty to record every detail. Since the recent introduction of the box roll-film camera, replacing clunky cameras that held twenty-foot rolls of paper, the grand duchesses have been enamored with photography, and the click of cameras echoes constantly around the palace.

The sculptress Rosa Koristanova is dressed in a starched white blouse with mother-of-pearl buttons. A rash is developing on her bosom, a testament to her aversion to anything remotely feminine. A petite woman, she stores unfathomable energy in her compact form. She is comfortable on the scaffolding, knows how to conquer it like an agile monkey, tackles massive blocks with the strength and dexterity of a wrestler, fashions sculptures of men in Herculean poses with such controversial titles as *Noble Savages and the Apocalypse*, *Feminine Mystic and the Male Controversy*, and *Murderous Gods and Their Victims*. She suffers from sculptor's asphyxia. Marble dust is stifling her lungs, yet she refuses to wear a mask. Worthy art, she believes, comes to life by engaging all five senses. The scent of her stones, the smell of dust and blood and history, determine the final shape of her sculptures.

Next to her is the choreographer Igor Vasiliev with his head bowed low. He keeps his hands at his sides. His patent tuxedo slippers tap to the dance shaping in his head, a waltz that might or might not have to do with the complicated relationship between the Tsar and his German cousin, the kaiser.

Dimitri Markowitz is known for his promonarchy caricatures,

images of a kind Tsar leading his people to unimaginable wealth—mines brimming with gold, wells spewing jewels, oceans vomiting all types of benevolent decrees—but in reality, he holds the Tsar responsible for the miseries of the people. Dimitri, however, makes every effort to conceal his true ideologies. He does not believe in becoming a martyr in the name of art.

Belkin Fyodor is among the invitees. Darya admires his landscapes that evoke a certain sense of familiarity, perhaps a sense of her having been there: flat stretches of sandy deserts, palm trees swaying in harsh winds, rippling sand dunes ablaze at sunset, camel caravans snaking around flapping tents.

The photographer Joseph Petrov Eltsin is not used to lavish palaces, imperial pretensions, and honorary awards that carry no tangible benefits. His blood is thick with the many tranquilizers he consumes, causing sporadic twitches in his knees and left cheek. He feels most at home in asylums, where he captures photographs of the mentally disturbed. His black and white photographs portray the anguished soul of beasts, the torment of lovers, and the solitude of monks, proof that man is born despondent and starving for attention. Here, in the salon, surrounded by intelligent personalities, each with a differently shaped head, he decides to embark on a crucial scientific project. He will compile a collection of photographs to prove that head shape does not evidence madness, as certain contemporary physicians claim.

Tamara, the Creator of Miniatures, the court's most beloved artist, is an honorary guest. Years of bending over her work have left their imprint. At the age of twenty-two, the outline of a slight hump and the stoop of her bony shoulders are visible under her sheer blouse. Her miniatures, carved into all types of precious woods, stones, skins, and roots, are coveted around the country, but the few she finds time to craft are for the sole enjoyment of the Imperial Family.

Darya walks to each artist, nods her greetings, congratulates Rosa Koristanova on being awarded the imperial gold medal for work of special merit in sculpture, tells Igor she has attended his Ballet des Aristocrats twice and wouldn't mind seeing it again, tells Dimitri that his caricature *Our Tsar in the Opera* hangs in the Emperor's study. She shakes Belkin's hand, "I love your *Blue Desert* painting at the Borodin Museum. I'd like to have one myself." She teases Joseph, "As for your photographs, sir, they're too intellectual for me, but the Tsar likes them." She kisses the cheeks of the Creator of Miniatures. "Thank you, Tamara. Alyosha is inseparable from the lovely enamel dog. Come visit him soon, will you?"

Having welcomed each artist, she takes her place behind two thronelike chairs awaiting their Imperial Majesties.

Something is amiss, Darya thinks as she takes note of the invitees. Something is not quite right. She counts once. Six. Then counts again, this time with greater attention. Panic strikes her like a slap of scalding water. Her heart misses a beat. Her hand creeps up to her Fabergé necklace.

Avram Bensheimer, the only artist the Tsarina personally invited, is absent.

The Tsar and Tsarina will be here soon. She has been in charge of establishing the salon, making sure the artists understand what is expected of them, recognize the sensitive nuances of court protocol. The blame for such brazen insolence, such unacceptable impertinence will rest on her.

She digs her fingers into her glossy hair that the pomade of honey wax and scented starch fails to tame. She is hot, perspiring. Releasing a silk tieback from the drapes, she gathers her hair back. She goes to a table spread with turnovers stuffed with meat and potatoes, tureens of borscht and pepper-pot soup, pheasants in cream sauce, fruits in wine, and ice cream. A waiter pours mint-scented vodka into a Baccarat tumbler. She swigs one shot of vodka, waits for the warming to take hold, for her heart to settle.

"Ladies and gentlemen, welcome to the imperial salon, where every day promises fresh creative fodder to embellish and use in your respective mediums." She allows a moment of anticipation, an exchange of opinions, some lighthearted banter, a few more seconds for her breath to normalize. "Consider this your sanctuary. A home where you may hone your skills, remain faithful to the demand of your art without fear of censorship. This is my solemn promise to you."

The artists exchange furtive glances. Is this the belief of the Imperial Couple? Are they being encouraged to free their imagination without concern of persecution? Or is this the opinion of the Tyotia Dasha?

A sudden chill scurries through Darya's veins. She is beside herself with rebuke. Did she really say this? Give permission to the artists to broadcast their every belief? Did she make the inexcusable mistake of granting them freedom of expression? What if they create art that raises questions about the monarchy? About the political situation? The artists are silent, expectant, poised to pounce upon any crumb of information Darya may toss their way. Voyeurism is part of their nature, a valuable tool in their arsenal, a way of digging deep to unearth precious details that will end up fueling their art. The Alexander Palace, its imperial inhabitants, and Darya, with her mesmerizing eyes, are intriguing sources to explore. Markowitz sketches the outline of her face in his head, her biblical-looking features, the patrician nose, the strong mouth, the tasseled tieback swinging below her earlobes. The ballet developing in Igor's mind is changing shape, the German and Russian cousins in a state of perpetual allegro, brisk, sharp, demanding. Tamara can think of nothing but her next gift to the little Tsarevich: a tiny deer like the one in the park, perhaps an aurochs, or the golden pony he's so fond of. Rosa wants to edge closer to Joseph, inhale his scent, sense his emotions, tattoo him in her mind. She wants to recreate him in stone.

The aroma of citrus blossoms from the lime trees outside wafts into the salon. A bird of paradise lands on the windowsill, its puffy chest heaving lightly, a worm dangling from its yellow beak.

Darya scrubs her concerns out of her mind, attempts a smile. "Ladies and gentlemen, I don't need to tell you that the Imperial Couple are fierce advocates of the arts. I don't need to tell you that you are here because their Majesties admire your work. So do not disappoint them!"

The mahogany doors swing open, and the master of ceremonies taps his ebony staff three times on the parquet underfoot, announcing their Imperial Majesties.

The Empress is regal in a flowing silk dress adorned with lace and designed by Worth in Paris. She touches the pink pearls hugging her white throat, reaches out for her husband's arm, and as if they were alone, he smiles at her and gives her hand an encouraging squeeze.

He is wearing his most simple military gear, cinched at the waist with a leather belt, his imperial medals left behind. The salon is his wife's brainchild, and he has no intention of eclipsing her.

The artists bow to their monarchs. Remain standing as the Tsar and Tsarina make their way across the expanse of gleaming parquet toward their chairs, above which hangs a Gobelin silk tapestry, depicting the ill-fated Maria Antoinette and her children, a thoughtless gift from the French government.

The Empress gestures toward the artists to take their seats, her smile softening her grave expression. She is pleased with her decision to establish a salon. No one will ever learn about her pain, her broken heart, her endless search for a miracle to cure her son. What the artists will project to the world are the vivid scenes of imperial life, vibrant, varied, and dramatic, a close-knit family whose only care is the well-being of their people.

She addresses the artists in a blend of British- and German-accented Russian. "Welcome to our court, ladies and gentlemen. I hope you will be inspired here to achieve great honors for our country. I will personally support you in your future endeavors as it is the belief of this court that our great culture is measured by the genius of our artists. I shall follow your progress and at year's end confer an honorary award upon the artist whose work best portrays the soul of our dear country."

An enameled easel, holding a large photograph of the heir apparent, Alexei Romanov, is brought in and set between the Imperial Couple.

The beardless Cossack of the guard runs forward to snap photographs.

The Empress gazes proudly at the image of her son. She thought long and hard about selecting Avram Bensheimer to paint her son's portrait, discussed the matter with the Tsar, who emphatically opposes the choice, and for the first time in her married life, she disregarded his advice in hope that Bensheimer will succeed in creating a masterpiece superior to *The Cure*. She studies each artist, groups them together in her mind, then separates them again, attempting to decide which is the Jewish artist. She settles on Joseph with his beady eyes and greedy ears. "Avram Bensheimer," she declares, "we commission you to paint a portrait of your Tsarevich."

Joseph is shriveling under her stare, glances around, subtly shakes his head. The silence is universal. Not a single tap of an impatient foot, a single rasp from an infected lung, a click of the camera, a shriek of swans, or a whoop of courting birds outside.

Darya's heart is drumming in her temples, the Fabergé egg necklace as heavy as the gallows around her throat. She struggles to collect herself, to appear calm, unruffled. "My apologies, Your Majesties, I don't know why Bensheimer did not come."

Rosa whispers in Igor's ear, who tugs at Joseph's sleeve, and a low murmur scurries across the salon like a rat on fire.

The Emperor's jaws are clenched. His face is splotched red with rage. He clutches the cane handle and squeezes the two-headed eagle emblem of his imperial house. He rises to his feet, offering his arm to his wife. They stand together at the head of the salon, regal in their indignation, their incriminating glares directed at Darya.

The flap of wings can be heard outside the window. A dog barks in the park. Count Trebla curses in his coarse voice.

"We will learn why!" The Emperor's eyes rest on Darya, and she wants to curl into herself and melt away. "And you, Darya Borisovna!" He stops there, handling his bottled rage, mindful of the Empress at his side, her affection for the girl. But he does not need to say more. His pronouncement echoes and agitates long after he turns on his heels and walks out with the Tsarina.

Chapter Sixteen

D ARYA REACHES OUT TO knock on the paint-peeled door, steals her hand back, stuffs it in the pocket of her hooded cape, and draws the cape around her as if to disappear inside its dark folds. Avram Bensheimer's apartment is on the third floor of a narrow yellow-brick building, a part of Tsarskoe Selo she has never seen. On her way here, the imperial horse-drawn carriage, out-of-place in these narrow streets, trotted past a few art studios, a butchery, a synagogue, a bakery, an elementary school, and closely huddled shops, houses, and galleries, as if no other space is left in all of Russia to accommodate these people.

The imperial carriage is at her disposal for the day, presumably for her bimonthly shopping ventures to back-alley stores and out-of-the-way antique shops to look for new fabrics—taffeta, grosgrain, velvets of all colors, silk brocades in various weaves—to embellish her dresses, feathers and scarlet flowers for her hats, and once every now and then, a special find for the Empress, such as a pearl-splashed ribbon the imperial seamstress weaves as a skirt waist or a bejeweled feather to adorn a hat.

She is not in this primarily Jewish section of town to purchase ribbons and laces and feathers, but to confront Avram Bensheimer. An unprecedented honor was conferred upon the artist, and in return, he offended their Majesties. The Emperor is expecting an explanation.

She knocks on the door once then harder twice. At first there is no sound from inside, then the squeak of wood. Footsteps. She takes a deep breath, locks her fingers behind her, steps farther away from the door. A cockroach scurries past, stops disoriented, and takes shelter under a dust ball.

The door creaks open on its rusted hinges, and a tall man appears in the dim light of the bare lamp overhead. A palette of dry paint—sands and russets and indigos—clings to his shoulder-grazing blond hair. His green-flecked eyes rest on Darya with a start of recognition. "Darya Borisovna!" he utters in an Austrian accent. "Tyotia Dasha of the Romanov!"

Darya is stunned into momentary silence. Has she knocked on the wrong door? That he recognizes her is not surprising. Her opal eye is her undisputable calling card, an immediate introduction. But the man appraising her with the attentiveness of an artist is the same man she saw defending the Jewish boy in court that day. "Avram Bensheimer?" She asks. "The painter?"

"Avram the painter," he replies, a smile lighting his sad eyes. "And you are the brave Darya Borisovna who defended me in the court of law. Here you are, when I need you again."

"Of course you need me, Mr. Bensheimer, but I don't think I can do much for you. What you have done is unforgivable. You offended the Imperial Couple. In fact, you wouldn't have been invited to the Artists' Salon if it were not for *The Cure*, which the Empress happens to admire." She appraises him, struggling to separate the twenty-four-year-old Jewish artist, who would dare keep the Tsar and Tsarina waiting, from the heroic man who stood up in court. "You did not come, Mr. Bensheimer. You were invited. You were expected."

He flicks his hair off his forehead and points at a fresh scar. "I needed medical help." He opens the door wide and gestures for her to enter.

She follows him into a small, tidy room, the walls covered with studies for his paintings—human anatomy, arms, legs, fingers, different shapes of eyes, some tearful, others curious or shocked, all types of wounds, bleeding, scabbed, healed, always a mark left behind. Despite the surrounding images, the room is pleasing to Darya. A pearly sun filters in through the sheer curtains, a faint sound of rustling leaves, the laughter of children playing in the street below. She points to his forehead. "What happened?"

"I was attacked," he replies, as if it was a minor accident. Nimble as a panther, he ambles across the room, grabs two of the four wooden chairs around a round table, and brings one to her. "Please rest. It's a long ride from the palace."

"Why were you attacked, Mr. Bensheimer?"

"Because I am Jewish."

"I don't understand."

He can tell that her sheltered life insulates her from the surrounding horrors. She has no access to *Bessarabetz* or *Svet*, the anti-Jewish newspapers, is unaware of the message Theodore Roosevelt sent Nicholas II to stop his cruel oppression of the Jews, the violent riots, mob attacks, killings, and destruction of their homes. She is unaware of the recent and most serious pogrom against the Jews.

"There was another massacre, this one worse than the other. I tried to save a neighbor, a child, from a police officer. We got into a fight. I was stabbed; it's a deep cut. I apologize."

He tells her that people had poured into the streets to protest the Tsar's political views, it seemed. Then, suddenly and inexplicably, the rioters turned against the Jews. They were ferocious, breaking windows, looting shops, dragging women by their hair. Glass was strewn underfoot, stuck in people's hair, shards blinding old and young. Blood-splattered horses trampled children to death under their wild hooves. Twenty-five hundred Jews were killed.

The wooden chair groans under Darya when she sits. She is pale, fraying at the edges as if her entire being is unraveling. How is it possible that she was ignorant of such atrocities inflicted upon a people in her country? And the Imperial Couple, are they aware? If so, why do they tolerate it? "I am sorry," she tells Avram Bensheimer. What else is there to say?

"I had no intention of putting you in a difficult position. Not after what you did for us in court. You are brave. Very brave, Opal-Eyed Jewess."

She does not know why he calls her Opal-Eyed Jewess, whether he intends to offend or praise her. "I am not a Jew," she tells him.

"No, of course not. But Jews can only depend on their own for help, yet here you are defending us in court. So make me happy, accept this honorary title. Or I could call you Opal-Eyed Queen, since you, too, like Queen Esther, came to our defense."

Accept both titles! The Ancient One levitates behind the sheer, billowing curtains, different today, her outline precise, solid, none of the earlier obscuring cloudiness. She is beautiful, Darya thinks, a certain soothing quality to her wise eyes, her message encouraging— *suitable titles*, she says, *yours to display like priceless medals*.

Avram is leaning back in the chair opposite her, observing her like a painter facing a blank canvas, an arena of endless possibilities opening up to him. "I'd like to paint your portrait," he says with a certain sense of entitlement.

She locks her eyes on his, the gravity of the situation hitting her with renewed force. "Mr. Bensheimer, you don't seem to grasp the seriousness of affairs. You are barred from the salon. The Empress is expecting an explanation." She gestures toward the wound on his forehead, a few drops of blood visible around the stitches. "This will not be enough. It's not life threatening. You could have come after you took care of it. Or at the least, sent a messenger to let us know you weren't coming. As for my portrait, I will not have you paint me. You paint all types of scars, and even naked bodies. I, alas, do not have a scar on my body, nor will I ever take off my clothes for you."

"You are angry with me, Opal-Eyed Queen. It makes me sad."

The muscles of her cheeks hurt. She does not know whether to laugh or cry. She has never seen such grief, such persistence, such warmth in a pair of eyes. He exudes a sense of anticipation that excites and scares her. "What am I supposed to do, Mr. Bensheimer?"

"Call me Avram. Please. Not many Bensheimers are left. Murdered in one pogrom or another. By their Imperial Majesties, the Romanovs!"

She flinches as if each word is a knife in her chest. "It's not true, Avram. Do not blame their Majesties. They would never tolerate such atrocities!"

He hears the hesitation in her voice, observes her tug at her necklace, lower her hand and tuck it into her velvet sleeve with the elaborate lace border. He pulls away from his pain. "I don't want to cause you trouble. Tell me how I can help and I will."

"You can't come to the salon, and you might not be safe at home. I want to help you, I really do. I admire your portrayal of the underbelly of society, the seedier side, as well as its beauty."

"If that's so, why won't you model for me? It is my greatest wish."

"You don't understand, Mr. Bensheimer. You are in danger. The Tsar has ordered the Ministry of Police to investigate your affairs. This is not good. No telling where you will be tomorrow." She reaches out a hand to bid him farewell. "I am sorry, Avram, I do not know what to do."

He raises her hand to his lips and holds it there for a long time.

Outside, the sun is flitting away. It begins to drizzle. There's a chill in the air.

A mysterious spark comes to life in her opal eye. An idea has dawned. She snaps her fingers as if to change the course of events. "You are an artist, Avram. Go and walk in a park, disappear, and don't even think of going back home or to your studio. Go to a museum, to a friend, do something, anything that will inspire you to find a way for the Imperial Couple to forgive you. If you do, then I'll pose for you. Know that the only way to the Tsarina's heart is through her son."

Chapter Seventeen

— 1905 —

S TEAM CURLS UP FROM a pot-bellied samovar in a corner of Portrait Hall. Limoges cups with the Romanov insignia stand on a gilded tray. Mead, brandy, buttermilk pancakes, pickled mushrooms, and herb-scented vodkas are set on a table spread with rose petals. Bowls of the Tsarina's favorite Crimean wild berries adorn the table. Her Imperial Majesty is expected at any moment.

A silver-threaded cloth covers an easel displayed on a platform at the head of the Portrait Hall. Avram paces back and forth in front of the easel, a nervous lion guarding his lair.

Darya walks around, stops at every station to oversee last-minute details. A leaden weight presses against her chest, and she thinks that if she survives this day, then she might survive any future hurdles fate may toss her way.

Avram's left hand creeps up to his forehead, he winces, runs his thumb over the scar. There is a new worry in his eyes, more depth, an added sadness. He knows the Empress has not forgiven him, knows that by inviting him to the salon, Darya has put herself in a precarious situation. He tugs at a loosened silver thread, pulls it off the cloth, twisting it around his fingers, rolling it into a ball. Nothing can be undone now. Whatever is meant to happen will.

Up on the scaffolding, Rosa Koristanova is preparing a massive block of agate alabaster. The Empress has paid for its transportation from Italy. The luminous, flesh-colored stone has been moistened with water, the fault lines and grain located, and the design of a triumphant Ipabog, god of the hunt, drawn with pencil on the stone. Mallet in hand and without protective gear, eye mask, dust mask, or fingerless gloves, Rosa strokes the alabaster, preoccupied with how to best shave off pieces of unwanted stone, careful not to leave bruises and sacrifice the heart.

"Who is your model, Rosa?"

The startled Rosa looks up to find Darya has climbed the ladder and is standing behind her atop the scaffolding. "Oh, my! You really shouldn't be up here with all this dust. It isn't healthy at all. Oh! You were asking me, weren't you, who my model is. Well, let me think, the truth is that this one is especially important to me…and…if I may, well, I would rather not tempt the devil by calling attention to it."

"Of course, of course," Darya quickly assures, certain she recognizes Joseph's profile drawn on the stone. "Many artists share your feelings. Good luck, then, and we'll talk later." She taps Rosa on the shoulder and, to the ceaseless click of Joseph's camera, climbs down the ladder.

In another corner of the hall, Igor Vasiliev is accompanied by two dancers impersonating the Tsar and his German cousin, Kaiser Wilhelm II. One of the dancers soars above a makeshift stage as if defying gravity. He embarks on a set of bold turns before landing in a graceful plié on the back of the other dancer, a Tsar impersonator, who is on all fours. With naughty twists of the arm, the kaiser slaps the buttocks of the Tsar, who all but carries his cousin on his back.

"What's the story of your ballet?" Darya asks Igor. "Why is this dancer riding on the back of the other?"

Igor bites his lip. He turns to Darya and his smile is free of malice. "It's the story of a kind merchant who made a pact with his donkey. In the spirit of equality, the merchant will ride the donkey in the morning and will allow the donkey to ride him in the evenings."

An expression of amusement scurries across Darya's face. "Does it work? Do they get along?"

"Time will tell," Igor replies. "It's just the beginning."

At that moment, the leg of one of the dancers cuts through the air like a swift arrow and inadvertently kicks the caricaturist in the shin. He jumps up and lands a punch on the dancer's nose.

Punches fly and legs flail as the horrified Darya tries to separate them, admonishing them, warning them that the Empress is expected at any moment.

The scaffolding rattles and Rosa, as if she were a Cossack of the imperial guard, jumps down, brandishing her mallet in the men's faces. "Shame! Shame on every one of your shit-stuffed heads! How dare you! Go out and piss on each other in the street. Stop acting like frustrated eunuchs." She grabs the men by their arms and marches them toward their assigned spaces just in time for the other artists to scramble back to their stations as the grand master of ceremonies announces her Imperial Majesty.

An immediate hush takes over, all eyes turning to her.

The willowy Alexandra Feodorovna sails in like an angel dressed in a four-tiered white skirt, white lace stockings, and suede shoes. Her hair is coiled high and kept in place with silver pins. Two tear-shaped pearls the size of pigeon eggs dangle from her earlobes. She has just returned from the Feodorovsky Chapel at the end of the park, where she fell to her knees and pressed her face to the cold stones, thanking the Lord for granting her son temporary relief.

She is in good spirits, radiant, smiling. Gesturing a conspiratorial forefinger behind the door, she invites her daughters to join her. They drift in like perfumed breezes, cross the hall, and walk straight toward Darya.

At their sight, the weight pressing on Darya's chest lightens, and she is able to draw some air into her lungs. Olga and Tatiana, the Big Pair, and Maria and Anastasia, the Little Pair, as she affectionately calls them, sail into her wide-open arms. She hugs them, drawing strength from their small bodies. Olga, the oldest, is only ten. Two years separate each sister from the other in age, but their elegant composure is breathtaking.

The Empress is observing the artists, fixing them under her stare, taking note of each face she was introduced to on the first gathering three months back. She catches sight of an unfamiliar face. "Who is this man?" she asks Darya.

"Avram Bensheimer!" Darya replies, grouping the children behind her as if to shield them from the predictable eruption.

"Bensheimer!" the Empress exclaims.

The pause is so long, the silence so complete. Darya can hear the soft inhale of breath behind her, can hear a small cough. The thought occurs to her that Anastasia might be coming down with a cold. "I invited Bensheimer back, your Majesty. May I explain?"

The smile flees from the Empress's lips. Her tightly set face turns to stone. She breezes straight toward Darya. "No! You may not explain! Hand this man to the imperial Cossacks and meet me in the reading room."

Darya goes to rest a trembling hand on top of the easel. Holds it there for a second.

The restive stamp of horses can be heard outside, a pale day moon sails behind a cloud. A breeze of white butterflies makes its way inside, circles the room, and then alights on Anastasia's left shoulder.

Darya tugs at the thread that binds the cloth at the base, pulls at a knot, and unwinds it. Grabs a corner of the cloth and, with one quick motion, flips it off the easel.

The Tsarina stands motionless in front of the easel. An artery throbs at her throat. She bites her lower lip. Her lips are dry, her eyes moist.

On the same easel that three months ago displayed her son's photograph, now stands a portrait of the Madonna and Child.

But this is not the image of the Son of God. This is her darling Alyosha. His blue-gray eyes twinkle. His full head of curls shine. His dimpled cheeks are the picture of health. He is safe in the arms of the Madonna, whose healing gaze falls on him like a benediction, her benevolent smile a balm, her caring hands resting on him like countless blessings.

The Empress lets out a sigh. Tears well in her eyes, remain suspended on her lashes. Her tentative forefinger traces the outline of the image of her son on canvas. Such artistic brilliance. Such an exceptional insight into her heart's desire. But what is the Lord's message to her, and why has He selected this Jewish man as His medium?

After an eternity that finds the artists scrambling for the optimal viewing position, the Empress lowers herself into the closest chair.

Darya gestures toward Avram, explains to the Empress that the portrait is his work as reparation for his insolence, explains that he extends his heartfelt regrets and profuse apologies and that a tragic event in his community kept him from the salon that day.

Avram is silent. There is not much fear in this man. There was not one tragic event, he thinks, but ongoing tragedies that are destroying entire communities, pogroms incited by the authorities, by the Tsarist secret police, by the military, even the mayor himself. His insides are a volcanic brew of resentment toward the Romanovs. But he will not jeopardize Darya's position in the Imperial Court. He will not lose her now that she will have to keep her promise and model for him.

The Empress rises, approaches the portrait to take another close look. She brushes her cheek with an open palm. She steps back as if in the presence of a holy image.

"Darya Borisovna, deliver the painting to my private quarters. Reward Bensheimer for his efforts!" Having conveyed her wishes, she nods to her daughters to follow her, turns on her heels, and takes her leave without as much as a single glance at the work of the other artists.

Darya waits for the echo of the Empress's steps to die, for her own heartbeat to settle.

She is unaware what a great risk Avram has taken. He presented this portrait to her Imperial Majesty, certain she would not recognize the woman who posed as the Madonna.

And he was right.

Cloistered in the Alexander Palace, the Empress failed to identify the face of the Madonna as that of White Thighs Paulina, an unknown proletariat whore.

Chapter Eighteen

D EFIANT, EVERY CELL IN her body rebelling, Darya orders the guards to exit the hall. Now that the Empress has left, she releases the soft-footed servants from their duties, and they melt away through the numerous doors.

She will honor her promise to model for Avram. She will do it in the nude. She will do it now. Do it to spit in the face of the Ancient One who appeared again last night, naked as Eve, a flamelike tear visible under her veil on an otherwise featureless face. Before stepping into the devouring blaze, she plucked the burning tear off and tossed it at Darya, but instead of catching fire, Darya's dress turned into an icy vise, stiff and irremovable and threatening to suffocate her. It is always something she is wearing in her dreams—a blouse, a cloak, a skirt— that the Ancient One transforms into a rigid, imprisoning curse.

Today, Darya is not dressed in her everyday fineries but in simpler attire of linen and Mechlin lace. She tosses her sandals aside, steps out of her robe, unbuttons the mother-of-pearl buttons running the length of her flounced petticoats, and drops them at her feet. One by one, she begins to release the hooks and ribbons of her corset. She hesitates, uncertain, gazes at the artists who, despite their efforts at civility, have their senses trained on her. She reaches out to Avram for encouragement.

"A screen can be brought in," he suggests, finding himself at a loss for words. Is this woman real, he wonders, or an apparition with no sense of fear?

"I have nothing to hide," she replies. This is not the truth. Her dreams, her opal eye, the woman she is, and the one at the beck and call of the Ancient One hold a million secrets.

Darya hands her corset to Avram.

She stands naked in the center of Portrait Hall. In full view of the artists and the painting of the Tsarevich and Madonna that will soon boast a place of honor in the Lilac Boudoir.

She comes down on the satin-covered dais and stretches out. She offers Avram an encouraging smile, although all she wants is to cover her naked body and crawl into herself.

Avram wrestles with the formidable task of reproducing on canvas the perfect curve of her breasts, the graceful hollow of her waist half-lit by the light coming from the window, the half-moon of her buttock, but most of all, the lovely translucency of her opal eye that projects her pleasure and suffering, courage, and vulnerability.

High on her scaffolding, Rosa attempts to banish the demons in her head, her hunger and desire. She glances at Darya naked as Venus, her prominent nipples luscious as chocolate, the soft flesh of her belly like burnished bronze. A lucky man, Avram Bensheimer, to have Darya as his model. What is she, Rosa, supposed to do with this spectacular block of stone when Joseph's head is constantly hidden behind his camera or shoved deep into his photographs?

Dimitri tears the half-finished caricature in his sketchbook, crumbles and tosses the page into a basket overflowing with rejected drafts. He has failed to embellish and exaggerate the expression in Darya's eyes, one sly like a slippery eel, the other obsessed and somewhat desperate, not unlike a betrayed woman. He leaves his station to pour himself tea from the samovar and adds a tumbler of vodka. He is a member of the Socialist Revolutionary Party and like the rest of his comrades prefers to be clear about the political affiliation of those who surround him. But the Jewish pimp is a mystery. On the one hand, he is enamored of Darya Borisovna, the imperialist bitch; on the other, he pretends to be against anything that might remotely reek of imperialism. Dropping four cubes of sugar into his tea, Dimitri stirs absentmindedly as he observes the painter and his model.

Two hours pass and Darya is becoming restless. Avram has yet to start painting. She tries to keep still as he continues to stare at her, at the canvas that faces away from her, back and forth, without lifting his brush. She does not want to disturb whatever is developing in his head, but the fire in the fireplace is like ice picks in her marrow, and she is desperate to cover herself, desperate for a cup of hot tea. "Avram, are you going to paint me or stand there and stare?"

As if startled out of a trance, he wipes his hands with a moist cloth, dips his brush in a jar of turpentine, and swishes it around. He measures her against the shaft of his brush, squeezes collaps-ible metal tubes of paint onto his pallet, arranging them like a rainbow. Small glistening puddles of Persian red and dragon blood, calamine blue and indigo, chrome orange and carnelian, and softer flesh tones of chrome primrose and shell pink. He dips the brush in paint and wipes the tip on a rag. His hand moves in fast, bold strokes, the brush licking the canvas like a possessed lover, transforming the stretch of canvas into a living entity, shaping her outline, her essence, capturing the distillation of this moment in her life.

The salon is in full session, the atmosphere electric. Rosa, normally respectful of even the most inferior of stones, is hacking viciously at the valuable alabaster. Dimitri is acting suspiciously, his pen scratching like a rat on dry wood planks, tearing into one sheet after another, not caring to toss the discarded paper balls in the wastebasket. Darya wonders what he is up to. She does not trust him. She attempts to think of anything and anyone other than Avram, who steps back now and then to inspect her with narrowed eyes. She thinks of the grand duchesses and the added joy they've brought into her life. She thinks of the Tsarevich, whether he will remain as attached to her when he grows into a young man. She thinks about her parents and how they were baffled by their daughter's growing ability to heal wounds and small sorrows. She thinks of her country, how difficult it must be for her Tsar to deal with a nation in turmoil, the populace pleading for even more reforms and all types of rights, a nation ignorant of the divine right of her ruler. And she thinks of the hateful Father Gapon, the priest and self-appointed policeman, who incited the working class to march to St. Petersburg to implore the Tsar for change. The result was tragic. A procession of peaceful workers, holding icons, singing "God Save the Tsar," had marched to the Winter Palace to hand a petition to the Tsar, calling for fairer wages, better working conditions, and an end to the Russo-Japanese War. The nervous army pickets near the palace fired directly into the crowd of more than three hundred thousand. Many were killed. The blame fell on the Tsar, who was not in the capital at the time.

"Avram, I want to see your work," she says, at last.

"Not yet. Do you need something? Are you comfortable?" His entire attention is aimed at the canvas, the smell of turpentine burning his eyes.

Two birds of paradise land on the window ledge and embark on a courting ritual. The male struts in a costume worthy of a Tsar—shiny black plumes, pale pink flanks, springy crown feathers, and velvety neck wattle. The skeptical female scrutinizes his flapping wings, fluttering whiskers, and flashing chest. At last, the quivering female bird lets out an inviting, guttural trill. The male leaps on top of her and they fuse into a feathered fuss.

Darya grabs the satin sheet and wraps it around her, pulls herself into a sitting position, slinging her legs down the podium. To Avram's great horror, and before he is able to protest, she has come around to face the canvas.

She forgets about her nakedness, about the sound of Rosa's

chisel overhead, the clicking of Joseph's camera at the window, Igor's music of Wagner echoing all around, the scratching of Dimitri's pen behind, and the passionate trills of birds of paradise on the window ledge.

This is more than art. This is magic.

Avram has given birth to the dark mystery between her thighs, the graceful indentation of her waist, her slim neck that slants toward voluptuous shoulders. Her mystical, eyes, the opal that flames in the outline of her face the shade of walnut husks. She does not recognize the hunger and sadness in her eyes, the scar on her forehead that is a duplicate of his.

"Why did you do that?" she whispers, indicating the painted scar.

"I'm branding you as my own."

In the future, when she is an old woman with a youthful face, wandering in her crumbling Entertainment Palace with her greedy rats, in the garden with the ravenous civets plucking coffee cherries from bushes, when she bathes in her banya while Little Servant attends to her every need, she will recall this as the moment she fell in love.

Now, Avram so close, nothing else matters, save her longing. She reaches out to him. She will take him by the hand and lead him out of the Portrait Hall, across marble and parquet and gilded woodwork, across the semicircular entrance hall with its *trompe l'oeil* ceiling, and into the park alive with the warble of aroused birds of paradise.

He inclines his head slightly toward the faint scent of ambergris emanating from her necklace and, conscious of all eyes pinned on them, whispers, "Later, Darya, later."

This is all he says, but it is enough to startle her senses back.

She will not tempt fate. Not now. Not yet.

Chapter Nineteen

WRESTLING WITH HER EMOTIONS, fear, and excitement, but most of all desire, Darya leads Avram across the bridge that spans the length of the artificial lake dotted with baroque follies, where swans intertwine with beaks buried in downy feathers.

Three months passed before she gathered her courage to approach him at his easel, when the others were engaged in the dining hall. They planned to meet in the evening, when the park is quiet, when the greater birds of paradise, tired from their flirtatious strutting, fluttering, and quivering, are snoozing on the branches.

Now, she leads him deep within the park, past fountains and fancy chinoiserie, and across the bridge toward a private island, where they will be safe. She tightens her shawl against the morning chill as she instructs him how to haul the bridge for privacy.

He is fast, efficient, his muscles straining as he follows her directions, unlocking the metal components, jaws, tongues, shifting, raising, and lowering the heavy locks that click into place with well-oiled precision.

They continue deep into the island, past a pillar in the center that commemorates a naval victory, and toward rows of massive urns leading to two yellow wooden pavilions: the banya erected by Catherine II for her beloved grandson.

Avram steps closer and murmurs into her hair. "You are delicious, my queen, and I'm addicted to your scent. Where are you taking me?"

Her voice shaking a little, she says, "To the banya, Avram."

He holds up a finger to warn her of the many dangers in store for her. The palace has eyes and ears. It is a den of informants. Spies might be lurking behind bushes and trees. The Tsar and Tsarina will not be pleased to discover that their admired Darya Borisovna is sneaking out with a Jew. He withdraws his warning. He wants her too, wants her badly.

They are unaware that, wet and shivering from his swim across the lake, Count Trebla, the court veterinarian, is trailing them in the shadows, skipping behind one tree, then another, a feral growl rumbling in his throat. He has been following Darya, her coming and going, certain he would catch her red-handed. And he has. Hand in hand with Bensheimer, no less, with his artistic nonsense and pompous ways, as if he carries royal blood in his veins. How dare she reject him, a count, an aristocrat, a descendant from a long line of noblemen who were all counts. He ducks behind a bush to avoid detection, scuttles to crouch behind the arbor surrounding the banya, nudges some branches back, and settles on his haunches to observe the two.

They enter the jasper and rock crystal Agate Pavilion, where eucalyptus-scented steam wafts off a sinking pool. Darya releases her gossamer shawl, and it drifts in the air, dazzling, diaphanous, light as butterfly wings. She steps out of layers of silk chiffon that fall to the floor with a peal of beads, tosses her pearl-studded suede shoes aside, and shakes her dark mane loose around her shoulders. Moonlight peeps through an arbor dotted with dahlias and zinnias, dappling her naked breasts, voluptuous buttocks, small waist. She plunges into the scented pool, her laughter pealing around the banya. Her stomach is tight with longing for Avram's feline suppleness as he peels off his paint-splotched pants, his aroused penis so unexpectedly beautiful.

He dives into the sunken pool, steam licking the sun-touched demarcation at his neck.

She presses her palms on his eyes, slides her tongue across his neck, a hum of pleasure in his throat, his breath in her hair.

He swims around her, his thighs brushing her buttocks, hands stroking her belly as if with a paintbrush. He takes her nipples in his mouth, one then the other, to experience their different tastes. "I'll take you to Vienna one day. We'll dine at Tomaselli, Mozart's favorite café. I'll show you the Vienna Court Opera. We'll see the manuscript of Mozart's *Don Giovanni*, the greatest piece of music ever composed. I'll teach you to swim in the Danube."

"I'll show you the gilded statues of the Imperial Palace in Peterhof," she whispers back, their breath mingling with eucalyptus steam. "In August, when the blue ageratum is in full bloom, we'll climb the azure-winged dragons and bathe under their water-spewing mouths. We'll play chess on the giant outdoor checkerboard and pretend that Peter the Great is looking over us."

"I will love you here and there and everywhere," he murmurs, sucking her wet earlobe, covering her eyelids with kisses. "I will lift you in my arms like this and anchor your legs around me. I will be patient and gentle and tell you how very much I want you. And you will feel pleasure and no pain, my Opal-Eyed Jewess, no pain at all."

Chapter Twenty

THE EMPRESS DIRECTS HER tear-filled gaze toward her husband who, hands clasped behind him, paces the room. Her ears register nothing but her fifteen-month-old son's moans and her failure to make his pain go away. What do doctors know about her suffering, her unbearable sense of self-blame and reproach? Now that Alexei has started walking and is prone to accidents, she and her husband have had long discussions about assigning two sailors from the imperial navy to protect him. But in the end, they had concluded that he did not require that kind of constant surveillance yet. How wrong they were.

To add to their grief, despite all precautions, rumors about the heir's failing health have found their way into magazines and newspapers. Special services are being held in cathedrals and churches around the country. The Empress, when not at her son's side, or finding refuge in the Feodorovsky Chapel at the end of the park, prostrates herself in front of Avram Bensheimer's portrait of the Madonna, in whose arms her son is the image of health.

The Emperor comes to stand behind his wife who, having been diagnosed with an enlarged heart caused by worry over the condition of her son, is temporarily confined to a wheelchair. Over the room hover the odor of grief and all types of medication. His son's internal bleeding is more serious this time. Months of civil unrest and a universal strike have left his country paralyzed. Ships dock idle along piers. Trains do not run. Factories, schools, and hospitals are closed. Food is scarce, and the streets are dark and empty at night. Crowds display antimonarchist sentiments. Red flags of the worker and peasant movement fly on rooftops. A new workers' organization with the preposterous title of "Soviet" or "Council" has materialized out of nowhere and is gathering clout. Peasants raid estates and set fire to mansions.

In order to bring a semblance of peace to the country, he has reluctantly accepted the suggestion of Sergius Witte and signed the imperial manifesto, transforming Russia from an absolute autocracy into a semiconstitutional monarchy, and granting his people the Duma, an elected parliament. Despite such concessions, the situation has not improved. What is a ruler to do? Everything he grew up believing is chipped away in small increments first, then in larger chunks until he does not know what to believe in.

Darya tucks a blanket around the Empress's legs, hands her a cup of hot tea. The Tyotia Dasha is screaming inside, pleading, demanding, furious at the Ancient One, who appears and disappears like an unwanted guest, yet is nowhere to be found now. *Ancient One, I need you! My Alexei is bleeding! Suffering! I can't help him. I've lost my powers!*

Then she sees her, outside the window, far away in the horizon. The Talmud rabbinic law in one hand and the Book of Ethics in the other, the Ancient One is wading through rivers of blood, leaving in her wake ripples of subliminal information about the nature of the bleeding disease. *A curse as old as man*, she whispers, *shrouded in mystery since ancient times. Pharaohs forbade women to bear more children if their firstborn was afflicted with the bleeding disease. The Talmud bars circumcision in a family if two male children had previously suffered fatal hemorrhaging.*

Show me a cure, Darya begs. *Tell me how to save him.* But the Ancient One is turning her back to her, leaving, shrinking, drowning in blood.

Dr. Eugene Botkin, the court physician, applies another compress to the swollen knee of the Tsarevich that is darker than burned eggplant. A gold watch chain swaying over his stout stomach, the doctor retreats into a far corner of the room and silently gestures to the Tsar, who gently unlocks the Empress's fingers from around his cane.

"The prognosis is dire, Your Majesty," the doctor says in a low voice. "The Tsarevich is hemorrhaging in the stomach as well as the knee. We tried to check the bleeding with medication, pressure, bandaging. Everything failed. It's time to call a priest."

The Tsar clutches the handle of his cane. "To administer the last sacrament?"

"I am afraid so," the doctor murmurs under his breath.

The Tsar seems to diminish, a lost expression creeping into his eyes. His right hand makes a twisting motion in the air as if puzzled at his fate. His voice shakes a little. "Publish a medical bulletin. Announce that the Tsarevich is critically ill. But under no circumstances mention hemophilia."

Darya kneels in front of the Tsarina, whose face has aged overnight, her lips blue with her effort to breathe. "May I speak, Your Majesty?"

"What is there to say, Darya? If you, too, want to tell me to rest while my son is dying, then, no, you may not speak."

"Your son *will* not die, Your Majesty, but you will if you don't eat. Constant fasting is taking its toll on your fragile health."

"What else is a mother to do?"

"Allow me to ask Father Grigori to come see the Tsarevich." Darya hates to admit that the vile man, with his cutting stare and disjointed way of speaking, who outbid her for *The Cure*, was right, after all. The Tsarevich needs him. Needs him badly. So she will swallow her pride and spit it out on her own face if Rasputin might be able to cure the Tsarevich.

"Nonsense!" Doctor Botkin interjects with an exaggerated gesture of his arm that raises the strong scent of his Parisian eau de cologne. "The best doctors in the country have examined the Tsarevich. An illiterate monk with no medical expertise is useless."

"Those so-called doctors," the Empress lashes out, "failed miserably."

"I beg of you, Your Majesty. Another unnecessary examination might dislodge the clot, add more suffering…hasten the inevitable."

The Empress grabs the handles of her wheelchair and raises herself to her feet, towering over the doctor, who seems to fade away in her presence. "This is my son you're talking about, doctor! Death is not an option. Am I clear?

"Darya Borisovna, summon Father Grigori!"

Chapter Twenty-One

ONE HUNDRED FIFTY GUARDS stand at attention as the imperial motorcade roars through the sweeping driveway and comes to a stop in front of the Alexander Palace.

Grigori Yefimovich Rasputin steps down from the first car in the motorcade. He stomps each boot on the stone path underfoot as if to rid himself of the dust of his long journey. Shading his eyes with one hand, he observes his surroundings, the velvet expanse of turquoise sky, the chatter of birds of paradise among rustling leaves, a rose petal floating on the breeze.

On the landing at the top of the stairs leading to the palace, Darya observes Rasputin march toward her, boots clicking underfoot. His stench of bitter almonds grows stronger with his advance, the same odor he emitted in the auction house fourteen months back.

Birds of paradise raise a racket, taking flight from the surrounding branches. The sun takes refuge behind a dark cloud. A shrill wind makes its way from the east, swallowing the pleasant breeze.

Darya waves a hand as if to banish his odor, banish any misfortune it might portend. She takes two involuntary steps up the stairs to get away from him, then quickly retraces her way back to welcome the little heir's last hope. It would not be wise to turn Rasputin away, even if she wishes to, even if his every approaching step feels like a blow. "Please, God," she prays under her breath, "let the monk, this self-proclaimed priest, heal my Tsarevich."

He ignores her extended hand, aims his bullet eyes at her, his odor nauseating, his smoke-infused beard too close, his brazen tongue flicking across wet lips. "A pleasure seeing you again. Strange! Very strange. A Jew in court."

"What do you mean?" she blurts out.

"You were born Christian. Yes. But I see a past. A Jew! You are of other times."

His stare ignites images that flash across the canvas of her life and strike her eye like lightning. She flinches. Her hand springs up to her eye. What are these images? Pomegranate stains everywhere. Menstrual blood? Israelites dragging her by the hair. She is afraid to enter a temple, or a church, perhaps. She is preparing for some kind of punishment. Why does she pray in Hebrew?

Rasputin lowers her hand from her opal eye. "Much mystery in your eye. Your Jewel."

She pulls her hand away. Suddenly she wants nothing more than to keep this man as far as possible from the heir, from the court, from herself. "Father Grigori, Her Majesty is not quite well and will not be seeing you after all. She will summon you back as soon as her health permits."

He reaches out, bunching her hair in his fist. His gaze wraps about her like a vise. "This is not true, is it! Think of Russia, of our people. Help me cure the heir."

Defiant, struggling to contain her rage, Darya reclaims her hair. Strands remain coiled around the grimy fingers he rubs under his nose. "Where is Bensheimer's painting? You promised to bring *The Cure* if I arranged an audience with the Empress."

"An art dealer bought it months ago. But why am I here? To save the baby or to discuss the silly painting?"

"So you broke your promise to me, Grigori Rasputin. But you better save the Tsarevich, or you'll never set foot here again!"

"Take me to him!"

He follows her into the grand foyer, handling an antique porcelain bowl on a side table, molesting the urns of malachite and jasper, his boots soiling the silk rugs, the ebony and rosewood parquet floors, the marble stairs as they ascend toward the Mauve Room. He lingers behind the door, fingers raking his matted beard. His gaze is boring into her opal eye, deep down to read her thoughts. She thinks he is polluting her. How wrong she is.

At the sight of Grigori Yefimovich Rasputin, relief softens the lines on the Empress's forehead, transforming her into the gracefully regal woman she once was. These days she is always in white, various shades and weaves of white—linen, damask, taffeta, satin, mohair, and silk cashmere—pure and innocent, gift-wrapped like a sacrificial lamb.

She is seated next to a lemonwood Becker piano, on her right an antique planter with a burst of lilacs next to a wood-framed glass screen. Shelves are crowded with photographs of relatives and friends, glass and porcelain ornaments, and jeweled Fabergé eggs.

The Tsarevich, bundled in a silk-lined coverlet crocheted by the Tsarina and three of her older daughters, is propped up on embroidered pillows on his mother's chaise lounge. He is small, pale, and listless.

The monk does not kiss the Tsarina's hand as required by royal etiquette but kneels in front of her, gazing into her eyes as if her son's future is reflected there. He rises, bends, and she allows him two consecutive kisses on her forehead.

"I received your summons in Siberia. I came right away."

"Thank you. It must be kept private."

"Always, Matushka. Always, Little Mother!"

Suddenly, he jumps up and shouts like a possessed creature, startling both women. "Out! Everyone! Out!"

The Empress gestures for Darya to leave the room.

He raises a calloused forefinger. "Not her, Matushka. You. Your son needs me, not you. You make him nervous. Make him bleed.

Go, have a cup of tea. Read a book to your daughters. They need you too."

The Empress gathers her skirts and crosses her boudoir, her heels clicking on the parquet. Hand on the door handle, she turns toward her son and takes a hard look at him. She crosses herself and steps out, shutting the door behind her.

Rasputin's stare swivels past Darya, who is standing next to the Tsarevich, holding his limp hand in hers, past the portrait of Our Lady of Tsarskoe Selo, and comes to rest on the portrait of the Tsarevich in the arms of the Madonna. Brows knit, he tugs at his beard. The shadow of his darkening face is a flat stain on his coat, stiff with sweat and dotted with oily stains. A series of low rumbles emanate from deep in his chest as if a string of inner quakes are shaking him. His right hand darts out, a long reach, as if the Lord Himself is about to tear the painting out of its ornate frame.

An expression of stifled fury on his face, he shouts, "White Thighs fucking Paulina!"

"What?" Darya interjects. "Who is White Thighs Paulina?"

"Paulina. You don't know her? Of course you don't. Neither would the Empress."

He leans forward to read the signature. He gasps. Straightens up. "Avram Bensheimer! He painted *The Cure*, didn't he? The portrait you wanted."

"Yes, Father Grigori. Bensheimer is the same artist. Why is this important?"

"This is no Madonna. Not at all! This is White Thighs Paulina. A fucking whore!"

Darya grabs her necklace, squeezes the jeweled egg. Pearls and diamonds dig into her palm.

The palace is quiet; not a sound comes from behind the shut door. She walks across the large room toward the window. The bright light hurts her eyes. The wind is gathering force, branches swaying like so many desperate arms.

What has Avram done? This is the end of him. Why did he do it? Now neither God nor His saints will keep Rasputin from revealing the truth to their Imperial Majesties.

Rasputin is at her side, his cutting stare aimed at her, as if to crush her with his powerful eyes. "You like this Bensheimer."

Her own gaze is steady, challenging. "Yes! I do. He is a brilliant artist."

He faces her, eye to eye, asserting his authority. He holds up a warning finger. "Yes, but his name makes you blush, makes you sweat." The anger on his face transforms into a conspiratorial grin. "We will be good to each other," he exclaims as if closing a deal. "I won't tell the Empress about Avram's appalling offense if you allow me entry into the mysteries of your opal eye."

Her spine stiffens, straight as the Tsar's cane. From now on she will fear this man, be vulnerable, exposed, a step below him.

She is unaware that a conspiracy is shaping in his mind. Unaware that his powerful stare will find a way to bore through her opal eye to steal a glance at much coveted secrets. Unaware that in six years she will eventually bow to this despised man's persistent manipulations and will reveal herself to him.

The Tsarevich opens his eyes and whimpers.

Rasputin pulls a chair close to the child, leans forward, flips back the coverlet, and lifts the small hand. His intense seerlike gaze examines Alexei's pale face.

"Precious son, listen to Father Grigori. Listen well. I will tell you a special story. A jewel you must treasure and keep to yourself.

"Once on a white planet of snow lived a little boy named Alexei. But no. No! That was not the name the Lord intended for him. Alexei? Never. This boy was meant to choose his own name and his own destiny. He did not want to be crowned Emperor. He did not want to be a prisoner of that snow planet. What he really wanted was to be crowned archangel of all the firmaments.

"One dawn, eighteen silver-lashed, filigree-winged angels fluttered their lacy feathers, swooping down to congregate around the little boy's palace of ice. Their honeyed voices rose to the seventh heaven heralding the good Lord. They prayed for the sun to shine upon the palace for forty days and forty nights and to melt the cocoon of ice. They pleaded with the Lord to have mercy on the little boy and thaw his bones that had become as brittle as his icy home. They flew around the palace, chanting hymns, praising the Lord and all His saints, their gossamer wings sheltering the boy from the ravages of hail, snow, and frost. On the dawn of the eighteenth day, the boy's blood began to warm up, his joints became supple, and his once dry eyes sparkled with the joy of experiencing warmth for the first time in his life. He smiled, laughed aloud, ran outside to thank the kind angels. But perched on a chariot of clouds, they were on their way to fulfill another promise.

"Overjoyed at the sight of young shoots, colorful blooms, and emerald leaves that had replaced the barren land and the carpet of frigid snow, the boy knelt to inhale the sweet perfume of possibilities. He raised both hands to heaven and shouted, 'My name is Life!'

"And this is who you are, Alexei Nikolaevich Romanov. You are life."

A hint of color appears on the heir's cheeks and soft breathing replaces his anemic moans. The lilacs in the antique planter vibrate, their fragrance inebriating. The scent of rosemary and mint floats through the windows. And for the first time since her parents' death, warm currents flow through Darya, thawing her own bones.

Rasputin rises to his feet, bends over the Tsarevich, his long coat concealing the child from her sight. An instant of silence passes, then another, and the monk's body begins to shake, weak spasms that grow stronger. His fingernails dig into his palms, drawing blood. His breath is loud and gurgling with phlegm. His long hair drips with sweat and another sound is rising from his throat, as if something is blocking his windpipe.

Darya lets out a cry of alarm. She puts her arms around Rasputin's sweat-drenched coat, pulling him with all her might, struggling to drag him away from the child. She helps him to a chair, knocking a vase over in the process. He slumps in the chair, eyes rolled back into his head, shaken by a series of powerful shudders. She picks up a pitcher of water from the nightstand and upends the contents on his head. A groan, a sharp intake of breath, and he staggers to his feet, disoriented, but only momentarily. Fishing out a soiled kerchief from his sleeve, he wipes his sweat-drenched face.

Darya steps back, rubs her eyes with her knuckles. She wants to grab the Tsarevich from the chaise lounge and flee somewhere away from this madman and his strange ways. Except that the child is no longer pale, no longer in pain.

Without any warning, and as though nothing out of the ordinary has just occurred, Rasputin bunches and lifts her skirt in one hand, grabbing her between the legs with his other hand, holding tight.

Disgusted and cursing under her breath, she slaps him away.

He waves his fingers under his nose. "A great, great pity," he declares in a fury of righteousness. "You are not a virgin!"

Chapter Twenty-Two

STROLLING WITH AVRAM IN back of the park, Darya stumbles across a sweet-smelling plant. She absentmind-edly examines it in the gray light of dawn and crushes the leaves in her fist.

A thin moon drifts behind a metallic cloud. Dew-mottled leaves sway in the breeze. The palace is quiet. Two months have passed since Rasputin healed the Tsarevich, and the Imperial Family is vacationing on the imperial yacht, *Standart*, while Darya has remained here. The change of the Cossacks of the guard is taking place, but Darya, with her healing herbs and miraculous potions, has ingratiated herself with them, so they know to turn a blind eye to the lovers as they stroll behind ancient trees and trellises.

She grabs Avram's arm, digs her nails in. She is furious. With the Tsarevich recuperating from his last bout of bleeding and the Empress needing constant attention, she could not meet Avram for two months and her pent-up anger spills out in her voice. "Why did you do it, Avram? Why did you choose a whore to model as the Madonna?"

He is surprised. Nothing can be concealed from this woman. Not even the identity of a prostitute who no one would recognize in this aristocratic part of town. "I chose her because she had the right face and the beautiful serenity of the Madonna. And I didn't think the Empress would recognize her."

"Rasputin did. And he knows you are the painter. He'll use it against you if he needs to."

"I put you in a difficult position again, haven't I?"

"Yes, you have, but I asked you to find a way for the Tsarina to forgive you and you did." She has no right to her anger when such difficulties must be expected in a relationship like theirs. Every star in the firmament has to be aligned for their love to flourish, two people from vastly different cultures and backgrounds, whose every encounter is a miracle. In the last year, their love has evolved and matured, layered like an iridescent pearl, and she will not allow this incident to tarnish it.

The birds of paradise are wild around them, their trilling cascading down the trees as they peck at bread crumbs Darya sprinkles behind. This is the time and landscape she likes most, when her dreams are left behind and dawn promises fresh possibilities. She searches around for the red-feathered bird of paradise, and as if in reply to her silent summons, there it is, strutting on one of the lower branches, her throat swelling with birdsong. Darya laughs out loud, but Avram is not amused. He has stopped to read the elaborate inscriptions on the tombstones at his feet:

Here lies Zemir, and the saddened Graces should throw flowers on her grave. Like Tom, her ancestor, like Lady, her mother, she was constant in her affections, swift of foot...The Gods, witnesses of her tenderness, ought to have rewarded her for her fidelity with immortality, so that she might for ever remain near her mistress.

"It's a mausoleum for dogs," Darya says. "Catherine the Great built it."

"Shame on the Romanovs! They care for their dogs more than their people."

"What a terrible thing to say, Avram!"

He directs his unforgiving gaze at her. "Listen, my Opal-Eyed Queen, you are not the only one who is cold. Everyone is these days, especially the Jews. Fight for us, Darya. You have the Tsarina's ear. Do something!"

"I don't know what to tell her. She thinks every revolutionary is a Jew."

"And here you are. With a Jew. What are we to do, Darya? Why do you tolerate the Romanovs? Can't you tell they are propelling Russia toward disaster?"

"Enough, Avram! Don't talk this way. Our political system is still the best in the world."

"Autocracy? Nonsense! It didn't work at the time of Peter the Great. And it's not working today. See what a relatively tame march to St. Petersburg turned into. Bloody Sunday! Our country will never be the same. Everyone is bitter."

"The Tsar was beside himself, Avram. It was a sad day for all of us. The order to fire on innocent civilians came from the anxious troops, not from the Tsar." She rises on her toes and tilts her face up to Avram. "No more politics, not today." And then, knowing full well that the truth is otherwise, she adds, "Our relationship has nothing to do with the Romanovs."

She sidesteps the graves, Avram guiding her by the arm. "Avram, do you detect an odor of decaying flesh around here?"

He brings his face close to the tombstone and pretends to sniff like a dog. He digs his hands into her hair, smiles at her with a lopsided smile. "Yes, I do. I smell the stench of corruption. I smell Rasputin. I smell treason. Durnovo, Gerasomov…" He traces the inscription on the tombs. "Leave them, Darya, come with me. Leave while your innocence is intact."

She wraps her hand around his wrist to count the bounce of his pulse. Rubs her cheek to the coarse weave of his coat. She loves this man, desiring him in her every cell, yet she hears herself hurt him in ways she does not intend. "My fate is sealed here, Avram.

I've been assigned a responsibility I don't quite understand. It's as if the survival of the monarchy depends on me."

Avram raises her chin with one finger. "Survival. Fate. Sealed. You're too young to think like this."

She does not know why these thoughts creep into her head, why her olfactory senses detect scents unnoticed by others, why fires that warm others send a chill up her spine. Grigori Rasputin has insinuated that he possesses the hypnotic ability to thrust her into a trance that will answer all these questions. But the notion of relinquishing control, even temporarily, to Rasputin's pale-eyed powers is not acceptable to her. Still, not only has he become a welcome guest in court but an essential member of the Imperial Family. Darya, too, encourages his visits to the palace, sends him a gift when he heals Alexei, compliments him on his ability to calm the boy, all for the sake of the Tsarevich.

She leans against Avram. She is sad today, and she doesn't know why. "Did you know that my name means sea?"

"I know. It's beautiful. The origin is Persian."

"But it's cold water and salt and freezing all the time, and maybe that's why I'm always cold. So I don't want that name anymore. Call me anything you want, any name that will warm me up."

"Opal-Eyed Jewess," Avram whispers to the birds of paradise that came here from New Guinea a century ago. "Darya," he calls out to the swans sailing across the lake. "My Opal-Eyed Queen," he murmurs to the rose garden behind them. "I love all your names. I didn't know you don't like Darya."

"I'm tired of being cold near fires. Tired of being different."

"But different makes you who you are. And I love different." He suddenly gestures to his left, motions to her to be quiet.

A shadow is ducking behind one bush then another, chuckling under his breath like a depraved, cloven-footed jester, an obsessed man unable to sleep, unable to eat, his head full of Darya. He is shaking, aroused, expecting his own moments of relief.

"Stay where you are," Avram whispers. "I'll be back."

Darya grabs his hand. "Don't go alone."

But he is walking ahead, fast, catlike, fearless. He ducks behind one topiary, then another, silent, edging ahead. He is sure-footed, good at eluding detection, good at concealing himself even if there's nothing to conceal. He lives in a part of town that requires this skill, this ability to slip away, fade unnoticed, escape Jew haters. Darya catches up with him. She is certain Rasputin is following them to punish Avram.

The two circle the topiary, slowly, quietly. Avram's heart is banging against his ribs.

Count Trebla is squatting behind the topiary. His sweat-drenched features are contorted as if in pain. He is pleasuring himself.

He jumps to his feet. Pulls up his pants. Wipes his soiled hand on his coat.

Avram grabs him by the collar, glares at him with the force of contained rage, ready to shake the fear of God into the man's thick skull.

Darya touches Avram on his arm, restrains him with a small tug at his sleeve.

He releases Count Trebla, shoves him away. "Go back to the kennels where you belong. Go!"

"Who are you to order me?" Count Trebla barks, assaulting Avram with a gust of sour breath. "I know what you're doing here. I will tell."

Darya steps forward, aims two fingers between his eyes like a pistol. It had scared him before, perhaps it will again. "Down!" She says as if ordering the Doberman who bit her that day. "Now!"

This man who titters on the brink of madness, who no longer cares for his dogs, forgets to feed them, slaps their licking tongues away; this man who has lost interest in his wife and the ledger he filled every night with frantic observations, falls to his knees at Darya's feet. He is mumbling under his breath, promising to be good, to serve her, to follow her every command.

"Go now," she says. "Go, take care of your dogs."

He clambers to his feet. Shakes himself like a wet puppy, bows to her, thanks her profusely, vows to remain her obedient slave.

He scrambles away, content, chuckling under his breath.

"I'm impressed," Avram tells Darya. "You, my queen, can talk yourself out of any predicament. Pity you are on the Romanov side."

"On your side too, Avram. We better leave now. This man is dangerous."

"And mad."

"Perhaps, but that doesn't make him less dangerous."

The city outside the gates is stirring; the sun is rising, gathering force. The scent of jasmine is in the air.

Avram kisses his forefinger and touches it to her eye. "Whatever happens, my queen, do not forget this Jew."

She turns away from him and walks past the parterres in golden boxes, across the Marble Bridge, and back toward the palace. She does not turn around to wave farewell. She does not want him to see her tears, her pain and conflict.

She does not want him to know, not yet, that she is pregnant with his child.

Chapter Twenty-Three

THE IMPERIAL COSSACKS OF the guard escort a veiled woman into the Alexander Park. Her dark hair, braided with ropes of fake pearls, quivers about her shoulders as she sashays ahead with the dexterity of a fawn, her bare thighs flashing in and out of lavender veils, her theatrical overtures casting a spell upon the men patrolling the park. Trailed by the clatter of hooves, she ascends the steps toward two Nubian guards who flank the entrance to the palace. They fling the doors open, and Jasmine the Persian Dancer is ushered in.

Servers in ceremonial livery, white tie and gloves, breeches, long socks, and nonslip-soled shoes race back and forth through the palace corridors. The aroma of spices—dill, parsley, bay leaf—rises from serving dishes of chicken and wild goat. The staff nod their greeting to Jasmine as she slips into the hall, wends her way between the malachite columns and toward the formal dining room.

Candelabras with masses of fragrant flowers crown the tables. Tsarskoe Selo crystal with the enameled Romanov coat of arms and gold menu holders, normally reserved for formal gala events, have been brought out. German salads, caviar, oysters, and aromatic mushrooms are set in silver and porcelain. Baccarat decanters brim with vodkas, permeating the air with the scents of mint, pear, and sour orange.

A luncheon is being held in honor of Grigori Rasputin.

Waiters serve the guests silently and discreetly. The privileged few, chosen to wait on the Tsar, are tall, strong, and handsome. They follow the Emperor from one Imperial Palace to another, grow old with him, their ears open to intimate gossip, handsomely rewarded by one minister or another.

Dressed in a simple army tunic with the ever-present epaulets his father conferred upon him, the Tsar does not move from table to table to partake of different courses along the way, converse with his guests, and honor them with his presence, as is customary. The protocol of serving *zakuski* in the adjoining hall has been dismissed too. The Emperor remains seated at the table of his honored guest, Rasputin. The Empress and grand duchesses are on his right. On his left, in a Georgian style mahogany highchair with claw feet, sits the eighteen-month-old Tsarevich, his face smeared with chocolate and raspberry sauce.

Grigori Rasputin reaches out to pinch the child's cheek, blows a kiss across the table toward Grand Duchess Tatiana and winks at Anastasia, who is telling a joke to Maria. He dips his fingers into the caviar dish, pinches the plump eggs between thumb and forefinger, and hand-feeds the Tsarevich, who spits it out. Digging into the creamy soup, he plucks out a meat pie and drops it into his mouth. Olga raises a surprised eyebrow. Maria and Tatiana exchange glances. The Empress averts her gaze.

Darya is at another table with Grand Duke Michael Alexandrovich, the Tsar's younger brother. He clicks his goblet against Darya's and drinks to her health.

She nods. Drinks a sip of wine.

The grand duke attempts to engage her in conversation, tell her about the few exciting days he has passed in the company of his brother, tell her all about dinner with the horse guardsmen and their military review the next day, about breakfast with the officers and their wives and the dinner later with the retired officers in the officers' club, where both he and his brother drank to their heart's desire. And he tells her that he was in attendance when the Semyonovsky Regiment returned from Moscow to inform his brother that the mutiny was successfully squelched. But a lot of sad things are occurring around the country—strikes everywhere, taxes not paid, bank withdrawals not honored. Peasants are seizing land, landlords are being killed, garrisons are mutinying, trains are being overturned by striking workers. In order to avoid a massacre, the Tsar agreed to sign the October Manifesto, granting basic civil rights to his people and allowing the establishment of political parties. "But," the grand duke tells Darya, "my brother felt sick with shame at this betrayal of the dynasty."

Darya is not listening. She is watching Rasputin. He has been assigned her usual seat next to Alexei, and she has been banished to another table. The temperature of her opal eye is rising, spreading onto her cheeks.

Grand Duke Michael is telling her something about Alexandra Kossikovskaya, his sister's lady-in-waiting. Darya attempts to collect her emotions. She nods her understanding. If it would not have been such an effort, she would have told him how deeply she feels for him. He is in love with Alexandra Kossikovskaya, a commoner, and has asked the Tsar and the dowager mother, Maria, to allow him to marry his love. But his mother and brother will not hear of it. They have threatened to remove him from the line of succession if he marries other than royalty.

He rests his hand on her arm. "Are you well, Darya Borisovna. You are very pale."

No! She is not well. She fears she might faint. Reaching out for the salt holder, she drops a few pinches of salt under her tongue to revive herself. "Thank you, I feel fine," she assures the grand duke.

She does not want to go to the infirmary, does not want Dr. Botkin to discover what transpired last night in her bedroom after an especially harrowing nightmare, where she was setting fire to everything and everyone she loved, to the palace, to the Tsar and

Tsarina, to the Tsarevich, burning everything dear to her, leaving unimaginable devastation in her trail.

She was startled awake by a vibrating metallic clank behind her eardrums. Her hand jumped up to her Fabergé egg necklace. It was wide open. She raised it to her nose to smell its sweet scent, but there was nothing to smell. The ambergris was gone. She searched everywhere, under her pillows, bedcovers, mattress, even the bed and carpet, but failed to find the ambergris. It was then that the Ancient One appeared on the windowsill, quivering as if uncertain whether to enter or leave the room. The flowing trail of her gown swayed and teased below the windowpanes. "Give my ambergris back," Darya commanded, certain the Ancient One had it.

A soft sigh, a breath of disappointment emanated from the specter before she flapped her wide-sleeved arms and drifted away, fading into the silvery dawn.

As she wondered how on earth the Ancient One had managed to unlock the clasp and why she would snatch away the ambergris, Darya remembered she was pregnant and softly, affectionately rubbed her rounded belly.

Thoughts of Avram prevented her from going back to sleep. When, she wondered, was the right time to reveal her pregnancy to him? He would want to marry her, take her away, care for her. Yet that was not what she wanted. But she was starting to show. How would the Imperial Court react? Some measure of leniency might be extended to Tyotia Dasha who, like many ladies-in-waiting throughout history, is of royal descent. Yet unlike those women, Darya pondered, the father of her child is not a king, a prince, or a grand duke, whose bastard might, in time, be accepted by the Imperial Court and perhaps even granted the father's surname. Neither the Imperial Couple nor any court of law would extend any leniency to her Avram, a commoner and a despised Jew. At that moment, without warning, and as if rebelling against her thoughts, her womb began to complain, squeeze, and twist to painlessly expel the embryo she successfully carried for four months and ten days.

And just like that, her child slipped out of her at dawn.

It was as if the little space in her womb was reserved for the Tsarevich, and Avram's child was an intruder. Only then did she understand why the Ancient One robbed her of her ambergris. She was being punished for desiring a child other than Alexei. Now, weak and bleeding, she wonders if she will ever have her own child.

She reaches out for her wine.

The grand duke hands her the goblet. He adjusts the medal of the Cross of St. George he wears with utmost pride, the highest military honor awarded for his command of the Caucasian Native Cavalry. He asks her a series of unnecessary questions to break the silence.

Her voice hardly audible she replies. Yes, she did attend Diaghilev's ballet. No, nothing has been purchased in auction lately. The salon is not held monthly, but every three months. Yes, she did go to see the *Three Sisters* in the Michailovsky Theater, but she did not care for the amateur company from Moscow. She did not attend the charity performance organized by Sonia Orbeliani at the Stanislavsky Art Theater, but she is planning to visit the exhibition of costumes in the Taurida Palace.

The Emperor's personal server, an old man with failing eyesight whom the Tsar inherited from his father, attempts to pour more wine for the head table. The Tsar supports his servant's trembling arm so no mishaps will occur. The honor of waiting on Rasputin is bestowed upon this most senior of servers, and he resents the task, resents the monk's crudeness, and resents him more than anything for positioning himself in the limelight and robbing the Tsar of his rightful place. The server ignores Rasputin and showers attention on the four grand duchesses, but especially Olga and Tatiana, whom he finds exceptionally gracious.

Jasmine the Persian Dancer bunches her veils and ascends the three steps up a platform, where a santour has been set. She curtsies, her thighs peeping out of transparent layers. She aims her stare at the Tsar and Tsarina, purrs in her smoky voice that blooms into a caress. "I dedicate my composition, 'Visions and Intimacy,' to our lovely couple."

Tsar Nicholas suppresses a smile. Few of his people are so ignorant of court protocol to address him with such informality as this Persian dancer who immigrated to Russia from Azerbaijan. She has not aged a bit since the days he was a carefree Tsarevich, sharing a simple meal in a remote restaurant, where the hours had breezed away in her company as she explained that the seventy-two-stringed santour is the grandfather of the piano, but with a far more tender soul.

The notes of her dulcimer take wing about the salon, enveloping and caressing every guest and momentarily erasing their daily cares. Before the echo of her melody dies and the guests have time to return to the reality of their present, she unleashes her hair and steps down the platform. Music in her fingertips, veils licking her feet, hair swaying about her hips, she whirls around like a dervish, whipping her hips into frenzy and transporting her audience away from their jaded universe and the formal setting of the palace.

The Tsar observes her with a mixture of nostalgia and fondness.

His betrothal to Alix of Hesse, the girl reared in Darmstadt and in England, devastated Jasmine, who once harbored the foolish hope of becoming his wife.

It was a sad day. His forty-nine-year-old father, Tsar Alexander III, was dying. Only then did he give his blessing to the union with Alix.

Alix was hastily consecrated to Orthodoxy. She became the truly believing Grand Duchess Alexandra Feodorovna. And he, a twenty-six-year-old Tsarevich who knew little about the business of ruling and was ill-equipped to shoulder the inherited responsibilities, became an Emperor.

A week later, his courtiers directed the Persian dancer into the palace. Strict orders were given to be discreet and under no circumstances to discuss the event. It was, by all standards of the court, a simple and private affair with a few close friends in attendance to welcome his bride to court. Jasmine's lovely music mourned the end of a great ruler, and her dance had cheered the ascension of the young Tsar. For a few fleeting hours, she succeeded in transporting him to a safe haven, even if temporarily, while his father's body was displayed in the capital and millions of mourning citizens shuffled by as high priests chanted the requiem.

Now, the Tsar observes Jasmine sway and twirl in her diaphanous veils, her breasts spilling out of her tight corset. She performed miracles that night, succeeding in lifting the spirit of his beautiful wife, the woman who came to Russia behind a coffin. This, he has been told, is how his people refer to Sunny.

The Tsar strokes his beard, pleased that his wife had agreed to lift her ban on the dancer. Did the unfortunate event happen last year, two years ago, perhaps? Time for his wife to forgive the dancer for having transgressed, as she had, that night in the Belovezh Forest. He rests a hand in the Tsarina's lap. She smiles and her complexion blooms to reflect the passionate woman she can be in private.

Energetic, gregarious, and boisterous, Jasmine slips out of her colorful veils to reveal the muscular legs of a horsewoman, folds her arms behind like broken wings, attempting to reach the snaps of her corset.

Darya holds her breath. Not again! The dancer would not dare end her presentation as she had that night at the Belovezh Estate, unhooking her corset and swinging it overhead as if to lasso her breasts. The night of her seventeenth birthday will forever haunt Darya, the night Sabrina and Boris marched straight into the jaws of aurochs, changing the course of her life.

Here she is now, her womb twisting and weeping, unable to adjust to its loss, her heart a reprimanding fist in her chest. She has no right, none at all, to keep their loss a secret from Avram. But she will. She will be kind, spare him this grief. Nothing will bring back their child now. The pain is all hers to bear.

Jasmine, having left her corset in place, curtsies to the cries of "Bravo" that reverberate around the salon. She takes her time to glance around at familiar faces: grand dukes, ministers, and princes with whom she has been intimate. Tugging and twisting at a strand of her dark, curly hair, she sends out a collective wink, enjoying the inevitable attention her every move stirs. Her eyes rest on the Tsar's sensitive hands, and the desire she folded into a tiny bud and tucked in a safe corner of her chest bursts into sudden bloom.

She sails toward the Imperial Couple, throwing herself at the Empress's feet. "My Tsarina, did my performance please you?"

The Empress is bouncing a silver kopek in her hand as if deciding whether to hand it to the dancer or to drop it back in her pocket. Her throat is very white, her eyes cold, calculating, a grim twist to her lips. She gazes at the worthless kopek for a long time, flips it around. Stares at the image of her husband on the coin as if to stamp him deeper into her heart. The air around them is damp. A buzz, a drone of surprise rises from the guest. All eyes are on the Empress. She gazes back at her guests, a decree to mind their own affairs. She reaches out a white-sleeved arm and tosses the coin at the dancer's feet. Her voice is colder than her eyes. "Amusing as always, dear. Do take your seat with the other entertainers."

A course of Dviena starlet, fish in champagne sauce, is brought in. Rasputin dislodges a bone from the soft flesh and deposits it on top of the woven imperial monogram on the starched linen. He wipes his beard clean and tosses the napkin on his plate. He rises to his feet. Lifts his goblet of Madeira. "Your Imperial Majesties. Ladies and gentlemen. I propose a toast."

The Tsarina clutches the arms of her chair to lift herself to her feet. The Emperor taps on her hand, and she settles back into her chair. Guests shuffle in their seats, baffled by the break of protocol. When has Rasputin become so influential that the important role of proposing a toast has been assigned to him instead of the Tsar?

Rasputin swivels the Madeira in the goblet, passes the rim under his nose, takes a sip. He cups his goblet in both hands, turns to his right, and extends it toward Darya. His voice echoes in the hall. "Let us drink to the sorceress."

Darya's womb contracts, releasing a trickle of warm blood between her legs. She registers the palpable sense of surprise, the disapproval of the Imperial Couple, the joy of Maria and Anastasia at the unfolding drama, and the concerned touch on her arm of Grand Duke Michael Alexandrovich. They are unaware that she has been thwarting Rasputin's insistent prodding to uncover the secret of her opal eye, wanting to understand the source of her healing abilities, wanting to know why she smells scents others don't.

"And to tight bonds," Rasputin continues.

"To your death," Darya mumbles under her breath.

"Tonight," he shouts, "let us drink to life."

Darya collects herself and slowly rises. She lifts her wine goblet. "I am not deserving of your kind toast, Father Grigori. It is our Tsarevich you should honor."

The room is silent. The Emperor looks at Darya. He lets the difficult moment pass. "Well said, Darya Borisovna. The toast is *yours!*"

Her heart pounding in her throat, she cuddles her goblet. "To the heir apparent and Tsarevich, Grand Duke Alexei Nikolaevich Romanov, our future Emperor, health and long life."

The crowd is on its feet and cheers of "Health and long life!" echo in the hall.

The Emperor offers his arm to the Empress, leading her to the adjoining hall, where tables are set with compotes, iced cherries, jellies, ice creams, chocolates, and sponge cakes from the imperial confectionery. Assorted liqueurs are served, and the Tsar partakes of his favorite 1875 brandy from Montleau and Hesse.

Rasputin is never far from the Tsarevich, one fist resting on his own chest as if holding the child's heart there. The Empress is content. The monk is present. All is well.

The Emperor indicates the end of the luncheon with a nod. It is customary for him to take his leave before his guests, but as previously arranged, the Tsar remains seated as the guests, flush with sugar and alcohol, are led out.

The servants transport the remaining food to the kitchen, where a crowd, among them the highest aristocracy, has gathered to purchase it. The money will go to the kitchen staff.

The waiters are dismissed. The clink of dishes ceases. The grand duchesses congregate around Rasputin, their magician of joy, the only one able to carve a smile on their mother's face, the man whose fairy tales paint their lives with delight and excitement.

The Tsarevich climbs into Darya's lap, and she wraps her possessive arms around him as if he might lessen the pain of her recent loss.

"Tell us a story," Tatiana begs Rasputin. "A story about yourself."

"Yes, Father Grigori," Darya echoes. "Tell us who you are."

"Me? Ah! Not much to say. Except…" He glares at her. Taps on his heart. "Heavy with untold secrets."

Having made his point, having reminded Darya of the power he continues to hold over her, he addresses the Imperial Family: "This story is about someone more interesting than me. So come closer. Listen. In a faraway kingdom, in a certain land and a certain time lived a queen."

Darya is ambushed by a momentary glimpse of an ancient time, another life in which *she* is queen. She is decked in opal ornaments as she wends her way between palm trees toward a place of prayer. She strains to hold on to the images, stop them from escaping. But they slip away, disappearing into the mist of her mind. She glances up to find herself held hostage by Rasputin's eyes, and she is assailed by a longing to spill out her innermost secrets to this man who reeks of vodka and donkey shit.

He frightens her, this man who seems to hold her future in his hands. Does he also know about her pregnancy, her miscarriage? He winks at her, breaking the spell.

"This queen lived in a land where flower pods froze in their kernels and lungs, unable to bear the cold, popped and collapsed like fat soap bubbles. But this queen was different from everyone. Her blood was hot. Blood boiled in her veins. When the weather plunged far below freezing, our queen did not suffer from the cold, the burning of ice to the touch, the awful ache in the lungs. And this is why she was the only one in that land who could achieve anything she put her heart to, any dream, any wish. Nothing was out of her reach!

"One day, her glorious skin the hue of diamonds, her fingers and toes radiating warmth, she went out naked and stood on the tallest mountain of ice to call out to the Lord.

"And the Lord, witnessing a woman of such valor, a woman who dared raise her voice in confrontation, stepped down from His throne to hear her plea.

"She turned her eyes to heaven and shouted: 'I accepted this terrible land as mine. I have lived here for many years and managed to maintain my youth and beauty. Because of that, I lured millions to Your land. You owe me a grand favor, my Lord, You do.'

"The Lord removed his top hat and bowed slightly from the waist, his baritone bouncing about the firmaments. 'Name your wish, my lady!'

"'To bear a son, my Lord. But not any son. Not like other people who freeze in your ruthless world. That I do not want. I want a beautiful boy with golden hair and lucid eyes. And I want him to carry my blood.'

"The Lord shifted on His throne, threw one long leg over the other, and dropped His top hat on the crown of His balding head. 'Are you certain, my lady? Is this truly your wish? Think long and hard before you reply. Know that once your wish is granted, it may not be changed.'

"'Yes, my Lord, I want this more than anything in the world,' the hot-blooded queen replied.

"And the deal was closed in heaven."

"Did the Lord give her a son with hot blood?" Grand Duchess Tatiana asks.

"A fair, blue-eyed boy who rode honey-gold ponies in the

snow and teased ice cubes from dark caves. Hot-blooded like his mother."

Darya squeezes the Tsarevich against her breasts, unable to clear her mind of emerging images—hot-blooded woman, perhaps a queen, a son or a prince—images that instantly evaporate like steam. What remains present and real is the blood of her loss trickling between her thighs. Did she lose a son, she wonders, or a daughter with eyes like her own?

Rasputin lifts a forefinger. "But this boy was different. Whereas his mother's blood was of equal temperature all over her body, her son's simmered and bubbled under his kneecaps, elbows, joints, causing excruciating pain that made him cry."

Darya glances at the Imperial Couple. The bags under the Tsar's eyes have turned a bluish hue, and his brow is knit in disapproval. The Tsarina rests her hand on his arm. He pats her hand absentmindedly.

"Poor boy," Grand Duchess Maria exclaims. "What happened to him?"

"All the Siberian ices and all the prayers of the land failed to cure the queen's son until a man of God came from a nearby town. He carried a pouch filled with gems as pure and smooth as ivory and as scented as myrrh. Not ordinary gems. Not at all. A blessing was tucked in the heart of each gem, which he tossed into a vast pool of ice water. The blessings multiplied and multiplied, expanding into colorful, translucent orbs of all sizes that kept on swelling and emptying the pool of all water until the pool became a giant container of sparkling spheres of blessings in which the boy was instructed to bathe. And from that instant on, day by day, his blood temperature began to adjust until it normalized as befits a proper prince."

"Bravo!" the Empress claps. "I love happy endings."

Chapter Twenty-Four

— 1907 —

WHITE NIGHT BATHES PEACH palaces, turquoise cupolas, green steeples, gilded churches, and elaborate colonnades in dreamy pastel lights. Boulevards, avenues, streets, and alleys have been swept and watered and decorated with imperial eagles and with the city's coat of arms. Hundreds of flags flutter in a mild breeze that has chased away the winter gloom, ruffling the surface of the city's canals and raising the faint scent of sweat and anticipation. The calm waters of the Neva mirror the festivities above. It is the month of July and the Tsarevich Alexei Nikolaevich Romanov's third birthday. Darkness will not fall on St. Petersburg, the city of his birth.

Theater Square throbs with excitement. Cheering spectators crowd the flower-strewn platforms, balconies, windows, rooftops, and sidewalks leading to the illuminated Mariinsky Theater. The stone façade arches and columns of the theater are lit from behind. Its windows are dressed in blue velvet drapes and frame glittering chandeliers.

The Imperial Family and its entourage are expected at any moment.

It is the opening night of *The Red Aurochs*, Igor Vasiliev's ballet.

In two short years, the imperial salon has refined the artistic taste of Russians and increased their knowledge, the people say. The belief is no longer rampant that the only art the family promotes is ballet, simply because a large number of the dancers happen to be mistresses of one or another grand duke. The Tsar has demanded that the ballet season open a month early in order to celebrate his son's birthday. It is rumored that the artists themselves will attend the ballet.

Such a talented group, these artists! Isn't she a wonder, that Rosa Koristanova, her sculpture in the Russian Museum a miracle to behold? What about Avram Bensheimer's nude portraits? Magical! Enchanting! So imaginative! Might the model be the Tyotia Dasha? No! The Imperial Couple would not allow it. Yet the resemblance is uncanny, wouldn't you say? And Igor Vasiliev's *The Red Aurochs*, strange to choose the word *red* in the title, not wise at all in these times. Surely he meant no harm.

An artillery salute of thirty-one guns from the Peter and Paul Fortress echoes around the city.

The imperial carriage passes through the crowded streets.

People cross themselves reverently. They greet the imperial arrival with the pealing of bells and thundering applause. A platoon of decorated officers stands at attention by the entrance to the Mariinsky Theater, which the Imperial Couple support with an annual subsidy of two million gold rubles.

The imperial carriage, all crystal, gilt carvings, and gold-wheeled, is ushered in by eight magnificent white horses led by grooms in blue velvet uniforms and white plumed helmets. The approaching horses, strong, muscular, and proud, paw the cobblestones with synchronized clicks as if digging for some hidden treasure to offer the cheering crowds.

Grand Duke Michael Alexandrovich is at the head of the procession, escorted by Life Guard Cossacks and an officer of the Life Guard Cuirassier Regiment, followed by pages of His Majesty. The applause intensifies. Second in line to the throne, the handsome grand duke is the Emperor's right hand, always present, always supportive. He is dear to the people, who follow his romantic escapades with much interest, cheering him on as vigorously as his family attempts to deter him from his inappropriate amorous liaisons.

The Tsar and Tsarina are dressed in full regalia. The Tsarina's hair is pulled back in an elaborate chignon; her suite of pearls and emeralds glitter on her earlobes and lace collar. The Tsar has donned his favorite uniform, a dark navy, double-breasted, gold-buttoned coat, the collar trimmed with gold stitching, and medals of honor prominently displayed.

The sky comes to life, crackling with its own praises. Northern lights perform a symphony of colors, burnt umber and pale green, which cast an added sheen on the city.

The Imperial Couple wave, smile, reach out for each other's free hands on the blue velvet seat. Their son is in good health. The salon has achieved its purpose. The arts are flourishing. The peasant population has been rendered powerless. The alliance between the peasants and the working class is frayed. Isolated uprisings have been quashed by the loyal army. According to his advisors, the many revolutionary factions—the Bolsheviks, Mensheviks, the Party of Socialist Revolutionaries, and the violent Maximalists that sprouted like wild weeds all over the country—are in disarray.

The Tsar gazes into the sepia evening. His lips curl into a contented smile. He is looking forward to a few hours of music and ballet. "Nice evening," he tells his wife.

"Lovely," she replies, squeezing his hand.

Darya is in the second carriage, holding the Tsarevich in her lap. She is wearing a taffeta gown of deep scarlet, scattered with diamond stars, her hair cascading down her shoulders. A hairpin of pink diamonds from her grandparents' Corinin mines harness a curl behind her right ear. She presses her cheek against Alexei's, whispers in his ear to remember this, his third birthday, when all the inhabitants of the city have spilled out into the streets to wish him well. She, too, will remember this night, her attending her first ballet with Avram, who has become far dearer to her than she imagined possible. He is in the Mariinsky auditorium now, having arrived earlier with the other artists, ministers, generals, and royal guests.

Olga, Tatiana, Maria, and Anastasia are in the third carriage, waving enthusiastically at the crowds that shower their path with snowfalls of rose petals.

Cries of "OTMA! OTMA!" (the first initials of the grand duchesses' names) rise and swell into a single unified roar of adoration. As certainly as Tsarevich Alexei Nikolaevich is the future of Russia, the grand duchesses are her heart and soul.

The Imperial Family, Darya, and Grand Duke Michael Alexandrovich are led through a separate entrance and up private stairs to the Tsar's apartment-sized box to the left of the stage. Two cherubs are perched on gilded arches above the imperial box as if to protect the precious Imperial Family in an auditorium already crowded with uniformed and plainclothes security guards.

The Emperor and his brother take their seats on both sides of the Empress. Darya settles Anastasia and the Tsarevich on her right, Olga, Tatiana, and Maria on her left. "Are you all comfortable, my angels," she asks them each. She kisses the tip of Anastasia's nose. "Try not to sleep, darling."

"I won't let her," Maria replies, pinching her small sister's arm.

"I'll tell Papa," Anastasia cries.

Darya pulls Anastasia's favorite doll out of the bag she has filled with all types of diversions for the children. "Here, Anastasia, little Lariska wants to see the ballet too."

The conductor raises his baton. An enchanting symphony, consonant and deeply introspective, curls up from the orchestra pit to fill the U-shaped auditorium.

The blue stage curtains of velvet and silk and lace rise.

The collective intake of breath can be heard in the auditorium.

The Mariinsky stage is awash in red.

A single aurochs is caged in the limelight.

The ballerino is disguised from head to toe in a shade deeper than the shade of ruby.

Four ballerinas, white and airy and purer than St. Petersburg summer clouds, fence the aurochs, circling and nuzzling, caressing, stroking, flirting with the graceful pliés of their arms, balancing on flat toes, closing on the prey, swirling in an adagio, slow, enfolding, tempting, then twirling into an allegro, light, soothing, curling, as weightless and graceful as the swans inhabiting the artificial lake in the Alexander Park.

Grand Duchess Tatiana whispers in Darya's ear that the aurochs seems to be swimming in a pool of blood. Darya nods her agreement. It is a chilling scene. But for now, she is basking in the aura of Avram's attention, who, occupying a seat in the mezzanine right below the royal box, glances up every few moments to find her lorgnettes aimed at him rather than at the stage. He is especially handsome tonight in coattails and brushed back hair with no trace of the stubborn paint that has a way of clinging to him.

She lowers her lorgnettes, rests her elbows on the balcony banister, and leans slightly forward. Their eyes meet. His eyes say, "I want you." Her eyes reply, "Me too." "Later tonight," his eyes say. "Yes," hers reply. Not a word is spoken.

The magical notes of flutes and clarinets swirl and rise and bounce like so many embraces, now melancholy, now with unprecedented rhythmic vitality. The audience is on their feet. "Bravo! Bravo!"

Alexei has left his seat and is on his toes, half his small body leaning over the banister. Darya grabs the back of his tuxedo jacket, lifts him up, and drops him in her lap.

"Alyosha!" she whispers, her heart hammering in her ears. "You were about to fall!"

Anastasia, finding her brother's seat vacant, shifts closer to Darya, rests her curly head of light brown hair on Darya's shoulder, and dozes off. Olga glances at her parents. Finding them engrossed in the ballet, she slips her hand in Darya's. Maria and Tatiana, having lost interest in the ballet, are whispering to each other, wondering whether their parents will invite the prima ballerina to have dinner with them. Their grandmother is the grand patron of the theater, after all, her bust exhibited in the formal entryway.

Avram is in a playful mood, now he taps on his wrist, where Darya loves to count his pulse. Now his arms are outstretched as if inviting her to fall into them.

Grand Duke Michael reaches out to touch Darya's shoulder. "Bensheimer seems more interested in you than the ballet."

Darya's cheeks burn. She raises her eyebrows as if she is not certain what the grand duke is referring to. She shifts back into her chair, clutching Alexei to her chest.

Michael winks at her. His tone is cheerful. "Shall we invite Bensheimer to the imperial box?"

"If it pleases Your Majesty," she replies with a mischievous wink.

The conductor flips his baton and the 150-piece orchestra bursts into a fortississimo of such magnitude, the Tsarevich digs his little hand into Darya's arm. The trombones, tubas, and horns blare. The trumpets and cymbals blast. The bass drums and tambourines boom. An aggressive war cry transforms the auditorium into a mighty acoustic instrument.

The aurochs is provoked into action! Its powerful right leg is pointing like a weapon at one of the dancers. He is jumping, brisk, lively, leg beating the air as if slicing everything into small pieces. And then an arabesque, then another and another, furious jumps and turns and kicks performed in the midst of a pool of red light.

The white ballerinas seem to fuse into a four-legged arabesque, their unity such that it is hard to tell one from another. But then, with sudden violence, they break apart, a savage battement of kicking that is soon transformed into en arrière, a backward tiptoeing as they sail farther and farther away from the audience, white specters fading into the fringes of darkness.

The strings raise soothing moans. The violins, violas, and violoncellos plead and implore, attempting to lure the dancers back.

But as the curtain falls and the applauding audience rises to its feet, it is the red aurochs who remains solid in the center of the stage.

Nine years from now, Darya will trace her thoughts back, identifying this moment as the instant a tiny seed of suspicion planted itself in back of her mind, a slow-growing seed that will bloom into a malodorous plant she will be forced to acknowledge.

Chapter Twenty-Five

— 1911 —

THE TSAR LEADS HIS seven-year-old son into Portrait Hall, with its smell of paint and ink and a cloud of stone dust that has settled onto everything. Since its inception six years before, the salon's fame has spread all around the country, becoming the talk of St. Petersburg, Ekaterinburg, and Moscow, the artists celebrated throughout the country, and the Tsarina admired for promoting the arts. Today, her sciatica having forced her into bed rest, the Tsar is shouldering her responsibility.

Darya follows a step behind. She winces, pressing her hand to her stomach. It has been a painful day, one of those days that pounce on her without warning. For five years now, since she lost Avram's child, her womb has been twisting and churning every now and then, refusing to settle, a constant reminder of her loss. Their love, hers and Avram's, has come far in the last six years, deepened and expanded, a wiser relationship. They no longer meet in the park. Count Trebla put an end to that. His blood poisoned with syphilis, his mind gone, he wandered around the park one dusk, grabbing anyone who happened to cross his path, holding the alarmed person hostage, rambling on and on about Darya and Avram, how they meet in the imperial banya, fuck in it, soil it.

Trebla was sent to the infirmary where, hands and feet bound, he was injected with malaria to induce a high fever to cure his syphilis. The treatment assaulted his nerves, rendering him numb from the waist down. The household officer in charge of the kennels released Count Trebla of his duty as veterinarian, but he was not banished from the court. His wife's miniatures have become too valuable, especially to the Tsarevich who can't wait to open the lacquered box he receives twice a year to discover yet another miracle to add to his collection.

Since the day her husband became housebound, Tamara is becoming more reclusive, dwindling in her skin. Her miniatures too are shrinking in size, so much so that details of some are invisible to everyone save the artist herself.

Now, she stands up with the other artists, abandoning her tiny tools—inspection loupe, mallet, file, hammer, tweezers, blade shears—rearranging her face and bowing low.

Hands clasped behind, the Emperor ambles from one station to another, lingering to take a better look at works in progress, nodding his head with approval, surprise, or a gesture of indifference. His temples are grayer, as if overnight. The dark circles under his eyes have turned soft with surrender, his broad chest a reminder of the numerous times he is forced to carry his incapacitated six-year-old son in his arms.

Darya is attentive, her gaze pouncing ahead of the Tsar, checking every station before he comes to it. Following the country's far-left tendencies, the political atmosphere of the salon has been shifting. Years of turmoil have emboldened certain artists, so that ballets and caricatures, once carefully designed to disguise antimonarchist messages, seem to be changing shape. The artists are shedding their masks and allowing themselves some liberties. Something must be done before they become too radical.

But the Empress is in denial; she does not want to see this change. What she chooses to see and relay to the Emperor is the extraordinary work that continues to be born in Portrait Hall: paintings, sculptures, miniatures, ballets, and caricatures.

In Germany, Igor's ballet about the Tsar and the kaiser won him both a knighthood and the honorary title of Ritter. The aristocracy, taken by Belkin's morbid paintings, is ready to pay exorbitant prices for his work. Dimitri Markowitz's caricatures express the impotence of the first and second Dumas and fetch high prices in the black market. His most popular caricature, *The Duma of Public Anger*, as the first meeting of the Duma came to be known, depicts moderate socialists, social democrats, and social revolutionaries hanging one another with their own cravats while the Tsar and Tsarina sunbathe on their yacht. In a show of blatant defiance, the caricature was purchased by none other than the minister of finance himself.

Darya brought this matter to the Emperor's attention. He raised his cane and pointed it at her as if to say she was too naïve to understand. "I admire Markowitz's caricature," the Emperor announced. "It depicts members of the Duma exactly as they are. A bunch of worthless idiots!"

Now, despite Darya's earlier warnings to the artists that the Tsar was on his way, she is not certain how the afternoon will unfold. Rosa scrambles down from her scaffolding and stands at the foot in case the Tsar has questions. She opens her mouth to greet the Tsar, but the marble dust in her lungs has taken a toll, and she doubles over coughing. The Tsar quickly guides his son out of harm's way and toward Igor's station.

Igor buttons his shirt and stands back with lowered head.

Darya directs an angry look at him. The sheets spread around his work area, renditions of dancers in different moves, are so poorly disguised that any attentive observer would recognize the underlying truth: a series of vignettes based on the 1904 Russo-Japan War that ended in an embarrassing defeat for Russia.

"Quite impressive," the monarch says. "Is this the norm? To test the ballet movements on paper first? And the rhythms and emotions, how do they come to life on stage?"

"Every artist has a different style, Your Majesty," Igor replies. "My preference is to test the entire dance on paper before transferring it to the stage. And as to Your Majesty's second question, the rhythms and emotions are added at different stages of practice."

In truth, these renderings were created for the sole benefit of the Empress, to be pulled out of Igor's briefcase and displayed whenever the Tsarina visits. Otherwise, Igor's choreography—concept, space, visualization, and so much more—is strictly born and shaped in his head. So today, having been forewarned of the Tsar's visit, he had dismissed the dancer who impersonates the Japanese Emperor Meiji and spread out the renderings, albeit with a few minor adjustments to reflect a measure of progress.

The Tsar nods, taps on one of the drawings. "Well done! We will eagerly follow your success."

Eyes downcast, Igor Vasiliev stands at attention, his respectful stance contradicting his utter contempt for the Romanovs. The salon has altered the public's perception of the Imperial Family's indifference to the arts. Despite that, Igor bristles, this is only the Tsar's third visit in six years, and even now his expression of boredom is quite insulting.

The photographer Joseph wants nothing more than to raise his camera, now that the Emperor is here in person, and capture the gray hairs in his beard, the strong jawline, the uneven teeth that he is known to neglect, the slightly large ears that speak of his intelligence, the dreamy blue-gray eyes, but most of all the shape of his head, a valuable supplement to his ongoing project. Despite years of grueling research, the photographer has yet to prove that head shape does not evidence madness, as claimed by some therapists, who themselves lack a single sensible cell in their brains. At the Tsar's perplexed expression at the scatter of photographs on the table, Joseph attempts to explain his project, name the many asylums he visited, the numerous madmen and women he photographed, the comparison he continues to make between the shape of their heads and those of supposedly sane people. But the Emperor has lost interest and moves on to Belkin's station.

The Tsar is confronted by a morbid painting—a coffin studded with copper nails and heavy bolts, as if to contain a dangerous living beast, rather than the bearded, long-haired corpse that rests inside. Nearby, lightning from an arid sky strikes a gaping grave from which emerges the painter's skeletal hand, holding up a decree.

Darya steps closer. "Perhaps Your Majesty might want to skip this station. The Tsarevich is too young to be introduced to such morbid painting."

Darya recognizes the corpse in the painting as Rasputin's. When his name first appeared in the press some months ago, opposing his influence on the Romanovs, the Tsar's primary reaction was to punish those who spoke out against the Imperial Couple for supporting a humble peasant who was known for his involvement with all types of questionable women he led into his bedroom, which he considered "the Holy of Holies." Their Majesties continued to lavish him with elegant garments and expensive gifts, welcoming him into their palace, allowing him to spend time with the grand duchesses, even late at night after they had changed. The governess to the grand duchesses had suggested Rasputin be barred from entering the girls' quarters. The enraged Empress discharged the governess. But lately, due to tremendous pressure, the reluctant Tsar has temporarily banished Rasputin from the court. And the decree held up in the painting is none other than the Tsar's decree, influenced by Rasputin, that appointed the controversial Vladimir Karlovich Sabler as minister for church affairs.

The Tsar slaps his cane against his leather boot. "Yes, let us move on, son. Mr. Bensheimer's work seems less gloomy."

The Emperor lingers in front of the portrait Avram is painting of Darya, her face filling the entire canvas.

A marvel of creation, the Emperor muses, admirable how the artist has rendered his model's every eccentricity, the emotional depth of her eyes in which her unquenchable curiosity blazes. Despite his talent and his portraits, which could have been valuable additions to the imperial collection, Bensheimer is a Jew, alas, and as such, a stain on his court. Yet his wife will not hear of dismissing him. That, she believes, is nothing short of tempting bad luck. She has become dependent on the portrait of the Tsarevich in the arms of the Madonna. She holds it dear, a talisman on which their son's health depends.

Avram stands silent by the easel. His portrait speaks for itself. The sensuality in his model's features is undeniable, the plump mouth, the flushed cheeks, the dreamy gaze. His eyes rest on Darya, studying her with the tentative gaze of a lover. There is concern in her veiled expression.

The Tsar turns his back to Bensheimer. "Come, son, let us visit our favorite artist. See what gifts she may have in store for us today. What tiny secrets they might conceal."

"How are you doing, Tamara Sheremetev?" he asks the Creator of Miniatures. "What are you working on today?"

She is blushing, her hand covering something. Despite having been in the service of the court for years, she has never become used to such attention. Her voice is gentle. "Perhaps you might raise your hand, Your Majesty."

He holds both palms up, and the Creator of Miniatures places a magnifying glass in one, and the pit of a peach on the other. Holding the glass over the pit, he brings his face close. The sharp intake of his breath can be heard around the hall.

Carved into the pit of the peach is Alexander Palace with all two hundred rooms. The music rooms, classrooms, playrooms, the tunnel leading from the palace to the kitchen building, the Empress's Lilac Room, the Emperor's study, Portrait Hall, the receiving room, and the private movie theater of the Tsarevich. And as if that were not enough to fit into the pit of a peach, the park with its flowers and fauna and the private island where the bridge can be hauled for privacy are all delineated with painful precision. The Tsar is riveted. What tools could be so precise, what hands so supple, what eyes so sharp, what patience so endless?

It would take him days to identify every nook and corner of his palace so accurately represented here.

"You could hold your entire court in the palm of your hand, Your Majesty," the Creator of Miniatures murmurs.

"Masterful!" The Emperor exclaims. "Impressive!"

"And for you, Your Majesty, a little car just like your father's."

She drops a small replica of the Tsar's Delaunay-Belleville Landau into the Tsarevich's cupped hands.

The child lets out a cry of joy. He rises on his feet to plant a kiss on her cheek. He holds up the miniature toy, carved out of a chunk of precious ruby, a million shades of reds, scintillating under the light of the chandelier. He twirls the steering wheel with one finger, all four small wheels rotating on gold hinges, the tiny spokes and studs, flicks the movable roof to reveal his parents in the back, their chauffeur in the driver's seat, every detail in place, including the Tsar's carefully trimmed beard and the Tsarina's pearl earrings, all in different shades of red, carved out of the gem's heart. The Tsarevich laughs out loud, kissing Tamara again. "Thank you, Tamara, thank you very much."

The Emperor clasps his son's hand as they walk toward the exit.

On his palm, the Emperor carries a treasure his wife will appreciate more than the Fabergé egg of green enamel and opalescent oyster he gave her this year for their anniversary.

The Tsarevich, in his cupped hands, carries a precious toy he will cherish for years to come, until the turn of history will force him to part with it.

Chapter Twenty-Six

D ARYA PICKS UP A pebble and tosses it into the depths of
the Black Sea, which is not black at all but blue as heaven.
She loves the Crimea with its native pine and sequoia,
vineyards that supply the sweetest muscat and headiest champagne,
trailing vines of rose and lavender, orchards of peaches and cherries
and almonds, and a range of hills that keep the cold northern winds
at bay and its handsome populace of Tartars content.

The Imperial Family and their entourage are here for the
inauguration of the new Livadia Palace. To Darya's great delight,
she succeeded in convincing the Imperial Couple to bring the
Tsarevich along, and under her tutelage and care, he has never
looked healthier. The Empress seems stronger and happier too.
And Avram, invited along with the other artists, is basking in the
success of his latest collection of portraits, the primitive-looking
nudes of his sole model: her!

The only cloud in the canvas of her clear sky is Grigori Rasputin,
whose encroaching shadow slithers underfoot, flat and ominous, as
she strolls along the fringe of the sea. Having been invited back to
court by the Empress, Rasputin is in good humor. The Tsarevich,
during a recent trip with his family, fell against the bathtub and
bruised himself. The bleeding was terrible. The Empress did not
leave her son's bedside for ten days. Doctors admitted defeat. An

announcement was drafted declaring the death of the heir. The desperate Empress sent Rasputin a telegram.

"God has seen your tears," he wired back. "Do not grieve. The Little One will not die." Within hours the bleeding had subsided. He had, once again, saved the life of the Tsarevich, and neither the most powerful of ministers, nor governess to the grand duchesses, or a single member of the Imperial Family dared to criticize him.

Darya detects something floating on the waves, bobbing up and down like a giant cork. Her hand shading her eyes against the sun, she squints to bring the shape into focus. An animal, she thinks, continuing to plow ahead. Warm sand sifts through her bare toes, but her gaze is riveted on the sea creature riding the waves, hissing and foaming like the Empress's Chantilly lace skirts.

Darya slows down, moves to the water's edge. The sea has vomited a silvery elliptical object onto the shore, an object the size of the Tsar's traveling valise. It glistens under the sun, as if imbued with a life of its own. Fossilized squid beaks and shells poke out of its hide that resembles brittle pumice stone, or some spongy material with the voluptuous scent of leather and tobacco and sea, a seductive perfume that curls up to embrace her like a womb.

Cherish it, the Ancient One says. *Its journey has been long and hard. It has crossed seas and oceans, has been cured for decades in salty waters and under hot suns to reach you. Valuable ambergris, Darya Borisovna. It is yours!*

Oblivious to the lapping waves and the warm sand, Darya falls to her knees. Rasputin's hunched-over body is so close, her skirt will inherit his donkey odor. She presses her forehead to the buttery surface, an impulsive act of a desert traveler thirsting for water.

She is thrust to another place, a queen teaching her disciples how to burn ambergris as incense to purify the air and to heal evil thoughts, how to flavor wine to enjoy long life, rub on wounds to stem bleeding, lace with hashish to alleviate pain, brew in tea to add sexual vigor, or consume in fertility rites to make the barren fertile.

"Ambergris is a powerful conduit." She hears Rasputin above her, relieved, for once, to find him close, as if they are partners on an imminent journey.

She rubs her temples. "I was in a strange place."

He gazes down at her, eyes warm, encouraging, saying she is safe with him.

"I don't know where I went. I was someone else, I think."

"Come with me. Will you? We'll go there together."

"The ambergris is mine," Darya echoes the Ancient One. "I won't leave it behind." Slowly, cautiously, she reaches out a trembling hand and breaks off a small piece.

And six years after the night she lost her child, she unlocks her necklace and replenishes its bejeweled egg.

Rasputin checks the chunk of ambergris this way and that, raises it slightly from all sides. It is heavy, but he is a strong man. He slides his arms under and lifts it as if he were carrying a woman in his arms. He follows Darya toward the Livadia Palace with its Florentine tower and 116 rooms, past the arched portico of dazzling Carrara marble, the Italian patio with its limestone columns and enclosing balconies, where the Tsarina has her afternoon tea, past inner chambers decorated in stucco and wood carving, and into Darya's apartments, all the way to her bedroom, where he deposits the ambergris on her bed.

Then, without considering the oddity of what she's doing, she takes a deep breath and stretches out next to the ambergris, inhaling its scent of musk and sweet earth and mossy forests. She is safe, safer than she has felt in a long time, her womb at peace as if she is forgiven, at last, by herself, by Avram and his dead son, even by the aurochs.

The drone of bees can be heard outside, the click of shears, the low voices of gardeners arguing. Sweet scents of ripe cherries and peaches drift in from fruit-heavy arbors.

Rasputin's voice wends its way to settle in Darya's head, weigh on her eyelids, and produce a subliminal sleep that transports her to caramel-colored sands and unblemished skies, where the sun and stars shine in symphonic harmony. The air is laced with the aroma of molasses and dates, and palm fronds sway in the breeze.

Rasputin stares at Darya with a freedom she would not have allowed when awake. He gazes at the delicate contours of her face, the vein pulsing at her temples, mouth parted as if to accept his kiss, and this man, who has never known fear, is terrified of the woman with the power to make him weak with desire. He approaches the bed and reaches out a cold hand to fondle her breasts. Steals his hand back, regards her with curiosity, and then comes down to take her in his mouth.

She lets out a long, drawn-out sigh.

He springs back as if she has been transformed into a deity who might strike him dead on the spot. He pulls a chair behind him. Shuffles backward, farther away from the bed on which she lies—this mysterious woman who will live to see the world twist and turn out of shape, live to hear the toll of millions of death bells, witness brother turn against brother and seas and oceans overflow with tears.

He wipes sweat off his forehead with the back of his hand. "Darya Borisovna Spiridova, who are you?"

She replies in a voice he does not recognize: "I am Athalia the traitor."

Chapter Twenty-Seven

— 842 to 830 BC —

I AM ATHALIA THE OMRIDE, daughter of Omri, queen of Judah. Swathed in silks and brocade, a headdress of silver tossed over my hair, opal headgear adorning my forehead, I wend my way in a procession across the halls of my palace. Slaves flutter peacock feathers above my head, men and women bow at every turn.

"A sip of rosewater, my lady."

"A spray of ambergris, perhaps."

I am the most beloved of King Jehoram's forty wives, also known as the Opal Queen. Merchants scour all four continents to bring me translucent opal, the rarest of all opals. So pure, it portends my future in its heart. The ignorant denounce opal as a vessel of bad luck. Such nonsense. Like life, opal symbolizes both the bad and the good, birth and death.

My red-haired jester prances in and out of sight, around my sandaled feet, behind the stone columns. His froglike eyes unhinged in their bony sockets, he flaps his short arms like wings, and as if propelled by some magical force, his hooflike feet scramble up Sari's plump thighs, hairless chest, and shoulders to land on top of the poor eunuch's head.

I laugh out loud. Others join in. My servants attempt to erase my sadness. My husband, Jehoram of Judah, the son-in-law of the house of Omri, is away at the battlefront. Seasons have come and gone; spring is here. Cisterns and jugs on rooftops flow with bathing rains. Roads and ditches are dried of lethal diseases, valleys and ravines are pregnant with wild flowers, palms are heavy with dates, yet no word of my beloved king, Melekh Israel.

"My lady, please rest, it is hot today. Tell us about the ambergris. It is time you revealed its secrets." Sari, my eunuch and confidant, breathes heavily, unable to keep up with my pace.

I gaze down at his freckled, balding head and pity this man who must have harbored his own dreams of wives and children. "We will rest, Sari. Here, chew on some ambergris to strengthen your heart."

Years have passed and I have honored my vow to the ancient spice merchant to keep the secret of ambergris to myself. But unable to shake my loneliness, I open my mouth and say what I should not.

"An ancient spice merchant with four fingers on one hand and a knapsack on his back crossed lands, seas, and deserts on foot, on horseback, by boat, and on camel to find me, Athalia the Omride, mistress of alchemy. He was tall. His handsome, sunbaked face was lined with wisdom, his silver hair braided and held back with many ribbons. Did I know how to extract youth from ambergris, he asked me, after which he opened his knapsack to reveal a waxy, flammable slice of heaven.

"It smelled of love and life. It smelled of death and renewal. I had to have it.

"We bartered.

"'Look at my opal necklace,' I said to the spice merchant. 'It is the rarest of its kind. Its color is deep like gold, but it is as clear and pure as air and water. I will give it to you in exchange for half your ambergris. And I will teach you how to stay young. Not with the help of ambergris. That I do not know yet. But I will teach you to reach deep into the heart of this pure opal to unravel the mysteries of the universe.'

"He laid his four-fingered hand on my shoulder. 'I will accept. And in return you must promise to hold the ambergris dear. Do not share its secrets. It possesses power beyond your imagination. Handle it intelligently. And never, ever use it as a means of…'"

Howls of a developing storm, followed by heart-wrenching wails, force their way into the palace.

A flash of lightning brings to life two silhouettes framed by the backdrop of the domed portal. Lit by dim torches, messengers of the king gradually emerge from the shadows, bows and arrows spent, eyes bloodshot for lack of sleep, feet blistered from the long journey.

"Our king is dead, my queen! By the hand of Jehu, his trusted general."

"An uprising!"

"A bloody revolt against the House of David."

"King Jehoram of Judah is dead!"

I gesture with an open palm and order my procession to keep their distance. My other hand presses to my chest to lock my grief inside. "Where is my son?" I ask the messengers. "Is he back from war?"

I listen, clutching my chest, holding on to the pieces of my shattering heart. My son, Ahaziah, is dead too. General Jehu incited an uprising. Murdered my husband. Murdered my son. Forty-two other Omride princes were also killed. Only five spared. I am in danger, they say; Jehu is bent on destroying all Omrides.

"Where are my grandson and daughter-in-law?" I ask. "Are *they* safe?"

"Yes, they were spared. But you must take matters into your own hand, our queen. The surviving princes are not worthy of the throne. Your grandson is a mere child. The survival of the monarchy depends on you."

Sari holds a vial of ambergris to my nose. I push his hand away. "I will be alone with my God. Do not follow me!"

He thrusts the vial in my pocket.

I cross halls of stone and marble, where rooms open into other rooms, into inner worlds of ambition and deception. I walk out of the palace and down stone steps. Gusts of wind blow sand into my eyes and the sour stench of carrion and urine into my lungs. Clusters of grieving stars congregate overhead. Tarantulas dig their way out of the earth, and vultures shriek into the wind. I weave my way between olive and palm trees, across the desert, and toward Mount Ephraim, seeking the temple between Ramah and Beth-El. I take shelter under the Etz Rimmon, the pomegranate tree of mercy by the main entrance to the temple. I hide my face in my hands and wail, "Why, Adonai? What have You done?"

An arid wind transports the odor of decaying dates and the sound of conversation in the sanctuary. The high priest, Jehoiada, must be here with his wife, preparing the temple for the day of mourning. I rise to my feet, straighten my spine, turn the knob, and open the back door. The air smells of incense and of the Ner Tamid, torch of eternal light. I step across the narrow corridor, separated from the main sanctuary by a stretch of embroidered fabric, and nudge the fabric back. Diffused light from the latticed dome falls on a circle of men. Desert-colored robes and delineated features come into focus—a square jaw, an imbecilic smile, a broken nose, twisted mouth spitting secrets.

What business do the remaining five Davidic princes, sons of King Jehoram from other wives, stepbrothers to my murdered son, have here?

They are congregated around the bimah altar scattered with sacred objects—havdalah spice boxes, Rosh Hashanah honey pots, sash of the high priest, glazed candleholders. Their heads come together, fists flashing gold and silver rings, their petulant murmurings a hum in the sanctuary.

They step up to the altar and unlock the holy ark. Remove a Torah, protected from harm for decades in the holy ark, where no outsider is allowed.

How dare they remove the Torah when such a sacred duty belongs to the high priest!

Why are they kissing the embroidered mantle that covers the holy book, kissing the jewel-encrusted breastplate that hangs over the mantle, unlocking the cover to reveal the holy scroll inside? Why are they removing the sash girthing the scroll, praying with eyes closed and foreheads touching the scroll? A word here, another there, a broken phrase and before long a string of remarks solidify around the hazy edges of my brain. "Accept us, Adonai... The glory of Israel...in our hands...King Jehoram of Judah is dead. His other son...We are Your servants...allow us to serve Your land."

My mouth fills with bitter ash. Treason! The princes are planning to rob my grandson of his rightful place as king of Judah.

I move away from the curtain and take the narrow back corridor toward steps that lead to a ledge behind the eternal torch. I step on the ledge and reach out for the light.

I grab and aim it at the traitors. Hurl it with the force of my rage.

They stare around. An accident, they think, trampling the flame, attempting to suffocate the anemic fire.

I snatch the vial of ambergris from my pocket, gaze at it with a sense of trepidation. It is buttery, glazed with oils and throbbing with possibilities. I think of the spice merchant, of the promise he extracted from me. I shut my eyes and toss the vial across the sanctuary. It shatters. Pieces of glass embed themselves in the men's flesh. The ambergris blooms like a dazzling rose, bursting into hundreds of blazing petals that roar into life with capricious explosions that soar to lick the ceiling, walls, windows, and doors.

The startled men scramble to find their way out, but the flames are spreading and encircling them like molten lava, scorching hair and fabric, melting skin and flesh and bone.

I make my way across the corridor and out into the dusty road, heedless of poisonous insects underfoot, the pounding in my temples, the screech of vultures overhead. Fire blasts behind, illuminating my path. A grove of palms ahead. Farther down, the horses' entryway to the stables. I slow for an instant, gaze back: wood planks come shattering down. Blazing fabric and smoldering parchments float above.

The roof of the temple collapses with a great wail.

My heart churns with remorse. The moon has turned its back to me. I am cold. I fall to my knees, hold my head in my hands, and call out to God: Adonai! What have I done? I burned Your holy book, Your sacred words. Pardon my transgressions.

I gaze ahead, gaze with unbelieving eyes. Struggle to comprehend the shifting landscape I face.

The branches of the pomegranate tree of mercy are shorn of leaves. They are steeped in fire. No! Not a burning fire! A lovely glow that does not consume the tree. And then…what do I see? Holy letters disengage themselves from fragments of parchment. The letters flutter overhead like luminous moths, like small blessings. Float down. Land on boughs and limbs, shoots and tendrils, adjusting and readjusting their placement to dress the tree with holy letters.

High above, a rainbow appears on the canvas of a night sky that leaks fat tears to extinguish the flames. And in the midst of the emerging ruins of smoke and ash and regret, the pomegranate tree of mercy, the keeper of the Torah, glows like a jewel.

I clutch my necklace and gaze into the translucent heart of the opal, searching for the image of the just-transpired miracle. I see my face instead. The face of a traitor. I razed the house of God. I murdered the king's sons. I unleashed a series of events that will forever stain Judah. I raise my face to the heavens and vow to ensure the continuance of the House of David. My raw voice shatters the hearts of angels, letting loose a torrent of stars.

I find my way to the palace. It is time to bathe. Change into royal attire. Announce the death of our king. Announce my leadership. Present myself to my people.

Sari assists me into the rooftop bathing tub. A specter of a pale moon glides behind a funereal blanket of smoke. The stench of burned wood and parchment and treason hovers above the realm. He removes layers of my pomegranate-stained clothing, pock-marked by fire sparks, the pungent odor of sin woven into the fabric.

We sit shiva for seven days and nights in the house of Jehoram. My one-year-old grandson Joash and my daughter-in-law Tsibia are by my side. My people beat on their chests and sway on their heels, reciting the mourners' kaddish.

On the eighth day, Tsibia and Joash bid me a tearful farewell. I ruffle my grandson's curly hair. "You will become king one day, my Joash. And it will be your sacred duty to preserve the royal seed."

The week after, I dispatch a messenger to invite my grandson and daughter-in-law to come live with me in my palace. We will raise Joash as befits a king of Israel. We will raise him with a firm hand and a compassionate heart.

Their house is silent, everything in its proper place, the messenger reports back. No sign of struggle.

The two are nowhere to be found.

And so it is that with the aid of the pomegranate tree of mercy, my loyal eunuch, and an army devoted to its murdered king, I have been ruling for six years a land bereft of an heir.

The first winter came with a deluge of rains, followed by a gray spring when the sun peered through smoke-tinged clouds, striving to purge the land of the stench of fires, grant a semblance of normalcy to our lives. Masons from all four corners of Israel toiled day and night to rebuild the temple on the ruins of the last.

Her boughs weighted with all 304,805 letters in the holy book, the pomegranate tree of mercy oversaw the completion of the magnificent edifice.

On the third spring, two saplings sprouted on each side of the tree, adorning the main entrance of the newly built temple with three rimonim of mercy in place of one.

On the eve of Rosh Hashanah, the land ablaze with scented torches and the air fragrant with amber and myrrh, a retinue follows me to the temple to celebrate the beginning of the seventh year of my reign.

The ram's horn is blown, resounding across the desert and in every home around my kingdom, heralding the arrival of another year of peace and prosperity.

The blare of horns of the cavalry announces my arrival. My soldiers, ministers, and advisers follow me into the sanctuary. It is dim and silent, devoid of all signs of festivity. Candles do not flicker on mantelpieces. Dust balls roll underfoot, and dried twigs beat against walls. The eternal light carves a solitary path through the sinister gloom. The shriek of a developing wind forces its way through an open window, blowing sand into my eyes.

Why? Why is the temple in a state of disarray on this day of celebration? Why is it besieged by menace? Why is Sari shaking like a palm frond and darting around like a sacrificial rooster?

Suddenly the sanctuary comes alive with hundreds of shifting shadows. A procession of disembodied faces—men, women, and children—appears from all doors.

From a shady corner emerges the high priest, Jehoiada, followed by lieutenants and cavalry of the army. Áhāh! Mutiny! My soldiers, at the command of my priest, are taking battle stations around *me*, their queen.

The bones of conspiracy I failed to see for six years glare at me now. I searched long and far in hope of capturing General Jehu, yet all the time, right under my watchful eyes, the high priest was plotting against me with my army.

Then all eyes swerve toward the commotion at the western portal. I, too, turn to look.

The love of my life, my seven-year-old grandson, Joash, olive-skinned, shining tight curls, and date-brown innocent eyes, stands at the threshold.

I open my arms wide. "My grandson!" I cry out.

The high priest's voice echoes against stone walls: "Athalia, you have sinned! You burned the house of God. You murdered our

Israelite princes. History will brand you as a daughter of Jezebel. Vilify you as the 'Other.' But your attempt to destroy the royal lineage failed. Joash was rescued from your wicked intents and raised in hiding."

The snub-nosed wife of the high priest steps out of the shadows and wraps an arm around my grandson's shoulders, the relief in his eyes more damning than the high priest's pronouncement.

Lieutenants and runners step forward and raise their weapons. A battalion of soldiers takes its place around the sanctuary. My grandson ascends the steps to the altar, a practiced precision that heralds the rightful crowning of our king, at last. He sits in a chair carved from a solid piece of yellow cedar, the latticed high back decorated with the menorah and with the crowning wreath and insignia.

The high priest opens the doors to the cabinet by the eastern portal and retrieves two objects. "Witness a miracle. The spear and quivers of King David were spared from the fire!"

But he does not hand the spear and quivers to my grandson, nor does he lower the crown upon the child's head. Instead the high priest raises his voice in the temple and appoints himself regent.

"Take this most evil of all women out to the columns!" He orders. "Let her not die in YHWH's temple. Whoever attempts to save her, kill by the sword!"

I am dragged to the horses' entryway. My opal ornaments are wrenched away. They bind me to a post that carries the long-ago stench of smoke and ash.

And as it had occurred on the night of the big fire six years before, plump drops of rain fall upon my head and a rainbow appears on the backdrop of the starry sky.

I shut my eyes and recite the Shema Israel, pray with my last breath to be forgiven.

The tip of an arrow pierces my left eye.

My soul rides on the wing of brilliant flames on a journey to another place.

Grigori Rasputin circles the bed on which Darya and the ambergris lounge like lovers. He is quiet, expectant, moving like an aroused beast. It is time to awaken Darya from her trance. The aroma of mint and fresh cucumbers, roasted lamb and goose, scent of pheasant in fresh cream and mushrooms sizzling in butter waft in from the window. The imperial kitchens are busy preparing tonight's dinner.

Rasputin pulls out a soiled kerchief from his coat pocket and wipes his face. He was right, after all. This woman harbors more secrets than he imagined. When he first saw her in the auction house six years back, intent on acquiring *The Cure*, her regal demeanor, opal eye, and biblical appearance alerted him to her exoticism. But he did not expect her journey to go so far back in time, back more than eight hundred years before the year of our Lord, back to Judah to reveal the magic of opal and ambergris.

He comes closer to stand over Darya, willing his breath to normalize and his heaving chest to settle. In her sleep and smelling of fresh leaves, she appears approachable. He digs one hand into his coat pocket and pulls out a folding knife. Flipping the sharp blade open, he passes it between his thumb and forefinger, rubs it against his lips, examines it under the light of the chandelier, where it flashes invitingly.

He leans forward, reaches out, and thrusts the knife into the ambergris, where it slides with unexpected ease. He twists the blade this way and that, his teeth clenched, his biceps bulging as he struggles to cut off a piece. But invisible jaws have grabbed the blade from inside, the bone handle sticking out like an insult. He falls on top of the handle, manipulating it with all his might, turning and pulling, sweat dripping off his face. A sharp metallic click is heard. He is sent stumbling back, the broken handle left in his hand.

Darya's eyes spring open. At the sight of Rasputin at her side, she jumps up into a sitting position. "Áhāh! What have I done? I murdered the princes! I burned the temple! I set the holy book on fire!"

Rasputin drops the knife handle in his pocket, cracks his bulging knuckles, pushes back the sweat-drenched hair plastered to his forehead. He coughs to recover his voice. "Darya Borisovna! Be vigilant. Know that the rest of your life will not be easy. You will experience many years of unprecedented chaos. Such tragedies, you might wish to die. You will live to be older than one hundred. Then, and only then, will a number of paths be revealed to you. Beware! Keep your eyes open. Choose the right path. Or you will be condemned to come back again and again until you…"

Darya jumps down from the bed, grabs Rasputin by the collar, shakes him violently. "Hear me, Grigori, hear me well! This is my last life. I am a different woman now. Aware of my sins. I will right the wrongs I committed in my other life.

"I will stand by Alexei Nikolaevich Romanov, protect him as if he were my own son. I will fight with my last breath for his right to occupy the throne. I will fight for the survival of the monarchy. This I vow on the grave of my beloved parents."

Chapter Twenty-Eight

— 1911 —

T HEY MAKE THEIR WAY gingerly across the bristling pine clover toward the Byzantine-style Church of the Exaltation of the Cross, where the religious ceremony preceding the formal gala to inaugurate the Livadia Palace will take place soon, awarding the architect, Nicholas Krasnov, the title of Academician in Architecture.

Imperial Cossacks on horseback patrol the perimeter of the park. Wearing scarlet tunics, boots and sabers shining in the moonlight, they raise fur caps to salute Darya and the Tsarevich.

Gardeners arrange water lilies in moonlit ponds, scoop out a stray leaf, a breeze-blown bud, collect objects one or another guest has misplaced—a silk fan, a half-empty goblet of wine, a jeweled hair pin, a shawl fluttering in the breeze.

Alexei stops in front of the imperial garage, nods at the chauffeurs, removes the Kodak camera slung across his shoulder. He snaps photographs of his father's cars, washed and polished to a high sheen—Delaunay-Belleville Triple-Phaeton, three Delaunay-Bellevilles, a limousine, two landaus, and a Mercedes Landau. Numerous other cars are housed in other palaces, the expenses of which the minister in charge of the imperial budget has been complaining about. But when it comes to his collection of cars, his pride and joy, the Tsar will not hear of curtailing expenses.

Imitating his father, the Tsarevich clasps his hands behind his back as he walks to each imperial chauffeur, reaches up to adjust a khaki coat that doesn't need adjusting, pats the coat of arms stamped on a uniform, and brushes a peaked cap that has been removed in his presence. He directs the men to pose around the cars. Pleased with his choreography, he takes a few more photographs. "Thank you," he says, snapping his hand up in a military salute. "Good-bye now."

A warm breeze ruffles his hair, like spun gold in the moonlight. Seagulls wheel overhead. The heady scent of ripe fruit wafts from the east. Notes of the orchestra tuning their instruments can be heard from the palace. Windows frame glimmering chandeliers and shadows of waiters completing last-minute tasks.

Perhaps later tonight, Darya muses, after the festivities, she might invite Avram to her quarters. Their relationship has had its share of twists and turns before settling into the grooves of her life. His compromises, she knows, have been far greater than hers. What man, after all, would remain loyal to a woman whose primary allegiance is to a sickly little boy? Only now does she understand the reason behind her fierce devotion to Alexei. Will Avram understand? Yes, she tells herself, he will. She will tell him what happened yesterday, tell him about Athalia, about her loss and sin and her attempt at redemption. Such knowledge will support his ultimate belief that she has always been two different women: the young, fierce Darya he loves, and the ancient soul he has come to admire.

The Tsarevich squeezes Darya's hand. "I'm going with father for a ride tomorrow, all the way from Yalta to Sevastopol."

"The Crimean highroad is great fun, Loves."

"I'll bring back many, many photographs for you."

"Bring me photographs of Chufut Kale on your way, a cave town perched on one of the Crimean plateaus. I've studied its ancient history, all the way back to the eighth century when the Khazar Kaganate adopted Judaism. It's called the Fortress of Jews."

"What's Jews, Darya?"

"Not what, Loves, but who. Jews are like us, except they believe in Moses instead of our Lord Jesus Christ."

"They're different then."

"I don't know, maybe, but not really; they seem to be a God-fearing people like you and me, except that we are Christian." Not completely true for one Israelite zealot who committed the most heinous of crimes in her past life. Some knowledge is better left buried, she sighs, longing for yesterday's innocence.

"Why do you call Chufut Kale fortress of Jews, Darya?"

"Because many Jews lived there once."

"Where are they now?"

She wraps one arm around his shoulders. "I'll tell you when you are older and the world is calmer. There's time, Loves, a lot of time to learn about hatred." Her glance falls on the amulet on the lapel of his tuxedo jacket. She holds him back, cups his elbow in her hand. "Come, let me straight your amulet. There, that's better."

"Come along, Darya. I'll not miss the fun."

She taps one finger on the amulet. "You won't, not while you have your good luck charm. No one will start without Alexei Nikolaevich, sovereign heir Tsarevich, Grand Duke of Russia."

He pulls his hand out of hers and continues his climb toward the palace church.

She trails close behind, trying not to touch him, to allow him a semblance of the independence he craves.

A sudden sound, a loud, startling boom bursts out of the sea.

He jumps back to grab her hand. She squeezes him tight against her thumping chest, waits for her heart to settle. She gazes at the horizon, far away, where the sky and sea bleed into each other and the entire Crimean night flickers on the surface of the Black Sea. "Look all the way out there, Loves, beyond that passing ship that looks like an illuminated Christmas tree. See that small gray hill? Good. Promise not to laugh, and I'll tell you something."

"I promise," he whispers, his cheeks trembling with the effort to keep himself from crying.

"That, Loves, is the hump of a sperm whale. And this is the sound of its complaining stomach. Sperm whales suffer from terrible tummy aches. So what you hear is the poor animal belching."

He raises his incredulous eyes to her, and she plants a kiss on each. "I learned this from my papa on our way here when your mama was pregnant with you."

He skips ahead, a few steps forward, hesitates, then stumbles as if not certain where to go, as if he changed his mind. A pebble rolls under the sole of his shoe, sliding, scuttling, his arms flailing as if he might fly. He opens his mouth but no sound comes out. The camera flies off his shoulder.

Darya screams, her arms dart out to steady him, catch him, leaping forward to cut his fall.

He comes crashing down on his back.

She drops on her knees beside him. "Are you hurt, Loves? Talk to me! Alyosha!"

He is still, wide-open eyes staring at the sky. A white kite glides overhead. The sperm whale rumbles in the distance. A lizard slips under a rock. A gardener whistles somewhere in the park. A flock of shrieking crows alight on the Greek cross on top of the chapel.

A chill like an ominous ghost slithers up her spine. She cradles his head in her lap. "Oh, God! You are hurt, Loves. Talk to me. Please!"

He sucks his breath in, licks his dry lips, swallows. His eyes are round with fright. "Don't tell Mama, Darya, please."

"Oh, Loves! Don't worry about that."

He is trying to prop himself on both elbows, struggle up to a sitting position.

"Wait! Don't move. Let me check you."

He pushes her away. Brushes clean his tuxedo jacket, pants, sleeves. "Please, Darya, I don't want to be sick. Let's go! Mama and Papa are waiting."

"I know, Loves," she replies, unable to keep her alarm out of her voice. "Tell me where it hurts." She unbuttons his coat and shirt, examines him from all angles, unfastening the waist of his trousers and passing her hands across his legs.

He holds up his elbow for her inspection. "Hurts here. Not much, Darya. I'm fine."

But she knows better. Nothing will stop the onset of bleeding now. There is no predicting how serious this episode will be. She tries to button up his jacket, but her cold, trembling fingers will not allow. "Come, Loves, we've got work to do."

"But I will not miss the ceremony," he protests.

"Either this, or you'll have to stay in bed for a long month, maybe more. Yes, I know, it's unfair." She kneels, wipes a tear off his cheek with her thumb. "Come, jump on my back. I'll carry you. You shouldn't be walking. Up, now, up."

His arms about her neck, his legs anchored around her waist, she descends the hill, her eyes combing every pebble underfoot, every gnarled root, every hidden sprinkler that might cause her to slip. She is drenched in perspiration under the weight on her back and the ache in her chest.

The whale's mournful cries reverberate in the distance, the shriek of seagulls overhead, the crashing waves below, and in her chest the thumping of her agonizing heart.

He will be fine, she repeats over and over to herself as she enters her apartments and sets him down on the sofa in her living room. "Don't move. I'll be right in the kitchen. Here, take a look at this picture book."

She chooses the necessary ingredients from jars of all sizes in the kitchen cupboards. A jar of oil extracted from sweet almonds, pounded and steeped in warm water and wrung drop by drop through a sieve. Pouring a thimble of the almond oil into a measuring cup, she adds a spoonful of nectar of black honey, a potent salve harvested in July from the hives of black bees who feed on pollen of a rare breed of purple Siberian rose. Next, she uncorks a bottle of red wine from Livadia grapes that ancient Greek immigrants fermented in oak barrels she obtained from a wizened blacksmith, who had inherited this last existing bottle from his great-grandfather. She adds a swig of wine, a few drops of melted saffron, and a palm-full of chickpea paste, known for its binding properties. She has done this before, with different herbs, roots, and barks for other ailments. As a cure for the Empress's insomnia, or as a potion to calm Avram's nerves whenever he brings himself to part with one of his paintings.

But she is hopeful to create a different elixir this time, something more potent, able to cure the incurable.

Ancient One, she cries out in her heart, help me! Help me make the right decision.

The Ancient One appears, a brilliant opal drop hanging from a chain around her white, throbbing throat. Never before has she been so close to Darya, so gloriously delineated, solid in her presence, her perfumed breath permeating the kitchen. *Darya Borisovna, I have come to bid you farewell. My mission has been fulfilled. You are a better woman today. You possess the knowledge of two women, a deeper awareness. Cherish the gift so recently granted to you. It will serve you well.* She turns around, her diaphanous train crackling with opalescent hues as it sweeps the floor behind her.

"Don't go yet," Darya cries out. "A gift? Tell me what it is!" But the Ancient One is gone, her fragrance intensifying in her wake. It takes an instant for Darya to identify the lingering aroma evoking the scent so recently introduced to her.

She runs into her bedroom, where the ambergris is lying like a lover she does not have the heart to banish from her bed. She takes shallow breaths, not wanting to be influenced by the musky, animal scent invading everything. She breaks off a trace amount from the buttery chunk that proves more brittle than yesterday when she had replenished her necklace by the sea.

Back in the kitchen, she crushes the ambergris, measures a teaspoon, adds a spoonful, and then a bit more. She does not know the right dosage, has no way of telling whether adding the ambergris to her healing potion will succeed in stemming the bleeding that must have begun somewhere inside the Tsarevich. But she is hopeful.

While Darya is busy in the kitchen, the Tsarevich leaves the sofa to explore the rooms.

Whether here, in the Livadia Palace, or any of the other palaces, Darya's apartments are a source of fascination to him. Every cupboard and closet is a fairy-tale world crammed with curious objects he likes to photograph—a hammered gold box, opal bracelets, gold chains and dangling earrings, shawls so light they flutter in the air like colorful balloons, picture books of strange places, men wearing headgear and long robes, sandaled women with kohl-rimmed eyes—but tonight his camera lies shattered somewhere on top of the hill in the park. He uncorks perfume bottles that smell of Darya, pulls a few strands of her black hair from a latticed wooden comb. He steals back into the hallway and enters the bedroom.

At the sight of something lying on the bed, he jumps back to conceal himself behind the door. He opens his eyes, peers back in. A soft light from the window casts a metallic hue over the oily carapace that resembles a giant turtle on the bed. It is still and silent as stone. Open-mouthed and clutching the doorsill, he waits for a movement, a noise. But either asleep, or dead, the creature remains motionless. He takes a few hesitant steps inside, approaches the bed, climbs up to take a closer look. The thing smells of the tobacco in his father's pipe and the leather gloves his mother orders from Paris. He looks around, searches for a sharp object. He unfastens the amulet from the lapel of his tuxedo and points the back pin into the carapace.

He probes the pin this way and that, becoming braver with each poke, pushing deeper here and there, breaking tiny pieces from a brittle section. He likes the softer areas, the squishy parts. He giggles under his breath. There! A fun spongy section. He shoves the pin deeper. He gasps, hand flying to his mouth. The amulet is slipping away. He fights to hold on to it, to snatch it back, probes his fingers in, tries to catch it. He can't lose his good luck amulet, can't let it go. Darya will be very, very angry. But the amulet has disappeared. Swallowed whole by the monster that is not dead after all.

He vaults down from the bed. Wipes his tears away with his hand as he runs back to the other room and jumps up onto the sofa.

"I made a delicious drink for you," Darya says, extending the elixir. She checks his arm. There is no sign of a bruise forming yet. Perhaps this time is different from other times, she dares to hope, perhaps blood will not pool somewhere in his joints, under his skin, inside his internal organs.

"Drink, brave boy. Go ahead. It's not too hot, is it?"

He dips his tongue into the warm concoction. His face puckers into a grimace. "Ugh! I don't like it. No! I will *not* have it."

"You must, Loves. One big gulp and it's all done. Pinch your nose and drink."

He raises his face to her, and she squeezes his nostrils with thumb and forefinger, bringing the cup to his mouth and keeping it there until he empties it. "There. Bravo, my boy. Relax now, try to rest." Her voice fills the large room, promising health, an evening of sweet ices and dark chocolates, soothing words that weave a hammock in which he peacefully sways.

"I like it," he says. "Some more, please."

"Maybe later, Loves." She observes him closely, checking for the usual signs of anxiety, fear, restlessness that such accidents trigger. Each of these incidents makes him appear older, wiser, more subdued. She covers his face with small kisses. "You're growing up, Loves, so fast I can't keep up with you."

"Some more of that," he mumbles, eyes heavy with sleep.

"Don't sleep, Loves. Keep your eyes open. I can't tell how you're feeling if you fall asleep. Stand up, Alyosha, try." She lifts him to his feet, holds him tight under the arms until he is stable. "Come, my boy, come bow your head and pray with me." She presses both hands to his temples, turning her vision inward, mustering the strength to will his blood vessels to contract, his blood to thicken and coagulate. "You will grow up to live a long healthy life. You will become our Tsar one day and rule until you are a hundred years old."

"I will become the best Tsar in the world. I will give them a lot of money. And I will never be sick."

"And here is a kiss to keep you doubly safe."

She strokes his forehead, touches her lips to the tip of his nose, tucks both hands under his arms and raises him to a sitting position, straightens his suit, adjusts his tie, and combs his hair. "Come now, Loves. You have a dinner to attend. Shall I carry you?"

He passes both hands over his hair and tugs at his collar, habits he inherited from his father. Slipping into the role of the Tsarevich of all the Russias, he snaps his fingers, gesturing to the smiling Darya to follow him out the door.

Chapter Twenty-Nine

H E CROSSES THE STRETCH of red carpet, past large porcelain stoves and orchid and lilac planters, across the marble and mother-of-pearl floors, toward his parents. He is preceded by footmen swinging aromatic pots of incense.

Thunder of applause and proclamations of "God save the Tsarevich" reverberate in the salon.

The Empress, clad in silver cloth and old lace studded with diamonds, a tiara of pearls and sapphires on her head, rises to her feet. The Emperor, regal in his court uniform, weighted with medals and gold braids, joins the Empress in welcoming their son.

The one-hundred-piece orchestra bursts into the national anthem.

The Emperor pats his son on the head. "You didn't come to the ceremony this afternoon, Alexei Nikolaevich, my sovereign heir. I sent our squire to look for you."

"I fell asleep in Darya's apartments, Papa."

The orchestra launches into a waltz. Reaching out to his wife and son, the Tsar leads them to the dance floor and into his arms.

The Grand Salon is filled with ministers, diplomats, and honored foreign dignitaries who have come from near and far to celebrate the inauguration of the summer palace. For the first time in history, artists of the salon, men and women born to no titles but who achieved fame by their own energy and genius, will share dinner with their Imperial Majesties.

Laughter of the grand duchesses can be heard across the room. They are gathered around the Creator of Miniatures. She is displaying her latest miniature: the Livadia Palace etched on a walrus tooth.

Count Freedericksz, the Minister of the Court, who has the delicate task of resolving disputes between the Tsar and members of his immediate family, joins the girls to discover the source of their delight. Olga, mesmerized by the exquisite detail, is examining the miniature. Tatiana reaches out for the walrus tooth and holds it up to the gold chain around her neck. "A necklace?" Anastasia giggles. "It might bite off your finger." Maria lets out a bored grunt and wanders in search of her parents.

"Fascinating," Count Freedericksz exclaims, tugging at his broad mustache. He digs into his pocket and flips out a thick wad of rubles. "May I entice the artist to part with her priceless treasure?"

Tamara turns red. She extends a trembling hand to reclaim her treasure, stuffing it into her pocket. "I apologize, Your Excellency, but this is for our Tsarevich."

"The apology is all mine, madame," Count Freedericksz replies. "May he enjoy it in good health." He clicks his boots, turns his attention to the sixteen-year-old Olga, and invites her to the dance floor.

Darya walks around, keeping an eye on the artists, proud of their achievements, wary of their volatile tempers. "Don't stand and chatter like chipmunks," she chides Belkin and Dimitri, who are in the midst of a heated debate. "Mingle and converse with others."

Rosa Koristanova is missed, Darya thinks. She became an important member of the salon, policing the artists, demanding order, creating sculptures that were acquired by the most reputable museums. But nothing could save the sculptress from her raging emotions and infatuations that catapulted her into the depths of madness.

She fell in love with every block of stone she worked on, every sculpture she created, but most of all with Joseph and his photographs.

One afternoon, after Joseph told her to mind her own business, she left the Portrait Hall, found her way into the palace kitchens and was about to plunge her head into a pot of bubbling oil. The chef grabbed her from the back. It took two men to restrain and transport her to the infirmary. After extensive medical tests, Dr. Botkin diagnosed her with cyclical madness, a chronic, severe, and debilitating brain disease that rendered her dangerous. No choice was left but to institutionalize her.

Now, Joseph is telling Avram about his visit to the Livadian asylum, where he had photographed Rosa. Evidence enough, at last, to prove that the shape of a head has nothing to do with madness. "The woman is mad. Mad as a rabid dog! Yet the shape of her head is like mine and yours. Are you listening, Bensheimer?"

Catching sight of Darya, he says, "Yes, my friend, your point is well taken. Well, I will be off for now. See you later." He wends his way toward her, steering her away from the crowd. "You look especially beautiful tonight. Why did you miss the ceremony?"

"Alexei had a small accident. I'm terribly worried."

"Not again! What happened this time?"

"He fell. I've a lot to tell you, Avram. Pray to God for Alexei's health."

"I always do, my Opal-Eyed Jewess."

She touches him lightly on the arm and then quickly tucks her hands under her beaded wrap. The name he gave her has taken a different meaning tonight. Tonight, the syllables tumble like sweet bonbons in his mouth and melt like syrup on his tongue. Accept the title, the Ancient One had advised six years back. She does now.

"I'll wait for you at dawn, behind the chapel," he says, wondering whether a day will come when they won't have to meet like thieves under the gray blanket of dawn.

"I want to, Avram, I really do."

"I'll walk you down to the beach. Make love to you on the sand. Bathe you in the sea."

"I'll come then," she sighs, glancing at Alexei.

Russian nobility in gold braid and scarlet sashes and jewel-studded medals on their chests follow the Imperial Family through the Reception Room and onto the verandas, where dinner is served on center tables and a legion of white-gloved servants runs around on soft-soled patent shoes.

Lilies and violets burst out of giant Chinese vases set about balustrades. The perfect disc of a moon casts a burnished halo on the marble façade of the White Palace. The spectacular outline of the grand mountains looms over the Black Sea in the horizon.

The Emperor leads his wife and son to the head table, and then visits one table then another to keep the conversation lively. He returns to his radiant wife and animated son. "Alexei Nikolaevich, are you well? Your cheeks are flushed, son."

"It's hot, Papa. May I take off my jacket?"

The Emperor helps his son remove his jacket and hangs it behind his chair. "What a beautiful evening," he says, squeezing his son's arm.

The Tsarevich winces, jerking his arm away.

The Emperor discreetly removes his son's cufflinks, rolls his sleeve up, and raises his arm for inspection. He stares at the swollen elbow, the taut, darkening skin. "What happened?" he asks, the terror in his voice alerting the Empress.

The boy moves his arm up and down, twirls his wrist. "Look, Papa, no pain. Please, don't send me to bed."

At the sight of her son's inflamed elbow, the Empress's hand springs to her chest. Her lips are smiling, her face a mask of horror as she exchanges glances with her husband. Where is Darya? How could she have allowed this to happen? Neglected to notify them?

Darya is standing alone, not far from the imperial table, on guard, following Alexei's every move. In answer to the Empress's summoning forefinger, she makes her way to the imperial table.

The Empress points to her son's elbow.

Darya no longer hears the orchestra, the click of crystal flutes, Rasputin's flirtatious boastings at another table, or the high-pitched hyena laughter of the minister of agriculture.

"A moment to explain, Your Majesty. We were on our way to the chapel when Alexei fell. I should have let you know, but I didn't want to alarm you. I was hopeful I'd found a cure in a chunk of ambergris I found yesterday. I tried it on myself first. It cured a weeklong stomach affliction. I applied it on one of the gardeners as an antidote to snake venom. I've been studying…reading about ambergris, and I think, hope, it might modify the chemistry of the Tsarevich's blood. Please, Your Majesties, be patient."

"I am hungry, Mama," the Tsarevich declares.

"How did you apply the ambergris?" the Tsar demands.

"I added it to a potion the Tsarevich drank."

The Empress gasps, grips her chair's handles, attempts to rear-range her expression.

The Emperor's face turns the color of red brick. "You did what?"

"Ambergris is edible, Your Majesty. It was used for medicinal purposes in ancient times."

"Ancient times! Have you lost your mind? When did he drink this thing?"

"Two hours ago."

"Call Father Grigori to our table," the Empress says in a low, urgent voice.

Rasputin's drunken laughter can be heard from across the terrace, where he is seated with the artists. His stained linen shirt, rough peasant coat, and soiled worker's boots have been replaced with a red silk shirt with flowers embroidered by the Empress, a pair of fine velvet trousers, and kid leather boots. Around his neck glitters a heavy gold cross, a gift from the Empress.

The party is in full swing, the orchestra playing Stravinsky's

"Petrouchka," the dance floor bustling with the swish of bejeweled ball gowns and drunken feet.

Darya's stare falls upon the lapel of the Tsarevich. "Alexei Nikolaevich, what happened to your lucky charm? I pinned it to your jacket this morning. It was there on our way to the chapel."

"I don't know, Darya. Honest."

Her hands turn as cold as abandoned tombs. Did it fall off during the hillside accident? But she had checked the amulet. Its lock was sturdy. No, it couldn't have fallen off. It must be a conspiracy. The scheme of one minister or another to rob the Tsarevich of the little good fortune he possesses. Michael Radzianko, the president of the Duma, must have stolen it to hurt the Empress. He despises Rasputin and his influence on her. Or perhaps it was the work of Alexander Fyorovitch Trepov, the traitor. He is doing everything he can in the Duma to curtail the Tsar's unquestionable sovereignty.

The Tsarevich digs a spoon into the bowl of caviar and devours a mouthful. He then moves to borscht, samples pepper-pot soup, and asks for pheasant in cream sauce.

The Emperor raises his knife and fork, stares at the mushroom patties, roast goose, and rissoles in cream on his plate. He pretends to take a bite, then sets his knife down.

An extra chair is brought in for Rasputin and placed next to the Tsarevich. His unhinged gaze skips around from Darya to the Tsarevich to the Imperial Couple. He slurs his words, "At your service. Who may I help? The little one?"

The Tsar gestures toward his son's elbow. "Take a look, our friend, it is bad."

"I am here now," Rasputin tells Alexei. "Relax. It is good. I will be gentle."

The Tsarevich holds his arm up like a trophy. He moves his arm this way and that, touches his elbow to demonstrate that he has no pain.

Rasputin raises the arm, stares at it, passes his palm over the bruise. The fate of the three-hundred-year-old Romanov throne is in his hands. This is how history changes. How the world changes. With a story, a hypnotic gaze, a prayer. The blue eyes he directs at the Tsarevich widen, wider than usual. His lips move in silence. He runs his index finger over the fine embroidered stitches on his blouse. He can hear the swish of wine in his head. Smell the scent of caviar. Feel the weight of gold around his neck. Life is good.

In the horizon a violet dusk has replaced the specter of the setting sun, a deep purple washing across the Black Sea and turning it aflame. The heady scent of champagne and wine is in the air, the peal of laughter, the sigh of silk on the dance floor.

The Emperor raises his son's arm, shows it to the Empress, they exchange discreet glances. They lay Alexei's arm in front of them, hold hands under the table, and wait.

The swelling on their son's elbow is abating in front of their incredulous eyes. The bruised skin is becoming lighter, less inflamed, turning a normal hue.

Darya wipes her left cheek, directing her stare at her wet fingers.

Her opal eye has released a single pearly teardrop. A gift from a stubborn eye that has remained dry for eight years, refused to shed a single tear since her parents died.

The sky comes to life with colorful explosions of fireworks. Thousands of sizzling stars burst across the sky and sea. The orchestra is playing Nikolai Rimsky-Korsakov's "Flight of the Bumblebee."

The Tsar seizes a bottle of champagne from a waiter and fills Darya's flute.

Chapter Thirty

— 1916 —

After Five Years of Turmoil

DARYA STANDS CLOSE TO Avram, snuggling into the scent of paint and canvas that is part of the fabric of the man she admires and loves with a passion that has not diminished over the eleven years she has known him.

The artists have collected their paraphernalia, cleared their areas, covered their stations, and left for the day. In half an hour the help will arrive to wash and dust and polish, remove all traces of the day's work in the Portrait Hall.

Avram wipes his hands and drops his brushes into their wooden case. He wants to touch his lips to the translucent shell of Darya's ear. She is lost in thought, tense, a tear glistening in her eye. "Why are you sad, my Opal-Eyed Jewess?"

"It's the salon, Avram. I'm so disappointed."

"Disappointed! You should be proud. Its universal success has prompted the Tsar's cousins to establish salons like ours. They've invited our country's best artists to England and Germany."

At the mention of the British king and the German kaiser, the Tsar's cousins, Darya's tongue puckers with the taste of ash. That she is not fond of the two men, finds them indecisive and weak, is undeniable. What she is unaware of is that in less than a year, their loyalty to their cousin will be tested. And they will both fail miserably.

She wipes her mouth with the back of her hand. "I've something to tell you, Avram, and I don't want you to be angry with me."

He lifts her chin to gaze into her eyes. "When have I ever been angry with you?"

"When we argue about politics."

"But not for long. What grand scheme is cooking in your head now?"

"Not a scheme, Avram. I have bad news. I'm devastated."

"Nothing can be this bad!" he says, touching her on the cheek, his gaze reassuring.

She casts her eyes down, reaches out to touch him, steals her hand back. She is churning inside, every muscle in her body aching, even her brain.

It is a gloomy afternoon, and the low gray clouds are creeping into the room. The light filtering through the sheer drapes is the color of stained silver.

"This was our last salon meeting, Avram."

"No! But why? You worked so hard for its success! I don't believe it."

"Things have changed, Avram. The salon has changed."

He looks her in the eyes with a razor-sharp gaze that slices through her heart. "And why is change suddenly bad? This is our only remaining sanctuary these days. Don't do it, Darya. Don't be foolish."

"Avram, please, it's not entirely my decision. But it's the right thing to do. We can't expect the Imperial Family to tolerate a forum for political debates in their own home. The salon has become a den of antimonarchist sentiments. Dimitri, whose promonarchy caricatures earned him a place in the salon, has gone wild. Have you seen his last one? The Tsar and Tsarina in the lap of Rasputin! No shame left, Avram, none. And I'm told that Igor Vasiliev's last ballet has been sold to the Bolsheviks, some subject about a German spy becoming a Russian Empress and falling in love with a bearded madman."

Why in the world did she not heed the subliminal message of Igor's ballet *The Red Aurochs*? It was there, right in front of her eyes, the hated Bolshevik color red, the violence, the war between the red and white factions. Did it have to take her nine years to acknowledge the seed of suspicion that was planted in her mind that evening at the Mariinsky Theater?

Avram's fingertips tease out the baldachin ruffles around her collar. "You chose popular artists, encouraged them to speak out. Now you want to shut them up."

"I was naïve, didn't think they'd turn against the monarchy. Please understand, Avram. We've suffered five terrible years." Darya thinks of how only twelve members remain in the newly formed provisional government, ruling by default. How they continue to draw new legislatures to further curtail the Tsar's power and freedom. Internal uprisings are tearing the country apart. The army was forced to call fifteen million farmers to the front. The war began with twenty thousand locomotives. Ten thousand or less are left. It is one of the most brutal winters Russia has suffered. Twelve million men have been mobilized. One million, perhaps two million, have perished. The wounded are too many to count. "The last thing we need, Avram, is another group of insurgents inside the palace."

"It's tragic, Darya, tragic! But if we won't have art to remind us of our human side, what will? Send Dimitri and Igor away, if you have to. They are the radicals, the ones inciting hysteria! Don't punish everyone. Alexandra wanted us to achieve great honors for Russia. We kept our side of the bargain. Keep yours!"

"I am on your side, Avram. Please, please don't be angry with me."

"Then show some backbone. Let the truth win, not the Tsar and his cronies."

"But I am one of them too. I can't turn my back on them. I'm sorry, Avram."

He steps closer, the feline lines of his body menacing. "Leave them, Darya. Come away with me. I don't want to hide forever, meeting you like a thief in the dark."

"You are breaking my heart, Avram. You know I can't do that."

A muscle in his left cheek jumps. His stare is like a cold slap. He seems to be edging darkly away from her and there's nothing she can do.

He yanks out a box from his pocket, tears the wrapping, and snaps the top open. He tosses it at her feet. He holds her by the shoulders, tattooing her in his mind, turns his back to her, and storms out the door.

At her feet, nestled in the box, is a magnificent gold band of twenty-four translucent opals. The promise of a life with Avram Bensheimer. She slips the band on her left ring finger. She reaches her hand toward the door to demonstrate the perfect fit of the ring as if he is standing there, waiting for her to say yes, of course, I will.

The door swings open on its heavy brass hinges and in runs the Tsarevich, his cheeks trembling with the effort to check his tears.

"What's wrong, Loves?" she cries out, rushing to him.

"Where have you been, Darya? I looked for you everywhere. Mother is upset. Very sad. You have to tell Papa to come back."

"We are all sad, Loves, very sad." How is she to explain to a twelve-year-old-boy that a two-year war with Austria and Germany has caused a shortage of food, fuel, ammunition, and the failure of the railroads to transport much-needed supplies. How is she to explain to the boy that his father, intending to raise the morale of his soldiers, has abandoned the capital to go to the front, leaving his people to fend for themselves. How is she to explain that every developing disaster is attributed to him now?

Internal peace has eluded the country since the inception six years ago of the Duma, the elected parliament that the Tsar so reluctantly granted. The Right remains furious about the weakening of the autocracy, the Left fears that the revolution will lose its momentum, the liberals do not trust the Duma, the masses are hungry and confused, and the police, having been stripped of power, encourage violence.

In the absence of the Tsar, the politics of the country are in the hands of the Empress and her wandering moujik, Grigori Yefimovich Rasputin, who evaluates ministers and provides baseless, ineffective political and military advice.

And the country, unaware that the Tsarevich suffers from hemophilia and that the Empress regards Rasputin as her son's savior, sees only a drunken imposter and womanizer who is allowed free access to the palace.

Darya gathers the Tsarevich in her arms. "Promise to take good care of yourself, Loves. You will rule our country one day. Will you promise me? Good! Come, I need your help. Your mother will listen to you. You must convince her to send Rasputin away. He's causing too much trouble. Once that's done, she has to send a telegram to your papa and ask him to come home. Are you up to the challenge?"

The Tsarevich buttons his jacket. "I'm ready, Darya. Let's go."

The Lilac Boudoir is dark. Drapes are drawn. The odor of putrid flowers and burning wood is overwhelming. A single floor lamp casts insipid shadows over the furniture, the vacant sofa, the Empress's curiously tidy writing desk, not a single half-written letter, not a pen or inkwell in sight.

They hurry out the door and take the grand staircase down, trailing the acrid odor leading them into the Red Living Room. The room is half-dark, silent, the unlit chandelier swinging like a bejeweled ghost. Flames roar to life in the fireplace, licking the blackened walls of the enormous grate. Morbid shadows flatten themselves on the ceiling and dance around the chandelier.

The Empress is hunched in a chair by the fireplace, huddled inside a powder blue robe, a heavy shawl wrapped around her shoulders.

Darya runs to her side. "Your Majesty, what are you burning?"

Alexandra Feodorovna leans back in her chair. She wipes her red-rimmed eyes with an embroidered handkerchief, gestures toward a pile of letters her husband sent her throughout the years. "Setting fire to my memories. I read and re-read them a thousand times, and then…" She tosses another letter into the flames, watches it curl back, the edges bursting into tiny fireworks, into ash. "There! Another memory. Gone!"

"Your memories are in your head and your heart, Your Majesty. But why are you burning your letters?"

"I have news from our friend. It is not good."

An icy tremor scurries up Darya's veins. She steps farther away from the fireplace, wraps her arms around herself. Her past life was revealed to her five years before. But awareness failed to bring relief, shield her from punishing fires. Was it not enough that she was blinded for her sin, burned at the stake? Does she have to suffer anew with every fire, suffer this agonizing chill in her bones? And now, to add to her misery, the survival of the monarchy itself is threatened. "Save some letters, Your Majesty, in case—"

"Of a trial? Yes. Sad, isn't it, that we need to prove our patriotism with these." She carefully stacks a handful of letters from her grandmother and from the Tsar and tucks them in a leather-bound folder.

Alexei rests his hand on her shoulder. "Mama, ask Papa to come home. We need him here. He will make everything fine again."

"Good advice, Your Majesty," Darya encourages. "The Emperor is needed in the capital."

The Tsarina smiles at her son, strokes his hair. "I've been trying to get in touch with Papa. I'll send another telegram and hopefully we'll hear from him." She reaches out a trembling hand for an envelope on the side table and hands it to Darya. "Take a look, my dear, this just arrived. Our world is coming undone!"

Darya pulls out a yellow sheet from the envelope. She recognizes the boastful title, the cluttered script:

The Spirit of Grigori Yefimovich Rasputin-Novykh of the village of Pokrovskoe.

I write and leave behind this letter at St. Petersburg. I feel that I shall leave life before January 1. I wish to make known to the Russian people, to Papa, to the Russian Mother and to the Children, to the land of Russia, what they must understand. If I am killed by common assassins, and especially by my brothers the Russian peasants, you, Tsar of Russia, have nothing to fear, remain on your throne and govern, and you, Russian Tsar, will have nothing to fear for your children, they will reign for hundreds of years in Russia. But if I am murdered by boyars, nobles, and if they shed my blood, their hands will remain soiled with my blood, for twenty-five years there will be no nobles in the country. Tsar of the land of Russia, if you hear the sound of the bell which will tell you that Grigori has been killed, you must know this: if it was your relations who have wrought my death then no one of your family, that is to say, none of your children or relations will remain alive for more than two years. They will be killed by the Russian people…I shall be killed. I am no longer among the living. Pray, pray, be strong, think of your blessed family.

Grigori

The Empress folds the letter and slips it back into the envelope. "I am beside myself with worry. I sent dear Anna to deliver an icon to our friend. She tells me that he is invited for supper to Prince Yusupov's, to meet his wife. But there must be some mistake. She is in the Crimea, I am certain. Here, Darya, this is for you. Father Grigori sent it."

The Empress gestures to a small packet tied with rough twine on the table.

Darya considers leaving the pouch unopened, tossing it away in the Empress's absence, but the Empress's gaze is upon her, and the Tsarevich is peering from behind her shoulder. She pulls the knot open and rips the brown paper to find a small, roughly sewn bag, secured with a safety pin. She undoes the pin, widens the mouth of the pouch.

It is filled with some type of seeds.

What is Rasputin up to now, she wonders. What need does she have for seeds?

"Flower seeds," the Tsarevich offers.

"Lilies," the Empress suggests.

Darya pokes a finger in, stirs the seeds around. She finds a small, tightly folded note at the bottom.

"Read aloud," the Tsarevich insists.

Darya Borisovna Spiridova!

I wish for you to have these seeds for your garden. For your mind. And for your soul. Do not share them. Keep them somewhere safe until you need them. You will know when.

Grigori

"Let's plant them," the Tsarevich says.

"Alyosha, no!" the Empress admonishes. "Didn't you understand the note? They must be planted at the right time."

Darya plucks a few seeds out of the pouch, tests them between two fingers, raises them to her nose, inhales their pungent, spicy scent, tosses the seeds back in the pouch she drops in her pocket.

She is unaware that in less than two years, she will send a prayer of thanks to Rasputin for having had the foresight to send her these seeds.

Chapter Thirty-One

— December 31, 1916 —

RASPUTIN LEANS BACK IN Prince Yusupov's chauffeur-driven car as it navigates through the snow-heavy streets of Petrograd.

He is wearing the embroidered blouse the Empress gave him. His boots are polished to a high sheen, and his black velvet pants are new.

He lets out a contented sigh, digs his hand into his coat pocket and fondles the icon the Empress had sent him this afternoon. Too late to save him, he muses. His death is imminent, but not at the hands of his trusted friend, Prince Felix Yusupov. And certainly not tonight, when Irina, the prince's beautiful wife, is back in town for the sole purpose of meeting him, Grigori Rasputin. And why not? The homosexual prince who struts across the boulevards at night in his wife's gowns is hardly a proper lover for the stunning Irina.

Rasputin peers out the tinted window of the car at the reflection of the moon on the snow-covered onion domes of churches and on the frozen surface of the Moika River.

His supporters warned him against going out so late at night. It is not safe. The Duma has denounced him, after all, accused him of influencing the Tsarina's political decisions in her husband's absence. Perhaps he does. He believes in the maintenance of autocracy, believes in the monarchy. Members of the Duma don't like his accurate prophesies, nor his close relationship with the

Imperial Couple, which they consider a direct threat to their authority. They complained to the Tsar. Well! In return, the Tsarina, with his guidance, of course, responded by dismissing the ignorant ministers and introducing a legislature that further curtailed the power of the ones who remain in the Duma.

Now, he, Grigori Rasputin, holds audiences, gives advice regarding matters of state, and forwards problems to the appropriate ministers. He checks the plans of prospective war campaigns, suggests the right timing, and prays for the success of the Tsar. He makes the sign of the cross. This is a monster of a war. Too much bloodshed. Too many corpses to count.

He lowers the car's window. The biting chill everyone complains about has a way of banishing his petty concerns.

The yellow silhouette of Prince Yusupov's palace, like a grand ghost ship anchored by the Moika, rises up against the dark skyline.

Rasputin chuckles with glee. He cracks his thick-knuckled fingers. He is impressed. The gates, the car door, the tall, heavy doors to the palace, all swing open to accommodate him as if by invisible, welcoming hands.

He follows a cherub-faced servant through halls lined with dimly lit sculptures and antiques, down a flight of stairs, across a stone hallway, and into a cellar of low-vaulted ceilings and gray stone walls. A white bearskin rug is splayed on the granite floor. A silver samovar hums on a table covered with embroideries. Cakes are set in ornate plates, two Madeira bottles on a silver tray. A cabinet inlaid with ebony and cut mirrors multiply his jovial image. At the sight of a rock crystal and silver crucifix above the cabinet, he straightens his spine and crosses himself.

"Yankee Doodle" is playing on a Gramophone somewhere upstairs.

He remains standing, hesitant, pupils contracting, nostrils flaring to identify an unfamiliar smell.

Prince Yusupov steps out of the shadows. He is slender, beautiful in an effeminate way, his long lashes enhanced with mascara. He embraces Rasputin, kisses him on both cheeks. "Welcome, my friend. Make yourself at home. Here, please, come sit. My chef baked your favorite cakes."

"Where is your lovely wife?" Rasputin chuckles, unable to contain his joy.

"She's upstairs at a party. She'll be down shortly," the prince assures him with an exaggerated wink that shows off his long lashes.

"And your servants?" Rasputin asks. "None to serve us?"

"Irina gave them the evening off. Why tonight, I don't know."

But, of course, Rasputin thinks, Irina must have taken all precautions for their meeting to be intimate and confidential. She is the Emperor's niece, after all, and word of their meeting should not leak out. He settles down in a carved wooden chair in front of the cabinet, leans back, and rubs his hands in anticipation.

"Please enjoy some cake," the prince offers.

Rasputin reaches out for the tray of cakes, hesitates, then drops his hand back in his lap. "No, I must not spoil my appetite. Well… maybe one or two."

He devours two cakes. Drinks two glasses of Madeira. He asks for another. The tune of "Yankee Doodle" turns louder upstairs. He coughs, his unhinged eyes acquiring a ghostly pallor. He is having a hard time breathing. "You should avoid the cellar, Felix. This humidity is not healthy. Some tea to clear my head, yes? Thank you. Please sing for me, will you?"

The prince fetches his guitar that leans against a wall. He likes to flaunt his beautiful voice, but not tonight. He wants this to be over. He hugs his guitar to his chest, his fingers strumming feverishly, his feminine voice filling the cellar. He sings song after song, one melody after another.

Rasputin's eyes feel disjointed in their sockets, his head becomes as heavy as lead, his breathing shallow. Perhaps he had too much Madeira, he thinks. He pours himself another cup of tea, drinks the hot liquid as if he is immune to heat. He drinks another cup. He is feeling better. He smiles, snaps his fingers, taps his feet, sways to the strumming of Yusupov's songs.

The prince's vocal cords are raw, his fingers ache. He glances at the monk. "Another glass of Madeira?"

"Tea perhaps. Don't stop, Felix. I love your songs."

Felix puts his guitar down. "Excuse me for a minute, I will be right back." He leaves the cellar and climbs the stairs two at a time to find his cronies. They have abandoned their idea of simulating a party and now huddle upstairs on the landing.

"What's happening downstairs? Why are you singing?"

"He is still alive!" the prince whispers urgently. "What shall we do?"

Lazovert, who already fainted twice from fear, slumps down again.

"We better drop the plan and go home," Grand Duke Dmitry suggests.

Purishkevich, the most senior and most levelheaded of the group, reminds them that they cannot afford to leave the half-dead Rasputin here.

"But you don't understand. He is not even half dead," Yusupov utters, rubbing his hands in desperation.

"Did he eat the cakes…drink the Madeira?"

"Yes, yes, many," Felix replies urgently.

"But it doesn't make sense. They have enough cyanide to fell a stable of horses."

"He is immune to poison. Something else must be done. Hurry, think, think…"

The men exchange glances, curse under their breath.

The prince adjusts his cravat, squares his shoulders. "Very well then, I will finish the job."

"Where did you go, Felix?" Rasputin complains as soon as Yusupov returns to the cellar. "Pour me some more wine." He has put Irina out of his mind and has other plans for the night. "What do you say we visit the gypsies?"

Felix positions himself in front of Rasputin. Hands behind his back, he observes Rasputin's face to see what it registers. Fright? Confusion? But all he sees is a drunk. No! Not even that, the man is just slightly out of sorts. He is nodding to signal for more wine.

"Look up at the crucifix on top of the cabinet, Grigori."

Rasputin leans forward, rests his chin on his hairy hands. "I like the cabinet better," he proclaims. He checks himself in the mirror, rearranges a wisp of gray hair, pushes it back, raises an eyebrow as if questioning his image. Something shatters upstairs. The thumping of footsteps on stone. Silence!

"Grigori Yefimovich, you better look at the crucifix and say a prayer."

Rasputin's eyes dart up to the crucifix then back to Yusupov.

The prince is aiming a Browning revolver at the monk.

Two shots echo around the cellar.

Rasputin lets out a savage scream. His entire body bounces out of the chair like a loosened coil. An instant of hesitation, as if wondering which direction to take, where to go from here. He topples backward onto the white bearskin rug.

Yusupov stares at the smoking revolver in his trembling hand. He stands over the prostrate body at his feet. Rasputin's eyes are open, his sizzling gaze aimed at his murderer. What type of a person, the prince wonders, could be immune to such large amounts of alcohol and poison? For a frightful moment there, he thought he might be immune to bullets too.

The prince's cronies burst into the cellar.

"He is dead!" Yusupov shouts, "Dead, at last!"

He tosses his revolver onto the table. It crashes against the bottle of Madeira and shatters it into small pieces that scatter. He succeeded, at last, succeeded in eliminating the mad monk intent on destroying Russia and her three-hundred-year-old monarchy.

He kneels down, checks Rasputin's corpse that seems to be made of iron and steel. How else could it have endured so much cyanide? Yusupov bends closer to the corpse. Plucks out a shard of crystal embedded in the right cheek. A drop of blood bubbles out of the wound. Yusupov's lips part in a self-congratulatory smile. He turns to his conspirators. "Look, the mad monk is made of flesh and blood, after all. All right, think now, what shall we do?

We have to get rid of him before the police come. Go upstairs and bring something to wrap the body."

He picks a napkin from the table and folds it around the piece of crystal, tucking it in one of the cabinet drawers, a reminder of his courage in the face of evil. The Duma will applaud him. The ministers will reward him. And the country will exalt him for his courage.

He lingers in front of the cabinet to admire his reflection in the cut mirrors, pats his pomaded hair into place, wets two fingers with saliva, and passes them across the length of his lashes. He steps back and congratulates his image in the mirrors. "Well done, Felix. Bravo, my boy!"

Two hands seize him from behind. Grab his throat and begin to squeeze.

"You bad boy," Rasputin whispers in his ear, his venomous eyes staring from the mirrors.

The prince jerks back. Struggles with all his might. He is not a strong man. He can't breathe. His lungs are bursting. He is going to die. Die by the hands of this madman!

He bends one foot back and kicks Rasputin in the crotch. He breaks loose with a series of coughs, sprints out of the cellar and up the stairs. "He is alive. He is getting away!"

Rasputin scrambles on all fours up the stairs behind the terrified Yusupov, who dashes into the safety of his parents' apartments. Rasputin crawls ahead, toward the front door, into the snow-covered courtyard and the gate. He pulls himself up, grabs the gate's lock. His voice tears through his throat. "Felix! Felix! I will tell everything to the Empress!"

A shot shatters across the night. Then another shot.

Purishkevich stands at one end of the courtyard, a revolver in his right hand. His left fist is stuffed in his mouth.

He has missed with both shots.

He bites hard on his hand to stop the trembling. Another three steps and Rasputin will escape. That will certainly be the end of them all.

A third bullet lodges in Rasputin's shoulder. The fourth finds his head.

Rasputin circles around himself like a dog chasing its tail. Blood spurts everywhere: on the bricks, the gate, the snow-covered courtyard. He topples backward onto the snow, a bloody hallow seeping around his prostrate body.

Purishkevich approaches the twitching body. Aims a hard kick at the temple. Grinds a boot into the face. Another hard kick between the legs, then another and another.

The hysterical Prince Yusupov runs into the scene. His face is blotched, cheeks smeared with mascara. He begins to batter the body with a club to the head, the stomach, between the legs until no sign of life is left of the man who had all but ruled Russia for the last few tumultuous years.

The men roll the body in a blue curtain and secure it with ropes. They take turns checking the knots, pulling, tightening, and fastening from all sides. They step back to observe their work. This is it, they think. Never again will the monk rise.

Torches in hand, they sneak through dark back alleys. The sky is a metal sheet overhead, the packed snow slippery underfoot. The alarming crunch of sleighs and carriage wheels can be heard in the distance. They stop every now and then to catch their breath, to curse the heavy load they carry like a rolled carpet on their shoulders.

They reach a secluded part of the Neva. Drop their load on the snow by the riverbank, stand back and gaze at one another.

Tall gas lamps cast a gloomy glow around them. At this time of the year the ice over the Neva is dense, troikas cross the river back and forth, people ice skate on the surface. How in the world will they manage to break the ice? The desperate Yusupov sticks his torch upright in the snow and falls exhausted to his knees, his vaporous breath coming out in gasps. Church bells chime in the distance. Not much time left before daybreak. One of the men stomps snow off his boots, rubs his hands, and blows out a cold plume of steam. "Let's break the ice."

"With our bare hands?"

The prince turns his torch upside down. The flame sputters and dies as soon as it comes into contact with the ice.

Purishkevich reignites Yusupov's torch with his own, gathers the other torches, and groups them together like a small bonfire. One torch is saved in case of emergency. He kneels and carefully brings the flames to the ice, pulling away before the flames go out, repeating the process again and again, and reigniting the torches when necessary. A shallow pool of ice water appears at his feet. The men surround him, a barrier against the rising wind as he stomps his boots on top of a small area in the ice that heat might, or might not, have thinned somewhat. They gather closer, pounding with their boots, soft kid shoes, Italian leather loafers. The ice moans under their feet. A thin crack appears. They attack it with whatever strength is left. The sun is rising on the horizon. Danger comes with daylight.

Purishkevich squeezes his hands into a narrow opening between two sheets of ice, scraping his skin. Blood worms its way into the ice. They all come down to help him, anchor their hands between the ice plates and push with all their might, forcing the ice farther apart, refusing to let go, well aware that they might lose their fingers when all is done.

They look down at the fissure they've created in the thick ice.

They slide the body to the edge and squeeze it through the crevice.

It will take three days for the body to be discovered.

An autopsy will reveal that the lungs are filled with water.

In the end, Grigori Yefimovich Rasputin did not die from poison or from bullet wounds.

He drowned.

Chapter Thirty-Two

— March 1917 —

THERE IS MUTINY IN Petrograd. Red banners flutter on rooftops and balconies. The roar of trucks and thump of artillery are constant. Large frenzied crowds populate the city, oblivious to giant-sized posters warning them to keep off the streets. Fists raised, red armbands flashing, they shout: "Down with the German woman! Down with the war!"

The Emperor scrambles to send reinforcements to the capital. But his diminished army, having suffered heavy military setbacks, is demoralized and useless. The Petrograd garrison, too, is unsuitable to fight back the sea of protesters. Sixty thousand of the Tsar's most loyal soldiers have joined the revolution. The elite Volisky Regiment and the legendary Regiment of Guards, founded by Peter the Great, refuse to follow orders. The entire country seems to be in flames: the Ministry of Interior, police headquarters, military buildings, even the Fortress of Peter and Paul with its arsenal of heavy artillery.

The events of Bloody Sunday twelve years ago ignited a series of revolutions that exploded into an irrepressible tidal force. Now, the entire country is a boiling pot of dissent. The Duma and the Petrograd Soviet of Workers' and Soldiers' Deputies have formed a provisional government, demanded the Emperor's voluntary abdication in favor of his son, with Grand Duke Michael Alexandrovich as regent.

The provisional government decided to sacrifice Nicholas II in order to save the Romanov dynasty.

The Emperor signed the documents that would pass the throne to his twelve-year-old son.

After bidding his troops farewell at Mogilev, the Tsar boarded a train that brought him to Tsarskoe Selo, where his wife and children are at the mercy of the provisional government and under house arrest in the Alexander Palace.

He buries his face in his wife's lap. His sobs can be heard across the palace corridors, in the rooms of the valets, by the aides-de-camp, and in the park, where revolutionary guards keep watch under the windows.

"Did you hear, Sunny? Did you hear what happened?"

She squeezes his icy hand, holds it up to her cheek. "You did the right thing, Nicky. You made the right decision. My poor dear, all alone out there. You showed such courage. You will become the proud papa of a Tsar one day."

Nicholas lifts his head from Alexandra's lap and directs his bloodshot eyes her way. "Sunny, I don't think you heard everything."

She dries his cheeks with the hem of her skirt. "So many rumors, Nicky! I don't know what to believe."

His face is bleached of color as he struggles to recount the recent events, to justify them to his wife. "Listen to me, Sunny. After I signed the papers, abdicating in favor of Alexei, I had six long hours to think. I summoned Dr. Fedorov. We had a conversation. He reminded me that there was no cure for hemophilia. That Alexei will always be subject to internal bleedings. He won't be able to ride horses, travel long distances, do anything that would stress his joints. Never grow to be a strong, healthy leader."

"Oh, Nicky! What do the doctors know? A cure will be found. Our son will become strong. He will rule our country."

"That's what I thought, Sunny. But Dr. Fedorov convinced me that the danger of exile loomed, and not to the Crimea."

"No, Nicky! It will never come to that. Our people love us.

They'll fight for us. The riots are temporary. I promise you. We are not leaving our homeland!"

"But if it does happen, Alyosha's upbringing and fragile health would be left to strangers. He won't survive. I had to think like a father. I was certain you would agree. So, a few hours after signing my abdication, I drew a different manifesto. I named Michael Alexandrovich as our Tsar. He is in the prime of his life, trained with a view to his possible succession."

Alexandra lifts herself to her feet, goes to the window. Her stiff back is turned to her husband as she struggles to collect her emotions. At last, she turns to him, her face aching, her voice low. "But it must be temporary, Nicky. Michael will abdicate when Alexei comes of age."

Nicholas holds his head in his hands. "This is not the end, Sunny. I sent a telegram to Michael in Gatchina. Explained why I took this step. Congratulated him. He immediately left for the capital. But rather than being welcomed, he faced fierce opposition. I suggested he meet with ministers of the provincial government to find a solution. But he was told that his life was in danger. Our people don't want us, Sunny. They don't want the Romanovs. They want a republic. Michael abdicated too."

"No!" Alexandra's head is tilted like a broken question mark. "Misha wouldn't do that."

"He did, Sunny."

She pushes papers and writing paraphernalia off her desk, lifts the imperial basket of jeweled lilies of the valley. Gold. Diamonds. Pearls. Worthless rubbish! She drops it on the table. A pearl gets detached from the basket and rolls onto the carpet. They might as well have this too, the heartless fools who are robbing her of everything dear.

Nicholas is squeezing his temples. "I'm sorry, Sunny. I didn't think separation from our son would be an option."

"Of course not, Nicky. And I want you to know that, whatever happens, whatever our future holds, you are far dearer to me as husband and father of our children than as a ruler."

The doors fly open and a revolutionary guard marches in, his boots leaving muddy imprints on the silk carpet.

Grand Duke Michael Alexandrovich appears at the threshold. The buttons of his military jacket are open at the collar. The medal of the Cross of St. George, the one he always displayed with great pride, is missing. He strides to his brother, embraces him. They hold each other, their eyes locked, all their emotions encompassed in their gazes.

A smoking cigarette dangles from the mouth of the guard at the door, standing watch over the brothers.

Alexandra pretends to look out the window. Her core is twisting with grief and fear. The absence of facts frightens her most. Where will they be tomorrow? The day after? How is it possible for their world to have collapsed with such speed?

A few fat raindrops land on the windowsill. A bird of paradise is huddled among the dappled leaves outside. Coarse laughter can be heard from somewhere by the gate.

Nicholas holds his younger brother at arm's length, unable to bear his haggard look, the deep pain on his young face, the silence that speaks more than any word.

Michael touches Nicholas's arm as if to hold onto him just a bit longer. He tugs at a button on his brother's coat. "Where will *you* go?"

"Our fate is in God's hands."

The Empress crosses the room and comes to Michael, crushing him against her chest, resting her wet cheek on his shoulder. She counts the seconds by the frantic beat of his heart.

He wipes her tears with his handkerchief. His forced smile is sad. "You'll have time to travel now. Enjoy the children. Nicky might even care for his teeth." Alexei runs in, his spaniel yelping at his feet.

Darya follows behind. "My apologies, Your Majesties. Alyosha wanted to say hello to Grand Duke Michael Alexandrovich."

"Come give your uncle a kiss, big boy," the grand duke says, then hugs the boy, kisses him on his forehead.

"But why are you crying, uncle?"

"Politics, big boy. Nothing to trouble yourself about."

"Is it because papa abdicated and I'm becoming Tsar?"

"No, not at all, big boy. I'm sure you'll make a great Tsar," Michael replies. Then he adds, "I don't know what to say. Everything happened so fast."

In the span of one horrific day his brother passed succession to his son as prescribed by law, and for a few hours the twelve-year-old Alexei became the autocrat of all the Russias. Then he, too, passed the throne to Michael Alexandrovich, who became Emperor for an hour before he was forced to renounce the already crumbling throne. The country was left at the mercy of the provisional government that is itself in disarray.

"We are all in a state of shock, big boy. It will be a long time before you become Tsar. We'll see what happens. What the future brings."

There is a heavy stillness in the room, the pungent taste of unspoken words. The biting odor of gunpowder makes its way from the windows. Grand Duke Michael raises Alexei's hands and plants a kiss on the back of each. "Be well, Your Majesty, take good care of yourself."

Michael turns on his heels and nearly runs out the door.

Chapter Thirty-Three

T HE MEDICINAL SMELL OF camphor and alcohol levitates inside the Alexander Palace. The sweet, tangy odor of the poultice Darya prepares from dried lemons, ground cloves, honey, turmeric paste, essence of chamomile, and sour oranges permeates the children's quarters.

Olga, Tatiana, and Alexei have all come down with the measles. Maria is delirious. She has developed pneumonia on top of measles, and Darya is rubbing the poultice to her chest.

Outside, in place of the imperial Cossacks, sentries march back and forth at the palace gates, their antimonarchist cries replacing the honking of swans and the trilling of birds of paradise.

Drunken laughter and pops of gunfire can be heard inside the palace corridors, where revolutionaries amble about in muddy red boots, march unannounced into bedrooms, and spew obscenities at the few servants who remain in the palace.

All telephone lines but the one into the guardroom have been disconnected, and the commandant rarely permits the Imperial Family to use that telephone. When they do, they must communicate in Russian, not French or English, and in the presence of a guard. All incoming and outgoing letters must remain unsealed. Food brought into the palace is inspected by dirty fingers, sampled, and the best is confiscated by the revolutionaries.

Only a handful of the Imperial Family's supporters—two of the Empress's friends, Count Benckendorff and his wife, two ladies-in-waiting, the children's two tutors, and Doctor Botkin—having refused immunity, remain in the palace.

A cup of warm passionflower and tincture of hawthorn in hand, Darya shuts the door behind her and walks across the corridor to Alexei's room.

"Where have you been, Darya," he asks. "Why can't we take the ponies out? When will the guards leave? What are they shooting at out there?"

She sits at the edge of his bed, takes his hand in hers. "I don't know how long they're going to be here, Loves. Not long, I hope. Before you know it, everything will go back like it was before."

How is she to tell a thirteen-year-old boy that members of the New Revolutionary Council of the village of Tsarskoe Selo are hunting the beloved family of deer the grand duchesses had tamed and fed for years? Or that Derevenko, the sailor and attendant who for ten years had been following the boy on his outings to make sure he does not have an accident, had fled at the first sign of trouble?

Darya hands Alexei the cup of elixir. "Here, Loves, it will help you to fall asleep."

She walks to the window, gazes out. Lost in thought, she twirls her wedding band around her finger, takes it out, toys with its opal stones, circling her forefinger around each smooth dome. It has become a habit of hers to glance out one door or another, one window or another, expecting Avram to amble through the gates with his feline stride and lopsided grin, expecting him to appear as unexpectedly as he disappeared eight months ago. Was it unexpected, his leaving as he had? Perhaps not. He had loved her far longer than any other man would have patience to do. As for her, she can still feel the bounce of his pulse when she held his wrist, count the thump of life in his veins. "I'm waiting for you," she mumbles, her voice hardly audible.

She gasps, clutching the windowsill, bending out to take a better look.

A gang of rebels in makeshift uniforms clamber up the steel turrets surrounding the grounds.

"Stop them!" she calls out to the palace guards. "They've no business here!"

The disheveled, unorganized guards glance up, offer her an indifferent smile.

Why, Darya wants to shout, did the imperial Cossacks turn their backs on their Emperor? Where was their devotion? Their vow to serve their monarch?

The rebels jump down into the park, come scrambling around the circular driveway. They skip around like possessed monkeys, raising their fists and shouting antimonarchist slogans.

"Shame on you!" Darya calls back. "Go away!"

"Come down from your throne, woman!" they yell. "Come down for a good fuck!" They grab their crotches, double over with laughter.

The young leader of the intruders keeps pushing away the mane of curly hair flopping over his face. His large brown eyes seek Darya with a mixture of reverence and curiosity. He cups his hands around his mouth and shouts, "By orders of the Soviet, we are here to take the Romanovs to the Fortress of Peter and Paul."

Darya steps back and shuts the windows.

Alexei has fallen asleep, his bed scattered with the collection of his miniatures.

She runs out and takes the steps down to Count Benckendorff, grand marshal of the court and the man in charge of the Tsar's safety.

"Sir, at least fifty men broke into the grounds. They want to take the Tsar away. Do something, please."

"I am trying, my dear. Trying very hard," he replies, his eye misting behind his monocle. "It is anarchy, I'm afraid. Go back to the children. Say nothing to the Imperial Couple."

Count Benckendorff straightens the lapels of his jacket, tugs at his handlebar mustache, passes a palm over his bald head. Every day a different group of self-proclaimed revolutionaries descends on the Alexander Palace. Men who are not answerable to a higher authority, free to abuse their newfound power, men who refuse to leave unless their unreasonable requests are met.

He steps outside, marching toward the young leader. "Gentlemen, it is unacceptable and unnecessary to intrude upon the family like this. I beseech you to leave immediately."

"Good day!" The leader raises his hand in a semblance of a salute. "Where is his Imperial…I mean…Romanov?"

"In the palace. The provisional government has him under strict house arrest. You have my word that he is not going anywhere. That small fenced-off area out there is the only open space he is allowed to walk around. He poses no danger. Kindly leave."

The leader wipes sweat off his forehead with the back of his hand. "It has been concluded that an inspection must be conducted. Right away!"

"An inspection?" Count Benckendorff asks, a muscle jumping in his left cheek. "Of what?"

"Of the deposed Romanov."

"To what purpose?"

"That is *our* business!"

Despite the cutting cold, Benckendorff's face breaks into a sweat. He turns on his heels and enters the palace that was once fragrant with lilac but now smells of the letters and satin-bound diaries the Tsarina destroyed in the fireplace.

Count Benckendorff steps into the study. Nicholas is sitting behind his writing desk, his head of graying hair in his hands. A thin film of dust covers the desktop. Benckendorff draws a painful breath and quietly shuts the door behind him. He clicks his boots and salutes formally.

The Tsar raises his head. He is haggard. Dark circles frame his eyes. "No need for such formalities," he says with a sad smile.

Benckendorff holds on to his formal posture. "Your Majesty,

another group of rebels has broken into the palace. They will not leave unless an inspection is conducted. I await your orders."

"An inspection?" Nicholas's eyes dart around the room. "Of what?"

"They want to inspect Your Majesty. Brute curiosity, I suspect. I apologize."

"A dethroned Tsar on display like some circus curiosity. Somewhat humorous, don't you agree? But you are not to blame, my dear man. It was my decision to abdicate, and I shall comply with their demand. Tell them I will be down in fifteen minutes."

His eyes burning, Benckendorff leaves the room to order the few remaining officers left in charge of the Tsar to post themselves along the corridor walls so as to buffer him from further insult.

Fifteen minutes pass and Nicholas Alexandrovich Romanov appears at the top of the stairs.

Hands clasped behind his back, he descends the stairs with the calculated precision of a commander in chief. The silent hallway is brightly lit, the odor of sweat and fear stinging. He paces the hall in front of the young revolutionary and his men, back and forth, back and forth, taking great care to slow his steps. He takes solace in the conviction that he is suffering this humiliation for the sake of protecting his family.

He comes to an abrupt stop in front of the leader and raises his eyes to meet the man's. "Why, my friend? What have I done?"

The young leader clears his throat, coughs twice. He is a common man with no political aspirations, a man at the mercy of his empty stomach. But now, face to face with the dignified Nicholas, he wants nothing more than to pray for the Emperor's health, to fall on his knees, and to ask forgiveness from the once omnipotent Tsar, who receives his authority from God.

The leader steps back, clicks his boots. He is about to salute the Tsar but thinks better of it. He turns to his men, his voice loud, cracking at the seams. "Citizen Romanov is not going anywhere!" he announces.

Chapter Thirty-Four

C OMMANDANT VASILIEV, THE LATEST revolutionary assigned
by the provisional government to watch over the palace, is
unable to sleep. His bladder is full, but he is having a hard
time giving up his warm spot under his coarse blanket. He checks his
platoon of five men, fast asleep under blankets around him. They are
volunteers—Chechens, Tatars, and Daghestanis—hard to discipline,
but strong, effective fighters, and accustomed to this brutal cold. An
unexpected winter snowstorm arrived out of nowhere, taking them
all by surprise; snow so heavy, it weighs down his eyelashes.

The commandant inspects the ashen sky, the sinister outline
of the Alexander Palace not too far off, the man-made pond, a
frozen, dark stain in the distance.

A movement behind bushes catches his attention. He jerks the
blanket off, sprints to his feet, his rifle aimed at the snow-covered
bushes. He lets loose a volley of bullets.

A family of rabbits scrambles out, dispersing into the night.

His men, awakened by the excitement, burst into laughter that
travels through the park and echoes in the grand square, where
Catherine II once watched her regiments march in parade.

"Form a line!" Vasiliev shouts. "Follow me! Bring your backpacks. What are you waiting for? It's time to take back what the
Romanov bastards stole from us."

A small, bony man with a skeletal face, Vasiliev twists his handlebar mustache into nervous knots as he reflects upon the treasures these vast imperial gardens might yield, a wealth of forgotten knickknacks that would fetch good money in the market as Tsarist souvenirs.

Their boots crunching on the snow underfoot, the men march deep into the park, across lagoons, inlets, and canals. Occasionally Vasiliev rummages in his backpack, pulls out a bottle of vodka, and takes a swig.

He leads his men across the Marble Bridge with its blue and white balustrades. He touches the tip of his pointy nose, bends it down toward his chin. Which path should he take? He flips a coin, decides to take the narrow path to the left that leads to an arbor with a four-sided granite pyramid. He holds one hand up. Signals to his men to stop behind the pyramid at the bank of a frozen stream.

He bends to brush snow off a marble slab, reads an inscription. He falls on all fours and begins to smash his fists on the marble. "Dogs! Dog tombs! What are you waiting for? Get to it! Destroy them! Bastard Romanov bitches."

The men attack the tombs with switchblades, rifle butts, and curses. They tie ropes around the broken corners and begin to heave and tug until the slabs break loose from their foundation. The earth underneath is wet and worm-infested. Vasiliev sweeps off a layer of soil with his boot, certain he'll unearth something valuable, a jewel or gold coin left with the dead to pay for transit to the other world. His boot catches upon something hard. He wiggles the tip until it snags the object. He carefully lifts his leg. The toe of his boot is stuck in the socket of a canine skull. He smashes his foot down. The skull shatters. Splinters of bone scatter. A sharp one lodges on the back of Vasiliev's hairy hand. He pulls it out and pins it like a medal of honor to his collar.

They reach the private island with its moving bridge, attack the metal joints, cables, and anchor, and smash the motor, rendering the bridge inoperable. They continue on their quest, deep into the park, leaving behind piles of smashed metal, marble, mud, and bleached dog bones.

Vasiliev's dark eyes narrow into greedy slits. He detects something red and shiny, poking out of the snow. He whistles, narrows his eyes, his mouth watering with anticipation. As silently and as quickly as a slinking cat, he thrusts his hand into the snow, closing his fist over his find. His back turned to his men, he unlocks his hand. On his palm gleams a miniature car, its steering wheels, spokes and studs, a tiny chauffeur, Nicholas and Alexandra in the backseat, everything intact, save for one of Alexandra's pearl earrings. Detached from its gold wire, it is buried in snow under Vasiliev's boot.

"A huge fucking ruby toy," he mumbles under his breath, dropping it into his coat pocket.

They continue their search, wander around the park, in and out of galleries, around leafless arbors and trellises, snoop into every nook and corner, uproot smaller sculptures, pile up deer carcasses hunted for food, and pilfer lilacs from the Empress's greenhouses to take home to their women.

Deep in the park, Vasiliev gestures for his men to halt again.

They are facing a small chapel.

The commandant aims his rifle ahead, taking a long time to assess the situation. He does not like the sense of eerie forlornness hovering over the place, the way steam curls out of its windows, the relentless way all types of hard-shelled and spike-legged insects hit themselves against the few intact windowpanes.

"What are you waiting for?" he yells to his men. "Come in!"

They are confronted by sad, condemning eyes in the damp chapel. Icons on shelves, on walls, painted on the ceiling. Sad eyes everywhere. A ghostly shaft of moonlight cuts a path through the broken glass of an upper window, illuminating a block of marble at their feet. Set flat in the ground in the center of the chapel.

The men are silent, paralyzed, afraid to breathe. They pull up the collars of their coats to shield their ears from the howling wind that forces its way inside. They do not fear God, or His saints, whose presence they certainly feel in this chapel. They are terrified of the mysterious man whose incriminating gaze is boring through layers of earth and stone, drilling its way into their chests.

They look down at Grigori Rasputin's grave.

Vasiliev yanks at his mustache. "What are you waiting for? Get to work."

The puzzled men shuffle in place. What is the order? What does their leader expect of them?

They have all heard about Rasputin's death. They know the Tsar's cousin murdered the monk, heard about the monk's prophetic letter. Like all Russians, they have lived to see his prophesies come true. They're afraid to disturb his grave, fearful that to do so might unleash his vengeance.

Vasiliev aims his rifle at the dark marble at his feet and fires round after round.

The men jump out of the way of bullets that ricochet off the headstone. They position themselves against a wall and continue to fire. One bullet after another pockmarks the marble slab.

Slowly, leisurely, like a geographical phenomenon that might take centuries to transform the shape of nature, veinlike fissures appear in the headstone and widen into arteries. A colossal groan shakes the small chapel and the arteries split to reveal an oak coffin in the ground.

"Pull his fucking body out!" Vasiliev shouts. "What are you waiting for?"

They jump into the grave. Struggle under the unexpected weight of the coffin. Curse with every unsuccessful attempt to haul it out of the hole.

"There's a rotting corpse inside, for heaven's sake, not lead," Vasiliev hollers.

More men step down to help. But the coffin refuses to budge.

Vasiliev jumps down to lend a hand.

As if Rasputin has been waiting for the commandant himself, the winds settle outside, the coffin shudders and sighs and reluctantly yields, at last, and is successfully raised and rolled out of the grave.

Covered with sweat and grime, the exhausted commandant sits on the coffin to catch his breath. He pulls out a nail clipper from his pocket and trims his nails. He is in a nasty mood. Why, he is not certain. It might be the cold. It might be the mere existence of the Romanovs. He licks his chapped lips and continues snipping his nails. He drops the clipper in his pocket, unfastens the dog bone and digs it between his teeth to dislodge leftovers. The wooden planks under him shift, a series of dry crackling pops. The coffin collapses.

Vasiliev falls into Grigori Rasputin's putrefied remains.

The men recoil from the stench, from the bones, some still sheathed in flesh. The matted long hair, the bared teeth in the grinning skull.

An ooze of indescribable color is bubbling out of the coffin.

Vasiliev crouches down, retching all over himself, drenching his coat with vomit. The stench is awful.

He straightens up, draws in a big gulp of air, wipes his mouth with his sleeve. He reaches out for an icon and a note tucked between the corpse's thighbones. He checks the icon, turns it around. It is signed by the Empress, a farewell gift to the monk:

My dear martyr, give me thy blessing that it may follow me always on the sad and dreary path I have yet to follow here below. And remember us from on high in your holy prayer. Alexandra.

Vasiliev crumbles the note and tosses it back into the grave with the icon. "Go outside! Now! Find logs to start a fire!"

The men spill out of the chapel. The cold is a welcome change from the putrid air inside. They scramble to fashion makeshift thongs from branches to gather a few of the scattered disintegrating remains in the chapel and pile them next to Rasputin on an intact slab of the coffin. They carry the plank with its load out and toss it on pine logs they gather from the many stacks around the park used for the palace fireplaces. Vasiliev empties his vodka onto the tinder. He tosses one match, then another, into the weak fire. The men step back. They wait. Fan the fire with their coats. The blaze will gather force.

But the instant the flames hit the wooden slab they sputter and die.

Vasiliev yanks down his pants. He aims a strong stream of urine at the fire. "What are you waiting for?" he shouts at his comrades. "Feed Rasputin! Feed him crude gasoline!"

The men hesitate, glance at each other, check their surroundings. Finding no other course but to follow orders, they aim their penises at the fire, attempting to encourage the flames with jets of urine the winds blow back in their faces.

A raging hiss rises from somewhere underground. Tongues of fire explode. Livid blue tips sparkle into millions of furious darts that bloom into a grand display of fireworks.

Rasputin is coming to life, his waist doubling over. He is sitting in the fire. His legs straighten, and what is left of his arms jerk down to propel him upright, his bottomless eye sockets aimed their way.

The terrified men spring away, scrambling to take refuge behind the trees.

"Come back!" Vasiliev orders. "Rasputin is dead! His tendons are shrinking in the heat, contracting his body."

One by one, the men reappear from behind the trees, their stares glued to Rasputin's corpse, which is recoiling and melting into itself. The relieved men pull up their pants, lock arms, and dance around the fire as it devours what the worms have left of the monk—hair, flesh, and bone—until nothing is left.

The commandant spits into the blaze, wipes his soot-blackened face. He is pleased. The mad monk is silenced, at last. "Well done!" he encourages his men. "Get the hoses and put the fire out."

The men scrabble around the park, collect hoses the gardeners have left unattended, and attach them to faucets. They attack the flames with powerful streams of water.

But rather than extinguish the fire, the water seems to feed it. They attempt to stifle the flames with snow and mud, then with their coats. But the inferno gains strength and momentum, climbing beyond the treetops and blinding them with ash and smoke.

An hour passes, and the priest in a neighboring chapel is awakened by the roar of fire and the wafting stench. Afraid that an unfortunate mishap might have struck the Romanovs, he drags himself out of bed.

Disheveled, the smell of mothballs emanating from his faded habit, a container of holy water in one hand and the holy book in another, he makes his way into the park.

"How can I help?" the priest asks in a birdlike stutter. "Is the Imperial Family safe?"

The commandant checks the priest's pockets to make sure he is not carrying a weapon. "They won't be," he says, "if you don't send up some prayers, do something, anything to put out this hell."

The priest retrieves a container from a paper bag, dips his hand in holy water, and sprinkles the flames, reciting the requiem once, then again and again, the repetitive act of a desperate man.

"Don't you see it's not working?" Vasiliev shouts. "Do something else!"

"And if thy hand offends thee, cut if off: it is better for thee to enter into life maimed than having two hands to go into hell, into the fire that shall never be quenched." Having said his piece, the priest hurls the container of holy water into the fire, turns around, and runs toward the palace.

An oily residue bubbles up from under the fire, a slimy liquid meandering around snow-heavy trees and bushes, slinking under thickets and dormant flower beds, snaking its way toward the Alexander Palace.

A sudden sense of horror, an unfamiliar emotion, shakes Vasiliev into action. He scrambles to gather his men and move them out of harm's way.

Darya is assaulted by the rising stench of burning flesh. A pillar of putrid smoke can be seen from every window, sulfuric plumes that spiral up and erase any demarcation between earth and sky.

She runs down the stairs and crosses the lower hall toward Count Benckendorff's bedroom. She bangs on the door. "Wake up, sir! You must call for help!"

A large squadron of fire fighters arrives at midnight. They toil for hours to smother the flames with water, salt, soil, and all manner of chemicals. With four-meter-long pikes they attempt to separate the fire into smaller, more manageable fires. But the flames join back like magnetic curtains. At dawn, defeated and drenched in sweat and soot, the firemen gather their hoses and tools. "The palace is in danger," one says quietly. "Evacuate the family."

A ghostly figure materializes from behind the forest of trees, ethereal in a sheer nightgown the shade of her pale face, her glowing eye cutting a path in the dark. She walks toward a petrified fireman, seizes his water hose with one hand, and waves him away with the other. Her hair darker than night, she secures herself against a tree trunk, the outline of her thighs fluid under her breezy gown. Hose anchored between her legs, she aims a strong jet of water at the fire, the hose twisting like a tortured being, the force thrusting her from side to side, her wet gown swirling around her slender figure, her hair flapping about her shoulders like so many raven wings.

The flames coil, twirl, and embrace like lovers in the throes of passion, changing color from cobalt to ruby to liquid gold. Without warning and without exhibiting any sign of losing its intensity, an enormous belch emanates from the fire.

The alarmed revolutionary soldiers flee into the park, abandoning their backpacks, knives, vodka, and stolen spoils.

Rabbits and squirrels scramble out of holes and bushes, their fur standing on end, their fleeing paws marking the snow.

The red bird of paradise flutters overhead, tempted to take flight behind the blanket of ominous smoke overhead, but instead it circles and settles on a frozen branch.

Rasputin's prediction that his corpse would be disinterred and his body tormented after death has come true.

Chapter Thirty-Five

Not long after the Big Fire, as the disinterment of Rasputin came to be known, hope arrives in the person of Alexander Fyodorovich Kerensky, the Minister of Justice of the Provisional Government.

The unassuming, clean-shaven man who has vowed to deliver the Romanovs to safety steps down from the deposed Tsar's automobile that has been selected at random from the imperial garage. At the wheel is the Tsar's chauffeur, who hurries to open the car door. He salutes Kerensky as if he were the Tsar himself, then leads him in through the kitchen door.

Wearing a blue buttoned-up shirt without cuffs, his right hand thrust into his jacket, Kerensky appears as uncomfortable as a peasant in Sunday attire. He is tense, abrupt, the creak of his boots announcing him at every turn.

He stops to assess the surroundings, his restless feet tapping. He talks loudly, incessantly, now to Count Benckendorff. "Assemble the soldiers of the guard, the servants, and every person who works here."

The count removes and inspects his monocle as if the solution to these never-ending horrors might be projected on the surface of the lens. He is caught in yet another thorny situation. Having no recourse, he scrambles to gather everyone in the hall.

But not the Empress, Alexei, or the grand duchesses. He will spare them the humiliation. Dr. Botkin, the chef, a few servants, even Vasiliev and his men, congregate around the new Minister of Justice.

Kerensky's voice can be heard throughout the palace, the salons, the Portrait Hall, the Red Room, and the dining room, where the Imperial Family is having lunch.

"You no longer serve your old masters. You are the servants of the people now. They pay your salary and expect you to keep your eyes open and report anything suspicious. Consider yourselves under the order of the Commandant and the officers of the Guard." Having ended his speech in this revolutionary manner, Kerensky addresses Benckendorff. "I am here to see how you live, inspect this place, and talk to Nicholas Alexandrovich."

"I shall put the matter before his majesty," Benckendorff replies curtly, having no intention of disturbing the family at lunchtime.

"A tour of the palace first," Kerensky says, running ahead like a squirrel with his tail on fire. He opens random doors, enters rooms, then rushes out again, as if unable to make up his mind why he entered the space in the first place and what he is searching for. He steps into the Emperor's private quarters, stands in the center of the room to assess the surroundings. He opens every drawer, inspects every corner with great curiosity, glances under the furniture, the large writing desk, the bookcase, shifts leather-bound books around to peer behind them.

Then, without warning, Kerensky turns to Benckendorff and addresses him in an uncharacteristically low voice. "The woman with the opal eye."

"Tyotia Dasha?"

"Yes, yes. I want to see her!"

"Allow me to inform her," Benckendorff replies.

But Kerensky is already marching into the hall, and Benckendorff is forced to run ahead and lead him to Darya's quarters.

"Pardon us," Benckendorff gestures to Kerensky, who marches

behind him into the room. "The Minister of Justice, Alexander Fyodorovich Kerensky."

Kerensky lifts a hand to the brim of an invisible hat.

Darya ignores his salute. She confronts him with her unwavering opal gaze.

The Tsarevich is at the other end of the room, watching a movie the Pathé Film Company gave him during better times. Darya had installed a projector she secretly took from the screening room, and a wall is used as a makeshift screen to project a scene of a royal entourage with liveries and dogs hunting for the legendary aurochs.

Kerensky coughs, shoves his hand inside his coat, taps his nervous feet, and turns toward the Tsarevich as if to put him at ease, then says, "Everything is going well."

"May the Tsarevich be excused, sir?" Darya asks.

"The *former* Tsarevich," Kerensky corrects with a frown. "He may leave. I need answers to some questions the party has."

"What could I add, sir, beyond what the party already knows?" Darya asks him after she shuts the door behind Alexei.

"A great deal, of course. You've lived with the family for more than twelve years. You're very close to them. But the family is a separate matter. This is about the Artists' Salon. Why was it terminated? What were the political inclinations of the artists?"

She digs her fingernails into her palms and struggles to keep her composure. "Are they under investigation, sir?"

"Yes, yes, they are."

"But why, sir?"

"For different reasons, among them, suspicious contact with the Romanovs and their close attendants. And there's the matter of a certain painting of the Tsarevich in the arms of the Madonna. The authorities have been searching for it. Where is it?"

"I know nothing about such a painting, sir," she replies, having no intention of guiding him to the Lilac Boudoir. "Why in the world, sir, is having a relationship with the Imperial Family a suspicious activity?"

"Please refrain from asking questions. The salon, in my understanding, was a façade for exploiting impressionable men and women into deceiving the masses with all types of bourgeois and religious art." He spits the last two words out as if he discovered a cockroach in his mouth. "And I have been told that the Madonna painting conceals political messages."

Darya smiles bitterly. "You have the wrong information, sir. The freedom and encouragement the artists received during that time was priceless. Do you know that *Murderous Gods and Their Victims* remains the Russian State Museum's most cherished acquisition? That sculpture was the work of Rosa Koristanova and was created right here in the Portrait Hall. And *The Red Aurochs* in the Mariinsky Theater was the longest-running ballet in our history. That, too, Igor Vasiliev shaped in our salon. I don't need to tell you, sir, about the international fame of Avram Bensheimer's portraits, I assume. So if giving birth to some of our most important contemporary art is a sin, then blame it on me, not the Imperial Couple. And as far as their political inclinations, if anything, the artists proved to be budding avant-gardes who found a forum to air their revolutionary ideas. That, I assume, would not displease you."

Kerensky gauges her with a suspicious stare. "You are fond of the artists, even more so than the Romanovs, it seems—"

"Of course not, sir," she interrupts. "It's just that I'm fond of art and what it has done for our country."

He glances at his watch. "Before speaking to you further, I ask that everything we say will be kept secret. Is that understood?'

The room is silent. The rumbling of an armored car can be heard outside the palace gates. Someone is attempting to haul the bridge over the private island, the metallic screech of its locks evidence of damage. Darya rests her hand on her heart. Her old scars refuse to heal; they throb and flare with every ignited memory of Avram. He had mastered the art of hauling that bridge with soundless speed and efficiency so as to startle neither man nor swan, nor deer, nor bird of paradise. Will the bridge operate again one day? Too tired to speak now, she assures Kerensky she understands his concern.

"An important resolution has been passed by the council of ministers. No one outside the family must learn of it. The family is to leave Tsarskoe Selo."

"Why, sir? Why? They like it here."

"Yes, I understand, but nothing can be done now. They will have to leave."

"Then perhaps they'll be allowed to settle in the Livadia Palace."

"No! The Crimea is too close to the capital. It will be dangerous. I am responsible for them and shall do everything in my power to send them as far as possible from danger. I don't want to become the Russian Marat," he says, referring to Jean-Paul Marat, the radical French revolutionary who was the cause of much bloodshed. "Our autocratic rule must be eliminated, no doubt, but without bloodshed."

Darya tries to swallow the lump forming in her throat. "Then send them to England, to the Tsar's cousin, if you have to. It's far enough."

Kerensky passes a hand over his full head of hair. "We will see. That is a possibility, it certainly is. Tell them to begin packing but do nothing to arouse any suspicions."

Chapter Thirty-Six

— August 13, 1917 —

"SAY BYE-BYE TO YOUR palace, *Gospodin Polkovnik!*" the oily-faced, unshaven Vasiliev shouts to the Tsar.

Nicholas II averts his eyes from Vasiliev's red armband. In the past months, Nicholas was called worse names than *Gospodin Polkovnik*—Mr. Colonel—and he will not react now, in front of his family congregated in the foyer, awaiting the train that will, according to Kerensky, transport them to safety, wherever that might be.

The Imperial Family has developed an odd friendship with Kerensky, who has made every effort to assure the provisional government of Alexandra's loyalty to Russia and has ordered the newspapers—*Russkoe-Slovo, Russkaia-Volia, Retch, Novoe-Vremia,* and *Petrogradsky Listok*—to end their campaign against her. Kerensky is not a bad sort, Nicholas thinks to himself, not bad at all.

Vasiliev raises his rifle and jabs the butt into the ribs of Nicholas II.

The startled Emperor groans and stumbles back a few steps, clutching his cane to break his fall.

Darya's hand flies up to her left eye. A crack is forming in the opal, a thin fissure in the center of the orb. For decades to come, every time she will gaze at her cracked opal eye in the mirror, she will be reminded of this shameful moment: the moment Russia lost her soul.

Vasiliev sneers, revealing his rotting teeth. "You, Citizen Darya Borisovna, unlike Mr. Colonel here, are free to go."

"Where are you taking my family?" she asks.

"None of your business! Grab your fucking luck and run!"

"To what do I owe this honor?"

Vasiliev holds up three fingers. "One! To the Big Fire you put out. Two! You have a way of scaring the fucking daylights out of my comrades, and they want you gone. And three! To rumors that you are an evil witch. So, go! Get the fuck out of here!"

Darya squares her shoulders. Crosses her arms in front her chest. "I will accompany Their Majesties to the end of the world."

Vasiliev doubles over with laughter. Finally, he straightens and sucks in his breath. The laughter is replaced by loud hiccups. "Well, well, Comrade Spiridova! Don't be shocked then if you *do* find yourself at the end of the world."

"Nothing shocks me these days. Not even the dreadful future inscribed across your forehead," Darya replies calmly.

Vasiliev's hiccups die in his chest. "And what is that future?"

"I see Rasputin's spirit looming over you, haunting you the rest of your life. I see you and yours forever burning in fires far worse than the Big Fire you experienced that night. I see your entire family—"

"All right! Stop this nonsense. Stay, if you're that stupid!" Vasiliev shouts as if reining wild horses. "Move! Collect your personal belongings. I'm talking to you, Comrade Spiridova! What are you waiting for?"

Darya hurries to her quarters, her most pressing concern the logistics of transporting the ambergris without attracting attention. Kerensky has promised to allow the family to take their portable valuables with them. But how is she to explain the ambergris without alerting potential thieves? She decides to divide the ambergris in two, stuffing the pieces into pillowcases she sews tightly. She places the pillows at the bottom of two suitcases and piles layers of clothing on top. She drags out a trunk from storage and sets it next to the suitcases. With the stubborn determination of a rebellious child, she crams the trunk with colorful clothes of all shapes, velvet and ermine and sable stoles, jewel-encrusted gowns with gossamer trails, the lightest embroidered damask skirts, and buttery kid gloves ordered by the Empress from Paris. Even if she is exiled to the heart of Siberia, Darya vows, where spit will freeze in her mouth and winters will snap her opal eye in two, she will make a point of flaunting imperial opulence that has become a thorn in the side of the revolutionaries.

The train that is supposed to transport the Imperial Family and its retinue to the unknown destination does not arrive. The sleepless night stretches into dawn. Boxes, trunks, and suitcases are piled outside the main entrance of the palace.

Dry-eyed, hair pulled back, Alexandra is seated in a chair in the foyer, Alexei's head in her lap. She tugs at a strand of hair tumbling over his forehead, pulling and coiling it around her forefinger. Every now and then, she attempts a sad smile at her daughters, who, huddled around her, doze off and on. They are beautiful young ladies. A world of possibilities await them. Olga is twenty-two; Tatiana, twenty; Maria, eighteen; and Anastasia, already sixteen. God willing, they would be allowed to settle in England with their British cousins, enjoy a peaceful life, wed, and raise their own families.

Darya sits on top of her trunk next to her suitcases. She grieves silently, bidding farewell to Tsarskoe Selo, to the twelve wondrous years she spent here, to the red bird of paradise that refused to flee the night of the Big Fire. But she is not ready to bid Avram farewell. The knot that binds them tightens with each passing day.

What will happen to him now? What will happen to all of them?

Kerensky is in the process of yet another endless argument on the phone, which was reconnected in the foyer for his personal use.

"Sir, where is the provisional government sending us?" she asks when he ends the call.

"To Tobolsk," he replies absentmindedly, his eyes bloodshot from lack of sleep. "The people of Tobolsk will not object to the family's move there. They remain loyal to Nicholas Alexandrovich."

"But for how long, sir?"

"Until the Constituent Assembly meets in November. Then you can all return here. Or go anywhere you like."

"When will the train arrive?"

Kerensky fidgets with his hands as if noticing them for the first time, thrusts one in his pants pocket, the other into the front of his jacket.

"They are not sending a train, sir. Are they?" she asks.

"The railway personnel are being hostile," he replies, turning on his heels and marching away noisily in search of the Emperor, who, hands clasped behind his back, paces back and forth by the main door.

"I apologize for the delay," Kerensky tells him. "But you have my assurance that the provisional government has guaranteed your safety."

"Thank you, my friend." Nicholas says, stepping out and gesturing to Kerensky to follow him. "I want you to know that you have done your best for us. And whatever happens in the future is the will of God."

The wail of an arriving train can be heard in the distance.

Nicholas offers his hand to Kerensky. "I feel tired and old these days and look forward to spending the rest of my life in peaceful anonymity with my family. I will pray for your success."

"The train is at the station!" Kerensky announces to the group inside the palace.

The servants are ordered to transport the trunks and suitcases to the station.

The morning sun struggles to penetrate the blanket of smoke that continues to cast a gloomy shadow over the village. Trees stand at attention like sentinels adorned with worthless medals. Ruby-eyed hawks take flight in the distance.

Inside, Olga and Maria awaken Tatiana and Anastasia, pat their hair into place, and tell them it's time to leave. Olga crushes a damp kerchief in her fist, turns her face away from her younger sisters, and attempts to swallow her tears.

Alexei has fallen asleep in his mother's lap, and his spaniel snores at his side.

Darya, eager for a resolution to this endless waiting, gently shakes him awake. "We're leaving, my Tsarevich. Say good-bye to your home. Take your time. Don't let the guards frighten you."

"Are you coming, Darya?"

"Of course I am. I'll always be at your side wherever you go."

The family and their entourage enter the automobiles that will transport them to the train station. Kerensky takes his seat in the imperial car at the head of the motorcade. Mounted Cossacks flank the retinue as the automobiles roar into gear and speed through the gates, spitting gravel across Alexander Palace, the imperial home of twenty-three years.

Count Benckendorff stands at the door to the palace, one hand raised in a formal salute, the other clutching a medal of St. Nicholas of Bari given to him by the Empress as a token of her gratitude.

He will remain behind to look after the personal affairs of the Tsar until the family returns—keeping the palace in order, paying the few servants staying behind, and assuring the remaining valuables and artwork are not plundered.

Chapter Thirty-Seven

— 1918 —

MIDNIGHT. DRENCHED FROM A continual drizzle, Olga, Tatiana, Anastasia, and Alexei huddle close to Darya, their trembling bodies seeking warmth from each other. They can hardly keep their eyes open from lack of sleep and fatigue from the long journey from Tobolsk to Ekaterinburg. The girls are scared, their aching legs trembling. A letter from their mother directs them to "dispose of all the medicines as had been agreed," a previously devised code and plan to bring along the gems they carried from Tsarskoe Selo to Tobolsk, which, having been ordered to depart on an hour's notice, the Imperial Couple were forced to leave behind. It took the girls several days to complete their task. Now, weighted down by their clothing heavy with diamonds, emeralds, pearls, and rubies sewn into them, they can hardly stand on their feet.

The wind smacks a burst of rain like gravel onto their faces. Darya wraps her arms around them. The thought occurs to her that the wretched Vasiliev might have been right in the end. After thirteen months of detention—five in Alexander Palace in Tsarskoe Selo and eight in Tobolsk—it appears they have reached the end of the world.

Nicholas, Alexandra, and Maria were transported to Ekaterinburg a month before. Unfit to travel, Alexei remained with Darya and his three sisters. Nagorny (the sailor in charge of carrying Alexei), Dr. Botkin, Kharitonov the cook, Troup the footman, and Leonid Sednev the kitchen boy now form a silent wall around Darya and the Romanov children.

The house looking down on them exhales a putrid breath. The façade's white stones, coarse with the city's violence and chewed up by time, are ominous in the dark of night.

"Welcome to the House of Special Purpose!" a revolutionary commandant—another of the many they have encountered in these months in exile—barks.

They are puzzled. What is the man saying? What is the House of Special Purpose?

Darya steps forward. "The last I knew, this was Ipatiev's house. What is the House of Special Purpose?"

He pokes a finger in his hairy ear to ease an itch. "Ipatiev is kaput! Gone! Ordered out by the office of the Ural Soviet!" He snaps his hand up in a mock salute. "Nicholas the Blood Drinker and his German woman are here now."

The house looks different, Darya thinks. With its window bars, painted panes, and surrounding high wooden fence, it resembles a prison rather than the handsome mansion it once was. Its first story overlooks the busy Voznesensky Prospekt. The second level faces a prominent hill in the distance on which the Entertainment Palace is perched.

She is unaware that fate will grab her by the throat soon and lead her back to the Entertainment Palace, where for year after long year, hundreds of butterflies will herald a new day and the aroma of Little Servant's coffee will force her out of bed. She is unaware that, made of a stronger mettle than she can imagine now, her relentless persistence and stubborn memories will carry her far into old age.

The revolutionary guard pulls back his lips, revealing a row of silver teeth. "Boy! Step forward for a thorough inspection."

Darya feels the girls squeeze closer to her, hears the rushing blood in their veins, the pounding of Alexei's heart, hears Joy, the boy's spaniel, skipping around and yelping.

Not once did she leave Alexei's side, not throughout the river voyage aboard the steamer *Rus*, nor at the Tyumen railway station when the commissar tried to separate her from Alexei, nor when Nagorny was there, able and ready to help. She carried the boy into the steamer's cabin, into the fourth-class carriage, all the way at the rear of the train. She is not about to part with him now. She glares at the commandant. He glares back. Her voice is sharp as a blade. "Search *me*, if you dare! Or step aside and let us in."

The commandant retrieves a smooth pebble from his pocket, turns it around as if his decision is inscribed in the stone. He bounces the stone from one hand to another, then drops it back in his pocket for later use. "You must be tired," he tells Alexei. "It's been a long night. All right then, go in, if you want. Your sisters will do." He rubs his cold hands. "Step forward, girls!"

Olga and Tatiana seem to diminish as if the heavy jewels are squeezing and shrinking them from all sides. The rain has gathered force, soaking their clothes, threatening to reveal the outlines of the precious stones.

Darya steps in front of the grand duchesses. Lifting her arms up toward the wet skies, she aims her cracked opal eye at the commandant, sucks her cheeks in, puckers her mouth, and spits out a burst of fire sparks at the man's face.

"Fire! Fire!" His shrill voice precedes him as he staggers back, slapping his face, his head, his ears. Lurching toward a muddy puddle, he plunges his head in as if his hair is on fire.

"Stop it, Darya," the frightened Alexei implores. "He won't let us see Papa and Mama."

"Don't worry!" Darya says. "I had to teach him a lesson, or he'd make our life miserable here." She bends and picks up some red seeds from the ground. "Pomegranate seeds I keep in my pockets for such occasions. I tossed them in my mouth when he wasn't looking. An innocent man would have acted differently."

She grabs her charges by the hand and leads them into the House of Special Purpose.

The summer months in the house progress to days of increasing horror. The occasional letters from relatives and friends in exile no longer reach the family. Local newspapers, which Nicholas once eagerly anticipated, even if few and far between, no longer arrive.

Their only source of knowledge is old newspapers wrapped around bread and eggs the local nuns send them, cut out magazines in the lavatory, a note from a friend concealed in a basket of fruit, but mostly stale information and rumors from the guards.

They learn that the German kaiser, cousin of Nicholas, facilitated the exiled Vladimir Lenin's entry back into Russia, and the man is wreaking havoc, encouraging uprisings, calling for all workers to take up arms. Civil war is raging, Red troops against White troops. No one knows who is murdering whom and who is winning the war.

The faraway rumble of artillery can be heard day and night.

The revolutionaries, afraid that someone inside the house might signal for help to a friendly White soldier or a monarchist crossing the Voznesensky Prospekt, do not allow the family to open any doors or windows and have coated the glass panes with lime, which traps the heat, turning the rooms into hellish furnaces.

Alexei is losing weight and spends most of his time in bed, Joy curled at his feet. His miniatures having been confiscated by Vasiliev at Tsarskoe Selo, he amuses himself with bits of wire, metal scraps, and a broken model of a ship.

The concoction of ambergris Darya rubs on his atrophying legs is not as effective in the absence of aged Livonian wine, sweet almond oil, vetivert, hashish, or ginger root. Desperate for a cure, she spends hours mixing whatever stale ingredients she finds in the kitchen—dried eucalyptus leaves, a clove of cinnamon, lemon peel, even salt—adding them to melted ambergris, until the pots and pans turn black and the smell alerts a guard, who marches in to order her out of the kitchen.

Alexandra and Nicholas hold classes for their children. They study the classics, practice French, discuss politics. The girls knit, crochet, embroider, or mend clothes.

They pray together—the family, servants, doctor, cook, and Darya.

They pray for food other than black bread and tea. They pray for an extra pair of boots for Alexei. They pray for the privilege of visiting the lavatory without being harassed and hassled by obscenities, without being assaulted by crude caricatures on walls of the Empress and Rasputin in appalling poses. But most of all, they pray for salvation, pray for the success of the anti-Communist White Army, pray that if any relatives and friends remain, they will hear their prayers and deliver them from this indignity.

And they all mourn together. They mourn Nagorny, Alexei's faithful guard who, arrested for having prevented another guard from stealing the boy's gold chain, was imprisoned and then executed.

They mourn when the revolutionaries celebrate the collapse of the provisional government that consisted of liberals from the last Duma. They mourn the fall of Kerensky and the rise of Lenin, who is systematically shattering their last hope of freedom.

They also celebrate together. Not birthdays. Those come and go without much fuss. The Empress turns forty-six, the Emperor fifty. Alexei is thirteen. They celebrate small daily freedoms. Being allowed afternoon walks in the garden, even if under the hooded eyes of the guards. Even if Alexei, all but crippled, sits quietly in a chair with his spaniel companion snoring at his feet. They celebrate walking, which oils their rusting joints. Nicholas wears his officer's coat, but the epaulets have been removed. Alexandra leans on a cane, her pulled-back hair almost all gray, deep lines framing her mouth.

They celebrate the blessing of being together.

Chapter Thirty-Eight

— July 16, 1918 —

YAKOV YUROVSKY MARCHES UP the stairs to the second level of the House of Special Purpose. His hands are deep in the pockets of his military coat, which is buttoned up to his chin, his mouth pursed tight. The bush of dark curls on top of his head, his thick eyebrows, and carefully trimmed mustache and goatee cast dark shadows on his thin face.

He stops outside Nicholas and Alexandra's room, the bedroom they have shared with their son during the five months they have been here. He stares at the door. He is not pleased. He is a member of the Bolshevik Secret Police, respects order, expects to be obeyed, yet despite strict instructions for all doors to remain open, this one is closed. Order seems illusive, although he has been in charge for twelve days now, after firing the previous inefficient commandant and his disorderly men.

He removes his left hand from his pocket. Knocks with a clenched fist. Steps away from the door before plunging his hand back in his pocket to stroke the hard, comforting coolness of his Colt revolver. He waits. Tugs at his coat sleeves. Whistles a tuneless war march under his breath.

The door is opened halfway. Nicholas peers out with alarmed eyes. Unwilling to awaken his wife and his sick son, he whispers, "Yes? What is wrong?"

"I apologize for the intrusion," Yurovsky replies with an exaggerated show of respect. "Because of the unrest in town, it's necessary to move everyone downstairs. It's dangerous to be upstairs while there's shooting in the streets. Please get dressed as soon as possible."

"New developments?" Nicholas asks.

"The White Army crossed into Siberia. They are regaining territory from the Red Army."

"Siberia is very large, my friend. It will take a long time for the Whites to get here."

"They *are* in the city," Yurovsky replies quietly, regretfully, discreetly.

Nicholas makes every effort to conceal his joy. It appears that the *thump-thump* of artillery, keeping them awake in recent nights, belongs to the White Army.

A note concealed in a basket of eggs the nuns sent them the day before yesterday brought news of the White Army's advance. But Ekaterinburg's geographical position deep in the heart of Siberia, and its large population of Bolshevik Reds, put the White Army in a difficult position, and victory seems unlikely.

Yet, tonight, the tall commandant's exaggerated politeness affords Nicholas a measure of hope. He turns on his heel and steps back into his room, sits down at the edge of the bed, caresses his sleeping wife, and squeezes her shoulders. "Sunny! Sunny! I have good news."

Alexandra is startled awake from yet another nightmare. She rubs her eyes, lifts herself on one elbow.

"Quickly, we must get ready. The Whites have invaded the city. See, didn't I tell you? Didn't I say our generals would save us? They are on their way. Hurry up. Get dressed."

"Could it be?" she asks as her husband helps her to her feet. "Our Friend is looking after us up there. Bless his soul."

Yurovsky proceeds to knock on all five half-open bedroom doors, awakening the rest of the family and their staff, ordering them to dress and congregate in the hall.

Having done his job, he coughs twice, slides his tongue over his thin lips, leans against the landing balustrade, and waits. Every now and then he tugs at his mustache and taps on the balustrade with his long fingernails, an impatient rap, rap, rap that can be heard in the bedroom of the grand duchesses, causing them added alarm.

As if she is about to attend an imperial soirée, Darya takes her time selecting a dress of fine damask, an embroidered guipure shawl, and a wide-rimmed feathered hat. Slowly, leisurely, she slips the dress over her head, feels the rich damask slide against her skin, the shawl caress her bare shoulders, the hat embrace her like a long-lost lover. Her Avram! One by one, she removes the hat, the shawl, the dress. What did she wear fifteen years back when they first bathed in the banya? She riffles through rich, colorful fabrics, beaded dresses, embroidered cloaks, crepe de Chine shawls, soft suede and leather shoes, until she finds what she is looking for. She buries her face in the gossamer shawl, inhales the scent of eucalyptus and desire, buttons the beaded silk chiffon dress that hugs her as gently as Avram did, slides her feet into the pearl-studded suede shoes, digs her hands in her hair and frees the curls into which he whispered. She avoids the mirror. She does not want to witness the damage the last months have inflicted on her thirty-one-year-old self.

Retrieving one of the pillows of ambergris she has transported from one place to another, she hugs it to her chest like a protective shield before stepping out of her room. She does not trust Yakov Yurovsky, does not believe one word he says, does not know where he will take them. Sixteen months of exile have taught her the importance of being on her guard and ready.

Nicholas and his son, dressed in simple military shirts, trousers, boots, and forage caps, are waiting in the hall. Alexei is in his father's arms, holding the pillow his mother instructed him to carry with him at all times.

"Where's Joy?" he asks Darya. "Will you find her?"

"Not now, Loves. Later."

"But Joy hates to sleep outside."

"Just for a few hours, Loves, promise."

Dr. Botkin, Demidova, Kharitonov, the cook, and Troup the footman join the family.

The doctor stands next to Nicholas. "Your Majesty," he whispers, "what is happening?"

Nicholas taps him on the arm, his composure reassuring. "Nothing bad."

"Please follow me!" Yurovsky's tone is level, polite. "We will walk down."

The hopeful exuberance of the procession sends a chill down Darya's spine. The Emperor's eyes have regained their youthful air, and he smiles at his son's attempt to brush away the last cobwebs of sleep. The tall, willowy Empress is regal, and despite relying on her cane, she carries herself with grace. The grand duchesses—Olga, twenty-two, Tatiana, twenty-one, Maria, nineteen, and Anastasia, seventeen—in wrinkled white dresses, resemble a garland of sleepy angels.

They are silent. No one complains. No questions are asked. They are drawing strength from Nicholas and Alexandra's demeanor, reminiscent of imperial days.

Darya steps behind the rigid Yurovsky, scrutinizing his detached manner, stiff back, hands deep in his pockets. She counts the twenty-three stairs they descend toward the cellar, counts them with the fanaticism of a lover, a religious zealot, a madwoman clinging to her last shreds of reason. They are led to another staircase, down into the bowels of the house.

She slows down, falls in step with Nicholas. "Your Majesty, I don't like this. Wherever we're going can't be good. There are eleven of us. We can ambush him. Flee into the streets."

"Follow orders!" Nicholas replies sternly. "Help is on the way."

"I beg of Your Majesty, permit us to try. It's not good at all! My mouth is stinging with bitter ash. This man is dangerous. Please, Your Majesty, please listen to me.

"Can I be of assistance?" Yurovsky asks, turning back.

Darya looks him straight in the eye. "I offered to carry the Tsarevich. He is not well."

"May I carry him?"

"Thank you. I can manage," Nicholas assures the commandant.

They cross a long corridor that leads toward a room in the basement. Yurovsky stops behind the door. His dark eyes stare at the procession, counting them in an even voice. He opens the door and steps back, gesturing for them to enter.

"Everyone, please. Thank you, yes, very well. You, too, Comrade Spiridova. Please hurry. Do not keep the others waiting."

They file into a small, wallpapered, empty cellar room. Graffiti is scrawled on a wall. The Empress in lurid poses with Rasputin. The grand duchesses in the arms of strangers. The moonless sky can be seen through a single barred window. A swarm of mosquitoes beat their wings against the rain-stained windowpane. The howl of a mounting summer wind makes its way through the cracks.

"What? No chairs?" The Empress utters, exhibiting the first sign of alarm. "May we not sit?"

Yurovsky thrusts his head out the door and calls out for two chairs. He grabs the chairs through the half-open door and sets them in the center. The Empress settles in one chair and the Emperor gently sits his son on the other.

"People in Moscow are worried that you might have escaped," Yurovsky says. "A photograph to prove that you have not. Comrade Spiridova, please remove your hat. I can't see your face. Thank you. This is better. You stand here and you here, there, across the back wall, thank you. Slightly further to the right, please," he says, kicking the hat Darya tossed at his feet.

Darya is assigned a place behind Alexei's chair.

Glaring at Yurovsky, she plants herself in front of the boy. "His Majesty does not like to be photographed," she growls. "What is the purpose of a photograph? He won't be escaping without his parents."

"Darya!" the Tsar orders. "Behind Alexei. Now!"

She tugs at her necklace that has survived the many thieves and robbers they encountered on the way here, pulls hard until the chain cuts into her skin, drawing blood from the back of her neck. She takes her time to walk around and position herself behind Alexei's chair. Nicholas is standing next to her, behind the Empress's chair.

The group of eleven is arranged in two orderly rows, distance between them carefully measured, the two chairs shifted closer and slightly to the center.

Yurovsky steps back, cocks his head, evaluates his choreographed setting. "It will be a very good photograph. Very good indeed. The people will see that you are safe. No one escaped. Yes, you are ready."

He shoves his head out the door and calls out for the photographer.

Darya rests her hands on Alexei's frail shoulders. "Listen to me, Alexei Nikolaevich Romanov. Don't you worry, not for a single second. I am here, right behind you. When we get out, I'll take you to Petrograd to visit the Hermitage Theater. We'll dine at the *Podval Brodyachy Sobaki*. You'll meet famous artists and poets and we will…"

The door opens. In burst eleven armed men.

Darya lets out a small gasp of pain. She grabs her head as if she is being pulled away by her hair, as if her eye is on fire, her flesh melting off her bones. There is the Ancient One, back after seven years, not whirling or churning in veils, but an embossed outline on the wall. Why did you abandon me? Darya is screaming in her head. How could you just say good-bye and leave me after revealing Athalia's deeds? You promised to guide me and watch over me. You promised to forewarn me of looming tragedies. Didn't you see our bleak future?

The Ancient One's sad gaze is on Darya. A single teardrop glistens like a crystal bead at the corner of her left eye. Her pale lips hardly move, but Darya can hear her loud and clear, see her gesture toward the pillow of ambergris in Darya's arms.

She snatches Alexei's pillow from behind and drops her own in his lap. "Hold it like a shield, Loves, press hard to your chest. The ambergris will protect you."

Yurovsky steps into the center of the crowded room that reeks of sweat, fear, and hatred. He holds a note in his left hand, his right hand stuffed in his pocket. He confronts Nicholas II. "In view of the fact that your relatives continue their attacks on Soviet Russia, the Ural Executive Committee has ordered your execution."

"Lord, oh, my God! Oh, my God! What is this? I can't understand you," Nicholas cries out, turning to his family, then back to the commandant. The veins in his neck stand out, his face white as the pillowcase on his son's lap.

Yurovsky jerks his right hand out of his pocket and aims his Colt revolver at the Tsar.

A point-blank bullet propels Nicholas's head backward and smashes his skull. His body wobbles in place before toppling sideways on Darya. She clutches the body, anchors the dead load against her, refusing to let go, her screams mingling with other cries.

The entire squad opens fire. Smoke and the acrid stench of gunpowder fill the room. Alexandra and Olga attempt to make the sign of the cross. A violent spatter of their blood blinds Darya. She releases the body of Nicholas.

Bayonets come crunching in on skull and bone. Bodies topple on top of one another. Guts spill, skulls crack, brain matter splatters. Necks and extremities bend and twist into lurid angles. Bullets ricochet against the pillow Darya clutches to her chest, hurtling her backward. She tumbles onto her side. She is being buried. Buried under a pile of bodies, her face jammed to the hardwood floor, the taste of blood and ash in her mouth, smoke in her eyes.

Footsteps shuffle everywhere. The door bangs shut. Silence. Darya struggles to remove a lifeless hand from her face. Alexandra's manicured fingers. Darya drops it with a silent cry. She struggles to breathe, to move under the load of bodies, search for a pistol, a bayonet, something to end her misery. Fragments of bone pierce her cheek. A foot presses into her armpit. Time passes. The pillow is jammed against her face. Emeralds, rubies, and diamonds are visible through bullet holes. Lord! What did she do? What in the world did she do! She should not have exchanged her pillow with the Tsarevich's.

The jewels in the pillow managed to shield her from the bullets. What if the ambergris didn't save Alyosha?

She hears the creak of the opening door, the squeak of approaching boots, bodies being shuffled around. She opens her mouth to invite them to finish her with a bullet, but only gurgling inhuman sounds tumble around her throat.

She is assaulted by a whiff of stale air. Someone grabs her by the shoulders. Removes the pillow from her face. A strand of pearls dangles from a hole in the pillowcase.

She grabs the pillow and plunges her face back in it, unable to face the smoke, the stench, the cursed world.

She is lifted up from a sticky pool of blood, squeezed hard against a rough coat, the buttons pressing into her breast, coarse beard bruising her cheek, her ear, a hand digging into her hair.

"Put me down!" She yells to the man with the yellow beard, unkempt hair, and wild eyes. "Alexei! Answer me. Loves! Where are you, Alyosha?" She directs her rage at the man, slapping him, kicking him.

She frees herself and lunges toward a bayonet leaning against the wall.

He grabs her around the waist and pulls her back. He is crushing her against him, his powerful hands imprisoning her in their grip, his breath on her neck. She spins around and pounds on his chest with her fists, her head, biting his neck.

"My love, my love," he cries into her hair, his tears wetting her neck. "It's me, Avram. What did they do to you! I came to save you. Come! I'm taking you away."

Chapter Thirty-Nine

THE MOONLESS NIGHT RATTLES with the nearby pound of artillery. Now and then, the black skies overhead ignite with a burst of cannon fire. The sound of marching boots, vehicles, gunshots, and troops grow louder, the rotting smell of refuse stronger.

Avram Bensheimer carries Darya over one shoulder as he maneuvers the city's back alleys and byways to avoid roadblocks, armored vehicles, and dangerous thoroughfares. He steps over something slippery and loses his balance, crashing against a nearby building.

She lets out a cry of pain.

He regains his footing and continues to sprint ahead, his breath coming fast, the impact of his steps on the asphalt underfoot constant in his chest.

She grunts, clawing at the air, at herself, at the world. "Where is Alexei, Avram? Where is he?"

"I don't know, Darya. I really don't," he murmurs into the dark. "I'm taking you to safety. I knew you'd be in Ekaterinburg with the Romanovs. So I joined the White Army regiment that made its way here."

"Alexei!" she cries out in her raw voice. "Alyosha!"

"Shh," he warns at the sound of approaching boots. "Keep the jewels in the pillow." He slips around a sharp turn and into an alley, ducking into a doorway.

A battalion of soldiers march by, a heavyset man at the head waving a red banner that otherwise hangs limp in the stagnant heat. A blast of artillery from somewhere nearby casts an eerie glow on the men's faces, blood-veined eyes, spit-dried lips, sweat-matted hair. A blood-splattered dog limps behind the passing soldiers, attempting to keep pace with a riderless horse.

A gray dawn is settling on the surrounding hills when Avram, at last, sets Darya down and doubles over to catch his breath.

She recognizes the birch, linden, and cedars surrounding acres of breathtaking beauty, which in the grip of this sinister dawn appears more forlorn than a ghost ship in a mist.

"You'll be safe here," he says. "At least for now. Come, don't stand here. It's dangerous." Finding her weak and unable to walk, he pulls her closer and leads her toward the Entertainment Palace, kicks the heavy door open, and helps her in.

A moldy smell meets them at the threshold. It is a long corridor, almost empty now. The Fabergé eggs in the glass cabinet are gone. The Persian carpets too. For now, a few paint-ings, a tapestry, and portraits of the Imperial Family remain in place. As does the entire collection of the family's books: a biography of Peter the Great, volumes of Chekhov, *Les Fables de La Fontaine*, a volume of *Tales of Shakespeare*, and the children's favorite fairy tale, *The Fire Bird*. These too, in the near future, will be plundered in front of her eyes, when she is still young and green and has not learned to use her opal eye and cursing tongue to scare away the enemy.

Avram gestures toward the pillow she clutches against her chest. "Put the jewels away." He turns a light on. Stepping closer, he holds her by the shoulders. He gasps at the sight of her cracked eye. "Who did this to you? Who? Tell me!"

She covers her eye with one hand. "It doesn't matter, Avram. Not now!"

"The Bolsheviks did it, didn't they? I'll kill them! I'll shoot every one of the bastards!"

"Don't bother, Avram. I said it doesn't matter now."

He kisses the tip of his forefinger and presses it to her eye. "I'm going, Darya. I hate to leave you alone, but you'll be safe here. Everyone thinks you are a witch. They'll keep their distance. Listen to me. I'll go back to the House of Special Purpose. I'll look for Alexei."

She does not turn away when he wraps his arms around her. She feels fragile in his arms as if the slightest pressure would shatter her into a million pieces. "I'm coming with you," she says.

"No! It's too dangerous. I'll have to do this alone."

She gazes at the door he shuts behind him, not caring to lock it, left behind in a palace she knows well, every corner, every room, the vast grounds she and Alexei once roamed, discovering miracles around every corner, the sweet-smelling herbs they crushed against their palms, the voracious squirrel they tamed with handfuls of walnuts, the banya they once converted into a grand pool of sailing toy ships, the sweet almond tree they climbed to scare away the mean-eyed cat that had a way of springing up from nowhere to frighten Alexei.

The need to wash off the blood, the visions, the stink of gunpowder is overwhelming. She wills her legs to take tentative, reluctant steps to nowhere. Her feet entangle in her skirts. She loses her balance, stumbles like a drunkard. She enters the guest bathroom opening to the garden, a shortcut to the banya. The alabaster sink is stained with the remnants of melted candle, shaving cream, hair. The sconce above the sink robbed of its crystals, the naked bulbs reflecting sorrow in the mirror below.

She confronts her image in the mirror, which she has been avoiding since their exile from Tsarskoe Selo. She stares at her unhinged, terror-stricken eye. Gazes hard and long at the opal, cracked like her heart and framed by a splattering of dried blood.

Their blood.

Chapter Forty

TWO DAYS PASS AND Avram is at the door, his arms loaded with two sacks he sets down at her feet. From one of the sacks, he plucks amulets, smashed icons, a broken emerald cross, bits and pieces of a lock, items of clothing, copper coins, nails, foil, and a Bible. "I found these in the Ipatiev House, thought you'd like to have them."

"Alexei?" she asks, the ache of his absence replacing the taste of ash in her mouth.

"I didn't find him," Avram lies, intent on protecting her, knowing she will not rest until she sees him for herself. "But I'm not giving up. I promise. There are rumors in town that Nicholas was killed by order of the Provincial Soviet and the rest of the family whisked away to different hiding places."

She folds into herself like a broken fan. "They shot the Tsar and Tsarina in front of my eyes. Olga too. Didn't you see?"

"No! They might have removed the bodies before I got there." He attempts to embrace what is left of her. "Shh, darling. Come, eat something. You've lost too much weight."

Her stomach lurches at the thought of food. She goes down on her knees and reaches out to leaf through the Empress's Bible, some pages torn, others heavily marked, dried leaves and flowers pressed between the pages.

"I found this too," he says, retrieving a pouch from his pocket.

She recognizes the packet of seeds Rasputin sent her. Useless, she muses fleetingly, the acrid stench of guilt in her mouth. Why did she care to carry it from place to place? She has no intention of planting anything, giving birth to anything, not now, not ever.

"And this," he says, pulling Alexei's pillow out of the sack.

She snatches it out of his hand, turning it this way and that, checking it for a long time. The pillowcase is riddled with bullet holes. What did she do! Why? Why did she listen to the Ancient One? She should not have exchanged pillows with Alexei!

She presses her hands to her eyes. A thought occurs to her. She grabs the pillow, pokes a finger in each hole, pulling and tearing the pillowcase to reveal the ambergris inside.

She raises the ambergris to the light, turns and checks it from all angles.

"Lord Almighty!" she cries out. "Look, Avram, come see. Alexei Nikolaevich is alive! A miracle! There are no bullet holes in the ambergris. It saved him! Remember this day, Avram! I swear on the souls of my parents that I will not rest until I find Alexei Nikolaevich and lead him to his rightful place as the autocrat of all the Russias!"

She suddenly jumps back screaming. One of the sacks, forgotten at her feet, is wriggling its way toward her.

Avram grabs the sack and unties the rope with one quick motion. The Tsarevich's spaniel scrambles out.

"Oh, Joy, my precious little darling," she exclaims. "Why are you so quiet? Why aren't you barking, wagging your tail? You saw everything, didn't you? You've gone mute, Joy, yes, you have."

She turns to Avram standing over her, the empty sacks in his hands like two limp carcasses. "Thank you." She gestures with her left hand as if to send him on his way. His opal band flashes on her finger. "Go find Alexei now."

His eyes light up. "You are still wearing my ring?"

"Don't talk to me about rings," she replies, stuffing her hand in her pocket.

He nods toward the scattered objects around them. "I'll put these away."

"No! I will."

"I'll help you then," he replies, following her into Alexei's bedroom, where she has spent the last two days, avoiding the rest of the palace, every corner a reminder of her loss.

The bedroom is large, with tall windows overlooking the garden. The sun is shining through the glass, casting a golden mantle over everything. Pamphlets and newspapers the revolutionaries left behind flutter in the breeze. A torn page settles on a lower branch. A raven alights on the newspaper and begins cawing until a stray cat appears from nowhere and scares the bird away.

A mechanical toy train remains lodged on the rails, its red engine lying on its side. The Emperor's cane dangles by its double-eagled handle from a hook. A round table displays photographs of the Imperial Family: Nicholas II with his officers; Alexandra at the piano in the Lilac Boudoir; the family during an outing on the coast of Finland onboard the imperial yacht; Nicholas and George V, who, in the end, refused to give asylum to his Romanov cousins.

Darya deposits her load on the bed. One by one, she lifts Alexei's pants, the blue sailor one with the piping, the cuffed gray flannel trousers, touches them to her cheeks, smells them, folds them with the utmost care. She presses her lips to his formal uniform, the two small holes in the right sleeve, his tuxedo coat, the pants missing, the collar having lost its sheen, inhales his innocent child's scent, gazes at the two pairs of socks the Empress had to mend several times. She doubles them into each other, strokes them with the tip of her fingers.

"I didn't leave you," Avram says as she walks to the closet, carrying Alexei's clothing like a child in her arms. "The Bolsheviks arrested me. It was a mistake to question our traditional statehood. I didn't know the alternative would be far worse. I fell prey to certain artists, believed they'd reform our stale ways. Little did I know that the tide would change and the same artists would start preaching nonsense like Dali's surrealism cultivates madness and encourages decadence, impressionism is antisocial and distracts citizens with fantasy…on and on until my own perception of things became distorted." He slaps himself on the forehead as if to force some sense into his head. "What was I thinking? Suddenly Igor's choreography, Belkin's paintings, even Dimitri's caricatures seemed to project the reality of our political state."

One by one, Darya lays Alexei's belongings in precise order on the closet shelves where a complete wardrobe of Alexandra's ball gowns—creamy velvet gown stiff with pearls, flowing peach-colored silk gown with all types of embroidery, mantles rich with brocades and studded with semiprecious jewels, all styles of taffeta, silk, and grosgrain—remain hanging.

"A year, perhaps even a few months after you ended the salon, my work came under attack for betraying the common people. I was ordered to direct my talent toward antimonarchist themes. I didn't know whether to laugh out loud or spit in their faces. I did both. Dimitri Markowitz reported me to the authorities. I was locked up for nine months with thousands of prisoners of war. And then we were freed one night. We were needed to reinforce one of the many anti-Bolshevik White Army regiments. There were reports that the Romanov family was transferred to the Ipatiev House. I knew I would find you there. So I joined the regiment that marched into Ekaterinburg."

Darya gazes up at Avram, haggard and reticent and so different from the man she once loved. She is changed too, unwilling to forgive, a dying woman hoarding the fuel of resentment for survival. She brushes her unkempt curls back from her face, goes to him, and rising on her toes, drapes her arms around his neck. She presses her mouth to his, hard. A savage force that surprises them both.

Chapter Forty-One

HAVING MOANED AND CREAKED for two months and twelve days, the palace begins to settle around Darya. Rats have taken shelter in every nook and cranny, snoozing in their holes and nibbling on anything they can get their teeth into. Like her, they survive on stale food the White Army left in the kitchen. After licking every last scrap clean, pattering paws and greedy eyes follow her everywhere.

She will have to dare the hostile streets or the rats will devour her alive.

Fetching her ambergris, she climbs the steps and walks down the hall toward the salon, glares at the mounted aurochs head above the door, all her misfortunes reflected in its glassy gaze. She shoves away shards of glass from the broken bottle of vodka she found in the salon yesterday or the day before, pulled out the cork, drained it, and smashed it against the fireplace. She turns away from the gold-framed mirror on the mantelpiece that projects the cheerless face of a thirty-one-year-old woman who has lost the will to live.

She kneels to gaze up the fireplace shaft. Despite the rats and not having been cleaned for years, the hearth is in good shape. Still, she wraps a cloth around a broom and wipes remnants of soot left from the last time the fireplace was used to celebrate the Imperial Couple's anniversary three years ago.

What an evening that was! The Imperial Couple and their 150 guests were dressed in robes from the reign of Catherine the Great. Wearing lightly powdered wigs and weighted down by ermine-trimmed robes studded with semiprecious jewels, women sailed ahead in glittering silver-threaded gowns imprinted with eagles. Replicas of the chain of the Order of St. Andrew shimmered across ample bosoms. Men sported helmets with rich plumage, gold-braided uniforms heavy with medals, epaulettes announcing high ranks. A thirty-one-gun salute from the Vladivostok Fortress rattled Ekaterinburg. Cheering crowds flocked to gather around the palace in hope of catching a glimpse of the guests as they arrived in open carriages drawn by horses wearing costumes of the same era. A concert was held, followed by dancing, choreographed by Josef Kschessinski of the imperial ballet.

What remains now is the forlorn chandelier above the stage, the sound-making machine for wind, thunder, and rain, and the device that raises the orchestra pit so the salon can be used as a ballroom. The Louis XVI sofas and armchairs, upholstered in Aubusson needlepoint tapestry, are here too, plus the French goblin and the silk carpet, a gift from Sultan Abdul Hamid II of the Ottoman Empire.

She drapes the two blocks of ambergris in layers of cloth, crouches in the hearth, and conceals them in a niche inside the fireplace. She checks around as if searching for intruders, spirits in the shadows perhaps, before locking the door behind her.

She returns downstairs to the kitchen, disturbing layers of dust on the balustrade. Opening one cabinet, then another, shifting a packet of dry beans, empty jars of marmalade, a jar of moldy pickled mushrooms, she passes a flat palm over the shelves. What is she looking for? Why is she in the kitchen? Yes! She remembers now. She pulls out a drawer and riffles through a collection of knives of all sizes. She chooses the largest, a hunting knife she had seen the chef sharpen and use to dress game.

The cellar that once held the family's provisions of rice,

potatoes, onions, dried mushrooms, and imported canned goods is cluttered with empty crates now. She shifts the crates, searching for what she concealed here some days, or months before, she is not certain since time has lost all meaning; days and nights neither pass nor matter as she wanders the rooms. There it is! The pillow of jewels she is looking for. She fishes it out from behind a crate. A cockroach scrambles away. She flattens it under her slipper.

She settles down cross-legged and forces the tip of the knife between the floorboards, loosens them one by one. The moist soil beneath the planks reeks of worms, mildew, and decay. She tosses the knife aside; it falls flat on top of a crate. She digs with bare hands, peels off clumps of earth that settle under her fingernails.

Widening the top of the pillowcase, she pulls out one jewel after another, buries each piece as if conducting a religious ceremony, not a funeral, not that, because she is certain she will return them to their rightful owner one day.

She buries the pearl necklace the Tsarina wore on her wedding day, a gold bracelet she wore when the Tsar returned from the eastern front, the good-luck ruby ring, a South Sea pearl belt, the pink diamond necklace Olga wore on their trip abroad the *Standart*, when the family traveled from Peterhof along the Baltic coast, the opal bracelet she gave Grand Duchess Maria on her twelfth birthday, and an emerald cross the Empress was especially fond of and wore to religious ceremonies. One by one, she buries her memories for safekeeping in the shallow grave, presses her palm on top, and keeps it there like a promise, then lays the wooden planks flat and piles the crates back on top.

She rifles through the closet in the upstairs room, strokes the formal gowns the Empress kept here for special occasions. She selects an embroidered dress of voile with ruffled sleeves, the beaded belt she bought for the Empress in one of the antique shops, and a hat with lavender feathers.

Armed with the Tsar's cane, hat pulled low over her brows, she steps out into the soot-covered Ekaterinburg streets.

She recoils at the sight of the bullet-riddled buildings, army trucks parked on Malysheva Street. Red flags everywhere. Red armbands. Posters with threatening fists lifted like so many curses. Posters of the Red St. George, Leon Trotsky, slaying the counterrevolutionary White dragon. Salutations that hurt her ears: "Hello, comrade." "Good morning, commandant." Is she the only one left to mourn the death of an empire? Russians will eventually wake up, too late and orphaned, not knowing what has destroyed them and for what purpose.

Her mouth puckers at the sight of the Ipatiev House, perched atop a hill, the fortlike fence still there. "Doom and damnation!" she shouts out to no one in particular, releasing a plume of ash from her mouth that curls up in spirals to float overhead like a halo and then rain down and settle on her hat, shoulders, lips.

She enters the neighborhood grocery. "Give me a loaf of bread, boy. A block of sheep butter and a can of sour yogurt too," she commands as if she were still Tyotia Dasha of the Tsarevich and the grocer, a thick-lipped youth with a fuzz-covered chin, was her servant.

"Right away, Your Eminence," he stutters, scrambling to wrap up the order, unable to take his eyes off her. He has never seen a more striking woman with such a strange, translucent, golden eye. Her plump mouth flecked with silvery ash, yet so frail she seems on the verge of melting in front of his awestruck gaze. He has an inexplicable urge to fall on his knees and press his face to the rich folds of her dress. Instead, he reaches out a reluctant palm to accept her money.

She drops a sliver of broken emerald from the Empress's cross onto his palm. "Keep this against my account! It's emerald, not glass, use it wisely or it will bring you bad luck." She is certain that the instant she steps out of his shop, he will open his loose mouth and blabber about a young opal-eyed witch being in the neighborhood, exaggerated tales of her supernatural powers, which will prove a blessing, since they will cast fear in the heart of the populace and keep them away from the Entertainment Palace, where not so long ago, crowds gathered around to enjoy the exquisite music wafting from its windows.

Darya steps out of the shop, gazing straight ahead, impatient to flee the blood-soaked streets and alleys, the flags and armbands like so many bloodstains, the buildings that are shameful specters of their old selves.

"Incantations, Madame, love potions, seeds for magic," a shabby, long-haired peddler screeches in her ear, following too close.

She raises her cane and smacks the pubescent boy on the shoulder. "Let me be, boy. Go somewhere else."

She continues on her way, a nagging thought at the back of her mind. Where else did she hear "seeds for magic" or such similar words? The thought bores into her brain like an insistent worm as she navigates through the somber lanes and streets to the palace and straight into the kitchen.

She upends the bag of groceries on the counter. Standing at the sink, she tears a piece of bread and chews it without tasting. Fills a glass of water from the sink and washes the bread down. "Seeds for magic," she repeats aloud. "Seeds for magic." And then she recalls the bag of seeds Rasputin gave her with a note:

I wish you to have these magical seeds for your garden and for your soul. Keep them somewhere safe. Do not think about them until you need them. I shall not tell you when that day is. You will know.

Where did Avram leave that packet? She searches the palace, one room then another, returns to the kitchen to rifle through drawers, shelves, inside ovens, behind blinds and drapes, on window ledges. Didn't Avram bring the packet with the family belongings he had found in the House of Special Purpose? She enters Alexei's room. The packet of seeds is sitting on the table next to photographs of the Imperial Family. She grabs it and goes out into the garden.

The sun is high in the sky, brutal in its brightness, melting the last few patches of snow. The sound of the city can be heard from somewhere far away. A bird flaps, squeaks, shits down on a tree bark. What will happen to the birds of paradise, she wonders.

She squats close to the damp earth, taking her time to dig holes that do not need to be deep, hoe earth before its time, haul pails of water back and forth when the hose nearby will suffice. As long as she keeps moving, rage replaces despair.

She plants Rasputin's gift, one seed at a time, all day long, dreading the inevitable arrival of night, deep and dark as her grief.

When the sun sets and the buzz of insects replaces the drone of the city, she seeks her bed, her complexion mottled with the sting of insects, red and raw from the sun. She drowns herself in a fitful sleep that repeats the sounds and images, the crack of bullets, snap of bones, shattering skulls, sigh of resigning lungs.

Startled awake, she sits up with the anxious gesture of a woman who has experienced horrors in her dreams. She shades her eyes against the sunlight slashing through the window. A plump, mean-eyed, wailing cat is perched on the windowsill. Its receptive tail is held high, its mottled fur covered with tiny butterflies.

What a strange creature, she muses, unaware yet that the uninvited guest caused Joy such alarm the dog fled into the streets. She tosses a cover over her shoulders and goes to the window. She lets out a faint sound of surprise.

Swarms of butterflies have invaded the garden she planted the day before. Their opalescent wings fluttering over a carpet of berries, they hop friskily, dodge and soar, skip and whirl, turn belly up, their wiry legs kicking in drunken ballets.

Overnight, Rasputin's seeds have yielded a crop of plump, juicy berries that pop out of the earth like tiny white balloons.

She goes outside and cuts a path through the shimmering cloud of butterflies, raising a faint smell of decay. She likes this invasion, this disturbing of the false balance of nature. She pulls a berry from the root, flicks the stem away, and squeezes the flesh between her thumb and forefinger. A milky sap stains her fingers. She licks off the pungent, sticky residue, tastes it under her tongue, sensing the puckering on the roof of her mouth.

Rasputin had predicted that one day she would cherish a gift to end the nightmares, the despair. She could not have asked for a better gift than poisonous berries.

She squats among the berries, hundreds of butterflies fanning her with tender wings, alighting on her lashes, burrowing into her curls, sighing in her ears. With giddy recklessness, even joy, she pulls out one berry after another and tosses them in her mouth.

She sighs, shuts her eyes, and lies down, her mouth filled with the sweet taste of earth and amnesia. She no longer hears the crack of gunfire, does not see the Tsar's skull explode, the Empress's hand rise to make the sign of the cross, Alexei thrusting his face into the pillow.

Her eyes raised to the heavens, she cries out, "Thank you, Father Grigori!"

The sun is forcing its way up. The air smells of rot and gasoline. Her back is slimy with crushed berries. Everything aches, her face, her bones, but especially her chest as if it has been left open to the elements all night. She is sprawled out on the carpet of berries that temporarily blunt the edges of her pain, the addicted cat with the mean green eyes snoring at her side.

She lifts herself to her feet, brushes her damp clothes clean, and goes inside.

Everything is different. Butterflies cover the silk-flounced lamp shades, the mantelpieces, and the Berger chair. They flutter under her skirt that hangs from a hook at the door, fluffing it up as if with tissue paper. She makes a few halfhearted attempts to shoo them out, flick a towel to direct them toward the open window. She throws her arms up. "Oh, what's the difference? You stay too. Invite the entire insect and animal kingdom if you must."

Three raps on the door send her heart into panic. Did she hear thumping boots, the click of a pistol? It took the bastards long enough to find her. Well, here they are, at last. She walks to the door and opens it as wide as a welcome.

Avram stands there, offering her an apologetic smile. His soldier's coat is the color of mud, the frayed collar pulled up to conceal his pale face, cap shading his eyes. The thought occurs to her that despite all the hardships he suffered, his green-flecked eyes have retained some of their spark.

"I want to be with you," he says. "Hide with you in the palace."

"If you want to," she says, "but you'll miss fighting for whatever you believe in."

"Not more than I'll miss you," he replies.

She shrugs her shoulders and steps back to let him in.

He sets down a toolbox and his painting supplies by the door. Opens the box and pulls out all types of locks, chains, and bolts. He hammers them the length of the door, testing each carefully, even if he is aware that more than locks and bolts would be required to keep out the madness in the streets.

Having finished his job, he silently follows her up the stairs to the upper hallway with its magnificent stucco and walls that once boasted the most prominent paintings of the time, follows her into the oval-shaped theater with its Corinthian columns, where the Imperial Family once held lavish theatrical productions and the walls still echo with music, laughter, and applause.

She settles into a chair and draws her knees up to her chest. "Paint me, Avram! Capture my grief."

"Pose for me the way you used to, my Opal-Eyed Jewess," he says, as if they were still lovers in Tsarskoe Selo and he was the most accomplished artist of the salon.

"It's different," she murmurs. "Nothing is the same."

He wastes no time setting up his easel, mixing the colors, and measuring the canvas. He gazes at her with agonizing intensity. Picks up his brush and embarks on the task of painting her portrait with the passion of a dying man whose days are numbered.

Day after day, he steps out of his bedroom to spend hours in the intimacy of the easel and more hours standing at a distance, examining his paintings of her set amid crumbling synagogues, corpses with bloody skull caps, and hungry-mouthed, skeletal children. He rips one canvas after another and then starts over again, as if to bring order to some chaos in his head. A shadow of his previous self, he can only create with tremendous discipline and with the help of the hallucinatory berries she feeds him.

When she seems lost in the past, unable to eat or drink, he pries her mouth open and drops a berry in, feeds her a spoonful or two of honey-sweetened yogurt, soft-boiled rice, marinated mushrooms, or a slice of smoked salmon he buys from the young grocer who keeps his shop open late into the night. Day after day, he feeds her like a child until her twisting stomach begins to settle and her eyes show a semblance of life.

He cleans his brushes, adjusts a canvas, and waits as he has the last weeks, hoping she will meet his eyes as she used to, lean back on the sofa perhaps, or curl on the carpet in a fetal position, maybe hug her legs to her belly and rest her chin on her knees. Something, anything, to show she is present, even if she does not care.

"It's impossible to work like this," he complains at last, after shredding another unsatisfactory portrait. "One day, you'll trust me again, perhaps even love me. For now, try to look at me, if you can. You're still wearing my ring, after all."

She considers telling him that she continues to carry the weight of his ring as penance for having expelled her child, their child, as if it were a tumor that did not belong. But it would take too much effort to explain, so she throws her shoulders up, curls further into herself, and, dry-eyed and listless, averts her face from him.

Another week goes by, a month, a decade perhaps, and life outside continues as if the world is the same and it matters what laws are being passed and by whom. What matters is the hope that one day someone will bring her news about the fate of the Tsarevich.

It is Sunday afternoon and black clouds are suspended in the hazy distance, heavy rains splash like marbles against the window-panes in the upstairs salon. Inside, the air smells of stale incense from the burnt ambergris Darya smeared on Avram's painful tooth from a recent habit of grinding his teeth.

He is absorbed in mixing a pallet of highlighting colors, a bit of pearly vanilla, pale citron, and a dash of transparent rouge. He selects a small brush from the cup that holds brushes of all sizes, strokes her portrait with a few touches, centers it on the easel, then steps back, narrowing his eyes for one last look. The calm of having completed a piece of art is a thing of the past, a time when he planned his days around the rewarding tilt of her head, parting of her lush lips, the smile in her mesmerizing eyes. Now, there is only anguish and the inexplicable necessity to inspire or be inspired by her, the need to make a difference.

He removes her portrait from the easel and leans it against the gold-framed mirror on the mantelpiece above the fireplace. Her eyes in the painting observe the world from every angle, sometimes puzzled, at other times sad, but always in perpetual admiration of the painter. He has not painted her as she is today, covered and huddling on the sofa, but as he remembers her in better times, gloriously naked, deeply in love, and devoid of all inhibitions.

"Do you like it?" he asks her.

"Very much," she replies.

He cuddles her face between his large hands and gazes at her for longer than she can bear. "Forgive me, my love. I have to leave. Go fight the Bolsheviks, or I won't be able to live with myself. They are slaying my people, every one of them."

She does not ask him about his loyalty to her. She does not tell him that his compromised genius had filled her empty hours. She does not tell him that she thinks he wants to leave because he is restless and, like her, knows that love cannot be nurtured in these surrounding ruins.

He tucks a curl behind her ear. "Whatever happens, my queen, don't ever forget this Jew." He raises her hand and presses his lips to the beating artery on her wrist, steps away and salutes like a Cossack of the imperial guards. "Lock the door behind me," he says before disappearing into the heavy fog.

Chapter Forty-Two

— 1991 —

"AND THAT IS MY story," Darya tells Grand Duchess Sophia Sheremetev.

In the tall windows a gray dusk has replaced the bright Crimean sunshine. The end of the day brings with it an unexpected chill that seeps into Darya's old bones. She wraps her arms around herself and waits. Her tongue is heavy with the load of the past, memories levitating around her like the grand duchess's cigarette smoke. Now that she has kept her end of the bargain, she expects to be escorted to the Tsarevich right away, or she will simply open her mouth and let loose the impatience mounting in her.

The grand duchess blows out a perfect ring of smoke, grinds her cigarette in the ashtray.

"Thank you, Darya Borisovna. I know it's difficult to recall such tragedies, but now that I know about the magical properties of ambergris, I understand why you think the Tsarevich might have survived."

Darya tucks her purse under her arm and stands up. "It is not that I *think*, but that I *know* he survived. And I will see him now!"

Darya waits for her eyes to adjust to the dim light in the Sheremetev mahogany-paneled library. Her heart is hammering in her chest.

She fears it will give up on her after 104 years, give up at a most inconvenient time. Her glance skims across the room, the volumes of encyclopedias on shelves, ancient looking, gold-embossed spines, a gurgling samovar in a corner, a set of gilded clocks on a pair of cabinets. She takes a moment to calm herself, to inhale the scent of leather-bound books that transport her back to the Emperor's study, where the Tsarevich crouched under his father's writing desk and played with Tamara Sheremetev's miniatures.

A chair scrapes against the parquet floor and someone rises from behind the desk. She blinks, unable to trust her eyes, unable to accept this devastating turn of fate. She was certain she would come face to face with the Tsarevich himself, but this tall, lean man in a wrinkled linen suit and a blue cravat loose around his collar is far too young to be the man her entire life revolved around.

He reaches out a hand and introduces himself in a firm voice. "Pavel Nikolaevich Romanov, Madame."

She pushes his offered hand away with her cane. "You must not introduce yourself as a Romanov, young man."

"But I am. And you, Madame, although not a Romanov by blood, have certainly earned that title. I know all about you and your past. You were close to the Romanovs, part of their lives, and this interests me."

"Have you nothing better to do than to stalk an old woman?" Darya controls her urge to blow a puff of ash into the impudent man's face. "If you *are* a Romanov, why didn't you come to me before, since my search for the Tsarevich is no secret? Tell me the truth or I'll spit out a curse that will turn your face the color of shame."

"I had to keep a low profile," he says, backing away from her. "Because it was impossible to trace my paternal ancestry. But now that the Tsar's remains have been exhumed and my DNA matches his, the results leave no doubt about my ancestry. So here I am."

"And why is such important news kept a secret?"

"You know better than anyone, Madame, that the government has no interest in publicizing the existence of a Romanov heir."

A sparrow flies into the library, lost and disoriented. It circles around the room, swoops past them, flaps its wings against the windowpane. Pavel shoos the frightened bird out the window.

"Come back here, young man," Darya commands. "You have a lot to explain!"

He stands under the chandelier, an amber glow pooling at his feet. He thrusts his right hand into his breast pocket, holds it there for a moment, then pulls out a tan leather wallet embossed with the Romanov insignia. The tip of his forefinger strokes a small silver padlock, flips it around to check for signs of damage. Having been assured that the lock is in good shape, he takes his time to pat his pockets and tug at his sleeves, as if he is about to perform some act of magic. At last, he flips out a zippered pouch from his other pocket, which holds a small key he uses to unlock the padlock. Inside the wallet is a light blue sheet, folded into a perfect square. He unfolds it with great care and hands it to her.

"Here you are, Madame. The DNA results!"

Her gaze skims the sheet, the heading, the signature at the bottom that confirms the document's authenticity. She takes a moment to reflect upon this information and a few more to shift her focus. The abacus of her mind begins to click, calculating, adding and subtracting years of the Tsarevich's life, possible dates of marriage, births of sons, daughters, and grandchildren.

She suddenly opens her arms and locks Pavel in her embrace. She was right all these years. The ambergris did shield Alexei Nikolaevich from the bullets! He did survive to find himself a wife and sire a son who fathered this fine young man. "Dear, dear boy, you must be Alexei's grandson and great-grandson of Nicholas II. A great honor, indeed. Now that I look closely, I see the resemblance, yes, I certainly do. You have your great-grandfather's eyes and your grandfather's smile. Do you know that I was more than your grandfather's Tyotia Dasha; I was also his friend and teacher. I cared for him as I would my own son. I was seventeen when your grandfather was born. He would be eighty-seven now. Still young when you know how to take care of yourself, and that I taught him well, yes, I did. I taught him to believe in hope and miracles. Hope is the elixir of youth, you know. Come closer, Pavel. Tell me who Alyosha married. Where is he now? What has he been doing all this time?"

She allows herself to be led to a sofa, to be offered a glass of hot tea, to be pampered again by a Romanov. Planting the Tsar's cane in front of her, she rests her chin on the double-eagled handle, embracing Pavel in her affectionate gaze.

His own gaze is intense, unwavering, as if nothing outside this room matters, as if the nucleus of his life centers in this old woman who carries eternal youth in her golden eyes. He leans toward her, the satin-upholstered chair creaking under him. "Surely you heard about the sacred relics, Madame. It was in the news. A box of relics that holds dug-up bits and pieces of a fire: bloodied earth, a few bullets, pieces of bone, and a small bottle of congealed fat. The box traveled from Siberia to Europe, from one grand duke to another, but none wanted to be associated with its bad luck. In the end, the Russian Orthodox Church abroad accepted the box for safekeeping. Recent tests have confirmed that the box holds remnants of Alexei Nikolaevich after his body was burned. The Tsarevich perished in Ekaterinburg with the family."

"I was there. He did *not* die!" she cries out, fumbling in her purse, searching for the piece of ambergris, for anything to temper the violent memories.

"Madame!" Pavel calls out from somewhere far away. "Are you all right?"

"No, I am *not!*" She fishes out a handkerchief with the Empress's initials and wipes her face. "And don't go on as if I don't know about the relics. I also listen to the news and know that the Tsarevich's remains weren't found among them. What I want to know is who *you* are?"

He leaves his seat and begins pacing the room. "The truth, Madame, is that I am not the descendant of any of the children

Nicholas II sired with Alexandra Feodorovna of Hesse. I am the outcome of a moment of Tsar Nicholas II's loneliness and fear. My grandmother, Jasmine, became pregnant with a girl the night the Tsar lost the battle of Galicia. I am that girl's son."

At the front in Mogilev, the Tsar summons his generals. Looking each one in the eye, he demands the unvarnished truth. And they give it to him: his campaign is crippled by flawed communication. Despite the most brutal of winters Russia has ever experienced, his men are being sent unequipped to the front to fight the devastating cold and are defenseless in the face of the superior German army. Germany has shifted its focus to the eastern front, driving Russian soldiers out of Galicia as well as Russian Poland. Casualties are staggering. He is losing the battle to the hated Germans.

The generals salute their commander in chief, snap their boots, and wish him a good evening before abandoning him to his thoughts. Night is falling on the barracks at the end of a series of dreadful defeats. The biting winter cold has settled on the compound; not a soul is detected wandering outside. Neither the thump of boots on snow, nor the howl of wolves, nor the sigh of branches can be heard. But the communal tent, where meals are served and strategies are conceived, is lit with oil lamps and humid with the breath of hundreds of aroused men.

Jasmine the Persian Dancer has been dispatched to the front to entertain the soldiers and lift their morale. She sways and whirls like a welcome apparition that breathes life into cold hearts and hope into wilted souls. She dances from one man to the other, touches her red lips to a forehead, a cheek, the crown of a head, purrs a compliment in an ear, the back of a neck. She is warm and splendid and reining in her impatience. She wants to leave. She has other plans.

At midnight, to the roar of drunken laughter and thunderous applause, she sails out, her expression that of utter sorrow, as if all she ever cared for is in this very tent and she regrets having to bid the tired soldiers good-bye.

Nearly naked, save for layers of sheer veils she gathers around her, she moves ahead with the agility of a panther, impervious to the cold jabbing into her skin and bone and turning her marrow into ice. Fate has handed her a dealing hand. Neither war nor the winter chill will snatch it away from her.

She is silent, her eyes stinging, unable to feel her bare toes, which she places one in front of the other, careful not to stumble over frozen branches, pebbles, and rocks as she sneaks past dozing guards and slips into the Tsar's bedroom.

She tiptoes closer to stand over him. She loves this man. Loves him dearly. Her every aching cell tells her that he, too, has never stopped loving her. She drops her veils at her feet, where they gather like plump rose petals.

The next morning the Tsar has a foggy recollection of the previous night's vodka-infused events when an exotic woman swayed into his room, her breasts trumpeting her entrance. Energetic, gregarious, and boisterous, she stepped out of her diaphanous costume to reveal the muscular legs of a horsewoman, unhooked her corset, the bones leaving red marks on the creamy flesh he licked as she opened wide her receptive thighs.

Darya presses her handkerchief to the unbearable pain in her opal eye, afraid it would suffer another fracture. She shifts in her seat, tugs at the worn edges of her skirt. This cannot be what her two lives amount to: a past of loss and devastation, a present repeating the same. A Romanov bastard claiming the throne. Decades of search cannot end here. "Jasmine was a good woman, Pavel Nikolaevich, but that didn't stop her from taking many Romanov lovers. And you, young man, could be the offspring of any of them." She glares at him to stop his objection, waves away the DNA document he has pulled out of his pocket again as proof. She knows he is telling the truth, knows he is the Emperor's descendant. The imperial handwriting, scribbled on a ripped off sheet she had found in the moldy folds of the valise, is proof enough. This one night with Jasmine is the torment that was tearing the Tsar apart, the secret he had hoped to take to his grave, now exhumed to sully the Romanov name.

She goes to the tall windows to draw air into her lungs, into her aching brain. She comes back, her determination towering over Pavel. "I hate to shatter your dream, young man, especially since I believe in the importance of dreams. But the truth is that our Slavic law forbids succession out of wedlock. Not only are you the product of an unequal union, but you are a bastard. So you better forget about becoming our Tsar and do something else with your life."

Pavel flips his hair off his forehead, his gray eyes blazing with conviction. "I promised my grandmother to do everything in my power to reveal my ancestry once the political tide turned, and I'm doing it now. Times have changed, Madame. Our laws of succession have changed." He replenishes Darya's stale tea from the samovar, stirs in two lumps of sugar. He stops himself from holding her hand, the hand that reminds him of Jasmine's fragile fingers at the end of her life, the skin thin as rice paper, the branching veins pulsating beneath his touch. "I wonder what my grandmother wants me to do now."

"To be honest, Pavel Nikolaevich, and respect the Romanov legacy. That's what Jasmine would have wanted you to do. So do the honest thing, Pavel! Do you understand?"

"Even if it's hurtful?"

"Yes, young man. Living an honest life never hurts, but a lie does."

The samovar becomes louder in the corner. Pavel lowers the knob and brings her another cup of tea.

She pushes his hand away. "I don't want tea, Pavel Nikolaevich. Sit down and tell me what you're hiding."

Pavel takes a moment to rub his temples. His face has acquired a pinched look of pain. He lifts the cup of tea Darya refused and takes an absentminded sip. "Soon after the revolution, my grandmother, God bless her soul, made it her business to follow every rumor about the fate of the Imperial Family. She, too, believed that Alexei survived that night. Since she was aware that you were searching the big cities, she concentrated on peasant towns, traveling from village to village, often by foot. The reality of her relationship with the Tsar changed shape in the telling and retelling of it in her mind, acquiring the attributes of a fable until she came to believe that she herself was of royal descent. She would press my finger to a blue vein on her inner arm, tell me that royal blood seeks the same artery, assuring me that even if she didn't find Alexei, he would find her. Well, she *did* find him."

"What are you saying, Pavel? Are you saying Jasmine found the Tsarevich?"

"Yes, Madame. I lied to be kind to him. Alexei Romanov is alive."

A volley of curses and questions crowd her mouth. "You lied! You lowly son of a one-kopeck whore! I will see the Tsarevich. Right now! Right away!"

"But he doesn't want to be found, Madame."

"He wants to be found by me! Listen, young man, I am old and tired and don't have much time left. One way or another, I *will* find him. We need each other, the Tsarevich and I."

"I'm not certain he needs you, Madame. He is settled down into a calm life. It would be cruel to rattle the foundation of everything he's become used to. I made a mistake. I shouldn't have revealed—"

"Let me tell you something, young man, you are in no position to decide who needs whom. So don't insult me. Although I don't want to hurt you, if it comes to it, I'll turn you inside out to spill the truth out of you. So let us make a pact. Take that paper and pen on the desk and jot down where I'll find Alexei, and I'll show you the secret way out of here. Go on! Don't keep me waiting."

"But I can walk out of here whenever I want. I'm not a prisoner."

She bursts into laughter, slapping both thighs. "Maybe not a prisoner, but certainly under strict surveillance. The grounds are dotted with plainclothes security guards hired by the Russian Nobility Association to monitor whoever enters and leaves the premises. In addition, Grand Duchess Sophia and Rostislav, a dangerous forensic anthropologist whom you don't want to cross, expect me to step out of this room to announce your candidacy to the throne. And, most important, a coup d'état is already in the planning. Too much is at stake for you to just walk out of here without giving them a convincing explanation. And that I forbid you to do."

"But I don't intend to walk out, Madame. Not when the throne is rightfully mine."

She curls her mouth in amusement. "No, Pavel, the throne belongs to Alexei Nikolaevich Romanov!"

"But I'm much younger, Madame. More able to reign."

An irrational affection for this stubborn youth is taking root in Darya's heart, and she tries to dismiss it. "My dear Pavel, you could never claim the throne. There's something else about your grandmother you need to know. Here, have some tea, something to calm you. I'd give you one of my berries if I had any left. All right! Are you ready? Your grandmother, my dear Pavel Nikolaevich, was a Jew. Yes, Jasmine was Jewish. I see your shock. She kept it a secret up to the very end. I don't need to tell you that the Russian people will never, ever accept a Jewish ruler. And if it becomes necessary, I won't hesitate to reveal the truth."

"No, Madame, I don't believe you. My grandmother couldn't have been Jewish. She would have told me if she was."

"I'm certain she did, in her own way. You must be circumcised, Pavel Nikolaevich, as all Jewish boys are at birth. Aren't you? Of course you are! That was her way of telling you the truth."

Pavel turns pale. A drop of sweat trickles down his forehead. His hand creeps up to his cravat. He folds it, twists it, rolls it in his hand. He lets go and the cravat falls limp and creased like his linen suit.

"All right, son, I believe we have a pact. There's paper and pencil on the desk. Write down where I can find the Tsarevich."

"I hope I am doing the right thing, Madame, and you'll be good for him."

She presses the folded paper between her palms. The air around her stirs as if Alexei followed her into the room as he used to in the past, when she felt his presence without having to look. All she wants now is to tuck away her jumbled emotions and go to Alexei. She drops the note into her purse, opens the French doors, and walks onto the terrace, gesturing for Pavel to follow her. Before them, a lavender-covered hill slants down to the sea and toward neighboring mansions on the lower slopes. The disk of a fat moon hangs low in the velvet sky. An owl alights on the balustrade and begins to hoot a melancholy tune.

Darya squeezes the young man's shoulder. "Don't worry, son, one day you will look back on this night and remember me with fondness. You have a bright future ahead of you. You might be sad sometimes, but never lonely." She retrieves the pouch from her purse and plants it in his hand. "Here, this will help. Enough jewels to support you for a long time. Bribe the security guards with a charm or two if they catch up with you. They'll let you go."

"No, Madame. I cannot accept what belongs to Alexei Nikolaevich."

"Take it. There's more for him. Listen to me well, son. Walk down the hill and out of the compound. When you reach the shore down there, keep to your right. You will pass a deserted dock, then an abandoned skeleton of a ship at which point, on your right again, you'll find a narrow staircase hewed into the hill that leads to a thoroughfare, where you'll find a taxi station. Lose yourself for a few months until you are forgotten. Go, before they come looking."

Pale hairs flutter in the breeze. His nimble downward steps gather speed. He hesitates for an instant, opens the pouch, and selects a few small items with which to buy his freedom, then turns back, and tosses the pouch toward her before breaking into a trot at the foot of the hill to lose himself in the thick darkness.

Chapter Forty-Three

DARYA WAVES HER CANE in salutation at the multiple images of Grand Duchess Sophia and Rostislav in the surrounding salon mirrors. Gilded consoles are set with delicacies and scented vodkas, above which a portrait of the duchess looks down, demanding the truth.

The Sheremetev Salon is pregnant with unspoken expectations, with the weight of the unknown. The afternoon has stretched into evening while Darya Borisovna and Pavel Nikolaevich were sequestered in the study. In this wing of the estate, Rostislav and the duchess were served afternoon tea and supper as they awaited word from Darya.

"Good news?" the duchess asks as soon as she sees Darya approach. She reaches out her cigarette holder for her attendant to reload. She draws deeply, letting out a cloud of smoke that momentarily conceals her pensive face.

Her bones aching, Darya settles in a chair the attendant pulls forward. "Unfortunately, not. Pavel Nikolaevich is not the person he pretends to be. I asked him to leave."

Rostislav jumps out of his seat. His burned profile is puckered in anger. "Why? Why in the world did you send him away?"

"I despise impostors, Rostislav! Either he had to go or I would have strangled him."

"Alert the guards!" Rostislav shouts. "Right away! Before he leaves the grounds."

The grand duchess points an accusing cigarette holder at Darya. "You were here to confirm or refute his authenticity. Other decisions were not yours to make."

"And that's exactly what I did. He is a charlatan, your eminence, with no ties to the Imperial Family."

Rostislav pours himself a glass of vodka, downs it in two gulps, upending the empty glass on the tabletop. "My dear woman, DNA tests have already proven his paternal ties. You must have insulted him. That is why he left."

A sudden rumble originates from faraway, a startling sound like cannon fire in the distance.

"An earthquake!" Rostislav shouts.

"We're under attack!" the attendant hollers.

Darya leans back, crosses her arms over her chest, and allows the fear of nature to work its magic. In another half hour Pavel will be beyond the reach of the security guards. She snaps open the clasp of her purse and finds a weathered berry in the bottom, flicks away a petrified butterfly from the stem, the dried fuzz disintegrating in midair. She drops the berry in her mouth and allows herself to celebrate the miracle of Jasmine's grandson leading her to the Tsarevich.

"What in the world is this dreadful noise?" the grand duchess demands.

Darya rises and goes out to the terrace, nodding, gesturing, and bowing as if conducting a private conversation with a higher authority, expressing her thanks to a miserable whale somewhere in the sea, beyond the fire-laced horizon.

She taps her cane on the marble underfoot, crosses the terrace, and steps back into the salon to confront her stunned audience. For the first time since that night in the cellar of the House of Special Purpose, she attempts to make the sign of the cross, but her hand will not obey, and she drops it to her side. "What you hear out there is the Lord's voice informing me that the Tsarevich is alive."

Rostislav's mocking laughter rises above the whale's thunderous interruptions.

The duchess's cigarette holder is poised as if to banish the intrusion from her realm.

"Call the guards!" Rostislav barks. "She's trying to buy time."

"My dear Rostislav, I was invited here to decide whether Pavel is a Romanov or not. Well! He is not. Must I repeat myself?"

"Stop this nonsense! I put up with your old woman imaginings, certain the true contender to the throne will find his way to you. Now that he has, you act like a Bolshevik!"

Darya swings her cane and, without as much as batting an eyelash, aims the tip at the artery on Rostislav's neck. "I'll skewer you like a rat! Then we'll see who is a Bolshevik!"

He freezes in place. He has observed this woman wield her cane with the force and speed of a dueling master's sword. He is certain she will not hesitate to plunge the silver tip into his artery.

The grand duchess crushes her cigarette among other lipstick-smeared stumps, rises to her feet, and gestures to her attendant to remove himself from her path. She grips Darya around one arm, reaches out, and extracts the cane from her. "What has come over you, Rostislav? Let Darya finish what she has to say."

"Stop jumping up and down like a monkey, Rostislav," Darya bristles. "Would you rather an impostor ascend the throne or Alexei Nikolaevich Romanov? Call the Russian Nobility Association and explain that my prayers have been answered; the Tsarevich has been found!"

Rostislav passes one hand over his profile as if to iron out the creases. "Dreaming again, Darya? No hemophiliac would ever live so long. Stop deceiving yourself!"

The grand duchess lifts a fleck of tobacco from her lower lip. "He has a point. Even if the Tsarevich survived the carnage that night, it's improbable he would live to be—"

"Eighty-seven," Darya offers. "Other hemophiliacs don't reach such advanced age because they can't get their hands on ambergris to stem their internal bleeding or keep them young."

Grand Duchess Sophia strokes the frown lines between her brows. She chases away some cigarette smoke with one hand. "You did mention a pillow stuffed with ambergris that might have deflected bullets. Very interesting. Do you have some ambergris with you?"

"Not much," Darya lies. "What about you, Rostislav? I gave you a generous chunk."

His lips turn the color of curdled milk. "I don't recall you giving me any ambergris!" He pats his coat, thrusts his hands into his back pockets, makes a show of rising to his feet to check his pants pockets. "We both know you never gave me any, Darya. But now that the matter has come up, I'd like some ambergris too!"

"Search your suitcase," Darya suggests, leaning back in her seat and thinking that Pavel must have made his way out of the compound and reached the Crimean thoroughfare by now.

Chapter Forty-Four

D ARYA STEPS DOWN FROM the taxi that transported her the twenty miles from the Warsaw-Moscow railroad to Biaroza on the banks of the River Yasel'da.

She sets her small suitcase down, leans on her cane, and gazes at the surroundings. Is it truly possible that this town is home to her beloved Tsarevich? Alexei Nikolaevich Romanov, who remains everything and everyone to her, who continues to temper the ache of her parents' loss, who replaces the sons she lost, who fills up the void of Avram's absence, which she will not call a loss because he is always with her. Is it possible that the child who once lived among unimaginable opulence is now living in one of these mostly decaying houses in this peasant town?

Part of the independent Republic of Belarus, Biaroza has witnessed its share of upheavals. The town was, throughout numerous historical unrests, tossed around like a rotting melon between Russia and the Red and Polish armies. During the Great War, the German army wiped out most of the town's population, seventy percent of whom were Jews.

She walks past the town hall and the ruins of the Biaroza monastery, which was looted and demolished in the distant past. The bricks were used to build the main prison. What is left of the monastery has been placed on the list of historic architectural heritage of Belarus to be renovated and restored, but little progress has been made. Pedestrians stroll around a fountain in the center of the marketplace. An emaciated donkey is tied to a tree. Shops display bolts of fabric, jars of spices, plastic toys. The scent of fresh bread emanates from a nearby bakery. The mix of old and modern surprises her. A few forlorn birches line the streets, a handful border the fountain.

Will Alyosha remember her? Will he remember the ambergris and its miracles? At the possibility of encountering an old, senile man who would turn his back to her, she settles on the ledge of the fountain, wipes her forehead, suddenly feeling the weight of the tiring journey from the Crimea.

A hydroelectric power station on her right comes to life, and her heart starts to pound like a mad woodpecker. According to Pavel's directions, the house in which the Tsarevich lives is on the far right side of the power plant.

She grabs her suitcase and walks ahead with the confidence of a young woman, savoring every step to cross the narrow street and circle the whitewashed wooden fence. Is this his home? This two-story building of fired brick with two balconies aflame with bougainvillea. Although modest, contrary to the surrounding houses, it is well tended. She pulls out the note, unfolds it, reads the directions again.

The air smells of grass and fire logs. The sky is a pure blue. A passing peasant with a thick kerchief on her head and a bundle in her calloused hand smiles at her. An emaciated donkey brays, clattering by.

She takes a deep breath, squares her shoulders, and climbs three steps to the front door that smells of fresh paint.

The thought occurs to her that she should have dressed for the occasion, purchased a new blouse, a pair of shoes. Wearing the Empress's old hat and maroon velvet skirt, she must look old and tired. "Nothing can be done now," she mumbles, lifting the lion-shaped knocker and tapping on the door once.

A wind wails around the corner, a handful of pebbles smacks

itself against her right leg. She rubs her leg, straightens up. Her back is aching.

She waits, knocks again. A face appears between half-drawn curtains at a side window. The swish of approaching slippers can be heard inside, then the clang of locks and bolts and a rattling of chains. Yes, she thinks, such precautions are necessary in a town with a history of numerous upheavals, but more so in a house that boards the Tsarevich.

The door is flung wide open, startling her. A tall, compact couple appears at the threshold. A man with an embroidered skullcap and coils of hair at his temples. A woman wearing thick stockings, with a flowered kerchief tied under her chin. The man grabs Darya's suitcase, the woman her hand, and almost pulls her inside. Their strange, synchronized movements unsettle Darya.

"Pavel Nikolaevich gave me directions to your home," she stutters.

"Yes. We were expecting you." The gentleman brushes yellow hair from a pale forehead shadowed with a network of veins. "I am Viktor. This is my twin sister, Greta. Come in, please. Pavel said you were coming. You must be tired."

Darya is led into a small, low-beamed, well-lighted living room with peasant furniture upholstered with chintz. Sheer drapes flank two windows, facing the street. Outside, a stray dog sniffs at something in the middle of the road. A garbage can rattles in the wind. Dry leaves and bits of paper drift past. She is reminded of the first weeks, months, even years after she had settled in the Entertainment Palace, adrift like these leaves, certain and hopeful that the force of her grief would blow her away. Yet here she is, at last, separated from the Tsarevich by no more than a wall.

Greta fluffs a couple of cushions on the sofa. "Please, sit. You must have had a long journey."

"No, thank you. I'm eager to see Alexei Nikolaevich. How did he react when he found out I was coming? He must be beside himself! Of course he is. I'll not keep him waiting another second."

"But you must catch your breath first. I'll bring some refreshments," Greta insists, stepping out.

"Tell me all about Alexei," Darya tells Viktor when they are left alone. "How did he come into your care?"

Before Viktor has a chance to address Darya's question, Greta is back with a tray of hot tea, honey cakes, and two candles. "We'll light the Sabbath candles. Do you care to pray with us? We are Hasidic Jews."

Darya struggles to harness her concern. How is it possible for Alexei Nikolaevich Romanov, born into a Christian Orthodox family and raised to rule Russia, to have been educated with beliefs so different from his? She gazes from sister to brother. Pray? She should know how to pray with these people, after all. Was she not a Hebrew queen in her other life? Why, then, is she unable to pray?

"Please," Greta says. "Pray in your heart, if you prefer, in your own language."

Darya joins the two in front of the lit candles on the mantelpiece, bows her head, and prays for a stronger, more patient heart to withstand all this waiting. She has endured seventy-three years of waiting, but another minute and she might die.

"I've prepared a room for you," Greta says. "Please spend the night with us. You can see Alexei tomorrow. It's already past his bedtime."

Darya's voice rises with alarm. "It's hardly seven. Why would he go to bed this early? Wake him up if you have to!"

Viktor rests a hand on Darya's shoulder. "Alexei likes photography. He wakes up at dawn to take advantage of the ideal light and works hard throughout the day. He's usually tired at this hour."

"But doesn't he know I am here to see *him*?"

"He fell asleep, and I don't have the heart to wake him up."

Darya slumps back in the chair, a million terrifying thoughts coursing through her mind. He has no recollection of her. She means nothing to him, less than a good night's sleep. How else to explain his lack of enthusiasm? She meets Greta's eyes with her own unwavering stare. "I'll wait right here, in this very room, for another eighty years if I have to, until I see him."

Greta casts her eyes down, adjusts her kerchief. "I'll wake him up then. But be prepared to meet a man who, like all of us, has been shaped by the innumerable atrocities he endured." She walks out and shuts the door behind her.

"How did the Tsarevich end up in Biaroza?" Darya asks Viktor.

"My understanding is that our uncle found him half-dead in a house during the revolution, concealed somewhere behind boxes. A dog was at his side. Maybe the dog dragged and concealed him, perhaps a sympathetic revolutionary did it, no one knows. Anyway, Uncle hid the Tsarevich with a family of peasants somewhere near Ekaterinburg. When it was safe to move about, Uncle brought him here to Papa and Mama. The Bolsheviks had their hands full in the big cities. Biaroza was the last place they were thinking about. Mama and Papa raised Alexei for twenty-three years. Greta and I were thirteen when our parents died at the outbreak of the Great Patriotic War, when the Germans captured Biaroza. The three of us—Alexei, Greta, and I—were left alone. We went into hiding in a hayshed with the animals. At first, it was too dangerous to move around much, especially for Alexei. German and Russian soldiers were everywhere, and later, well, this is home, and we didn't want to leave."

Darya struggles to sit still. She is a tangle of nerves, unable to deal with the seed of doubt hardening into certainty.

Viktor gestures toward the door. "Come with me, please. I want to show you something."

She musters all of her strength to follow him across a narrow hallway. The walls on both sides are crowded with photographs: scenes of Biaroza engulfed in a desolate dawn, portraits of peasants carrying their scant wares, sad-eyed children playing in an alley, a shopkeeper dropping a coin into the outstretched hand of a beggar, a bald-spotted puppy. She slows down to better observe the forlorn photographs that seem to be layered in smoke.

"Alexei's," Viktor replies to the question she has not voiced. "He is quite a photographer."

Viktor opens a door, ushers her into a dining room, stepping aside as if the room is not large enough to accommodate this woman's passions.

Darya's hand springs up to her Fabergé necklace. Her cane rattles to the floor.

There, facing her on the wall, is a rendition of the baby Tsarevich. His blue-gray eyes, fair hair, and dimpled-cheeks are a vision of health. Perhaps no other painting, Darya muses, managed to achieve its potential as well as this painting of the Tsarevich in the arms of White Thighs Paulina. Not only did the painting give the Tsarina great hope when she needed it most, but it also caused the revolutionary bastards to bristle with a million indignant questions.

Darya reaches for the cane, but Viktor fetches it for her. She gasps. In front of her unbelieving gaze, leaning on a simple wooden easel on the opposite side of the room, is another portrait.

In this small home in Biaroza where her Tsarevich lives, she has her face to the portrait Avram was most proud of and her back to the only portrait he was ashamed of.

She steps close, touches the canvas, the scar on her forehead that mirrors the scar Avram carried like a defiant introduction to the persecutions he endured. She is lounging on a satin-covered dais, her nipples swollen, the soft curve of her waist and chiseled hip half-lit by a chandelier. Her eyes gaze back at the painter with a blend of wonder and adoration.

Throughout the years, several of Avram's paintings were purchased by museums. Many found homes in palaces and aristocratic mansions. But this one he kept for himself. He believed this portrait, more than any other, revealed the energy, passion, and confrontations that transpired between the two of them, the artist and his model, during their hours spent together.

"You must have known Uncle Avram well," Viktor says.

"Not as well as I should have. How in the world did he acquire this portrait, the Madonna and Child?"

"I don't know why he disliked this one," Viktor says. "It's a lovely portrait, isn't it? He spent a great deal of time and energy searching for it. He bought it for an exorbitant price from a Bolshevik commandant, I understand. Someone named Vasiliev."

That bastard Vasiliev! Darya curses under her breath. It was not enough that he invaded the Alexander Park, disinterred Rasputin, set fire to everything in his path, but he had to plunder the Lilac Boudoir too. "Have you more of Avram's paintings?"

"No. But he painted a lot after the revolution. He produced numbered lithographs, posters, and ceramic replicas of your portraits. They became very popular. He made friends in high places, ready to do him some small and large favors in return for one or another of his paintings."

"I followed his success in the newspapers. He became rich."

"But he was always lonely, up until he died in 1943."

"Twenty-five years after we parted," Darya murmurs. She crosses her arms over her breasts. "Maybe he wasn't that lonely. He certainly knew where to find me. I was waiting."

"He tried. More than once. The first time, the newly formed Cheka arrested him as he was approaching your doorsteps. They were following Lenin's orders, imprisoning dissidents and confiscating right-wing bourgeois art. Uncle Avram fit the profile. And you, because of your loyalty to the Romanovs, were under constant surveillance. Uncle Avram tried to contact you a year later, when he was released from prison."

"That was a terrible year," Darya says. "Lenin's Red Terror was in full force, and people were executed in plain sight. I couldn't bear to go out."

"Uncle Avram tried to see you again. I think it was his third or fourth attempt, I'm not certain. A bullet meant for someone else lodged in his lungs. Doctors decided to leave the bullet in place. It would have been too dangerous to remove it."

Viktor Bensheimer takes a deep breath, adjusts his skullcap, and hands Darya Borisovna a glass of ice water. "He survived that incident too. He had survived wars and revolutions, prison, torture, and bullet wounds. He was sixty-three and had seen enough of the world. He decided to travel to Ekaterinburg again."

———

Avram Bensheimer stands in front of the main entrance to the Entertainment Palace. He passes his hand over the massive door in front of him; the weather-beaten, cracked oak has lost all semblance of its past glory. The brass hinges are dull and rusted. Despite the heavy doors and thick walls that separate him from Darya, the eucalyptus and clover scent of her hair is all around him. He raises a hand, wincing at the pain from the bullet lodged in his lung, which left him with an imperceptible limp, compromising his feline walk. He lets his hand fall to his side, takes a long-drawn breath and knocks twice, harder the third time when no answer comes. He steps away from the door that remains closed in his face. Disappointment, rage, and sadness curdle within him.

He is unaware that Little Servant is in the distillery in the garden, engaged in sampling vodka, and Darya is bathing in the banya, shampooing her hair with eucalyptus oil and Bulgarian evening primrose. As she has done every day for the last twenty-five years, she twirls his opal wedding band around her finger and relives the joy of the first time she gave herself to him. Avram! Her first and last love. She had immersed him in the imperial banya, a rite she insisted they perform despite having no imminent wedding plans. Youth and arrogance blinded her to the enormity of the risk she was taking that day, allowing a Jew, no, tempting him, into the inner sanctum of the Imperial Court. Still, despite all the suffering she caused them both, she does not regret that day. How she had delighted at that first glimpse of his arousal, unexpected and utterly delicious.

He turns his back to the door and descends the steps he had climbed an hour ago. He is having difficulty breathing, the pain in his chest excruciating. The bullet is dislodged, and traveling toward his heart.

He pulls a revolver out of his coat pocket and aims it at his pain.

According to rumors, his still warm body was discovered at the threshold to the Entertainment Palace. Since there were no known relatives, the body was dispatched to a mass crematorium designated for war victims. Other rumors say that a passing peddler attempted to give him a proper burial, but in view of the fact that the artist had committed suicide, he was refused a Jewish burial.

And an overwhelming number of bystanders swear that at a certain moment and time, they witnessed the painter's prostrate body cloaked in a white light emanating from within. In a matter of seconds, and in front of their disbelieving eyes, nothing remained of him but a phantom glow that illuminated the entire Entertainment Palace as if it were a sacred shrine.

Darya wipes her wet cheeks, rubs her stinging eyes. She curses the banya, the berries, Little Servant, and his vodka. Why did she have to bathe that day, at that specific hour, gorge herself on berries? She is a patient woman, after all. She should have sat at the door, waited for years if necessary, left her door wide open for Avram. She should have known he would come.

Viktor retrieves a brown-wrapped parcel from a drawer and hands it to her. "Uncle Avram left this for you,"

She takes her time opening the package, ripping layers of wrapping off to reveal the treasure inside. A portrait of hers she had not seen before, smaller than any of his other paintings. She is swirling in white veils that fall over her hair and face, the sheen of her raven black curls and golden eyes palpable behind tiers of gossamer. Her joy illuminates the canvas. She is a bride. She allows herself a rare instant to treasure this moment so master-fully captured beneath a cloud of veils, to acknowledge his love, his hunger for her, perhaps stronger than for his art. She passes her palm over the signature, smiling at his message: *Fare Well, My Opal-Eyed Bride.*

Chapter Forty-Five

H E APPEARS AT THE threshold, tall and elegant, silver curls coiling at his temples, an embroidered skullcap kept in place with hairpins. He holds on to the doorframe with one hand; the other seeks the locket strung with a leather strap around his neck. Greta gives him an encouraging nudge forward. He tugs at the camera hanging from his shoulder. Takes a few guarded steps toward Viktor and reaches out to seize his hand.

"Alexei, Loves. It's me, Darya!" She controls the urge to cross the room, hug him, squeeze him to her chest.

He tilts his head and gazes at her with startled eyes from which the smile has long fled, checks her from head to toe: her hat pulled down over knitted brows, the threadbare jacket with ermine trim, the velvet skirt. "Mama? Is it you, Mama?"

"Not Mama, Loves," she whispers, removing her hat and letting loose her silver curls that remain as wild as they were in her youth. "Look at my eye! Take a good look. Don't you remember how you liked to touch my strange eye?"

He reaches out a finger to trace the outline of her face, her chin, the bridge of her nose, the length of her eyebrows, around one eye, then the opal eye, without displaying the slightest surprise. He fumbles for his camera case, retrieves a Polaroid, the lines on his handsome face deepening as he twists a black knob. He raises the camera to check her through the viewfinder.

Long before he opened his mouth to utter a single word, she knew that something is terribly wrong with the old Tsarevich, with his faraway gaze and disconnected gestures.

She is dumbstruck and grieving anew, hope taking flight, crumbling around her like ancient ruins robbed of their flimsy buttresses.

He lets out a sudden sound of surprise, lowers the Polaroid, takes a few steps toward her, and bends to take a closer look at the amulet pinned to her blouse. He breaks into a wide smile. "Darya! Is it you?"

"Yes, yes, Loves! Your Darya! Look at you! Handsome as ever. Come! Give me a hug!"

He does not step into her wide-open arms but continues to stroke the amulet. "You found it? Where? Tell me."

Her hand springs up to her chest. "The amulet?"

"Yes. Can I have it?"

"Of course, Loves. If you want it."

"Yes, I really do." He unlocks the locket from around his neck and takes out a small piece of ambergris. "See, just a tiny bit left. When it's finished, I'll start bleeding again. But now that you brought my good luck amulet, I'll be fine. Remember how you stopped my bleeding?"

Yes, she remembers all too well. She remembers the different concoctions of ambergris that had successfully stemmed his bleeding, remembers how the amulet became part of his uniforms when he was a child, present in formal photographs, there when he played with his sisters, his companion every waking hour. Even when the two sailors of the imperial navy were assigned to follow him everywhere, to protect him from falls and injury, he did not step out of the palace without his good luck amulet.

Having been deprived of a normal childhood, he, too, had searched for a miracle in small things.

As if they are back in the Crimea, and she has just dressed the young Tsarevich in formal attire on his way to the inauguration of the Livadia Palace, she detaches the amulet from her dress and pins it to the lapel of his coat.

He wraps his arms around her and covers her face with kisses, her cheeks, her forehead, the back of her hands. "I thought I killed you too. I murdered them all, you know. Is this why you didn't come to see me?"

"What are you saying?" Darya exclaims, unable to rein in her shock. "Who did you kill?"

"Mama and Papa and Tatiana and Anastasia, all my sisters, and you know—all of them." He flops down on the sofa and pulls her down beside him, hugging his camera to his chest.

"No, Loves, don't ever think like this. I was there. You didn't do anything wrong." She strokes his hair even as she reprimands herself for resorting to the childlike voice of decades ago, when he was a small boy.

"But I did. I'll tell you what I did if you won't punish me."

"What a thing to say, Your Majesty," she says, bowing her head. "Who am I to punish you?"

He gazes down at his hands that hold the locket. "They all died after I lost the amulet that day in your apartments. I don't remember exactly what day, I think it was a week ago, or today maybe. I found a monster on your bed, a turtle, or the whale with the tummy ache that cries a lot. It was slippery and smelled of father's tobacco and mother's leather gloves. I prodded its tummy with the amulet's pin. Don't get angry. You promised. I just wanted to take the pain away and make the whale all better. But it suddenly swallowed my amulet. And then Papa went away to war. Mama cried a lot. We were sent away and became prisoners. And everyone died."

Darya covers her eyes with her hands. So it was not a conspiracy, after all. The Tsarevich himself had shoved his amulet into the ambergris, where it remained buried for decades, right under her ignorant nose.

Suddenly his eyes light up and the mischievous boy of another era reappears. "You know what I did that night?"

"What night, Loves? There were so many nights."

"No! There's only one night. The night of bullets. I snatched a bit of ambergris out of the pillow you gave me and hid it in my fist for a very long time, until Avram gave me this locket for my ambergris." He holds up the locket that had been hanging around his neck.

An icy wind stirs in Darya's heart. She opens her purse, snaps it shut, then opens it again, digging her hand in. She can hardly bear to think of Alexei suffering as he has. She finds the kerchief-wrapped ambergris in her purse and hands it to him. "Here, Loves, replenish your locket. There's more in my suitcase, more than you'll ever need. You'll never run out of ambergris again."

He fumbles with the latch to unlock his locket. He does not ask how she survived that night or how she managed to find him. His world is enclosed in his head and in the four small rooms in which he wanders, his camera in constant frenzy as he searches for knickknacks—metal sheets, electrical wires, copper coins, nails, and pieces of rope to fashion primitive toys. On rare instances when unsolicited snatches of memory emerge, he locks himself in his room and sucks on a piece of ambergris until blessed amnesia takes over. The mind of a thirteen-year-old resides in the body of an old Jewish man who remains imprisoned in the cellar of the House of Special Purpose on the hot, humid night of July 16, 1918, when his family was slaughtered.

Chapter Forty-Six

DARYA TOSSES THE BLANKET off and, in the same clothes she traveled into Biaroza the day before, sits on the edge of a bed and rubs her eyes. She did not sleep all night, although the Bensheimers made every attempt to make the guest room comfortable. A vase of wild flowers and a jug of water stand on a coffee table in front of a sofa. A portable heater warms the room. Extra blankets and pillows are piled on a reclining chair. But such amenities mean nothing when decades of search have led her to this bitter truth.

Alexei Nikolaevich Romanov is a damaged man.

He is not up to the task of ruling Russia.

And she is not up to the task of redirecting her loyalties.

She, too, remains a hostage to her dreams and nightmares, to bathing rituals that take her back to her youth with Avram, to berries that keep her hope alive and her will steadfast.

She spent so long trying to find the Tsarevich that it never occurred to her that he might not want to be found.

The cold wind in her heart develops into a blizzard, and she fears she is about to die. Die at the worst time and in the last place she wants to be buried.

She tidies her clothes in front of the full-length mirror, then steps closer to examine the fan of wrinkles girthing her eyes, the sad turned-down corners of her lips, the burst of tiny lines around her mouth, and for the first time in her life, sees herself as the old woman she is. Did the deterioration begin decades ago when she left Tsarskoe Selo and entered the House of Special Purpose, a week ago when she left Ekaterinburg for the Sheremetev Estate, or yesterday when she came face to face with Alexei Nikolaevich Romanov?

A hesitant knock at the door startles her. She checks the green fluorescent numbers on the clock on the bedside table. Five a.m. She crosses the room and opens the door.

Wearing yellow checkered pajamas, uncombed hair falling over smoky eyes, Alexei offers her a timid smile. "Can I take your photograph?"

He sets on the coffee table a clothbound portfolio tied with twine, the cover embossed with the image of Moses. He directs his attention to the black focus knob on the camera, concentrating with the seriousness of a mathematician, fully engrossed in the process of manipulating the universe enclosed in the frame of his viewfinder, a tiny world over which he rules as he once had over the Alexander Palace. He begins to snap one photograph after another, capturing her forced smile, then her impatience at the consecutive flashes of light that startle her eyes shut, the frantic clicking of the camera that rattles her already frayed nerves, and her annoyance with pointless, expensive cameras that deliver immediate photographs like some sort of easy birth.

One by one, he pulls photographs out of the Polaroid and arranges them on the coffee table. First three, then six, eight, on and on. Every now and then, he locks his puzzled gaze with hers, wondering why she has stopped smiling, whether she is sad or upset at him.

He arranges the photographs on the tabletop, observes the developing images as they come into focus. Slowly, carefully, he shifts them around as if he is assembling a puzzle and it's of utmost importance that each piece fit properly into the other.

She traces the growing rows of pictures, arranged in some order that eludes her. The collage seems to highlight a slow, inexplicable deterioration at the corners of her eyes, dark crescents under them, a sagging of her once round chin, a slight drooping of her arched eyebrows.

She slumps back on the sofa, holds her head in her hands, feeling faint and disoriented. "I am confused, Loves. Tell me what your pictures are about."

"About you, Darya."

It occurs to her that just as Avram's paintings had introduced her to the young evolving Darya, these photographs, brutal in their bluntness, reveal the desperate woman she has become. Her hand plunges into her purse for a bit of ambergris to drop in her mouth, but finding none, she throws her shoulders up in resignation.

"Tell me, Loves. Are you happy here?"

"Happier now that I have the amulet and more ambergris."

She shuts her eyes to ponder the profound simplicity of his reply. It never occurred to her that happiness could hinge on so little. A sense of peace she has not experienced for a long time washes over her. She wraps an arm around his shoulders and shuts her eyes to better enjoy a feeling of warmth that permeates her opal eye.

"Darya, are you still angry with me?"

"Don't say that, Loves. I'm never angry with you. Do you remember our ritual? Good. Bend your head. Just like this. Now, repeat with me. You'll grow up to live a long, healthy life. You'll become our Tsar and rule until you are a hundred years old. I'm impressed. You remember every word. And here's a kiss to keep you doubly safe."

He smiles, a perplexed smile, as if not certain whether he is allowed to give free rein to his joy, to his sense of unexpected euphoria.

"What are you thinking, Loves? Do you want to say something?"

"Will you take me with you?" he asks.

"Oh, Loves! Nothing would make me happier. Nothing in the world!"

She suffered the Bolshevik Revolution, civil wars, and seventy years of Communist rule to hear these words from the Tsarevich. Yet she opens her mouth and says, "But this is your home, Loves. And I'll have to go back to mine. An old woman like me can be a great nuisance. I can't take care of you."

"But look at the photographs, Darya. You are not old at all."

She is taken aback by yet another developing scenario spread out on the tabletop, the closeup of her eyes that stare back at her from the photographs. A look of gentle acceptance floods her right eye, yet it is the left that makes her realize that what she felt in her opal eye just now is connected to the photographs. She holds one picture up to the light, places it back on the table, and leans over to scrutinize the rest. She rises to survey the reflection of her eye in the sheen of the lacquered tabletop, in the windowpanes, and one last time in the mirror. "Am I going mad, Loves? Is this true, or am I imagining this?"

"Your eye?" he asks without a shred of surprise.

"You see it too?"

"Of course. It happens all the time."

"People change in your photographs?"

"For real. See, you're not broken anymore."

"Thank you, Loves. It's wonderful to see myself and you… well…everything in a way I didn't before."

She unclasps her necklace, strokes the enameled Fabergé egg, and snaps it open to inhale the sweet and bitter scent of her joys and sorrows, the ups and downs of her two lives. She locks it around Alexei's neck. "Here, Loves. Now you have two lockets."

She digs out the pouch of jewels from her purse and plants it in his hand. "Give this to Viktor and Greta. They raised you well."

Chapter Forty-Seven

C LAD IN THE TSARINA'S once white tulle gown that had inherited the dusty shade of the roads she traveled, Darya sets her valise down and leans on the Tsar's cane, the double-headed eagles, the shaft smooth with the patina of time and polishing oils. She is home at last. Tired from days of traveling from Ekaterinburg to the Crimea to Biaroza and back again. A month away from home seems like an eternity, and she expects to find her Entertainment Palace surrounded by a hostile army, even razed by one or another political faction. Instead, a few birch and linden saplings and a handful of cedars raise their emerald shoots out of the earth, startling the gray landscape of her coffee bushes.

She inhales deeply, surprised to find the air laced with the sweet vanilla and chocolate scent of the coffee Little Servant brews for her, rather than the stink of rot that the hallucinogenic berries have a way of scattering in all directions.

She lifts her suitcase and takes a few steps toward her home, a breeze sighing about the treetops. She gazes up at the scattering of white clouds overhead. A change is in the air, a damp drift that foretells rain. The chatter of birds reminds her of the birds of paradise, and she wonders whether they, too, were forced to readjust their loyalties.

She is startled by the sight of two people walking out of the gateway to her back garden, a swirl of white butterflies on their trail. Her butterflies are not social creatures. Why, then, are they out en masse as if drawn to some fragrant nectar? Who are these strangers with wide-brimmed hats concealing their faces, a veil tossed over the face of one?

Darya retreats into the tree boundary surrounding the vast grounds of her palace and shades her eyes against the sun to take a better look.

The outlines of the intruders move seamlessly under loose, capelike coats with flowing sleeves as they continue to glide ahead, one adjusting the veil, the other waving a hand in front to clear their field of vision. They amble through the bushes, cats and wild civets weaving in and out of their legs. They stop to study the crumbling façade of the palace, gaze up behind them to appraise the gathering clouds on the horizon, then take their time to stroll around, as if surveying the grounds.

Are they waiting for her, Darya wonders? She pinches her cheeks to instigate a blush, pats her hair into place, and brushes leaves off her skirt. What a useless act, she muses, to tidy herself in case of company. Avram is dead. Alexei is imprisoned in his own world. The Ancient One has abandoned her. Who else is left to pay her a visit?

The strangers come to a stop in front of the house, and as if on cue, the door opens and out walks Little Servant, wrapped in a blanket and shivering uncontrollably. A metal watering can in hand, he glances this way and that as if to make sure his mistress has not returned and is not watching him. The two flank him like angels or thieves, collaborators perhaps in a plot as he kneels down, pries the can open, and places the lid at his feet. He pours liquid from the can over a bush. He plunges his hand under the folds of his blanket and pulls out a small box, strikes a match, holds up the flame like a miniature beacon, the breeze transporting the smell of phosphorous. He drops the match on the gasoline-saturated bush. He empties the can, striking match after match while the couple fan the growing flames with their flowing sleeves.

Darya sits on her suitcase, concealed behind the gathering of trees. She stares into the fire as if she is young again and gazing into Rasputin's unforgiving eyes, which had the power to thrust her into her past life and into a fire of death and renewal. The steady rhythm of her heart drowns out the chirping of birds, the yowl of cats and wild civets. All she hears is the blood running strong in her veins.

Little Servant picks handfuls of coffee cherries off the bushes, tosses them on the sputtering fire, upends the can of gasoline, and steps back. A sudden flare blooms like a corsage of red roses, and the plump cherries melt like sugar in hot tea, the sap snaking in and around shrubs, stumps, and saplings, making its way toward the foundation of the Entertainment Palace.

Darya is startled into action. She steps out from behind the trees to hurry ahead and stop the fire from consuming her home. She hesitates, settles back on her suitcase. She sees no reason to save a home that has inherited the stench of her memories, neither is she in a hurry to retrieve the rest of the Romanov jewels that remain concealed under the wooden floor planks in the cellar. What use would these jewels be to the Tsarevich now? She thinks of her friends, the beady-eyed rats that have grown fat on stolen provisions. She thinks of the ambergris, thankful she had the foresight to deliver a large part of it to the Tsarevich. But most of all she thinks of her portrait on the mantelpiece in the upstairs salon, a gift of love from Avram. This she will certainly miss.

The silence is broken by an explosion of slick, golden flames that illuminate the surroundings, the crackle of bushes, the wails of cats and wild civets, the cacophony of birds, and the squeal of squirrels. A flock of birds bursts out of the branches and soars overhead, disoriented in the fragrant smoke and flames that hiss and dance in concert.

Her butterflies, wings rainbows of livid colors, soar to unimaginable heights and disappear from her field of vision. Are they gone, her butterflies? Left without a flutter of a farewell? And then she sees them appear from behind a low cloud, a flurry of white snowflakes floating down toward her, adorning her ermine collar, enfolding her arms and shoulders, crowning her hair, and cascading over her curls like dazzling bridal veils.

Little Servant is astonished at the ferocious determination of the blaze to clear everything in its path. His intention was to light a small bonfire to warm himself, but this beastly fire seems to have a will of its own, spreading uncontrollably in all directions.

He flings his blanket into the flames and flees toward the city.

Darya's gaze follows her servant's flight into Ekaterinburg, a city of cement and concrete, a city of shame teeming with an amnesic generation that keeps igniting mindless wars that will devastate for centuries.

The strangers, with their cloaks as graceful as diaphanous wings, continue to amble around the grounds, as if enjoying the vista of burning saplings, flaming birch, the smoldering of every blessing and sin in their path.

Darya lifts her suitcase, steps into the open, waves, and calls out, "Who are you?"

They beckon to her as they stride toward the flames, their flapping cloaks and sleeves scattering delicious warmth her way. One raises an arm and gestures toward her with open palm. The other flings the veil back with one fluid motion. Darya recognizes her mother's face that is dazzled by the flames and her father's inviting smile, before the two hold hands and walk into the fire.

A delicious breeze strokes Darya's cheeks as if the blaze has opened a door. She is hesitant, uncertain what she might find on the other side of the door, whether it will be better than what she will leave behind. Rasputin had prophesied that she would be doomed to come back again and again until she rights the wrongs committed in her other life. Has she? Did she turn her back on Alexei? She is not certain.

She snaps her purse open and rifles inside for any cash. Enough to purchase a train ticket back to Biaroza. She lifts her suitcase and raises a hand in a gesture of farewell to her parents.

Then he emerges. Avram Bensheimer. As if summoned by some incantation, he ambles toward her with that feline stride that challenges gravity, staring into her face with those green-flecked eyes, tall and defiant as she had seen him for the first time in the St. Petersburg court. His shoulder-grazing hair reflects the colors of his palette; his crooked smile appears the instant he catches sight of her. He comes closer, nodding his salutations, gesturing to the opal wedding band on her finger, promising her that this time is different and that he will not lose this last chance to be with her.

Author's note

When I embarked on writing my first two novels, *Harem* and *Courtesan*, I did not know where and how my story would begin, nor did I know when and how it would end. Yet, I was intimately familiar with my main characters, with their looks, their likes and dislikes, strengths and weaknesses, and their many eccentricities. I also knew they were determined individuals, even if I was unaware yet of the extent of their bullish tenacity. Having been blessed with a colorful cast of eccentric family members, grandparents, aunts, uncles, cousins, and friends, I've gathered a treasure-trove of fodder to draw from, all types of traits that would find home in my protagonists, men and women, who led me through the ups and downs of their lives, surprising me at every page. And I utterly enjoyed the element of surprise, the excitement of not knowing what they would do next and how their story would unfold.

But the way I came to write *The Last Romanov* was quite different.

I was introduced to the shattered, acid-drenched, and burned bones of my main characters, the last Romanovs, on July 18, 1991, after the dissolution of the Soviet Union and the fall of Communism. The advent of *Perestroika* by Gorbachev and the policy of openness enabled the government to announce to the world that the remains of the Romanovs were discovered after seventy-three-years. Yet, the mystery surrounding the 1918 Bolshevik executions of the Tsar Nicholas II, Tsarina Alexandra, and their five children remained unsolved. About one thousand bone fragments were exhumed, but only nine skulls discovered, whereas eleven people—the Romanov Family and four servants—had been murdered in the cellar of the Ipatiev House in Ekaterinburg. Russian scientists began the lengthy process of skeleton identification. With the help of photographic superimposition, initial tests concluded that the missing bodies were those of the Grand Duchess Maria and the Tsarevich Alexei. Another forensic team, this one American, travelled to Ekaterinburg in 1992 to analyze the dental and bone specimens. This time, it was concluded that the missing daughter was Anastasia. To make sure, a Russian DNA specialist took some of the bones to Britain for genetic testing. The mitochondrial DNA—passed down only through the female line and sharply dissimilar from one family to another—from the remains of the Tsarina and three children were compared with that of Prince Philip, the Duke of Edinburgh, whose maternal grandmother, Princess Victoria of Hesse, was Alexandra's sister. The match was identical.

I was captivated by every emerging detail that raised one question after another. Why did the Tsar neglect to care for his teeth, while the Tsarina had sophisticated dental work, even porcelain crowns? Who was this cold-blooded Yakov Yurovsky, the primary Bolshevik executioner, who left a note, detailing the executions, in addition to the gory details of the destruction of the bodies? How and why would the mysterious Grigori Rasputin, known as the mad monk, find such great favor with the Imperial Family? Was he a man of God, a charlatan, or a sorcerer? Was it true he caused the downfall of the three hundred-year-old Romanov Dynasty? But the most pressing question gnawing at me was the looming mystery of the missing remains of the Tsarevich Alexei Nikolaevich. Did he survive? And if so, would he be in a position to reinstate the Romanov dynasty?

I have often asked this same question, albeit in another form, in the context of another revolution, which I witnessed in my own lifetime. Thirty-two-years have passed since the 1979 Islamic Revolution of Iran and the overthrow of the Pahlavi Dynasty. I spent my formative years in Iran. I remember well, the day my life changed in profound ways. Huddled around the TV screen, my family and I watched the Ayatollah Khomeini step onto the tarmac at the Mehrabad airport. His dark, glaring stare and condemnatory wave dismissed Mohammad Reza Shah and ushered in an era of chaos and uncertainty.

Now, after more than three decades in America, I am a changed woman, an American author with the freedom to write honestly without fear of censorship, without fear of imprisonment. With the freedom to ask "what if?" What if the Islamic Republic is overthrown? What if the Pahlavi Dynasty is reinstated?

Questions about the possibility of the fall of Communism and the reinstating of the Romanov Dynasty became tantalizing seeds that bloomed into a novel. I chose 1991, the year the Romanov bones were discovered, as the opening and closing of my novel that spans the life–one hundred and four years—of my main character. So, although the missing remains of Alexei and one of his sisters were discovered in 2007, while I was still in the process of writing the book, I saw no need to alter the storyline. As always, drawing from the amalgam of different cultures I experienced, I weaved my own fictional protagonists, such as the opal-eyed Darya Borisovna and the Jewish artist Avram Bensheimer, among epic historical figures. And as always, I allowed myself a measure of authorial liberty, imagining a meeting between the young Nicholas and Alexis in the Belovezh Forest or an anniversary in the fictional Entertainment Palace in Ekaterinburg.

After extensive research, I became intimately familiar with Tsar Nicholas II and Tsarina Alexandra Feodorovna, the four Grand Duchesses, and Alexei, the hemophilic heir to the throne. I learned about Alexandra and Nicholas's great love for each other, which might have been another cause for their downfall, how their only son's suffering affected their private lives, the political future of Russia, and arguably the entire world. Against the backdrop of one of the most tumultuous political eras in Russian history, years of unrest, a chain of revolutions, the Russo-Japanese War, World War I, and the Bolshevik uprising, I set out to give the reader an intimate understanding of a decadent court steeped in myth, superstition, and denial.

Reading Group Guide

1. When we first meet Darya, we see her waking from sleep and covered in clouds of butterflies. The messenger at her door asks questions seemingly designed to let us know how others fear her—believing she is a sorceress—and are also in awe of her due to her rumored connections to a monarchy from so long ago; it seems like a fairy tale. How does this introduction set the tone of the story and present the threads of magical realism weaving through the history?

2. On page 19, Sabrina and Boris debate the meaning behind their daughter's golden-opal eye. Boris is certain God means to punish him for past sins, while Sabrina interprets the message as a gift, something that will "further embellish their love." Do their interpretations strike you as naïve, or wisely cautious? What did you suspect the true meaning of Darya's magical eye was at this point, having read the opening chapter?

3. Boris and Sabrina conceived Darya out of wedlock, and Sabrina sometimes fears her daughter will be punished for this sin. But she comforts herself in knowing that Darya was conceived in love, so believes God would only care for her and never harm her. Identify other traditions broken throughout the course of the novel, and discuss how the characters suffer or benefit from these departures.

4. On page 37, Mossanen writes, "The Romanov executions are regarded as a legend rather than a stain on the canvas of history." What do you think this means? How do you see this sentiment played out in the novel? Discuss the difference between these perspectives and how each might influence the Russia of Darya's old age. Can you think of other historical events that fit this characterization? What might make a people more inclined to remember something as a legend rather than "a stain on the canvas of history," or vice versa?

5. Born with the gift of second sight, among others, Darya sees signs everywhere. Incredibly, she finds the amulet she gave to the Tsarevich Alexei hidden within her chunk of ambergris decades later, when she splits the chunk of ambergris with the intent to bring a piece to the supposed heir. She interprets the timing of her discovery as a sign that she has finally found Alexei. What other signs occur throughout the novel, and how does Darya interpret them correctly or incorrectly? Do you think Rasputin similarly sees signs, or do you think he's the manipulative charlatan the rebels purport him to be?

6. When Darya first asks the Empress for permission to bring Rasputin to court, Alexandra rejects the idea, claiming on page 80, "We will put our trust in the Lord. He will heal my son." Why does Darya want to bring Rasputin to see the Imperial Family? What finally makes it possible for her to do so—and why isn't she thrilled with the prospect? Describe the complicated relationship Darya and Rasputin share at the Romanov court, and discuss their feelings for one another.

7. According to Darya, popular gossip and political intrigue paint Rasputin as responsible for the destruction of the Romanov's three-hundred-year-old dynasty, and yet when we see him with the Romanovs, he seems like a friendly monk, even if he is unaware of court protocol. Why does the Empress tolerate Rasputin, given her evident disgust with his lack of manners

and general crudeness? What makes the Tsar banish Rasputin from court, and why does he later invite the monk to return?

8. Darya is dubious about helping the Romanovs establish the Artists' Salon at court. What does she worry will happen? Does she think she made a mistake in her choice of artists? Do you think she made a mistake? What would you have done in her place? Identify the many enemies Darya and the Romanovs have lurking in court, and discuss their motives. Do you think the Salon helped or hindered the Romanovs' slow slide into disgrace?

9. Rasputin recognizes White Thighs Paulina, the whore Avram uses as a model for his virgin and child portrait of the Tsarina and the Tsarevich. When Darya confronts Avram, he swears he used Paulina as a model because she had the right look. Did you believe him? Does Darya? Discuss the role of this portrait in Mossanen's version of the Romanovs' downfall. Which other portraits claim important roles in the story? How does art influence the events of the novel?

10. Though the Tsar would dismiss Avram, a Jew, from his court, Alexandra won't hear of it, certain Avram's painting of the Tsarevich keeps the poor boy healthy. Darya continues her secret relationship with Avram, also despite his being Jewish, for six years. Why doesn't she leave with Avram, or simply break it off if she fears her own disgrace? What ultimately causes him to leave her? Discuss the ways she and Avram influence one another throughout the novel.

11. Though there are hints all along that Darya's gifts are magical in nature, it isn't until Rasputin finally gets to put her in a trance that we learn the true origin of her strange abilities. Did you suspect Darya's secret past? Did this information change how you feel about her and her attachment to Alexei? Why or why not? Compare and contrast the details of her past life with her current one.

12. There are many dramatic turning points for the Romanovs and for Darya in *The Last Romanov*. What moment does Darya pinpoint as the moment Russia loses her soul? What relation does this event have to the crack in her opal eye and the unfolding of her own future? What ultimately heals her eye?

13. Finally, after years of searching, Darya receives word that an heir to the Romanov Empire has been located by the Russian Nobility Association. But when they bring her to meet him, she's dismissive. Why doesn't Darya accept Pavel, whose DNA and story reveal him as the grandson of Tsar Nicholas II? Why does Pavel, who thought to become Tsar and revive the Romanov dynasty, cave so quickly and agree to Darya's escape plan? Do you believe it's necessary for him to escape and hide, as Darya convinces him? Why or why not?

14. On page 195, Rasputin warns Darya that she will be forced to live life after life until she makes amends for the sins of her past self. But she counters, "This is my last life. I am a different woman now." She interprets the messages from the Ancient One as admonitions to care for the Romanov Dynasty and its young prince in particular. At the end of her life, she wonders if she has fulfilled her promise to the Ancient One and redeemed herself for Athalia's transgressions. Do you think she has? Why or why not?

15. How did you feel about the ending? Do you think Darya was right to dismiss Pavel? Why do you think she chooses not to announce to the world that she's finally found the Tsarevich? Why do you think Avram never told her that he'd found Alexei? What would you have done?

16. Who do you think is the last Romanov alluded to by the novel's title? Alexei? Pavel? Darya herself?

A Conversation with Dora Levy Mossanen

1. Both of your last two books, Harem and Courtesan, are intergenerational in that they follow the lives of three related women—mothers, daughters, and granddaughters. But *The Last Romanov* mostly follows Darya, who loses her mother at a young age and who never has a child of her own. How did writing a novel with one protagonist differ from writing the multigenerational stories you've previously told?

   DLM: To me, this, too, is a multigenerational novel. Sabrina Josephine, Darya's mother, is an important character in the story, and although she dies when Darya is still young, she influences Darya in significant ways that continue to reverberate throughout the novel. And although Darya does not have a child of her own, to her, Alexei is no different than a son. And she certainly loves and cares for him as a mother would. So, in the end, this story, too, is influenced by three generations.

2. Historical fiction by its very nature requires meticulous research, infused with a healthy dose of imagination. What kind of research did you do in preparation for writing *The Last Romanov*? How did you decide what facts to include, revise, or ignore?

   DLM: Research was voluminous, and it was not easy to sift through the plethora of tantalizing information I gathered.

Fascination with the Romanovs continues even today, nearly a century after their death, and new information is constantly uncovered. After all, it was only in 1991 that the Romanov remains were exhumed, and it was as recently as 2007 when the missing bones of Alexei and one of his sisters were eventually found. One of the most important jobs of a writer is to exercise control when it comes to which researched fact to include and which to ignore. If even the most intriguing information does not help advance the story, then it does not belong there. And as imagination is an important player, even in historical fiction, the responsibility of the novelist is critical in what facts to leave alone and what to tweak without harming the integrity of the historical tale.

3. Darya, our protagonist, is one of the non-historical characters in this novel. She's also one of the strangest in terms of her magical gifts and exotic appearance. What led you to give Darya a golden opal eye and mystical powers? Did you use any sources as fodder for her abilities and concoctions, or was it all straight from your imagination? Is Queen Athalia a historical figure, or is she based on one?

DLM: Opal is a mythical precious stone, purported to carry all types of healing, aphrodisiac, and magical powers, so I thought it would be fitting for Darya, who has supernatural powers. Perhaps it is my background, the culture where I come from, that's rife with myth, magic, and superstition that compels me to create such characters. Plus, I truly enjoy the freedom of imagination magical realism affords me. Athalia is based on a Biblical figure, who might or might not have been the daughter of Jezebel. Athalia, who ruled Judah, or Israel, for six years, is the only female monarch in the bible. Since there remain so many unsolved mysteries about her life and her intents in the Bible, it is with this controversial historical figure that I took the most authorial liberty.

4. Now that you have three novels under your belt, have you seen any changes emerging in your writing process or style? Tell us a little bit about that process.

DLM: My writing style is constantly evolving, and that's why once my books are out, I never go back to read them. Not even a paragraph. Because that is crazy-making for me. I know that if I ever start reading, I'd want to change this and that and then curse myself for not having added this or that. As for the writing process, some habits remain the same, but others have changed. I still prefer to start writing early in the morning until my brain tells me it's time to quit. I still like to write in a central corner, where I can tell what's happening around the house. I still like the ritual of steeping a cup of tea before I sit to write with all the intention of drinking it, but which invariably turns cold and undrinkable. What has changed is that I mostly work on my laptop rather than on the desktop computer. If I'm stuck in the story, I've learned to get up and take a short walk, sometimes no further than the other room, and the solution comes to me. And now, I don't panic if I don't have an idea for another book right now and right here. I'm confident that I have enough stories to tell in my lifetime.

5. Legends of Rasputin range from portraying him as a crazed priest with political ambitions to a sinister sorcerer with ties to the Devil himself. How did you balance the true historical record of Rasputin with the many legends that abound? What busted myth or unknown fact surprised you most?

DLM: Rasputin was the most compelling and contradictory historical figure I researched. He had crude manners and was a notorious drunk and womanizer, who was a member of the Khlysty sect, who shared the orthodox belief that the body is a sacred gift that should not be debased, yet maintained that sin was an essential part of the human life and that man can attain grace through sin. This doctrine was attractive to Rasputin, who took advantage of it to justify his debauchery. What surprised me most was that Rasputin did indeed possess certain healing powers. It is documented that he was able to stem the Russian heir's bouts of hemophilic bleeding. Doctors now credit this to Rasputin's hypnotic power that succeeded to soothe and calm—essential in stopping hemophilic internal bleeding—the heir and those he was surrounded by, especially his mother.

6. Besides their tragic execution and the mystery of possible lost heirs, the Romanovs are most famous for the intricate artistic wonders created for them by masters such as Peter Carl Fabergé. Are any of the items you so beautifully describe in the novel real? Of those you researched, which was your favorite and why?

DLM: The jeweled Fabergé eggs I describe in the novel that were created by the House of Fabergé from 1885 to 1917 are all real, except one. The Fabergé egg pendant the Empress gifts to her friend, Sabrina Josephine, and Sabrina then gives to her daughter Darya. These Fabergé imperial eggs, with the intricate secrets they reveal, are truly works of wonder, one more stunning than the other. My favorite is the Alexander Palace Egg, which Nicholas II presented to his wife, Alexandra. The Alexander Palace Egg is made of Siberian nephrite, diamonds, gold, rubies, and tiny paintings of the Imperial children on ivory. The initial of each child is monogrammed in diamond above each portrait. The surprise inside the egg is a detailed replica of Alexander Palace, including the adjoining gardens, the Imperial Family's favorite residence. In 1917, Kerensky's army confiscated it from Alexandra's Lilac room. Perhaps I favor this egg, not only because of its beauty and historical value, but also because it represents Alexander Palace, where most events of my story take place.

7. Your first novel, *Harem*, takes place in the fourteenth century. *Courtesan* takes place in the late nineteenth century. What first attracted you to the fairly modern period of history (mostly

twentieth century) portrayed in *The Last Romanov*? What attracted you to the story of the Romanovs?

DLM: I am attracted to periods when major historical events reverberate around the globe and change our world in major ways. I am also fascinated by eras of unimaginable decadence that end up imploding. This is what happened in Tsarist Russia, when the enormity of excess on one hand and poverty on the other ignited a chain of revolutions that resulted in Communist rule.

8. So far, all of your novels have an element of danger or forbidden love, and Jewish characters experience more difficulty. What special interest does this theme hold for you?

DLM: Having spent a good part of my life in Iran, surrounded by all types of prejudices, and having experienced wars, revolutions, and even a *coup d'état* in my own lifetime, it's not surprising that the prospect of some type of looming danger is never far from my consciousness. Jews have faced tremendous difficulties throughout history. And as my Jewish identity is part of me, it is understandable that my Jewish characters, too, face great obstacles.

9. In many ways, reading The Last Romanov is like an extravagant trip through Imperial Russia. Did you travel to any of the locations described in the novel? How did you infuse your descriptions with such detail?

DLM: Just as I did not need to travel to Ancient Persia to recreate the details of the Jewish Quarter for *Harem*, I didn't need to travel to Russia to picture, for example, Ekaterinburg, Alexander Palace, or the Mariinsky Theater, in realistic detail. These days, we have powerful tools of research at our disposal, a treasure trove of images and information that allows the author to visualize places, events, and characters as if inhabiting that world.

10. Ambergris is still a popular essential oil and scent. Is there any scientific or historical basis for its use as a healing substance, particularly for hemophilia, as it's used in the novel? Is it really the product of whale indigestion?

DLM: There is historical evidence of using ambergris as a healing substance, although I'm not aware of any scientific basis for using it to cure hemophilia. Arabs used ambergris to heal heart or brain diseases. Ambergris is still used in the Orient as an aphrodisiac. The Greek added it to wine or inhaled it before drinking wine to boost the effect of alcohol. When sperm whales are unable to digest the sharp, hard beaks of squids, they expel a chunk of fatty substance, sometimes hundreds of pounds, into the ocean. Whether this substance is a whale's vomit or fecal matter is open to debate. What's certain is that this rare, valuable ambergris has a foul smell, until it has a chance to be cured or aged for years by sun, air, and salt water.

11. One might expect a happier ending for Darya and her lover, Avram, who stays by her side longer than any man probably ought to and who returns for her time and time again. Why did you choose to separate them? What does it mean for you that her loyalty to Alexei is stronger than her love for Avram, who would marry her?

DLM: A different ending for Darya and Avram would have been unrealistic in an anti-Semite court to which she was deeply loyal. Still, this ending, although not what we would traditionally call a happy ending, is not that bad for a 104-year-old woman. Darya believes it's her responsibility to save Alexei, her only hope for salvation. Loyalty and love are close relatives, I believe, and carry different meanings to different women. Alexei is as dear to Darya as a son would be. A mother's loyalty to her child often takes precedence over loyalty to a lover.

12. Can you give readers any hints about what eras and stories you might explore next? What's interesting you right now?

DLM: I am working on a historical novel that takes place after the *coup d'état* of Reza Pahlavi and the fall of the Ghajar Dynasty in Persia. It is the story of a Jewish dentist in court. As my own grandfather was Reza Shah's dentist, this story is especially close to my heart.

Acknowledgments

My first deep felt thanks are for Nader, whose endless support, patience, love, and understanding are crucial in every aspect of my career. Carolyn, Negin, and David, Leila, Adam, Hannah, and Macabee, my shining stars, are always there when I come up for air. I am grateful for your love, encouragement, and unconditional support.

I owe a special debt of gratitude to Anna Ghosh, my literary agent, who believed and persevered. The wisdom, inspiration, and superb guidance of Shana Drehs, my wonderful editor, enhanced every facet of my book. Thank you. My appreciation goes to Dominique Raccah, whose vision and respect for the written word has energized the book industry. A million thanks to my publishing team extraordinaire: Holly Bahn, Sabrina Baskey-East, Katie Casper, Ed Curtis, Heather Hall, Beth Pehlke, Will Riley, Lindsey Tom, Danielle Trejo, and Sarah Zucker.

My heartfelt gratitude goes to Marcela Landres for her advice, insight, encouragement, and for her steadfast friendship through the many ups and downs we experienced together.

As always, words cannot convey my eternal gratitude to my generous friends and colleagues, Paula Shtrum, Maureen Connell, Joan Goldsmith Gurfield, Leslie Monsour, and Alex Kivowitz, who read and reread draft after draft and on whose invaluable feedback I've relied year after year.

Writing might be a solitary process, but completing a book requires the support of an army of family, friends, and colleagues.

I am fortunate to enjoy such support from my beautiful mother, Parvin Levy, my dear siblings, Ora, Nora, Laura, David, and Sol. Thank you! My father, Sion, of blessed memory, continues to cheer me on by making his presence known in his own extraordinary way.

Special heartfelt thanks go to my dear friend Ann Kirsch and to Jonathan Kirsch, my mentor. Your continued guidance and friendship have enriched my life in numerous ways. I'm indebted to John Schatzel, Lita Weissman, Judith Parlarz, Piera Klein, Megan U. Beatie, and Lynn Goldberg, who are instrumental in smoothing the path, facilitating the journey, and ensuring the book's ultimate success.

About the Author

Dora Levy Mossanen was born in Israel and moved to Iran when she was nine. At the onset of the Islamic revolution, she and her family fled to the United States. She has a bachelors degree in English literature from the University of California-Los Angeles and a masters in professional writing from the University of Southern California.

Dora is the bestselling author of the widely acclaimed novels *Harem* and *Courtesan*, which have been translated into numerous languages, and is the recipient of the prestigious San Diego Editors' Choice Award. She blogs for the *Huffington Post*, reviews fiction for the *Jewish Journal,* and has been featured in various publications.